Apoca

MW00881714

Omnibus 2 (Episodes 4-6)

By

Joe Nobody

Copyright © 2018

Kemah Bay Marketing, LLC

Edited by:
E. T. Ivester

www.joenobodybooks.com

This is a work of fiction. Characters and events are products of the author's imagination, and no relationship to any living person is implied. The locations, facilities, and geographical references are set in a fictional environment.

Other Books by Joe Nobody:

Apocalypse Trails: Episode 1
Apocalypse Trails: Episode 2
Apocalypse Trails: Episode 3
Apocalypse Trails: Episode 4
Apocalypse Trails: Episode 5
Apocalypse Trails: Episode 6
Secession: The Storm
Secession II: The Flood
Secession III: The Surge
The Archangel Drones
Holding Your Ground: Preparing for Defense if it All Falls Apart

The TEOTWAWKI Tuxedo: Formal Survival Attire
Without Rule of Law: Advanced Skills to Help You Survive
Holding Their Own: A Story of Survival
Holding Their Own II: The Independents
Holding Their Own III: Pedestals of Ash
Holding Their Own IV: The Ascent
Holding Their Own V: The Alpha Chronicles
Holding Their Own VI: Bishop's Song
Holding Their Own VII: Phoenix Star
Holding Their Own VII: The Directives
Holding Their Own IX: The Salt War
Holding Their Own X: The Toymaker
Holding Their Own XI: Hearts and Minds
Holding Their Own XII: Copperheads
Holding Their Own XIII: Renegade
The Home Schooled Shootist: Training to Fight with a Carbine
Apocalypse Drift
The Little River Otter
The Olympus Device: Book One
The Olympus Device: Book Two
The Olympus Device: Book Three
The Ebola Wall

Episode 4 Prologue
The day of the eruption

Sheriff Hewitt Langdon reached for the phone, his sleep-fogged mind instantly annoyed by the machine's obnoxious tone. "Sheriff," he croaked into the receiver.

The dispatcher's unwelcome voice was thick with embarrassment. "Sorry to bother you, sir, but Mr. Prichard believes Mexican illegals have crossed over the border onto his ranch and are intending to relocate his cattle south of the border. He sounded mighty upset, and he said he's heading out to the barn right now with his shotgun. He asked to speak with you specifically, and when I told him you weren't on duty tonight, he told me not to worry about it 'cause he needed a little target practice anyway. I hated to call, but I thought you should know … before he shoots somebody … or himself. Lord knows his eyesight ain't what it used to be."

"Where is the night shift deputy?" growled the lawman, once his sluggish brain engaged.

"Bo's answering a similar call up north. Seems to be the night for rustlers and horse thieves. I tried to call one of the reserves, but he didn't pick up."

A mental parade of excuses and protests came next, harsh words of rebuttal forming in Hewitt's mind. *Tell that paranoid, old fart to go back to bed*, he mentally retorted. *Doesn't he know I'm about to retire and need my beauty rest?*

Yet, serving 31 years as Ventura County's only elected law enforcement officer wouldn't allow such a response. A natural leader and reluctant politician, the sheriff had learned to think twice before he spoke. "Okay. I'm on it. Tell that crusty, ole codger I'm on my way down to his place. And for gawd's sakes tell him to unload that damned scatter gun. My mug is hard enough to look at without adding a lot holes from buckshot."

"Yes, sir. Will do. Be safe."

Sheriff Langdon rose, rubbing the sleep from his eyes while cursing the hour. After brushing his teeth and splashing a handful of water on his face, he opted for blue jeans and flannel rather than his official uniform. It was too damn early for starched collars, neckties and dress shoes. If he started answering pre-dawn calls appearing all prim and proper, folks would get the idea it was okay to call anytime, day or night. "Next thing ya know, they'll have me rescuing cats from trees by the light of the moon," he muttered, pausing long enough to give himself a once over in the mirror. As a last-second addition to his casual attire, he rubbed a squirt of Old Spice across his stubble.

He topped off his ensemble with his duty belt, complete with .45 caliber sidearm, extra magazines, handcuffs, and spare badge. A pair of well-worn boots and tan Stetson hat rounded out his wardrobe.

He paused as he walked by the kitchen, his brain subconsciously wandering toward the stained coffee pot resting on the counter. "No," he mumbled. "Better get going before Prichard's trigger finger ruins the rest of my day."

He noted the stack of dishes in the sink and swore again. He'd meant to wash them last night, but somehow the unwelcome chore had been forgotten. "Just another sign of old age," he grunted, heading toward the door. "Miss Kelly is probably rolling over in her grave."

The unruly rose bushes surrounding the front porch caused him further despair. His wife would have never tolerated such overgrowth. For a moment, he could see her image brandishing a pair of pruning shears, snipping away just enough to reveal a properly manicured, English garden. "Kelly, I promise I'll trim them this Saturday," he grunted, glancing toward the heavens. After receiving no acknowledgment or forgiveness from above, he continued for the Crown Victoria police cruiser occupying the driveway. Like his landscaping, it had seen better days.

Fumbling to secure the keys in his pocket, Hewitt instinctively felt the need to hike his pants. The act generated more disdain. "I'm getting so old," he hissed. "I don't have enough ass left to keep my britches on anymore. Barely any place to hang a firearm. No question. Retirement was the right decision."

The Prichard ranch was situated at the southern end of Ventura County, Arizona, about as far away from the Hewitt's house as was possible given the sheriff's jurisdiction. The commute gave him plenty of time for pre-dawn reflection.

He thought about the tattered calendar hanging on his office wall, sporting neat rows of days that had been crossed off. Just five more weeks before the new sheriff would be sworn in. That left just over 35 days of chasing down Mrs. Chavez's perpetually lost terrier, a bit more than 800 hours of dealing with the rare fender bender and serving the occasional foreclosure notice for one of the Tucson banks.

Hewitt didn't write speeding tickets anymore. Despite pressure from the county's district attorney and elected commissioners, the sage law dog had figured out years ago to let his deputies generate the much-needed revenue from traffic fines. In a jurisdiction of fewer than 900 voters, Sheriff Langdon figured every citation was a ballot cast for an opponent in the next election. Political awareness was a necessary evil for the man who felt a deeply engrained love for the law. Early in his career, he had carefully defined the acceptable parameters of politics and law enforcement within his daily duties. For decades he enjoyed sleeping like a baby, evidence of his successful balance of the two opposing elements of his job.

The Crown Vic's headlights tunneled through an arid, rocky landscape, Hewitt hardly paying any attention to the familiar surroundings. It wasn't until he reached the county's only town and namesake that his attention wandered beyond the roadway.

The Ventura County seat shared its name with the county itself. Meaning "luck" or "happiness," the founding fathers must have hoped for a double portion of good fortune. However, it, like so many small communities in the desert Southwest, had seen its fair share of ups and downs.

Recalling local history as he motored through the small village, Hewitt tried to visualize a booming Ventura as hundreds of prospectors and miners spent their paychecks in what the historical society described as a series of brothels, saloons, gambling halls, and establishments of nefarious repute. The 1830s had witnessed that first population explosion, copper and silver discovered in the surrounding mountains and drawing men from all over the world to seek their fortunes in the desert. "Now that would have been an exciting time to enforce the law," he chuckled.

Then, 40 years later, a second economic boom had struck, this one driven by the railroad. Ventura had been a marshaling yard and water stop for the ever-expanding network of iron horses crisscrossing the Southwest US during that era. The town's population had blossomed to rival Phoenix and Scottsdale. After the rails were laid, the crews moved on, and again, Ventura had fallen on hard times.

Now, as his car passed through the small, dark community, it was difficult to imagine such multitudes of people and a flurry of commerce occupying what now was essentially a crossroads with a courthouse and two street lights.

The modest settlement consisted of a single-room post office, a feed store, the courthouse, and Carlos's Diner, which was basically an all-in-one gas station, convenience store, and half-assed greasy spoon. The antique "mall" had closed a few months ago, it being the last eviction Hewitt hoped he would ever have to serve.

Again, his mind drifted to a bit of morning brew as he approached his favorite breakfast spot. Checking his watch, he grunted. Carlos wouldn't be opening for another hour. Coffee would have to wait.

Just like that, Ventura was in his rearview mirror, more of the same rocky, arid terrain now rolling past the cruiser's windshield. "A man can't even get a pre-dawn cup of java in this one-horse town," he mumbled, regretting not taking the time to microwave up a cup of instant for the drive. "Maybe after I arrest Prichard's Mexican horse thieves, he'll pour me a cup of joe."

Through the years, he had questioned why he and his bride stayed in Ventura County; Kelly never did. But then, she was the real people person.

Sure, the place was backwater. It was a two-hour drive toward Tucson before you could hope for the convenience of a strip shopping center. Even the few local children citizens suffered from the isolation, having to be bussed over 90 minutes each day to Nogales to attend school. The lack of convenience and availability of everything from a new pair of boots to a dentist was damn unhandy. Ventura wasn't the kind of town where you wanted to run out of toilet paper in the middle of the night.

Yet, there were good, honest folk all around. If he didn't count the occasional border crosser's body surfacing in the desert, there hadn't been a murder here in nearly 15 years. Old man Prichard might be in the early stages of dementia, but he wasn't a bad sort. Carlos's eggs were greasy but fresh, and the waitress always kept his cup full with a smile. There were a lot of positives about Ventura.

7

None of that, however, was going to be Hewitt's concern in five weeks. As he accelerated south, a chest-deep yawn reminded the sheriff that his retirement was long overdue.

Truthfully, his decision not to run for reelection hadn't been all that tough. Sheriff Langdon, now a regular feature at the diner since Miss Kelly had succumbed to the tumors in her breasts, had casually announced his intention almost a year back. Between heaping fork-loads of scrambled goodness, he declared, "I'm going to hang up my gun belt and badge … focus on fixing up my place. I'm *not* going to throw my hat into the ring this year."

He still remembered the stunned look on Carlos's face. For months, the local entrepreneur hadn't believed Hewitt would truly keep his name off the ballot. "You're an institution in Ventura County … a legend … an icon. You can't quit."

The lane to Prichard's Ranch then appeared in the circular radiance of Hewitt's headlights. The sheriff slowed and turned onto the washboard, hardpan path that he suddenly remembered was over two miles long.

"If I lose a filling on this call, I'm going to have the county send Prichard the bill," he grumbled through gritted, jarring teeth as he bounced along the uneven path.

Eventually, the dim outline of several buildings became visible on the horizon. Between the dips and minefields underneath his tires, Sheriff Langdon could discern the main house, an oversized, metal-roofed barn, and a dozen or so lesser outbuildings.

Prichard met the lawman at the edge of the drive, double-barrel shotgun resting in the nook of his arm. "Thanks for coming, Hewitt. I already made a tour of the perimeter. I can't figure out what's got the livestock stirred up, but they sure are spooked," the leathery, old rancher announced.

Sure enough, the anxious bays and whinnies of both cattle and horses tumbled across the pre-dawn desert sand. Something had the animals on edge … or riled up … or both.

"Let's go take a look," Hewitt responded, hiking up his pants with a frown.

As the two men marched toward the livestock pens and corral, the sheriff felt a genuine sense of relief. At least he hadn't yawned, nodded and zipped across half of Arizona for nothing.

After twenty minutes of Hewitt's flashlight identifying no tracks, cut fence, or rustlers, the duo returned to the driveway. "Beats me," the sheriff muttered, rubbing his wiry stubble in puzzlement. "Maybe there's inclement weather moving in? Maybe there's a big cat passing through the area? Hell, Prichard, I don't know, maybe they're just tired of seeing your ugly face every morning?"

The rancher grunted at the tease, his gaze traveling toward the still-restless animals. "Could be," he sighed in disgust. "But it's just damn odd, Hewitt. Almost 50 years in the bovine business, and I've never seen an entire herd so upset."

The cattleman then shrugged, evidently coming to grips with the fact that the mystery was going to remain unsolved. "Thanks for coming out, Hewitt. Sorry about the hour."

"That's what the citizens of Ventura County pay me for," came the softer-than-expected response. "At least for a few more weeks. I'm going to head back into town ... call if anything else comes up."

"Can I get you a cup of coffee for the drive back? There's a fresh pot on the burner."

For the first time that morning, Sheriff Langdon smiled. "Do you have a to-go cup?"

Ten minutes later, Hewitt was pulling onto the paved highway, again cursing Prichard's uneven lane for causing half of his java to end up on the Crown Vic's vinyl seat. With a deep breath, he managed to check his frustration, "No worries. Carlos's is only 20 minutes away."

The sun was squirming over the horizon when the sheriff rolled into the diner's parking lot. Out of habit, he scanned the small collection of vehicles present. The usual crowd was already there.

Steering past the two gas pumps, he aimed the Crown Vic into an empty spot next to Henry's twentieth century, Chevy pickup, noting the feed store's owner was yet again testing the truck's rear springs with a bed full of bagged corn. "I hope he isn't going to try and navigate Prichard's lane with that load. Bust an axle for sure," he whispered.

The sheriff opened the hefty, glass door leading to the combination gas station and convenience store when his lawman's sixth sense perked. Something was wrong. The cash register, surrounded by the usual displays of beef jerky, peanuts, disposable lighters, and colorful lottery ticket dispensers was abandoned. The drowsy kid, ordinarily parked on the stool behind the cash box, was nowhere to be seen.

Subconsciously moving his hand toward his sidearm, Hewitt's gaze swept the wall of glass refrigerator doors stocked with soft drinks and beer and then traveled up and down each aisle. No one was manning the store.

"Maybe he had to take a bathroom break?" Sheriff Langdon muttered, not wanting to accept that a robbery was in progress just a few weeks before he turned in his badge.

Before he could move toward the door marked, "Restrooms," excited voices drifted from the diner.

Now fully alert, Hewitt patrolled the interior of the establishment and entered the section where a few booths and a long counter announced the restaurant. There, at the far end, he spotted a crowd, including the cashier, gathered around the small television mounted on the wall. Again, he had the bone-chilling sense that something was awry.

Angie, the waitress, covered her mouth with her hands as if in shock. Carlos was rocking from toe to heel, his arms crossed in stress-induced knots across his chest. Henry was shaking his head in disgust as all eyes were glued to the television and the broadcast received courtesy of the satellite dish on the roof.

"What's going on?" Hewitt asked, strolling with purpose toward the throng.

"Yellowstone is erupting," someone said, pointing toward the TV. "And it's a big one."

Nearly an hour passed before the sheriff realized the muscles in his legs were growing stiff from standing at rigid attention, his eyes mesmerized by the events materializing on the screen. He was so enthralled, he hadn't even bothered to hike his pants or ask for a cup of coffee.

The disaster was hypnotic in a way, the small group of onlookers barely managing to utter the occasional, "For the love of God," or "Unbelievable," comment as a parade of apocalyptic images scrolled across the square glass. At 90 minutes, Carlos summed it up, saying, "Thank the good Lord above that this is all happening five hundred miles away."

That sense of security-via-distance soon evaporated, however, as the cable news network began interviewing various experts on volcanic upheavals. "This catastrophe is heading directly for us," Hewitt grumbled after another hour. "We've got to do something," he added a few minutes later.

Dire predictions and computer generated models now dominated the broadcast, countless scientists touting how the weather patterns would certainly spread Yellowstone's output across North America ... and perhaps the world.

"The only empirical example in modern history that we have to compare with this incident is the 1883 eruption of Krakatoa in the South Pacific. That event is believed to have disrupted weather patterns across the globe for nearly a decade," proclaimed one grey-bearded intellectual. "If Yellowstone continues to spew ash for an extended period of time, we could be witnessing an extinction level event."

It was mid-afternoon before the county's commissioners joined Hewitt and a host of other citizens on the courthouse steps. About half of the elected officials dismissed the issue, waving off those who voiced concerns as paranoid.

The meeting became heated when Carlos and Henry, the town's two most prominent businessmen, asked about emergency preparedness or any sort of disaster plan.

"What disaster plan?" answered a commissioner. "We've never had a flood, or tornado, or earthquake. Why would we have a plan for something that never happens here? Good Lord ... next you'll be asking for the tsunami plan."

After another 30 minutes of heated exchanges, the gathering soon polarized into two distinct camps. On one side stood those who thought the distant eruption was nothing more than a mild curiosity. Hewitt, along with several other concerned citizens, disagreed.

"First, we need to calm down, pull together, consider the situation, and agree on a survival strategy," Hewitt continued, overriding the confused fragments of conversation occurring on both sides. "While not even the experts can agree on the extent that this event will affect us, we definitely need an organized approach to this threat. If that volcano keeps hurling crap into the air, we could all be in danger. We should plan for the worst and hope for the best," Sheriff Langdon concluded in an effort to unify the populace.

Given his position, the sheriff's voice carried weight – but not enough. "What kind of plan are you proposing, Hewitt? Should we all board up our windows and rush over to Carlos's and empty the shelves of canned soup?" someone snickered.

Angie piped up from the crowd. "Hey, y'all can share all the chicken noodle soup. I just want the milk chocolate and potato chips," she giggled. "Can't leave THEM behind. Now THAT would be a real disaster."

Eventually, the meeting disbursed without any form of resolution. "We'll all be fine," stated one of the commissioners with confidence. "By tomorrow morning, this will all have blown over. You folks know reporters – always making a mountain out of a molehill."

For his part, Hewitt wasn't so sure. He found himself wandering back to the diner, surrounded by a group of worried faces who seemed to be looking to him for an answer, or at least some sort of guidance.

All eyes remained glued to the television for the rest of the afternoon until late into the night. Carlos eventually shooed the gawkers away, stating that calamity or not, he needed to sleep and bathe. "We can all meet back here in the morning. By then, maybe we'll have a better idea of what to expect and what is needed to be prepared."

By the end of the second day, Sheriff Langdon was convinced that he and his neighbors needed to take drastic action. California, or at least a large part of it, was uninhabitable. Reports stated that tens of thousands had succumbed to toxic gas. Contact had been lost with Kansas City, grey ash falling in blizzard-like conditions. Roofs were collapsing all along the eastern seaboard, surrendering to the weight of Yellowstone's exhaust. The president had just declared martial law.

Again, Hewitt found himself the center of attention, a swarm of anxious citizens turning to the man who had been the image of authority and the keeper of the peace for as long as most could remember. Despite the bright, cloudless sky outside, the sense of melancholy inside the diner continued to build at a pace equal to the endless waves of bad news streaming across the airwaves. He sensed that his neighbors were near panic, desperate to take action that might save their lives.

The sheriff noticed Prichard, Henry, Carlos, and a host of other friends hanging on his every word. Yet, despite his years of maintaining a clear, cool head under pressure, Hewitt wasn't sure what to do. If what the "experts" on television stated was true, the situation seemed hopeless.

How could a rural area like Ventura ever hope to provide the food, water, shelter, and the breathable air required to keep them alive? Even for folks who had heeded the warnings and had stored staples for years, the seemingly insurmountable list of basic needs to survive this disaster was daunting. Now, with only hours to react, it seemed that they were all doomed.

Hewitt, pacing up and down the diner's floor, fell back on his training and years of dealing with complicated problems. "Take it one step at a time. Maintain control. It's more than your job now. It is more than just carrying a badge and gun. One step at a time," he whispered to himself.

The first requirement, he determined, was shelter. The courthouse was sturdy but old. Given the images he'd seen on the TV, he wasn't sure about the safety of any of Ventura's buildings considering the weight of the falling ash. "What we need is a big cave," he grumbled.

That thought incited a eureka moment in the lawman's mind. "The Cliff House!" he turned and spouted to Carlos. "We need to get everyone up to the Cliff House and fill it to the brim with food and supplies!"

The diner's proprietor instantly connected with the sheriff's idea, his face brightening into a broad grin for the first time since the volcano had begun launching death into the atmosphere.

From the time he'd been a snot-nosed kid, Hewitt had known about the Cliff House. During the 1960s, local lore postulated that the place was haunted by a tribe of massacred Indians. He and his pre-teen friends would climb into the hills at dusk, scaring the hell out of each other with ghost stories while huddled inside the mysterious structure.

A few years later, pot smokers and hippies had attempted to organize a commune on the property. Ventura, they soon discovered, wasn't *that* progressive.

The late 1970s had seen the first real attempt at reviving the architectural gem. A visiting businessman from Scottsdale had lost a lot of money trying to convert the place into a tourist trap, bulldozing and widening a driveway while building a new, separate structure that was to house an art gallery. Unfortunately, that specific business plan was all the rage in rural Arizona at the time, dozens of tiny hamlets launching nearly identical efforts to draw artists from Southern California and New York. The investor, like the sheriff's back side, didn't have enough ass to hold up his entrepreneurial pants, and the business ran out of money before it opened.

Creative minds flocked to Bisbee and Tupac. Painters and sculptors prompted Flagstaff to flourish, while songwriters and poets kick-started Sedona's unprecedented growth. Ventura, all the while, floundered.

Despite the roller coastering economic outlook of its hometown, the Cliff House remained a local landmark, rich in history. A cowboy by the name of Honeycutt Jones was credited with constructing the original structure. According to legend, he'd discovered a vein of silver while riding down strays in the area's plentiful box canyons.

For a period, Honeycutt had evidently tried to keep his windfall secret, fearing claim jumpers and other villainous scoundrels would abscond with his newly found wealth. The story claimed that Jones had built a stone wall to camouflage his diggings. As the silver continued to produce, the structure had eventually morphed into a home, then later, a secreted, clandestine mansion.

Another version of home-grown lore presumed that Mr. Jones was a cattle rustler, and he used the odd rock formation to hide his stolen livestock. Hewitt had often wondered if this alternative history wasn't more accurate, as there was a subterranean cathedral large enough to house a significant number of head inside the cavern. A small stream of spring-fed water ran through the formation, and at one end there were large, man-made pens that looked like modern-day hay slots used to feed cattle.

Regardless of which version the public subscribed to at the time, Honeycutt eventually married a local gal named Hope, and the couple continued to expand the Cliff House together. By the time they both had passed on in the 1930s, the structure was well over 8,000 square feet and contained modern features such as indoor plumbing, electric wiring, and glass windows.

"The Cliff House has water, strong shelter, and there's plenty of room," Hewitt said, continuing to expand on his best and only idea. "We can hole up there until this whole ash-thing blows over."

"We're going to need a lot of food," Angie stated. "If the reports on television are accurate, we're going to need some sort of air filter as well."

Sheriff Langdon turned to Prichard and said, "Can you load up 30-40 head and transport them to the Cliff House? We can have beef and milk at the very least."

Nodding, the old rancher replied, "Sure. I'll get a couple of my hands to fill our stock trucks with my best. We're going to need feed, too. Cattle eat a lot."

"I can fix that," Henry stated with confidence. "I'll start hauling up as much grain as I can. We just got in two semi-loads, and my pickup is full as well."

Carlos picked that moment to chime in, "I'll lock up the shop here and have my people start boxing as many provisions as we can. Plus, we have a delivery scheduled for today. How long do you think we have, Hewitt?"

"I don't know, but we better get moving. And ... spread the word. Tell people they're welcome. Tell them to bring as many supplies as they can. We're going to need medicine, food, blankets, salt ... everything."

Chapter 16

Jack had never feared the wind – until now.

Despite his chosen career in the Navy, the commander had only considered atmospheric conditions as part of the operational environment. He had been taught not to navigate through hurricanes or sail small boats onto high seas, and he had avoided those dangers at all cost. He'd never seen a tornado, and he had zero experience with wind-driven forest fires. No, until today, the impact of moving air on his life had more akin to gravity than a dangerous element. After all, playing golf was harder with a robust breeze. Flying a kite was easier.

Jack scanned the landscape, sighing deeply at the scene before his eyes.

The desert was flat here, a tabletop of open spaces that not only numbed the mind, but allowed the carpet of volcanic ash to race, swirl, and ultimately drift without interference.

Rivers of the charcoal-colored powder streamed across the interstate, some as deep as the commander's waist. Yellowstone's entire output, combined with a squall straight from the depths of Hades, seemed intent on burying him alive.

Riding the bike was now an impossibility, his two-wheeled chariot converted into an anchor of rubber, spokes, and sprockets. More than once, he'd pined for a pair of snowshoes.

"How ridiculous," he grumbled to the empty roadway. "Snowshoes in the desert. You're losing it, Commander Cisco. Going stark raving loony."

Yuma had passed without incident. Of course, having several, well-armed Marines alongside tended to guarantee safe passage through just about anywhere short of hell itself.

In truth, Jack's new friends had made an agreement with the few surviving locals of the western Arizona town. There was some level of trade and barter between the two groups, as well as some occasional community outreach. The guys at the air station had delivered a baby; the townsfolk provided a plumber to repair a leaking water tank. No one was shooting or looting. Yet, no one was getting fat either. "I wonder how peaceful things will be after the grub runs out?" he pondered.

After Yuma, things became real mind-numbing, real quick.

While western Arizona hadn't exactly been jam-packed with people before the eruption, Jack found himself riding through what could only be described as a wasteland. The commander soon realized that his water supply was going to quickly be an issue.

The further east he traveled, the deeper the ash became. Not only was plowing through with his bike and pack physically difficult, the terrain itself was draining his morale and resolve.

All points of the compass were the same, a darker grey horizon melding into the somewhat lighter sky. He hadn't seen a shadow since arriving back in San Diego. He wondered if he would ever feel the sun's warmth on his face again.

There were no buildings, dead trees, or even bridges along this stretch of road. Not a single exit for miles, not even a billboard to tease him with some vestige of civilization that no longer existed. Jack carried the isolation with each footfall, the weight seemingly as heavy as his gear and weapon.

The mask across his mouth and nose had worn the skin of his face raw. Shaving was out of the question – not that he would have wasted the water anyway. His boots were continually filling with Yellowstone's talcum, his eyes reduced to narrow slits to avoid the stinging, biting grit. The dust permeated everything, including his underwear. For a moment, he questioned if he would have any hair left below the waist.

A gust kicked up just then, the battering gale causing Jack to lose his footing as both he and the bike flopped to the ground.

He laid there, uttering vicious, scathing curses directed at everything from Mother Nature to the planet as a whole. Why had Yellowstone picked now to erupt? Why had God forsaken them all? Why hadn't the government been better prepared for such a catastrophe?

His wrath then reflected inward. "You fool! Why did you leave the base and your loyal crew? Everybody knows there is safety in numbers. What are you doing out here in the middle of fucking nowhere? You don't even know if your wife and daughters want you to join them. What kind of idiot pushes his family away like you did?"

17

Rising to his hands and knees, Jack lifted a handful of the pewter grit, spreading his fingers slightly and watching the sand-like substance drain from his palm. "This is your life force," he whispered. "It's drifting away in the wind. Ashes to ashes, dust to dust."

He pondered turning around. Shelly and the Mud Lake crew were decent people. Archie possessed the only green living things he'd seen since making shore. The people of Pinemont knew how to party and more importantly, they had eggs. He could even return to *Utah* and help his brothers in arms start anew.

Rising, Jack stared to the east and Texas, the barely discernable outline of the interstate's lanes leading off into a grey tunnel of doom. "It's pointless to keep going. Mylie and the girls are either dead or not. No way you are going to pedal to the Lone Star State. Might as well forget that pipe dream. Besides, that soulmate of yours kicked you to the curb, Commander. She doesn't want you around."

Hell, even hanging out with the Marines in their underground bunker was better than dying out here in middle of some charcoal wasteland.

Yet, defeat was a scenario Jack Cisco couldn't accept – in any form. To turn around now would be an admission that he'd been bested. How many times had he wanted to throw in the towel at the Academy? There had been hostile upperclassmen, instructors he was sure wouldn't stop until he'd failed, and an academic workload designed to crush any mortal being.

Submarine school had been nearly as bad, as had his first assignment on a real boat.

Even in childhood, Jack had met his fair share of insurmountable obstacles. His father had lost his job, begun drinking, and started abusing his mother. Jack and his mom had nearly given up before convincing what was otherwise a good man to seek help with his addiction.

Finally rising, Jack began pushing the bike again, switching to the opposite side of the handlebars to provide relief to his sore and aching back.

Given the blowing blizzard of grime, the commander didn't notice he was on a gradual incline. Suddenly, in the distance of a few steps, the entire landscape changed.

A long valley spread out below Jack's vantage, the commander so distracted by the view that he nearly ran headlong into metal posts holding up a roadside information sign. "Rest Area – 1 Mile," it read.

"Thank God," Jack exhaled through his mask. There would be shelter against the wind. He could empty his boots and pants, make a meal, and perhaps even sleep for a few hours.

The interstate began to descend here, Jack's passing of the summit bringing about an abrupt and stark change in the environment. Within a few hundred yards, the carpet of ash thinned substantially, less than an inch of the powdered inferno covering the earth.

The wind seemed reluctant to travel here as well, the constant din and buffeting reduced to occasional, weakening gusts.

At 500 yards from the rest area, Jack stopped.

Standing still in the middle of the eastbound lanes, the commander removed his weapon from its handlebar-mounted cradle and used the optic to study the road ahead.

The first image to appear in the circle of magnification was a line of relic automobiles snaking alongside the highway as if waiting in line to enter the rest area. "Everyone else had the same idea," Jack whispered, studying the queue of ash-covered machines. "We're almost out of gas, honey. We'll stop at the rest area and wait for help," he continued, imagining the conversations that led to the overflow of visitors. Help had never arrived.

He tried to look for footprints but wasn't close enough to discern that level of detail. Next, he attempted to scan for any movement or structures. Again, geometry was against him, a slight hill blocking his view.

For a moment, Jack considered just riding right up and barging in like he owned the place. "Who would still be there?" he muttered through his mask. "How could anyone still be alive?"

Yet, if the commander had learned anything during his post-apocalyptic life, it was that human beings were full of resolve, could represent a mortal threat, and were difficult to overcome. He'd encountered groups of people living off the contents of over-the-road trucks. Could a similar community be surviving at the rest area?

The proper tactic would be to find a hidden overlook and observe the objective for at least several hours, perhaps longer. Jack's sore back, raw skin, and aching feet didn't support that idea.

Then there was the weather.

He'd been lucky so far, having been able to find shelter during the lethal electric tempests that now seemed to rage across the planet. If he were caught out in the open….

He didn't even bother to consider the potential for acid rain.

About then, the commander's stomach rumbled with the pangs of hunger, adding fuel to the internal argument calling for Jack to sit, rest, and eat.

A few moments passed before the commander arrived at a compromise. He would observe the rest area for at least two hours before going in.

The small rise between him and the rest area's structures was the logical site to perform the task. With a deep breath, Jack began pushing the bicycle toward the edge of the road.

He found a shallow drainage culvert and hid his bike, taking only his weapon, a spare magazine, and his water along for the uphill portion of the hike. Jack didn't like leaving any of his gear behind, but his body was too weak to manhandle wheels and pack along the bumpy terrain.

Cautiously, he approached the apex of the hill, eventually finding an outcropping of sandstone that provided a good view and reasonably comfortable place to lie.

He was 150 yards away from the main cluster of buildings that made up the rest area. Jack had seen similar configurations before, such facilities standard along practically every interstate in North America. In less than a minute, he was making an educated guess as to which rooftop belonged to the restrooms, visitors' center, vending machine shack, and maintenance shed. There were even phone booths.

The architect had chosen a southwestern theme, the exterior walls appearing to be adobe. Red and orange tiled roofs added to the effect. Weighty boulders, obviously hauled in from some other part of the state, rounded out the design.

Jack studied each building, paying particular attention to the entrances. Here, if the location were occupied, there would be footprints, signs of packed ash, or other indications of habitation. He spotted nothing but abandoned cars, minivans, pickups, and a few semis. All had been looted.

It was tempting to head on in. Jack could just tell the place was unoccupied. He could sense it.

It then dawned on the commander that most rest areas were twins. The eastbound oasis below him should have a sibling on the other side of the interstate. After a quick scan with his optic, Jack located the opposite, higher companion facility on the opposing embankment on the far side of I-8.

"Shit, you've got to be kidding. Not more climbing," he cursed, able only to see the rooftops from his already-elevated perch. "Should I bother?"

As he studied the west side on the freeway, an unusual object came into view. A moment later, what Commander Cisco observed caused him to inhale sharply.

There, high on the hill, laid an overturned truck … a water truck! It was the kind that delivered big plastic jugs to office building water coolers so people could stand around and gossip. Jack was stunned, elated, and relieved all at the same moment.

As his gaze swept downhill, his heart began to race faster. There it was … an abandoned treasure…. One of the large, plastic containers rested at the bottom, undisturbed, where it had landed after tumbling out of the upturned vehicle. Jack's mind instantly avowed that it was probably full of clear, crisp, unpolluted water. Enough for a man to take a bath if he wanted – definitely enough to keep the weary traveler alive until he found another source. He began calculating how to tie the massive jug to his bike. Could he drag It along behind on a rope?

His brain screamed for him to stand, dash across the interstate, and verify the huge container was full. His mind was working the math, quickly estimating that the jug held at least 10 gallons of liquid gold. His heart demanded that Jack go right now and hide the prize before somebody else came along and snatched it up. His gut shouted the loudest, however, sounding the age-old alarm that only came with wisdom and experience. If it looked too good to be true, it probably was.

Yet, Jack wanted so desperately for it to be true.

Instantly, his mind began to justify the existence of the water. The driver had been trying to escape a frantic throng who could clearly see his precious cargo. The mob had surged for his truck, and in desperation, he'd tumbled off the edge of the hill. The accident had killed so many, the survivors had overlooked that last jug at the base of the hill.

"Yeah. Right, Commander. And if you believe that line of shit, I've got some great bottom land I'll sell you cheap."

How *had* the water survived? Was the jug empty? Had that container been consumed before the truck rolled over? Was the driver hauling empties back to the plant?

More and more questions bombarded Jack's thoughts. Practically all of them had no answers.

Again, he suppressed the urge to rush across and satisfy his curiosity.

It then occurred to Cisco that if people still occupied the rest area, it would be only natural for them to hold the higher ground, or the westbound rest area. It was clearly the highest point in the vicinity, and from there, they could detect anyone approaching from either direction. In fact, they might be watching him at this very moment, the spider waiting for the bike-riding fly to tumble into its web.

For a second, panic rushed through the commander's veins. Pulling away from the crest, he did a quick 360-degree scan just to make sure no one was sneaking up on him. Finding nothing but ash-covered desert all around, Jack forced his heart to slow.

Frustration began to swell in Jack's chest. His previous dilemma of how long to scout the rest area had now grown exponentially more complicated.

There was no easy way to study the higher ground across from his current position.

He couldn't enter the shelter below him without fear of being seen from above.

He couldn't just keep going and pass on by without exposing himself to a potentially deadly ambush. Even utilizing the bike's superior speed wouldn't be enough to get him out of serious trouble.

Jack was just beginning to work out the steps of waiting for darkness before trying to sneak between the two rest areas when movement drew his attention.

Sure enough, there on the other side of the pavement, something had disturbed the ash into a small puff.

Now that Jack's eyes were focused, it was easy to observe the next occurrence. Fascinated, he watched as a figure rose and advanced three long strides before again diving prone. Another wisp of powder rose a few inches into the air.

He was only slightly surprised when a second human shape joined the first. For nearly two minutes, Jack watched the duo leapfrog each other as they advanced toward the water bottle lying on the hillside.

With hoods and masks covering their heads and faces, Jack had no clue regarding the identity of the two forms he was observing. He was sure, however, that they had been exposed to the ash for some time as their clothing was nearly identical in color to the surrounding hue and his own wardrobe. "We have the same tailor," he whispered, glancing down at his own charcoal-colored sleeve.

After their ultra-stealthy approach, the larger of the two shapes was now within striking distance of the jug. Jack watched with anticipation as the figure stood and rushed for the water.

From Jack's perspective, the jug was evidently full. The mystery thief tugged once, again, and then was joined by a partner. "Damn, that must be heavy water," Jack whispered, watching them struggle through his optic.

With four hands now trying to lift the container, Jack saw the spout end of the clear plastic begin to rise, then a straight line appeared in the ash, immediately followed by a cord pulled taut by the bandits' efforts.

Jack's eyes followed the trip line up the hill where it was attached to a bulky piece of rusty, metallic framework. Just like that, a basketball-sized rock toppled from the top of a semi. Jack cringed in anticipation as he watched the stone fall, wincing as it struck a wide section of sheet metal.

A surprisingly loud, gong-like sound thundered across the valley, informing anyone within half a mile that someone had just tugged on the water jug.

The commander's gaze traveled back to the two thieves, the body language of the hooded shapes indicating they were near panic. Both of them turned and scampered west.

They hadn't made it more than ten steps before Jack spied activity at the rest area above. Something was moving up there, but he couldn't determine exactly what it was. Still, it wasn't difficult to hazard a guess. The booby trap had been well planned and executed. It had probably snared many passersby.

Several men boiled over the hill from the rest area, a rough-looking bunch of masked figures who despite their ragtag appearance, seemed to know exactly where to go.

The two thieves tried to pick up the pace of their westward departure but were quickly cut off. Jack spotted another three men rise up from the east. The would-be water-jackers were now surrounded on three sides.

The commander also noted that for crooks, they were extremely slow. Their movements appeared clumsy, almost child-like as they tried to scurry in the only open direction, which meant running directly at Jack's hide. For a brief, déjà vu moment, he was reminded of the starving man he'd been forced to kill in San Diego.

Less than a minute had passed before the ambushers surrounded their prey. Jack, still lying on the eastbound rise, had a perfect seat to observe the festivities.

At that point, it became apparent that the two thieves were an adult and a child. The larger of the two bandits pulled the youth close in an embrace as if to protect it. There was a female and a pre-teen, probably a boy. "A mother and son? No wonder you had trouble lifting the jug," Jack whispered.

For their part, the ambushers appeared more like cavemen than modern humans. Layers of filthy, tattered clothing and makeshift head wraps created the visual effect, which was further accented by the haphazard collection of personal gear secured by ropes, belts, and shoelaces. Unruly, oily hair protruding from beneath their masks only added to the menacing façade of the wolf pack.

The ambush's leader stepped forward from the circle of Neanderthals, ignoring the woman's pleas for mercy. "Please. No. Please. Don't." He reached for her hood, unaffected by her recoiling from his touch. As he yanked it off, she nearly fell over. A head of long, dirty-blonde hair appeared, causing a wave of renewed interest to pass through the ring of surrounding men.

It was easy to read his cohorts' minds, and with a swift motion, the leader grabbed the woman's thick coat with both hands and easily tore it from her shoulders.

The onlookers audibly moaned in disappointment, and Jack didn't understand why. Finally, one of the men facing the commander's position clarified the reaction. "There ain't enough meat on her bones to bother fucking or cooking!"

Commander Cisco shook his head, wondering if the desert air was playing tricks on his ears. Did that guy actually say *cook? Cannibals?* Had things degraded that far?

The child was next, Jack's attention now riveted and focused with more intensity than before. He had no dog in this fight, and the woman *had* tried to take the water. Yet, cannibalism was another story. It made his stomach hurt to think about such an act.

Again, the top layer of clothing was torn away from the child, exposing a rail-thin boy who was maybe ten years old.

This discovery caused another round of grunts, guffaws, and comments. The leader waited them out and then declared with a loud voice, "At least this meat will be tender!"

Without further ado, one of the larger examples of hair dressed in rags stepped forward, a machete appearing from under his robes. The woman screamed at the sight of the blade, the surrounding throng cheering in support of their comrade.

Disgusted, confused, and fighting an overwhelming desire to vomit the bile from his empty stomach, Jack didn't know what to do. As the butcher stepped forward and raised his blade, the commander pulled the trigger.

The shot from nowhere surprised the mob below, but only for a moment. Jack didn't give them a chance to recover.

There wasn't much cover where the gang had formed its ring. One by one, Jack's 62-grain bullets tore into the cannibals, as they rushed, darted, dove, and scampered.

Only two of them managed to fire a shot in his general direction, but neither bullet was even close. After pumping half a magazine into their midst, Jack paused to assess the damage he'd inflicted.

Four of his targets were down and unmoving. Two more were still alive, rolling back and forth and thrashing in pain. The rest were running for the west side of I-8 like Satan himself had risen from the ash and was out to harvest their souls.

The woman and boy were scurrying as well, heading directly toward Jack's perch.

Knowing he didn't have much time before the highwaymen would regroup and come back for revenge, Jack hurried down the hill and waved to the frantic woman. "Come with me if you want to live!"

She hesitated, but only for a moment. With a hand on the boy's shoulder, she guided him directly behind the commander.

There was no time for introductions. "This way," Jack ordered, pointing in the general direction of his bicycle. "Please hurry…. They'll be back."

No other words were exchanged as the trio made their way back to the bike.

Jack pointed for her to head west, back the way he'd just come. He was reasonably sure the bushwhackers had made the elevated rest area their home, and at that very moment, distance was life.

The woman and boy were slow, apparently weak from hunger or dehydration. Glancing over his shoulder and scanning for the inevitable pursuit, Jack spied a larger group of men assembling alongside the road.

"We have to move faster," he informed his new friends. "They're going to catch us if we don't pick up the pace."

"I'm sorry," she responded in a weak voice. Then turning to the youth, "Try harder, baby. Come on honey, I know it hurts, but we have to make time."

Less than a minute later, Jack knew they weren't going to make it. A posse of 15 men was now behind them, closing the distance at a surprising rate. Jack had to slow their pursuers down.

Visions of the wind-strewn plateau he'd just crossed then darkened Jack's mind, another hindrance to their desperately needed speed. "Climb to the top of this rise," the commander pointed. "I'm going to see if I can discourage them from chasing us."

Without waiting for her response, Jack pivoted and moved to the edge of the pavement and dove prone. The M4 was against his shoulder, and within seconds a man was centered behind the red dot.

He judged the distance to be less than 300 yards. He raised the glowing circle a few inches and squeezed the trigger.

The carbine barked, a single brass casing arching through air. Before that cartridge landed, Jack was centering on another of the shadowy forms.

Jack managed three shots before the mob on his tail scrambled desperately for low ground. A quick scan revealed one visible body lying on the pavement, the downed hunter jerking in spasms of pain.

With no clear target available, Jack thought to stand and catch up with his bike. The woman hadn't made it very far, he noted, so he decided to keep the war party behind him busy until she'd managed a bigger lead.

They were a patient lot for flesh-eaters, he judged a minute later. Now and then, Jack could see one of them clamber forward, either trying to find a better hide, or advance on his position. At two minutes, one of the stupid ones actually stood and charged. Jack killed him before the ignorant gent could manage five steps.

The woman and boy were now a football field's length further up the incline. Jack decided he'd wait until she'd doubled that distance before catching up. His attention returned to the cannibals.

For another five minutes the round circle of his optic swept the area where he knew they were lying in wait. "How long before you give up?" he whispered. "How desperate are you? Go back and eat your dead friends, assholes."

Jack rose up from his cover, knowing good and well that the men below could see him. The commander jogged backward several yards, ready to snap off a round if any of the wolf pack exposed themselves. None did.

He turned and continued at a controlled run, pausing every 20 steps to turn and see if he were still being chased. He nearly caught up with the sluggish woman when bravery overrode common sense, and the men behind them stood as a group and charged again.

Jack repeated his tactic, rolling into the drainage area beside the pavement and using the ground to steady his aim. Evidently, the flesh eaters still had some brain cells functioning. Their group spread wider this time and ran while bent at the waist in order to provide smaller targets.

When they noticed Jack hit the ground, they mirrored his move and dove for cover before the commander could squeeze off a single shot. "We gained some distance, assholes," he grunted, noting their forms looked smaller through his optic's magnified circle. "You're losing. Go home. You're not worth my ammo."

Again, the zombies' tactics changed. Now, rather than lie and wait for Jack to move again, they started advancing low along the ground. Some crawled, some hopped up and rushed a short burst before diving back to cover.

"Okay, you're not losing," Jack grunted. "But how long will you keep this up?"

He fired one well-aimed shot, saw his target's hands fly into the air, and then waited for the woman and child to gain additional distance. His snipe had the desired effect, the crawling and scampering advance stopped instantly by the lucky shot.

That act repeated two more times before the wooly gang behind them finally stood, flipped Jack the bird, and then turned around to go home. The commander's trust in mankind, sorely shaken by the entire affair, forced him to watch their retreat until the disheveled shapes faded into the distance.

Jack's flush of relief didn't last long. After catching up with the struggling duo pushing his bike, the commander thought, *"Okay, now what in the hell am I going to do with these two?"*

"We can rest for a second," Jack informed his new companions. "Put the kickstand down and have a seat."

"Thank you," the woman croaked, her throat parched and her legs weak from the exercise. She turned to help her son with the bike. "I'm Sarah … and this is my son Justin. Thank you for saving our lives."

As Jack dug in his pack for a bottle of water, he returned the introduction. Sarah seemed not to hear him, her eyes so intent on the clear plastic bottle in his hands. When the commander handed it to her, she started crying.

She passed it to the boy first, the lad's hands shaking as he raised the bottle to his lips. Mom let him drink half before gently pushing the bottle from his mouth.

Sarah drained the remainder in a few hardy gulps, the hydration seeming to give her strength in short order.

"When was the last time you had something to eat?" Jack asked in a nonchalant tone.

The question seemed to puzzle her. Realizing her lack of an answer probably seemed odd, she grunted and offered, "Several days, I suppose. So long ago that I'm having trouble remembering."

Nodding at her response, Jack then turned toward the cannibals' lair. "I have some food I can share, but right now I'm more worried about those animals back there. We need to get off this road and find a defendable place to hole up for the night. We can't be sure they've given up."

Sarah didn't argue, her frightened eyes following Jack's back to the location where she and her son had almost become a meal. A minute later, the trio was up and again pushing the bike toward the windy plain.

Just as he thought, the breeze started picking up the moment they approached the crest. Jack could see the wind kicking up the ash in the distance. He chest tightened with dread at the thought of having to venture near that perilous area again.

"We should cut to the southwest," Sarah announced. "There is a county highway about two miles over that will take us into Ventura."

"Ventura?" Jack asked, his dread of the windy flats so intense he was willing to listen to just about any alternative.

"Yes, I'm trying to reach a town named Ventura. My husband is there … or at least I think that's where he got stranded."

While the idea of taking the bike off the road wasn't appealing to the commander, the direction Sarah was pointing appeared to circumvent the worst of the flats.

Again, Jack engaged the bike's kickstand and then began digging into his pack for the folded map he stashed there.

After straightening the unwieldy paper, Jack confirmed his new companion wasn't delusional. He remembered crossing over the two-lane highway that led to the tiny village several miles before. There hadn't been an exit or any road sign for that matter announcing the community.

"Why do you believe your husband is still in Ventura?" Jack asked, still skeptical about taking the alternative route.

"He managed to get through just before the cell towers went down. He told me about a delivery he was making, and he said that the people of that town were creating some sort of shelter. His truck was having engine problems, and as soon as his company got a mechanic out to help, he'd be home. He never showed up."

Jack, rubbing his chin, pondered the woman's story. It didn't make any sense. "Look, lady, I don't mean to be a cynic, but if my wife and son were as close as you claim your husband to be, I would wade through hell to get back home. Hell, I'm crossing half of the United States to try and find my family, and my better half doesn't even like me all that much. Don't you think your hubby would have shown up by now if he was still alive?"

She shook her head. "I told him I was going to my sister's house during that call. I just know he thinks that Justin and I are safe at her place up near Taos in the mountains."

"And why didn't you go?"

"We tried, but the roads were all gridlocked, and I couldn't buy any gas. We turned around and went back home and have been praying my husband would come back ever since."

Jack pondered her account, briefly wondering how many families had been separated by the volcano. Then, with his eyes studying the map, he finally nodded. "It's a good 50 miles out of my way," he announced, "but there's no better route around the rest areas … or their restless natives."

They trudged across the desert, Jack managing to push the bike through the softer sand and dirt. It was more difficult than the pavement he'd been following but not impossible. Besides, becoming some flesh-eater's culinary delight just didn't seem like a viable option.

Eventually, they approached a boulder field running alongside a low set of foothills. Jack spotted an enclave that would afford them protection from three sides. "That way," he pointed. "We'll spend the night over there."

Given the dim light, he decided a fire was worth the risk. Smoke would be difficult to detect at night, and if he kept the flames under control, his rock fortress would prohibit anyone from having a view. Besides, he desperately needed a hot meal and thought his new friends could use one as well.

Sarah's eyes widened to the size of saucers when she saw Jack pull the can of chili from his pack. Her gaze never left the modest, metal container as it sat heating on the small fire. She stared at it as if she were eyeing a T-bone steak.

When the thick, soup-like meal began to boil, Jack used a rag and pulled the can away from the flames. "Here," he said, handing it to his two refugees. "You two can split this. I'm going to cook up an MRE. I'm sick of chili."

Without hesitation, Sarah and Justin began shoveling the food into their mouths with dirty fingers. Neither seemed to care about getting burned, or sanitation, or social amenities. Sighing, Jack said, "Stop. You're not animals. Here, you can use my fork. The MRE has plastic utensils."

Jack was a bit surprised when his two starving guests began sharing the fork. Although her dirty face didn't allow a clear view, the commander was sure Sarah blushed from embarrassment.

Jack had never seen a cleaner chili can by the time they finished eating. Not only did the hungry duo scrape every last morsel out of the tin, Sarah then filled the container with water and shared the bouillon with her son.

Their transformation was amazing. With just a few quarts of water and one meal, Jack could see the light and life returning to their eyes. Sarah even managed to stand and begin tidying up around the camp.

"So why did you choose now to leave and find your husband?" Jack asked.

"Because of the chaos in Prescott," she answered with a shaky voice. "Our neighborhood … my street … well, it had turned into hell. If you think those guys back at the rest area were bad news, they were nothing compared to the vicious beasts roaming around my house."

When Jack didn't respond, she continued, "At first they only ate the ones who had already died. But the bodies rotted quickly, and pretty soon they discovered that fresh meat was far tastier and more accessible. They even started keeping cattle pens full of the people they caught. Those poor souls, waiting like beef on the hoof to be slaughtered and eaten. It was horrible."

Jack didn't know whether to believe her or not. "So without any food or supplies, you and your son just decided enough was enough and left?"

He regretted the question as soon as it had left his throat. "I'm sorry," he quickly added. "I didn't mean for that to sound so harsh. I'm exhausted and having a little trouble believing everything that I have been witness to today."

She managed a smile, nodding an acceptance of his apology. "We were out of food and water. The toilets were backing up, and the roving gangs of body snatchers were getting closer and closer to finding us. The night before we crept out, they almost caught me in the backyard burying the contents of our chamber pot. That's when I decided we had to leave."

Again, Jack remained silent, watching Sarah take another drink of water. After she'd swallowed, she continued. "I filled a couple of backpacks. I had water, a few scraps of food, our sleeping bags, and Billy's pistol. We made it to the edge of Prescott before the sun came up, so just before dawn we hid in the back of an old storage shed to get a little shuteye. While we were asleep, somebody must have discovered us and absconded with our packs. All of our supplies were gone the next morning, and we've been struggling to find anything to eat or drink since."

"How long ago was that?" Jack asked.

"At least a week. Without food or water, Justin has had trouble walking more than a few miles at a time. He's always been a thin kid, and I guess he just doesn't have any fat reserves to burn. The lack of water has been the worst though. When we saw that overturned truck back at the rest area, I thought my prayers had been answered."

Jack nodded, registering the important lesson he'd learned that day. Evil didn't translate into stupid. "I was probably a few minutes from bumbling into that snare myself. It was a very, very sophisticated booby trap. Whoever constructed it was a genius."

Sarah's eyes rolled back into her head as her thoughts returned to the moment when the mob surrounded her. "I thought that was it…" she started with a shiver. "When that animal pulled out his oversized knife, I just knew we were dead."

Wanting to change the subject, Jack said, "So tell me about Ventura. What did your husband say? What kind of shelter were the locals building?"

Again her eyes drifted back in time, "Not much really. He called it the Cliff House … or something like that."

Sheriff Langdon scanned the herd, his lips moving silently as he counted head.

Beside him, old man Prichard was doing the same and feeling silly. Finally, the rancher said, "We didn't lose any overnight, Hewitt. Why are we counting them again?"

"I don't know," the sheriff replied, shaking his head at the interruption. "I guess I keep hoping they'll multiply or some shit. Hell, can't a man have some optimism around here?"

The two were standing next to the rock corral, a wide, natural bowl of erosion that was completely covered by an enormous overhang of the hill above. Years ago, probably by the hand of Honeycutt Jones, somebody had filled in the few openings with piles of stones. It was an indoor pasture, complete with a small stream of water winding across the floor.

Not only had cowboys or rustlers of old built up the walls, they had also constructed a clever set of feeding pens that held a surprising amount of hay or grain.

Prichard estimated the grotto claimed at least three acres of completely hidden floor space, more than enough for 30 to 40 bag-fed head of cattle. About the only shortcoming of the ingenious design was that the odor from the animal's waste could not vent to the outside, and eventually it permeated the entire complex. After a while, Sheriff Langdon became immune to the stench, although others in the community still grumbled an occasional complaint.

Hewitt reflected on the day he'd devised the idea of moving his friends and neighbors into the Cliff House. It had been a gamble bringing Prichard's animals into the underground corral, their ability to filter the air supply his most daunting challenge.

Years ago, as a teenager, Hewitt and his pals had explored the upper reaches of the complex formation, discovering a series of small shoots and cuts that led to the surface above. Would they be enough to filter Yellowstone's ash?

The sheriff believed there were so many twists and turns in the air's path that it would be difficult for the powdered pumice to remain suspended and float through the entire route. Just to make double-sure, he and several of the men had used everything from cotton bed sheets to burlap bags to add additional filtration to the incoming oxygen.

It had worked, and for the first several weeks, Hewitt felt like the smartest man on the planet. Load after load of grain, food from Carlos's storeroom, hay, and any edible foodstuff had been hauled up the narrow path to the Cliff House along with Prichard's prize cattle.

The sheriff recalled a convoy of pickups, farm trucks, trailers, and SUVs snaking their way up the mountain path. Ventura hadn't seen anything like it since silver was discovered in the hills over 100 years ago.

The cows would provide milk, what Carlos had termed a "renewable" food source. Occasionally, they would butcher a cow for table meat. The plan had been to keep the herd's headcount stable, only eating a mature animal when a calf was born. In total, the old rancher had provided 42 cows and two bulls.

Everything was going according to plan until the end of the first heavy ash fall. Seeing the desert covered in a carpet of grey seemed to motivate the skeptics and naysayers of Ventura County. Hewitt, and the citizens who had worked so hard to provide for their future, suddenly found their sanctuary's doorstep crowded with non-believers who arrived desperate and pleading .. but were accompanied by very few provisions. *I wonder if Noah's sleep was interrupted by soaking wet cynics pounding on the door of the ark?* he mused.

Yet, the sheriff was proud of the surrounding community. The majority of folks heartily pitched in and worked around the clock in what could only be described as a superhuman effort to ensure their survival. Before the volcanic slag began to fall, they had been heckled by their neighbors who either didn't believe or wouldn't accept the dire predictions coming across the airwaves.

Still, Hewitt let the skeptics in.

Many of the above-ground refugees were already having difficulty breathing. Practically all were dehydrated. Few offered any supplies or skills in exchange for their room and board. With every family, Hewitt had to reduce the duration of time their supplies were projected to last, yet he couldn't find it in his heart to turn the desperate away.

Despite the extra bellies to keep full, the strategy was working well. While the accommodations were a bit crowded, everyone had a dry, warm place to sleep; and for the time being, there was still enough food and water for all. Hewitt figured that with careful management, they could survive for months with the supplies on hand. By then, they all hoped, either the world would heal or help would arrive.

That sense of optimism was now beginning to fade, however. Four days ago, they found a dead cow lying next to the feeding pens. Prichard's assessment wasn't good news. "She didn't have any lung or respiratory issues. I think she passed from a parasite-borne infection called Coccidiosis."

"You see, we moved them into this damp environment," the rancher reported when the second animal succumbed yesterday, "and these cattle are not acclimated to moist air and the bugs who live in it. If we don't get our hands on the right treatment, we could lose the entire herd within a month."

Having no background in ranching, Carlos voiced the obvious question. "What do we need?"

The cure, Sheriff Langdon soon learned, was a drug called Coccidiostat.

The feed store, according to Henry, had none of the remedy in stock. "We just don't see Coccidiosis much in the arid Southwest," he had stated with disappointment.

Yesterday, Hewitt had sent masked search parties out to the surrounding ranches, seeking out the substance and with permission to barter. They found no survivors and zero medicine.

Without a source for beef and the milk the cows produced, Hewitt estimated the longevity of their food supply was cut nearly in half. People couldn't eat hay, and while ground feed corn made an acceptable flatbread, the former residents of Ventura needed the milk and meat the herd could provide.

"The last time my vet needed that drug, he sent off to Tucson and one of the universities there," Prichard stated. "We might be able to slow down the spread if we up the percentage of grain in their diet, but that's only a delay, not a cure. We need that medicine."

"Let's get Puff fired up and head into town then. I'll get Henry and Billy to ride shotgun with us. We can't afford to lose any more of these animals," Hewitt stated.

Chapter 17

It came as no surprise that Ventura was a ghost town. Other than an odd set of tire tracks in the ash, Jack could find no sign of recent human activity.

"This little settlement probably didn't compete with Times Square *before* Yellowstone blew," he commented to Sarah. "Still, I have to wonder where all the people went. I've been asking myself that question a lot on this trip," he continued, pausing to study the streets almost vacant of vehicles. "Most of the time, the thoroughfares have been blocked with vehicles that stopped in gridlock, containing the remains of families who didn't manage to escape. But not here. This place looks like it was evacuated."

Neither of his guests offered a response, which didn't surprise Jack in the slightest. While food and water had given both mother and son more energy to travel, neither seemed very talkative or willing to engage in anything but basic conversation. *Given what they've been through, I can't blame them*, Jack thought.

Pushing his bike down the eerily silent main street, the commander motioned for Sarah and Justin to follow him across to the convenience store's parking lot. After a few circular strokes to clear a peephole through the accumulated dust, the commander pressed his nose against the glass door and peered inside.

At first, Jack thought they might have just gotten lucky. Bright colors filled his hazy view, several display cases around the cash register showing promise. After wiping the window a bit more, he exhaled in disappointment. "You can't eat lottery tickets," he sighed.

Other than the instruments of state-sponsored gambling, the establishment was empty of any object. Bare shelves met the traveler's gaze, not a candy bar, bag of chips, of soft drink in sight. "Cleaned to the bone," Jack stated with disappointment. "A church mouse couldn't survive on what's left in there."

They continued their tour of the abandoned community, visiting the courthouse and feed store before finally arriving at the antique mall.

It was here that Jack noticed the first sign that people in the area were still alive. Several clear footprints were visible in the thin layer of ash by the side entrance. There were at least three different pairs of shoes. The commander's grip on his carbine tightened, his head now scanning right and left, scrutinizing the landscape, on high alert for any threat.

"We need to find shelter," he instructed his companions. "It gets dark so quickly these days, and we're way overdue for another lightning storm."

That thought led Jack back to the courthouse, the building's stone façade and stout-looking roof giving the commander a sense of comfort. He was surprised to find the front door unlocked.

They stepped into the interior, finding the marble floor covered in a thin layer of grit. Jack saw signs announcing the various county offices, brass plaques denoting the "Assessor," "Clerk," and "Justice of the Peace."

It was a larger sign next to a stairwell that drew Jack's intense scrutiny. Large black letters boldly announced, "Sheriff's Office," printed above an arrow that pointed downward. He might find ammunition there or other valuable tools for his journey.

With Sarah and Justin in tow, he proceeded down a single flight of stairs and into the basement. Another hallway was waiting on them, darker, but still sporting the same brass signage above each door. Most of the rooms were designated for records and other storage.

Jack found the sheriff's office unlocked as well. Beyond the frosted glass door was a small interior of three desks, a wall of metal cabinets, and a single jail cell that was barely large enough to hold a cot. Amazed at the diminutive size allocated for processing lawbreakers, he sauntered into the middle of the room. Just then, Cisco found himself in a déjà vu moment, flashing black to old black and white TV shows his mom liked to watch. "My Lord! I feel like I just strolled into Sheriff Andy Taylor's office on Mayberry R.F.D.," he laughed, scanning the room as if Deputy Barney Fife might bumble in.

Convinced that a lawman's office, no matter how small, held promise for obtaining much needed provisions, Jack began searching its contents. A radio set rested on the first desk, an old style, wooden name plate declaring that the chair belonged to the dispatcher. The cleanest work surface belonged to the deputy; the one stacked with the most papers declared it was the sheriff's. So far, nothing of real value in sight.

Wandering around the small space, Jack began testing the cabinets which reminded him of high school lockers. They, too, like the doors to the courthouse, were not secured. Upon opening each one, Jack's sense of disappointment grew. Someone had apparently carefully picked them clean of anything of value in the post-apocalyptic world. There wasn't a single flashlight, battery, bullet, or candy bar to be found, much less any weapons or ammunition. Jack's mounting discouragement was burgeoning into full-blown anxiety.

The commander turned, finding Sarah and Justin standing just inside the door. Already frustrated by the lack of treasure, his voice conveyed more anger than he intended. "Can you at least help me search? Look in those desk drawers for anything that might help us."

Sarah didn't argue or protest, moving quickly to the dispatcher's workstation and opening the top drawer. Justin followed suit, choosing the deputy's desk.

Shrugging, Jack plopped down in the sheriff's chair and began rummaging through the contents of each drawer. He found the prerequisite "catch all" area in the top center opening of the old oak desk, a haphazard collection of paperclips, rubber bands, and half-used ink pens. Only mildly disappointed, he then moved on, coming across a stack of unopened mail in the next.

It was Justin who hit pay dirt first, pulling out a half-eaten bag of salted peanuts while saying, "Mom! Look!"

Before Jack could say a word, the kid tilted his head back and poured half of the stale snack into his mouth. Ignoring the shocked expression on the commander's face, the kid then bolted out of his chair, rushing to give his mother the remaining morsels.

Sarah got it, accepting the plastic bag and flashing Jack a look that said, "I'm sorry. He's thinking with his stomach and not his heart."

Instead of eating the peanuts, Sarah rose without speaking and handed Jack the rest. "Sorry," she whispered. "We've been so desperate, for so long...."

"At least he finally spoke," Jack replied, waving off the dozen or so nuts left in the bag. "You go ahead. You guys have been without for a lot longer than I have."

Indeed, both refugees from Tucson were in sorry shape as far as the commander was concerned. During their trek to Ventura, Jack had been afforded the opportunity to study his new friends with a more scrutinizing eye, and the picture wasn't pretty.

Justin's physique was nothing more than skin and bones to say the least. At one point, the boy pulled up his sleeve to scratch, and the commander had been shocked at the appearance of the kid's limb, the skin sagging, his body seeming to have been emptied of muscle and fat. "I bet my wedding ring could reach his elbow," Jack had muttered.

Sarah wasn't in much better condition. After they had put more distance between them and the cannibal camp, Jack did a visual assessment of her general health. He found her skin was pale and waxy, the bones of the woman's fingers protruding in a way that declared she hadn't eaten well in months.

In fact, on their journey across the desert, Jack's biggest fear was that one of them would stumble and fall. Surely their very skeletons would crumble under the slightest stress.

Yet, the scrawny pair had soldiered on, putting one foot in front of the other and somehow managing to keep up with the commander's pace. Sarah, at one point, had even offered to take a turn pushing his bicycle through the rough terrain.

Jack excavated the next prize, extracting two individually wrapped mints from the back corner of sheriff's bottom drawer. *Those little breath fresheners probably accompanied the chief lawman's fried rice takeout box,* the commander assumed. *Too bad … looks like the entrée must to have been wolfed down months ago.*

Studying the two red and white spheres, Jack crinkled the plastic packaging. He was struck by how people had ignored the simple things before the catastrophe. The mints in his hand were now exciting and rare, his own mouth watering in anticipation of something sweet. The irony of his exhilaration did not escape the commander; before the collapse, these goodies would have hardly been noticed by the average person. The restaurant probably had an overflowing bowl of them by the cash register.

Tossing one of the candies to Sarah, Jack said, "Take your knife and split this into three pieces. It's by no means a gallon of mocha ice cream, but it will help with the aftertaste of that damned chili."

The remainder of their search produced no additional finds, but the discovery of the mints gave Jack inspiration. "We'll set up camp in here for tonight. There's the cot in the cell, and I found some blankets in that locker over there. We're as safe here as anywhere. In the meantime, I want you and Justin to check every office and desk in this building. Who knows what people left behind?"

Sarah nodded, motioning for her son to follow. "What if the doors are locked?" she asked as an afterthought.

"Don't destroy anything. We're scavengers, not looters. There's a difference."

His labels seemed to puzzle her. "There is?"

"Yes," he nodded. "At least in my mind there is. The people of this town expect to return here one day. They'll probably be faced with difficult challenges, and I don't want to add to that burden. A few missing breath mints and stale peanuts won't be an issue. Busted locks and broken glass will."

Chapter 18

They called her Puff, Hewitt unsure if the moniker were due to the belching smoke or a reference to the literary dragon. Either way, the nickname had stuck.

She was a 1913 J.I. Case steam tractor, her brass plate announcing she was number 17101 and had been built in Racine, Wisconsin.

For years, the relic had sat as eye candy in front of Ventura's antique mall. Hewitt had no idea where the owner had found the old tractor or how much it was worth. What the sheriff did know was that by the time he served the foreclosure notice on the property, the green and white behemoth was surrounded by weeds and suffered from fading, chipping paint. An eyesore at best.

It has been Carlos's idea to try and restore the prehistoric machine. Shortly after the last pickup had stopped working, it had become clear that carrying heavy supplies up from Henry's feed store was going to be a back-breaking, if not impossible, task.

For three days, they had worked on the old beast, wearing heavy painters' masks and scavenging parts from the courthouse's steam boiler. Hewitt didn't trust the Case, even after Henry had managed to figure out how to engage the gears and the damn thing had actually moved.

The foggy glass gauge on Puff's dash indicated there were over 150 pounds per square inch of pressure in her boiler. Given the massive amounts of rust they had flushed from the inside, Hewitt was always worried the antique was going to explode and kill them all.

The two substances still plentiful in Ventura were wood and water. Given every stem of vegetation was dead or dying, it hadn't been difficult to gather bundle after bundle of dried mesquite and scrub oak. Carlos had joked that the rusty boiler would be the one resident that wouldn't suffer from consuming ash-laced water.

Her wheels were iron with a thin, worn layer of hard rubber that did little to cushion the kidney-jolting ride. Puff managed almost five mph in the higher of her two forward gears and could pull practically anything they loaded onto Prichard's longest horse trailer.

Once a week, the men of the Cliff House filled her water tank and stuffed as much wood into her boxes as possible. She could run for three hours without refueling.

In the end, Hewitt had finally accepted Puff and the dangers the old tractor posed. The cattle consumed massive amounts of hay and feed. That, combined with the fact that their last working pickup had failed over a month ago, left the people of the Cliff House with a difficult problem. Toting hundreds of pounds of cow food up and down the mountain would have been impossible using nothing but strong backs and knees. When the late-model Ford truck had finally given up the ghost in a billowing cloud of blue exhaust, Puff had come to the rescue.

Puff wasn't the only old-school machine salvaged from the now closed antique mall. Two of the women had found a butter churn, oil lanterns, a set of candle molds, and even a hand-cranked meat grinder. Pre-electric technology was definitely playing a role in improving their lives. Given the dry nature of the corn dodgers that now made up a significant portion of their diet, Hewitt especially appreciated the butter.

Now, walking beside the mammoth, chugging machine, Hewitt noted one of the sentries posted high above them on Buzzard Ridge. The sheriff waved to a rifleman, receiving a "thumbs up," in return.

The day that Puff moved under her own power was also notable for another important event and the reason why the sentry was monitoring their progress. That was the same day the first strangers had arrived at the Cliff House.

Sheriff Langdon had never thought about posting guards. Ventura County was so remote and off the beaten path, any effort to secure the isolated Cliff House would have been a waste of manpower according to his way of thinking.

Hewitt and some of the men had been congratulating Henry on getting the big tractor to roll when a ruckus broke out. The sheriff heard a woman scream, and then a shot rang out.

Thirty years of habit and a wide streak of stubbornness saved them that day. Hewitt had his .45 caliber tucked into his belt, the old lawman always having felt naked without a weapon. Rushing around the stone corral, he discovered three men standing over George's prone and bleeding body. The intruders laughed while they watched the dying man gasp for breath. One of them poked George with the barrel of his hunting rifle, smirking as he taunted the incapacitated man lying at his feet.

Hewitt's trained eye summed up the situation as his palm closed around the Smith and Wesson's grip. He didn't know the men, had never seen them before. Their soiled clothing and ragged appearance announced vagrants or drifters. Henry's prone form convicted the trio of murder. The sentence was death.

The sheriff drew and began firing, catching the vagabonds by surprise. Again and again, Hewitt's finger squeezed the trigger, the pistol's 11-round magazine feeding flawlessly as his aim held steady.

The first man dropped without raising his rifle, the second falling before he could pivot. The third ran.

While the sheriff had never considered himself a marksman, Hewitt felt competent enough with his skills, in particular with an up-close gunfight. Hitting a fleeing man with a pistol, however, proved to be difficult. With his target now zigging and zagging in a desperate effort to make his escape, the sheriff fired three more shots. All missed.

He stood for a moment, watching as the last assailant disappeared behind a small outcropping of rock. A few seconds later, Bo and a handful of the other men arrived, the younger deputy then rushing off in pursuit.

"Don't! Stop!" Hewitt ordered, halting the brave subordinate before he had taken three steps. "He's got a long gun and might decide to turn and pick you off. Besides, the way I figure it, he won't stop running until he hits the California state line."

That prediction proved to be erroneous. The third vagabond returned two days later, this time with five other men, all of them desperate and well-armed.

Bo, Peach Gentry, and Jimmy Wadlow all died during the ensuing firefight. Hewitt would never be able to forget the flickering glow of their funeral pyre, the distant flames throwing an eerie, red hue onto the surrounding cliff faces.

That first meeting with outsiders had exposed the people of the Cliff House to the fact that the world was now a much more dangerous place. Sheriff Langdon and the elders began organizing random patrols and ordered that the rifles and shotguns be unpacked. There was a heightened sense of awareness to their surroundings. When workers did venture outside into the ash, they were more alert to potential threats.

Until that point, Hewitt had welcomed any peaceful souls into the stone-walled safety of their community. George's murder and the second ambush by the invaders, combined with their dwindling food supply, forced the sheriff and other leaders to declare that the Cliff House was officially closed to new arrivals.

"We will turn them away," everyone had agreed. The sheriff, however, knew that policy wasn't good enough.

It was clear to the community's leadership that the thug who had escaped had recruited the others. The sheriff could just hear the murderer bragging to his friends, "You are just not going to believe what I saw. There is this big group of people. They have food and water, and they live in a castle built into the side of a mountain. Come with me, and we will kill them all, eat their food, and live like kings!" Those six marauders had nearly taken the Cliff House and slaughtered three of Ventura's best men. How would they be able to handle 20, or 30, or even more looters?

It was quickly determined that secrecy was the key to their survival. If outsiders didn't know their community existed, they would be safe. "But what do we do if someone does wander through and finds us?" asked one of the women.

Still stinging from the loss of his friends, Hewitt's initial thought was, *Off with their heads! Dead men tell no tales*. That hardline thinking, however, went against his natural grain. Not even an apocalypse could reverse decades of enforcing the law and playing the role of the white hat.

"We'll extend our perimeter," the sheriff had finally determined. "We'll intercept people before they get close enough to discover our secret. We'll chase them away before they have a chance to figure out what we have here."

It proved to be a daunting task.

The community's best hunters were the first volunteers for guard duty. Hewitt remembered how strange they looked, covered with thick coats and all wearing white painter's masks, a leftover from when Carlos had last remodeled the interior of the diner.

Over the days and weeks, the newness wore off and being posted as a sentry became one of the least desirable tasks associated with living in the Cliff House. Other than the constant need to shovel manure out of the corral, it was hard to find a job more loathed.

Wearing a mask while outside was difficult enough. Spending hours staring out at a barren, pewter-colored landscape was enough to drive a man crazy. It was cold, dreary, and damned uncomfortable. Worse yet, a man began to feel like he was a target out there. Carlos summed it up best, "Being a sentry is like playing the outfield on a baseball team. You spend hours bored to tears, and then for five seconds, life gets far, far too interesting."

Someone had drawn up a rough map of the surrounding hills and assigned each of the six men to either an elevated perch or a known trail. It wasn't the most secure perimeter Hewitt had ever seen, but it was better than nothing.

They had also drilled the 80 odd residents of the Cliff House on what to do if trouble did rear its ugly head. Men were to keep firearms handy at all times, women assigned to gather up the young ones and move to the interior of the facility. Most of the gals had weapons too.

The first drifters the sentries encountered were three brothers from Ohio. There was a heated exchange when the Ventura men offered challenge, the intercept occurring less than 400 yards from the Cliff House.

The men from the Buckeye State had been in Arizona on a guided hunt when Yellowstone spewed her fury. They had survived at a hunting ranch until the food started to run out. At that point, the staff had asked them politely to leave … at gunpoint. Their rental car had failed after traveling for less than two hours.

Hungry, exhausted, and lost, the three Midwesterners began walking, hoping to find food, shelter, and a way home. They had their rifles and some ammo, outdoor gear and packs, and a determination to survive.

It took a shotgun blast a few feet over their heads to convince the men from Ohio that they were heading in the wrong direction.

The next encounter didn't go as smoothly. Sheriff Langdon had been unloading bags of feed from the wagon when all hell broke out on the next ridge south of the Cliff House. He and a dozen others had rushed to retrieve their long guns and join the fray.

A protracted firefight ensued, the attackers more organized and cautious than any of the previous intruders. For over an hour, the two sides launched bullets at each other, Hewitt and Prichard finally managing to scramble up the next hill, rush through a narrow draw, and hit the attackers from behind.

When the ash settled, they found a dozen dead Mexicans strewn amongst the rocks. The contents of their pockets led Hewitt to believe they had crossed over the Rio Grande in the last few days. They were all males, all in their 20s, and all carried military-grade weapons. The superior marksmanship of Ventura's hunters had saved the community. That, combined with Hewitt's knowledge of the local terrain, had barely carried the day. About the only positive outcome from the encounter was the fact that now the defenders of the Cliff House were armed with AK47 and M16 rifles, as well as a proper amount of ammunition for both.

Sheriff Langdon retrieved one of those rifles, his respect for the Soviet-era AK based on its reliability and proven performance in sandy, gritty environments. "Ventura County and its ash aren't that far from the Iraqi desert," one of the younger men had noted.

Given Puff's slow speed, Hewitt easily kept pace with the lumbering tractor as it rolled toward town. The sheriff appreciated the chance to get out and stretch his legs, but that sentiment wasn't shared by all. Billy and Prichard, deciding to ride along in the old rancher's wagon, seemed deep into a conversation about how long it would take the earth to heal. "Another good reason to walk," the sheriff grumbled, scanning the surrounding hills. "I've got a bad feeling we're in for a longer fight than anyone knows."

Jack had just managed to manhandle the bike down the courthouse's basement steps when the most unusual noise reached his ears. The carbine slung to his back was in the commander's hands in a flash.

Sarah heard it too, and she darted out of the tax assessor's office with a frightened-looking Justin in tow. "What is that?" she murmured.

Jack ignored her question, his ears focused solely on the mechanical clunking that was coming from outside. With M4 high and ready, the commander moved toward the structure's front door and peeked through a window.

In all his years, Jack and never seen anything like the procession that rolled down Ventura's main street. In front was a tall, thin man wearing a huge, Western hat, well-worn boots, and a leather duster. His face was wrapped in a fashion that would make any Bedouin proud, the effect enhanced by the AK47 strapped across his chest.

Behind the cowboy-Arab was an enormous machine that Jack initially had difficulty identifying. Finally, it dawned on the commander – a steam-powered tractor of some sort. Amazing.

Behind the old steamer was a first-rate, shiny, new aluminum trailer with whitewalls and mag wheels. Two more men, rifles pointed skyward, rode on the back.

Jack hadn't seen a moving vehicle of any sort except for Shelly and Philip's golf cart. There was no comparison between that compact, electric powered buggy and the monster that was rolling down Ventura's main drag. With a thick column of smoke billowing from the stack and tires as tall as a man, the old tractor would have been a sight before the apocalypse. Now, it was a true jaw dropper.

Justin and Sarah were at Jack's side a moment later, gawking at the procession as it passed in front of the courthouse.

The commander was just turning to warn his guests to remain quiet when the boy burst through the door yelling, "Dad! Dad!" and chasing the wagon.

Sarah spotted her husband a moment later, dashing out after her son before Jack could react.

The men on the back of the wagon seemed surprised to look up and see a skinny kid running after their parade. A second later, one of the riders leapt to his feet and jumped from the trailer, rushing to meet his wife and son in an emotional embrace.

Jack stayed by the window long enough to make sure his two new friends were truly welcome and then pivoted for the sheriff's office and his bike.

The commander dashed down the steps and raced to his ride, securing the hefty pack as fast as his fingers could work the bungee cords and straps.

Back up the stairs he climbed, lifting the heavy bike over each step and the hustling toward the back door.

Pushing open the emergency bar with his boot, Jack had managed to move the front tire of the bicycle through the opening when the barrel of a pistol was shoved into his face. "What's the hurry, sir?" sounded a gruff voice.

"Just passing through," Jack managed to answer, instantly regretting the line from a B-grade Western.

"Why don't you pull off that rifle, son. Nice and slow, and hand it over your left shoulder to me," the voice commanded as it moved to stand behind Cisco.

Jack's mind raced to find a solution, his body tensing to strike at the pistol holder and then make his getaway. The man behind him seemed to know what the commander was thinking, however, and warned against such a move. "Don't son. Don't even think about it. I've been the sheriff in this county for better than 30 years, and I promise you won't make it."

Nodding, Jack reached for his sling using slow, deliberate motions. A few moments later, the man behind him confiscated his M4 carbine.

"Now," the voice insisted, "you walk that bicycle over to the feed store, nice and slow. No sudden moves or bullshit, just a casual stroll. I'll be right back here, behind you all the way."

Jack did as he was instructed, something in the voice behind him telling the commander that it belonged to a man who could more than handle himself in a fight and wouldn't hesitate to kill. Halfway to their destination, two of the sheriff's friends arrived to help.

One of them took over pushing the bike, the other patting Jack down for other weapons. The commander was relieved of his knife. "He's wearing body armor, Hewitt," one of the newcomers announced. "I can't tell what is underneath it."

Sarah was there, along with Justin and her husband. When she observed Jack being detained, she quickly interjected, "Billy, he's the man who saved our lives … he's a friend. We wouldn't have made it without him."

None of the men now pointing guns at Jack seemed to give her words much weight. Cisco could hear two of his captors talking, but couldn't make out the words.

"Come on, boys; we got to load up this trailer with feed before it gets dark. We can figure out what to do with our new guests later. Let's get moving."

For 30 minutes, Jack watched the masked men load bags of feed onto the wagon while the one they called the sheriff stood well behind him.

When the load was finally ready, Jack was forced to walk in front of the tractor, now taking his place leading the parade out of town.

Five miles outside of Ventura, the sheriff motioned for Jack to turn onto a lane that showed the same unusual tracks he'd spotted in town. "The tractor," he whispered, finally putting it all together.

The procession wound its way up a meandering trail, entering an area of sheer cliff faces and narrow canyons. Along the way, Jack spotted a rifleman standing on a nearby ridge. Given the sheriff's friendly wave, the commander assumed the guy was standing watch.

They rounded a bin, and Jack spotted the Cliff House for the first time. It reminded him of an ancient, Indian cliff dwelling his family had visited when he was a child.

This structure, in contrast, was new and modern-looking, complete with glass windows, large doorways, and smooth, professionally constructed masonry in certain sections. There were also dozens of people, and from the smell that drifted past his nose, some number of cattle or other manure-producing livestock.

How on earth have they kept cattle alive, Jack wondered. *That would be a miracle.*

Sure enough, Jack saw three men scraping a pair of fresh cowhides suspended by ropes between two nearby boulders.

Jack was escorted into a long, narrow room lined with hooks on both walls. "Take off your clothes. We try to keep as much ash out of the interior as possible."

Seeing the other members of the tractor-team removing their coveralls helped lessen the commander's apprehension.

It was just as cold inside the Cliff House as it was outside, a fact that left Jack standing in his skivvies and shivering. The others had clean clothes hanging from assigned hooks, and wasted no time in redressing. Finally, the man they all called "the sheriff," threw Cisco a blanket. "Come with me," he said, making sure the prisoner noticed the AK that was ready for action.

They proceeded through a second door, the entire setup reminding Jack of an airlock. It was a damn good idea, he had to admit. Wrapped in the heavy, wool cover, the commander was led through a series of halls and rooms.

They passed at least 15 or 20 people who gave the commander nothing but hard looks. Obviously, strangers weren't welcome here. In fact, they were apparently feared, and that wasn't good.

Jack was guided to the back of the enormous complex, the route winding further into the bowels of the rock mountain. There were no windows, and the commander got the distinct feeling that he was far underground. The occasional candle, flickering light on the stone, made the ceilings and walls seem all the closer. *It's a tomb*, Cisco thought. *Let's hope it's not mine.*

"Step in here," ordered Sheriff Langdon. "Stand over there and face the wall."

Entering a tiny area that looked to be the lawman's makeshift office, Jack spotted two simple chairs and a plain, wooden table. A single, small taper was the only light. He did as instructed, stepping to face the stone façade.

The sheriff took his time searching the commander's gear.

First was his load vest, then armor, then the contents pulled from his pockets. Finally, the sheriff was finished, taking all of Jack's possessions and placing them into a large cardboard box.

"Why am I being treated like a criminal, Sheriff?" Jack finally asked, breaking the silence he'd maintained since being captured an hour before.

"You're not," came the cold reply. "You're being treated like an intruder. You need to understand one thing right here and right now – the law here in Ventura County is me, and me alone. There are no courts, or lawyers, or inalienable rights. It's just you and me."

"Okay, then why am I being treated like an intruder? All that I am guilty of is reuniting a family. I saved that woman and child from some very dangerous men, and now I'm the one who is being treated like the bad seed."

"Sit down," the sheriff responded, completely ignoring the question.

Again, Jack complied with the instructions, then watched his captor take the opposite chair behind the table. "What is your name?" the lawman asked.

"Commander Jackson Cisco, United States Navy."

His military rank brought a low grunt from the sheriff, but that was the extent of his reaction. The questioning continued, "And what brings you to Ventura County, Commander?"

"I am on my way to Texas. My family is there," Jack replied.

"Deserter?"

"No, sir," Jack hissed, straightening in his chair. "I am on leave, officially granted by my commanding officer."

"And what is a Naval officer doing with Marine Corps equipment?"

"I was issued this gear before I left San Diego," Jack replied. "Again, it was authorized by my boat's captain."

"How long ago was that?"

Jack was already tired of the interrogation, now convinced that the sheriff was simply fishing to see what sins had been committed. "I'm done answering questions, Sheriff. Now please return my possessions to me, and I'll be on my way."

The man across the table didn't respond right away, instead he seemed to be studying Jack with a scrutiny that could only be described as intense.

Finally, the sheriff sighed and responded, "I'm afraid I can't do that, Commander Cisco. We have a rule here at the Cliff House – no one is allowed to leave."

"What? Why? I would think the fewer mouths to feed, the better."

The sheriff nodded, and then said, "What makes you think we would allow you to live? Dead men don't eat, sir."

For the first time since being captured, Jack felt the pangs of fear gnawing at his gut. The man across from him didn't smile, or wink, or show any sign that he was anything but serious.

"So, no good deed goes unpunished? You kill people who risk their lives to help innocent strangers?"

"Not at all," Hewitt responded with a wave of his hand. "Your reward would be a painless death. You wouldn't want to see what we do to the really bad intruders around here."

"Why? Why take an innocent man's life? You just don't seem like the type of people to do such a thing."

"We have let a few strangers go before, and every time, they come back with a lot of friends, and our people end up dying. That's why we have the sentries in place … to chase stragglers away before they figure out what we have. Unfortunately for you, we were driving Puff today. And the fact is," he paused, staring at Jack sternly, "I just can't let you go running all over the countryside, telling every hardcore badass still walking the earth what you have seen here today."

"I wouldn't tell anyone you were here," Jack replied with honest eyes.

Hewitt grunted, "If someone has a knife to your balls, you would tell them anything to live. Don't kid yourself, Commander. You may be a brave guy, perhaps even an honorable fellow, but every man has his limits."

Jack thought about the sheriff's response for a moment, struggling to come up with a valid counter argument. "Sounds like I was in the wrong place at the wrong time," he finally said, still having trouble believing he was going to be killed.

Someone rapped on the doorframe just then, the sheriff rising to see who was interrupting the interrogation. It was one of the men from the wagon, bringing Jack's clothing. His pants and shirt had apparently been brushed clean and searched. They had even knocked the ash off the commander's boots.

"Get dressed," Hewitt demanded, handing over the articles. Then he turned to the man who had delivered the clothing and said, "Stay here. I'm going to need your help for a few minutes."

While Jack buttoned, zipped, and laced, the commander's mind struggled to come up with a way out of this trap. Was the sheriff just trying to scare him? Were these seemingly civilized people actually capable of such an act? On one side, he wondered why he was being allowed to dress if his execution was next. After the commander was finished, he looked at Hewitt and said, "What if I want to stay here? I have certain skills that might prove useful, and I'm not a bad hand with a rifle."

The lawman grunted, "I thought about that, but I'm pretty sure you would run off the very first chance you got. Obviously, to have come this far, you're a determined man, Commander Cisco. And I can't say I blame you. In your shoes, I'd probably be hell bent on getting to Texas and willing to do just about anything to get there."

Without waiting for any further debate, Hewitt turned to the lingering man in the doorway. "I'm going to go talk to the elders. You stay here and keep our guest inside of this room. If he tries to get out or does anything at all to offend you, kill him. Understood?"

"Yes, sir," the newly-minted guard responded with a nervous voice, before throwing Jack a look as if he expected the commander to grow horns and hoofs.

For a moment, Jack thought the sheriff was going to leave the box containing his equipment behind. Hewitt had no such intent, however, bending to pick up the commander's gear and exiting without another word.

Chapter 19

Hewitt hadn't been gone five minutes before the door opened, and an elderly woman entered his cell carrying a tray. "Sheriff Langdon said we should feed you," she said. "I'm sorry. It's not much, but it is the same as everyone here is eating today."

While she set the tray on the table, Jack observed the fidgety guard outside. The young man was obviously scared to death, his white knuckles plainly visible when he gripped his rifle.

The woman backed out as Jack mumbled, "Thank you." Moving to the tray, Jack pulled back a cloth napkin and inhaled sharply.

On the plastic plate was a steak the size of Nebraska, fried beans, some sort of flat bread, and a large glass of milk. "I've not seen anything like this since before I boarded *Utah*," he whispered, taking special note of the butter dripping from the hot bread.

The commander dug in, partly because the aroma was wonderful, partly because he knew it might be his last meal, but mostly because in these times, a man never knew when he might eat next.

The steak was tender, fresh, and so well prepared, that the plastic knife sliced right through. The beans appeared to have been canned right out of a local garden … and had been cooked in some sort of oil or fat, probably to add calories to everyone's diet. The bread was horrible, only made tolerable by the butter. All in all, Jack savored every last morsel, including the warm, rich milk.

After wolfing down the meal, the commander got back to focusing on his primary task – escape.

The plastic knife and fork that had been provided on his tray were worthless. So was the candle. Basically, Jack had his clothing and boots, and nothing else but the table and chairs. Unless he planned on taming a lion, the furniture sparked no opportunity to vacate the premises. Deeply engrossed in his mental initiative, the commander was briefly distracted by his bloated gut, happy to have been nourished, but at the same time protesting the work involved in digesting the now unfamiliar cuisine. He stood to stretch out his core and allow a little breathing room for the heavy meal to be processed when an odd thought crossed his mind. "That was some feast. I just hope these folks aren't of the same mindset as those flesh-eaters we met at the rest stop. They might have just been fattening me up for the kill."

The mental image of his body stretched over a pit boasting an apple in its mouth reinvigorated the military man's search. Studying the room for the Nth time, Jack noted the total lack of windows, vents, or other openings besides the door. The walls were solid rock, some of the surface natural, other smaller, smoother sections exhibiting tool marks where a natural indentation had been expanded. The ceiling and floor were stone as well.

Jack thought about calling the guard and jumping the nervous fellow but dismissed that option. The man was so scared, the commander was surprised he hadn't accidently shot himself already.

Scanning the walls one last time, Jack found that just above his reach, no one had bothered to smooth out the rock. There were natural crevices visible all around, especially over the door.

"You have to do something before the sheriff returns," the commander whispered to himself. "Think, Jack … think hard."

He pulled over a chair and began feeling the area above the door. There were several indentations, some deep enough for Jack to stick in his arm up to the elbow.

Stretching higher, the commander found several rough sections that could serve as handholds. He could climb to the ceiling, but what good would that do?

An idea came to the commander.

Using two hand holds, he pulled his feet off the chair and began swinging like a kid on a tree branch. After a couple of passes, Jack caught his boot in another crevice. He was now hanging above the door, suspended nearly horizontal in the dim candlelight. "Just call me batty," he grunted, dropping back down to the chair. "I hang upside in caves," he added, rubbing his strained hands.

The problem with hovering above the door was how to lure Mr. Nervous in from the hallway, drop down, and disarm the sentry without the guy getting off a shot that would surely bring Hewitt and a bunch of others running. It was a safe bet that the guard's finger would be on the trigger.

But, he had to try. The alternative wasn't appealing.

Jack surveyed the room again, trying to formulate a plan. The empty tray of food was still on the table, only a puddle of grease from the beans left the plate.

Smiling, the commander picked up the cotton napkin and dabbled one corner into the oily slick. "I bet that would make a lot of smoke if it got too close to the flame," he whispered.

It took five minutes for Jack to practice his moves, rehearsing the most important physical feat of his life.

Soaking up every last drop of the oil, Commander Cisco took a deep breath and then lit the cloth via the candle. He set it next to the door and watched as a small spark began to flicker, a column of smoke rising from the fire.

He jumped from the chair and caught the rocks. A second later he was suspended, hanging on for dear life and waiting for the napkin to become fully engrossed.

"Fire!" he yelled. "Fire! Let me out of here!"

For a second, Jack didn't think the guard was going to take the bait.

After what seemed an hour, he heard the latch, and then the door opened about an inch.

Seeing the smoke and flames, the guard opened the door the rest of the way but didn't venture inside. Jack had anticipated that move.

Swinging from the ceiling, Jack's legs shot through the opening and struck the sentry directly between the eyes with a vicious kick, slamming him backward into the rock wall.

Jack was on him in a second, but there was no need. The guy was out cold and would awaken with a broken nose and a goose egg on the back of his head.

There in the hall was the cardboard box of Jack's gear. After picking up the guard's AR15 and checking the magazine, the commander pulled the unconscious sentinel into the room, latched the door, and then rushed down the hall carrying his box of equipment.

After two turns, Cisco was lost. Cursing himself for not paying more attention as Hewitt had led him through the maze, the commander identified a small, closet-like nook and snuck inside.

Pulling on his equipment in the dark, Jack tried to recall the turns and general direction to complete his escape. He remembered the men from the wagon leaning his bike against an outside wall. But how to get there?

Now fully armed and feeling more secure wearing his armor, Jack considered taking a hostage and making the captive guide him outside. He opened the door an inch, scanning up and down the deserted corridor. "Just my luck. Not an ounce of hostage material roaming these halls," he murmured.

Deeply inhaling, his chest now full of air, Jack bolted from the secluded niche and sprinted, weapon up and ready.

He made two more turns before realizing something was wrong. First, he noticed the eerie echo of his footfalls on the stone floor. Knowing that the ricocheting sound was an indicator of hollow spaces, Jack's stride slowed as he evaluated his surroundings. On the way in, the commander had passed rooms packed with cots and people. Once teeming with life, those same rooms now were vacant of any human population. Only the bedding remained. Jack hadn't seen a single soul since his escape. Where had everybody gone?

Another section of hall brought a voice to Jack's ear. He couldn't make out the words, but clearly a man was speaking. "Finally, a live body … hostage material … somebody to hold at gunpoint and get the hell out of this nightmare," he hissed, moving toward the sound.

He crept carefully to a half-height rock wall and peeked around the corner. There, in a cavernous, open area, gathered at least 40 people. Behind them, a herd of cattle rested on the cool, stone floor. Hewitt stood on a wooden box, apparently in the process of delivering a soliloquy.

Jack was stunned. He'd seen the cowhide when it was scraped and had devoured the fresh meat offered to him. Despite both of those hints, he had no idea the Cliff House was equipped with a makeshift, indoor corral, or that the locals had managed to move a whole herd inside.

The image of Hewitt perched on a soapbox put the commander in mind of an old-timey snake oil salesman touting his wares or an itinerant preacher saving souls. But that was not what was going on here. Realizing he had just bumbled into a town meeting, Jack ducked back out of sight and tried to regroup. All the while, Sheriff Langdon continued making his statement to the gathering.

"We know from Billy's wife, Sarah, that Tucson has degraded to the point where roving gangs scour the streets, searching for living, human captives to round up and then eat. I know this is gross and shocking, but it is our new reality. Furthermore, both she and our captive believe the rest area on I-8 hosts a similar group of cannibals," Hewitt explained.

Jack could hear the gasps and mumbling from the throng, some of the voices calling on God to protect them. Most of the Cliff House residents, however, simply sounded angry.

"On another note, according to Prichard and two of our other ranchers," the sheriff continued, "we will lose the entire herd in less than two months if we don't find a way to obtain sufficient amounts of a chemical called Coccidiostat. As far as any of us know, Tucson is the only place in this area that stocked such a substance in the quantities we need. Now that the city is in complete anarchy, we have an even bigger problem on our hands than before. That is why I called you all here."

Leaning back against the rock, Jack listened as the meeting progressed.

"We neither have the manpower, nor the capability to invade Tucson," Hewitt continued. "Our original plan was to take 15 men, walk in, and carry enough of the chemical home to save our beef. That option, given what we've heard about the state of affairs in the city, is no longer executable. It would be suicide to try and fight our way in and out, all the while carrying hundreds of pounds on our backs. Now we are faced with the potential of losing our entire herd of livestock. That would leave us little to eat but corn dodgers and flatbread."

The crowd was obviously deeply concerned. Jack sat for a moment, listening to the murmurings. The sheriff, having given enough time for his audience to digest his bad news, then opened the floor for suggestions.

Jack listened for another 15 minutes, hearing nothing but anger and disappointment. He then realized that he should be running, not hoping that the people who were about to execute him would come up with a solution.

The commander quietly rose from the cranny and darted toward freedom.

Figuring the underground corral must be located in the back of the Cliff House, he scurried the opposite direction. A minute later, he discovered the local armory and his own rifle along the way. For a second, he considered helping himself to some additional ammo but dismissed the idea. Why prove the sheriff right?

Another series of turns and rooms, and then he found himself at the main entrance.

Wrapping his head and face, both as a disguise and to protect from the ash, the commander emerged and strolled calmly to his bike. Having to cover his skin while outdoors sucked, but at least it afforded the benefit of anonymity.

Jack found his bike exactly where he'd seen it parked.

He mounted his 2-wheeled getaway and began pedaling down the lane. He figured the main entrance to the complex would have the most lookouts, but it was the only way he knew. The commander started pumping the pedals hard.

A shout came from a ridge when he was less than 300 yards down the trail. Waving with a friendly nod, Jack kept on going, praying that the sentry wasn't an expert marksman and that the speed of his bike would throw off the man's aim.

"Hey! Where are you going! You know nobody can leave by themselves!" the second challenger bellowed.

Again, Jack waved and then flashed the thumbs-up signal, just like Hewitt had on the way in.

Confused, not wanting to injure a friend or neighbor, and having only instructions to shoot at anyone *approaching* the Cliff House, the guard didn't fire a single shot.

Five minutes later, Jack arrived at the blacktop highway that led into Ventura … or back to I-8. A critical decision needed to be made, and he hadn't thought this far ahead.

Going back to the interstate was the smart thing to do from the standpoint of finding his way in this monotone grey, post-apocalyptic world. Getting lost would be more than a simple inconvenience; it could lead to his demise. *No,* he thought, *best to stay on this path and just sneak past the rest areas. After all, it will be dark in a matter of hours*.

That still left Tucson, and the thought of trying to travel through a large colony of cannibals sent a shiver through Jack's core.

He needed time to think, study his map, and lay out a new course. More immediately, Jack needed to rest and regroup. Sleep had been difficult to come by the last few days, and the commander knew he needed to be at the top of his game.

Interstate 8 was about to turn into I-10. El Paso, Texas wasn't that far away, and while the thought of finally reaching the Lone Star State was uplifting, news that cannibalism was the newest survival technique made Jack second-guess his decision to continue on the main highways.

But right now, at this moment, what he needed was distance between himself and the people of the Cliff House. "They'll anticipate that I'll run for the interstate," he whispered. "Let's not do what that sage, old, bastard of a sheriff expects."

Jack turned toward Ventura.

Chapter 20

Cisco reached the tiny village in less than 15 minutes, his body still keyed up from his escape and his legs pumping the pedals hard.

Once in town, his next job was to find shelter.

The courthouse was out, as were the antique mall and feed store. Not only was Hewitt smart enough to track an outlaw, but it was also evident that the people from the Cliff House still visited those facilities on occasion.

The post office, however, showed no signs of being disturbed, the enclave of the front entrance having nearly a foot of undisturbed, drifted ash.

Jack rode around to the back of the unpretentious, red brick building and checked the rear door. Again, there was no sign of human visitation.

While the small structure wouldn't be Jack's first choice during a lightning storm, it was better than nothing at all. The accommodations offered shelter from Mother Nature's wrath, but also offered too many avenues of approach for any ne'er-do-wells in search of a meal. And if the sheriff did pick up his trail, the men from the Cliff House could be on him in a heartbeat.

No, staying in town was just too dangerous.

The commander rode on, heading south out of the tiny community, hoping to find some other lodging.

Ventura thinned out quickly, lowering Jack's hopes of sleeping anywhere but on the ground – again. Still, every mile gave relief. The commander didn't see any other bicycles at the Cliff House, nor any sort of vehicle except for the steam tractor. That meant he was outdistancing any pursuit with each rotation of his wheels.

He saw the utility line cut to the east for several hundred yards before the driveway came into view. There, nearly a half mile back from the road stood a modest, adobe home and a few metal outbuildings.

The terrain here was as flat as a pancake. The wind had blown most of the ash off the pavement and gravel lane leading to the structure. *I could cut off the highway and make it tough to follow my tracks,* he mused, smiling at the shriveled undergrowth on the shoulder. Jack examined his surroundings and determined that the sheriff's posse, if they decided to give chase, could be seen for nearly a mile in any direction.

Turning off the main artery, Jack dismounted, and with a grunt, picked the bike and heavy pack off the ground. He stepped gingerly through the dead weeds alongside the home's drive for nearly 50 yards to ensure he didn't leave any sign. The effort was exhausting but well worth the energy.

Jack approached the ranch's residence cautiously. While he seriously doubted anyone had survived outside of those boarded at the Cliff House, he could not be sure.

"Anybody home? I mean no harm," he yelled from the end of the drive. As expected, there was no answer.

He patrolled around the perimeter, keen for any sign of habitation. The were no tracks in the ash, no trash or garbage accumulated, and no movement from within.

He stepped on the tiny porch, opening the screen door and grinning when a small river of pumice ran out. No one had been through the entrance since the eruption.

He found similar evidence at the back entrance. "If anyone is home, they haven't stepped outside for a long, long time," he whispered.

Again, he shouted a warning. "Hello! Is anyone home? I'm coming in. If someone is here, let me know, and I'll just leave." There was no response.

He tested the doorknob, thinking he would have to kick or pry away the lock. The home was unlocked. *Small Town, USA*, Jack thought. *Crime evidently isn't an issue under the sheriff's watch.*

Still, Jack hesitated. He had never entered anyone's home without being invited. Despite being sure that the place was abandoned, an odd sense of guilt seized his gut. This had been some family's domain. Their castle. It just felt wrong.

For a moment, Jack considered the outbuildings. They were second-rate, at best. The roof of one "barn" looked near collapse, the commander reasonably sure the structure hadn't been in the best condition before Yellowstone spilled her guts. The others were really sheds, and he doubted they would be far from airtight.

The thought of a lightning storm striking in the middle of the night compelled him into the home, rifle high and ready.

Stepping into what was a small utility room, Jack spied an old washer and dryer, sink, and several pairs of workbooks lined up against the wall. No gunshots or shouting interrupted his tour.

Now the commander's advance was halted by another concern. What if there were dead, decaying bodies inside? It was an image he didn't want to be ingrained in his mind's eye. What if it were women and children? "The nightmares would never end," he whispered.

Taking a deep breath, Jack decided to follow his nose. The commander didn't detect the noxious odor of rotting flesh. In fact, the place smelled a little stale and musty at the worst.

He continued, entering a small kitchen. *Looks like someone had to rush out to the PTO luncheon*, he mused, noticing the crusty, morning dishes stacked in the sink. Otherwise, the place was tidy. Too neat, in fact. Jack found every cabinet had been cleared of anything edible. Holding his nose and preparing for a mold-infested swamp of sour milk and rotten bologna, he opened the fridge and was surprised to find it showroom empty, void of even the basic condiments. "So much for having mustard on my MRE meatloaf," he snipped.

Room by room, Jack searched the home. He blew the dust off the photos in the living room, revealing several images of a middle-aged man and his wife. Evidently, they had one child, a girl. As the pictorial chronology continued, he noticed where the daughter had gotten married and had produced two cute grandbabies. In an odd way, the images were warming.

Jack carefully returned every picture frame exactly where it had been. He wasn't here to loot and destroy. He only wanted a roof over his head for the night. Maybe the owners were squirreled safely away at the Cliff House. Perhaps they hoped to return one day and live out their lives on their own land again.

The bedrooms indicated more order and organization. The master's bed was made. The towels were folded in the modest bathroom. The sinks and toilet were dusty but clean.

Finding wide spaces of empty racks in the closets, combined with the clean refrigerator, Jack assumed that the owners had made an orderly withdrawal. He arrived at the conclusion that indeed, they had moved to the Cliff House and were now enjoying home-canned veggies and fresh steak. It comforted him to assume they were alive and well.

He decided to sleep on the couch rather than disturb their bed. There was something sacred about that … the difference between being an invader and a guest.

Checking the perimeter in the last of the natural light, Jack observed nothing but empty fields of ash and dead undergrowth. "Thank you for inviting me in for the evening," he announced to the pictures. "You have a lovely home."

The commander awoke before daybreak, the howl of the wind rousing him out of a very deep sleep. "Your couch is very comfortable, thank you," he croaked to the photographs.

Sipping from his CamelBak, he decided on a substantial breakfast. Food was soon going to become a problem, as was water. Sarah and Justin had both been bottomless pits, but they had needed the nourishment far more than he.

Removing the "meal heater," from a previous MRE, Jack used one of the kitchen stove's burners to warm a can of chili. "What I wouldn't give for a hot dog to go along with this," he complained, smacking his lips while watching the thick liquid begin to boil.

At first light, he again checked his surroundings. No posse of riflemen were sneaking up on the farmhouse. Hewitt wasn't leading a pack of bloodhounds in pursuit.

What Jack did notice was a pile of bones sticking out from behind the barn, and the sight troubled him greatly.

With face re-wrapped and rifle in his hand, Jack stepped out the back door to investigate. Dreading the thought of finding the owners dead, he approached with a grimace, weak tummy, and hesitant legs.

It was a small relief to find several dead cows versus human skeletons. Evidently, the animals, suffering from the ash, had come to the barn for relief. There were at least 50 expired carcasses lying in various stages of decay. Now, with the gusts becoming more intense, Jack could smell the decaying stench.

The small herd had probably been the rancher's primary source of income. Obviously, the commander wasn't visiting in a wealthy household, and given the state of the outbuildings, times had probably been hard on the owners.

There was more, however, to the melancholy cloud that now descended over Jack. His mind drifted back to the indoor corral at the Cliff House, and how wonderful it had been to see the living, breathing cattle. Other than the chickens at Pinemont, they had been the only non-human creatures the commander had seen since the catastrophe.

The protected enclosure was probably an ultra-rare occurrence on the planet. Unless someone had the forethought to move sheep or goats into a domed football stadium, it was difficult to imagine any other place on earth where a herd of livestock could have endured.

"They were surviving," Jack whispered, scanning the boneyard. "Now they're doomed, just like these animals."

Turning to go back inside and get out of the wind, Jack felt a profound sense of sadness swelling in his chest. "How will mankind survive without animals?" he pondered. "Even if the ash clears and the sun comes back out, how will we repopulate the earth?"

Commander Cisco returned to the couch, sitting down just as if he'd stopped by for Sunday brunch after church. "I started on this voyage to find my wife and daughters," he explained to the snapshots. "Now, I'm wondering what I'm going to do if they are still alive. How will I provide for them? What hope is there?"

Archie and his gardens had provided a glimmer of optimism. Pinemont and those precious eggs had been uplifting. The people of Mud Lake and the underground Marines exemplified the resilience of mankind. But these isolated incidences did little to build his belief in the long-term future of the species.

"Quit being such a fussbudget, Jack," Cisco scolded himself. "If the people of this backwater, hick town can survive, there are probably thousands of other creative souls who will save humanity."

Still, what little confidence he could muster seemed to drift away like the ash that now covered North America. The negative retrospect just wouldn't stop.

"The truth is that more often than not we're turning on each other rather than banding together to survive. Few of us can see the big picture. No one is worried about anything other than where their next meal is coming from," he complained to the charming couple smiling back from the photographs.

"Hell, even Hewitt was going to kill me…. Tucson is home to a den of wild cannibals. What possible future can my girls inherit? What dreams will they hold for themselves? Or will the mark of success be avoiding the flesh-eater's knife?"

The doom and gloom then turned to introspection. *And what have you done to improve the situation, Commander Cisco?* he mused. *Sure, you helped Archie get water. Yeah, you saved the people of Pinemont's ass, and you stopped the campers at Mud Lake from losing their water supply. But what have you actually done? What contribution have you made? You're no better, sitting here on your fat butt, bitching, moaning, and complaining about everyone else.*

His mind returned to the cannibals. How had something like that gotten started? Who had taken the first bite of human flesh?

Jack knew the disgusting practice wasn't anything new. During his survival classes at the Academy, the topic had been discussed while studying the recent wars in the Congo and Liberia.

In fact, history was full of examples where famine had driven normal people to feast on their friends and neighbors. There was the documented story of an airplane crashing in the Andes mountains in the 1970s. The survivors had little food or water and heard on the radio that the search for them had been called off. Until rescued, they had consumed the dead bodies of the passengers and crew, preserved in the snow. And that was not an isolated incident. Lifeboat survivors had seen cannibalism, as had early expeditions into the unknown.

Still, Sarah had claimed that the body-snatchers in Tucson were now hunting the living. That was a new low, as far as Cisco was concerned. But maybe that would become the new normal?

Without freezers or a boatload of salt, the dead would be nearly impossible to preserve for any period. Living people, on the other hand, were just like cattle, or sheep, or swine. They could be harvested as needed. Meat on the hoof. Jack wanted to puke at the concept.

The commander remained on the couch, dreading travel in the building flurry. As he sat listening to the persistent breeze buffet the home, his thoughts began to darken.

"Why am I being such a nice guy?" he asked himself.

"Why am I one of the few people walking the earth that is taking the high road? Maybe I'm the one playing the fool. Maybe self-centered survival is really what it takes to ensure the future of the species. Perhaps in another few weeks, well after that last can of chili is gone, it will dawn on me that taking what I need from others is the only option."

"I'll go rogue," he warned the montage of photos. "I have leadership skills and training far and above anyone I've met since the fall. I've become deadly with a rifle and have survived several firefights. Maybe it's time I stopped being Mr. Goodie-two-shoes and started getting all Darwinist on my fellow man. I'm more fit, smarter, stronger, and clearly a higher achiever. I should rule the roost. I should run the show. I should get what I need before the rest of these lower life forms."

His mind then shifted to Hewitt and the folks at the Cliff House. They had managed to revive the old steamer, which was quite brilliant. They had moved a large number of survivors into a safe location and were feeding them. No easy feat in the post-Yellowstone world.

Yet, Jack could ruin their day without much issue.

His mind began to wander … fantasize … plotting the downfall of the sheriff and his tribe. The commander could go back to Ventura, pick a good spot and wait for them. When Hewitt and the boys came to pick up feed, he would ruin their day. He would ruin their lives.

It would be easy to ambush the tractor crew. They were slack, far from diligent, and Commander Cisco had a strong notion that only Sheriff Langdon had any real fighting experience.

Jack would snipe the lawman, take him out with the first shot. He'd nail one or two more of them before they even realized what had happened. The commander would leave a single man alive. The messenger.

Jack would hold their precious tractor hostage and send back the lone survivor with the ransom demand. "As much food, fresh water, and ammunition as a man and bicycle can carry. Do it now or I'll destroy the tractor, and you'll all starve," he hissed at the portraits.

He recalled Mud Lake and the divided leadership there. How easy would it have been to play one side against the other? He could have been their President, Monarch and Emperor in less than two weeks. Shelly would have experienced a "firearm malfunction," her husband accidently slipping and drowning in the spring.

He had held Pinemont's leadership hostage in a garage. He could have played that differently and ended up running the town. Archie, and his precious greenhouses would have been child's play to control.

"No," he sighed, "You are missing your opportunity. You should be building a new empire, Commander. You should have marshaled and managed the assets you've encountered along the way and headed east as an invading army, not a lone drifter. Between the Marines at the air station, the men of Mud Lake, and the people of Pinemont, you could be consolidating all of Arizona and New Mexico. A warlord. A strongman. The new sheriff in town, with a huge, unstoppable posse."

The thought made Jack laugh, something his troubled soul desperately needed. Endorphins surged through his brain, his chuckling at the mental images continuing for longer than it should have. He just couldn't stop.

It then occurred to him that perhaps his comedic line of reasoning wasn't so humorous after all. He was the highest-ranking government official he'd encountered since leaving San Diego, except for the Marine commander at Yuma. *Should* he be taking an authoritative perspective?

"Hi, I'm from the federal government, and I'm here to help," Cisco snorted. "I've been granted authority on behalf of your elected representatives to come here and take control of the situation. Job one – feed me. Job two, send out your best men to find my wife and kids. Priority three, draw me a bath."

Again, Jack's laughter filled the empty house. After a bit, he suddenly stopped and then sat in silence.

"You're losing your fucking mind, Jack," he finally whispered. "You would suck as a king or dictator. Get your ass off this perch and get moving toward Texas. Finish this quest."

He trudged to the bike and retrieved his map.

After a quick review, he sighed in disappointment. Avoiding Tucson was going to be difficult at best. It wasn't so much the distances involved that troubled him, but the terrain. He would be wandering through one of the most unpopulated regions of North America for at least three days. He only had one MRE and one can of chili left. Perhaps two days of water if he was careful. What were the chances he would encounter food or drink along the way?

Still, there was little choice. He knew for certain at least one hostile group occupied the rest areas. After that encounter, he believed Sarah's tale about Tucson. He would wander the wilderness.

Pushing his bike out the back door, Jack paused to glance at the dead herd again. "More than anything, that is what's bothering you, isn't it, Commander? You've lost all optimism. You no longer have faith in the future or your fellow man."

Shrugging, Jack mounted his two-wheel steed and steered for the road.

He arrived at the pavement, stopped, and glanced to the southeast. The land looked barren, inhospitable, and daunting.

Anger welled up inside him. Hewitt's cows were going to die, followed soon after by the people of the Cliff House. While it sickened him to think about the loss of human life, what really was eating at Jack was the opportunity the cattle presented. He wasn't an expert on animal husbandry, but surely that number of head offered a big enough gene pool to ensure a healthy population. Was he riding away from the one source of future protein that might feed generations to come?

Hewitt wanted to kill him, and that fact merely added to Jack's frustration. Some inner voice within the commander's head wanted to prove the old law dog wrong. There was an injustice to the whole affair, and in the commander's experience, injustice was a sign of weakness.

Glancing back toward Ventura, Jack said, "Why don't you people grow a pair and go get whatever you need to keep those cows alive and breeding?"

"Why don't you?" he then asked himself, growing more agitated by the second. "If it is so important, why don't you go back and confront them? They haven't seen what you have. They don't realize how bad things really are!"

While his head shouted for Jack to turn toward the empty desert and Texas, the commander's heart won the internal argument. Not knowing why, not having a plan, with no idea what to expect, Jack turned the bike toward Ventura and the Cliff House.

Knowing the sentries were there was half the battle. With that intel, Cisco could hang back, take his time, and proceed with metered caution.

He realized where the first man was stationed after being challenged during his escape. Circumventing the perimeter around the Cliff House, Jack observed the second guard rise and stretch from his rock perch. Given the census of the Cliff House's residents, the commander was confident that there would be no more than five or six men posted as lookouts.

He spotted the third armed gun during the guards' shift change.

It was relatively simple to identify a hidden approach between them. Three hours after leaving the ranch, the commander was spying on his nemesis from less than a football field's length away.

Taking up residence in such rugged terrain was a two-edged sword. It was easy to hide – for both the stalker *and* the stalked.

Nestled in a patch of rock that had slid off the cliff above some thousands of years ago, Jack rested, hydrated, and asked himself again, "What in the hell are you doing here, Cisco?"

He was operating more off instinct and emotion rather than cold calculation or level-headed analysis. For the Nth time, he questioned his own sanity. A whiff of cow manure, normally a repugnant experience, now served to reinforce the commander's commitment.

The activity around the Cliff House was exactly what he had expected. Jack watched as small gaggles of men and women meandered here and there, each group obviously busy with some designated chore or activity. The sheriff, the man he actually wanted to chat with, never showed his face.

Jack spent the hours rehearsing what he wanted to say to his former captor. As the time passed, a high-level plan began to form in the commander's head.

Just then, Hewitt appeared at the main entrance, stopping to chat with two females who were heating clothing in a large, black kettle.

"Finally," Jack hissed, tensing in preparation.

Sheriff Langdon sauntered over to a group of men standing around Puff. Jack watched as one of the gents pointed out a feature on the old steamer. Somebody cracked a joke, waffles of laughter spreading through their masks and across the desert.

That's when the commander caught a break.

Patting one of his friends on the back, the sheriff stepped in Jack's general direction, away from the Cliff House.

"He's got to take a leak," Jack snickered.

Standing quickly, Jack followed Hewitt as if he belonged in the community. Every exposed step made the commander's heart pound, the blood rushing through his ears. Twice he paused, thinking to turn, sneak away, and forget the whole thing.

He rounded an outcropping and spied Hewitt some thirty yards ahead. Sure enough, the sheriff ducked into an alcove of rock, already reaching for his fly.

When he'd finished his business, Hewitt zipped up his trousers and turned. If the old lawman was surprised to see Jack's eyes staring down the barrel of his carbine, the sheriff didn't show it.

"I knew you'd be back," Hewitt growled in a low, mean tone. "How many murderers did you bring with you, Commander? How many innocent people do you intend to slaughter today?"

"I came alone," Jack replied, trying to make his voice sound as friendly as possible. "The only person who has to die today is *you* ... if you reach for that pistol in your belt."

"What do you want?"

"Just to talk. You and me, man to man. If we can't come to an agreement, then I'll leave without troubling you further."

Hewitt took a few moments to mull over Jack's words, finally nodding as he responded, "Okay. Talk."

"I came back because of the cattle," the commander began. "I don't give a rat's ass about you ... or the people here. The cows, however, have to survive."

For a second, Jack noticed surprise flash behind Hewitt's eyes. It was fleeting, but the commander knew he had earned the sheriff's attention. "Go on," the local leader prompted.

"I have a plan ... of sorts ... about how we can get into Tucson, load up the chemical you need, and get out. It's dangerous, probably deadly for a few, but in the end, we have to save that herd."

"I'm listening," Hewitt responded.

"I need more information before I go spouting off like a crazy man. I want to talk to Sarah and your people. If my scheme isn't workable, then I'll march out of here, and you'll never see me again. I want your word that I won't be taken prisoner or executed. Do we have a deal?"

"Why should I believe you? Why shouldn't I start shouting at the top of my lungs? You might get me and a couple of our men, but you'll die for sure."

"What choice do you have, sir? Has anyone *here* come up with another option?" Jack paused to collect his thoughts, a kaleidoscope of his journey's memories swirling through his mind. "You've not seen the mass devastation that I have seen crossing the country. You cannot imagine how truly uninhabitable it is out there. You might possess the only living livestock within a thousand miles or more. We have to try. At some point in time, we're going to have to rebuild, and that's why I'm here."

Spreading his hands wide, Hewitt glared at Jack with a skepticism born of years as a cop. One thing was for sure; his stint in law enforcement hadn't kept him in constant contact with the crème de la crème of mankind. Yet, there was a sincere note in the commander's tone that struck a nerve. "I suppose we should at least hear you out. You could have been halfway to Tucson by now if you wanted, and there is some weight to your coming back. All right. You have my word. We'll let you go if our powwow doesn't produce results."

Jack nodded, lowered his rifle, and stood waiting. Hewitt pivoted and began his trek back toward the Cliff House. After a few steps, he waved, calling over his shoulder, "Well, come on. Time's a wasting, Commander.

After reassuring everyone that Jack was, "Okay," Hewitt quickly gathered his flock. Jack was led through the airlock again, this time being allowed to brush the dust from his clothing with a small whisk broom.

Twenty minutes later, Hewitt and the local brain trust were gathered in what had probably been the stone mansion's great room. Most of the dozen attendees sat on the floor or leaned against the wall as the parley was called to order.

"The commander has returned," Sheriff Langdon announced. "Somehow … I'm not quite sure how … he has managed to convince me that his intent is peaceful. He is not to be harmed unless he threatens one of us or tries to take something that doesn't belong to him," he instructed. Then turning to the interloper, "Go ahead, Cisco. Tell them why you are here."

Jack stepped forward and cleared his throat. "Outside of your sanctuary, the world is a dismal place, devoid of life. Only small pockets of refuge have managed to protect any plants or animals. We have to save the cattle," he stated. "They represent the only animals of their kind that I've seen after crossing two states … and maybe the only herd left in the United States. Hell … maybe the world."

The gathered were not impressed. "Yeah? So? We figured that much," commented one older gentleman. "What are you going to do, Navy man, put on a cape and fly into Tucson to secure the meds we need?"

"Not exactly," Jack laughed, appreciating the man's humor if nothing else. "My plan isn't entirely formed. I need some information first. Maybe I'm wasting everyone's time, but I couldn't go on without at least talking to you folks and giving my concept a good skull secession."

Jack then turned to Sarah and Billy, a much healthier-looking Justin standing with his parents. "You talked about the 'body snatchers' in Tucson. Can you describe them for me in a bit more detail? How many were there? What kind of weapons did they have? Are they organized? Where do they stay?"

Sarah squinted her eyes as an involuntary shiver whipped through her frame. Billy instinctively responded by pulling her close in an embrace. After steadying his soulmate, the husband glowered at Jack and protested, "Honestly, Commander, do we have to do this? She has nightmares every night, and while I am thankful you brought her back to me, I really…."

Gently resting a hand on her husband's chest, Sarah interrupted, "It's okay. I can do this. Jack is right; we have to save the cattle."

She took a deep breath and started explaining. "I think there are twenty to thirty of the body snatchers, although the most I've ever seen at one time is five or six. I saw them stalking their prey on my street once. They all have rifles like Hewitt carries, with the funny-looking banana clip sticking out the bottom."

"Young? Old? Mixed?" Jack asked.

"Mostly young," she nodded. "I can't be positive, but from their clothes and the few tattoos I could see, I think they were a gang before Yellowstone. They are a rough-looking bunch. Mean eyes. Despite the cold, they all walk around in sleeveless shirts and jackets with belts of ammunition crossing their chests like they were some kind of macho banditos or something."

Nodding, Jack continued to probe. "You said they were taking people alive to eat later. How many do you think they have captured? Do they have a lot of prisoners?"

Shaking her head, Sarah answered, "I don't know. I watched them pull Mr. Goodyear out of his house down the street. They beat the crap out of him because he fought back like a wild man. Jennifer said she saw them marching a bunch of captives away, laughing and joking about having a feast."

"Where do they keep these prisoners?"

"I don't know," she sniffed, her eyes becoming wet from the memories.

"I do," piped up Justin, glancing up at Sarah as if he were in trouble. With a timid voice, he continued, "I followed them one night after mom was asleep."

An eerie hush descended upon the room as everyone leaned in, intent to hear what the lad had to say. Sarah was stunned at her son's disclosure, her brow knotting as she scolded, "You did *what*?"

His words tumbled out in a defensive rush, "I needed to know where they were hanging out, Mom! I was afraid they were going to catch you, and I had to know where I could find you if they did."

Bending low and getting face to face with her son, Sarah growled, "I don't know whether to punish you or kiss you."

Billy made the decision, rustling his kid's hair and saying, "That was very brave, Justin. Clearly stupid … but brave."

"So where are they detaining these people?" Jack prompted softly, hating to interrupt a family moment.

Justin became even more excited as he explained, "They take them to that big resort you used to work at, Mom. I saw them. The swimming pools have been drained, and they keep the people in there until they want them."

"The Tucson Mirage?" Sarah asked. "They took over the Mirage? Well, I guess that makes sense. If you are going to establish a private headquarters to slaughter and roast your neighbors, it certainly beats the Traveler's Inn. As a matter of fact, it's the finest hotel in the whole city. Beautiful place. Very posh. Nice digs."

"Thank you, Justin," Jack nodded, smiling broadly at the young man. "Now, the next issues involve the chemical you need to save the herd. Does anyone here know where it is located? In what part of town?"

An older man stepped forward to introduce himself, "My name is Prichard, and those are my cattle. We don't normally worry about Coccidiosis around Arizona because our environment is so dry. The last time I saw this, was 14 years ago when we had a very, very wet spring. I had to travel to the university in Tucson … to their school of veterinary medicine and brought back a truckload of the stuff."

Jack asked if anyone had a large, detailed map of Tucson. No one did, but another man from the back spoke up and offered, "I had one on the wall at my store in Ventura. We used it to help people who were lost when they wandered into town. It's back by the ice cream freezer, next to the restrooms."

"We'll need that," Jack nodded, "In fact, if we decide to pursue this crazy scheme, we're probably going to have to hunt and gather quite a few items."

What followed was another 30 minutes of Jack trying to create a mental picture of Tucson's general layout, more specifically, the proximity of the university to the resort. Someone produced a large piece of cardboard and a black marking pen, and before long, the locals gathered around, helping the commander generate a hand-drawn map of the region.

For the next two hours, Jack held court in the great room. At first, several of the locals dismissed his ideas as pure hogwash and a suicide mission. Not Hewitt, however, nor Prichard, nor Carlos. The elders remained stoic, listening intently, and even nodding agreement on occasion.

As the afternoon wore on, a few of the men began submitting suggestions or improvements. Before long, Jack felt like he was back on a well-run Navy ship, even enjoying the give and take from individuals who all shared a common goal. It was like being a member of a society again. He belonged.

"One other thing that may prove to be challenging. Sheriff, did your department have portable radios?"

Hewitt nodded, "Yes, but the batteries are long dead. We have no way to charge them."

"Leave that to me," Jack smiled. "If we have communications, we have a huge advantage over the cannibals or anyone else who tries to stop us. I'm in if you all decide you want to run with my idea. The radios seal the deal for me."

Then another thought occurred to the commander. Sighing, Jack said, "I have a final question, and this one is for Hewitt. How many spare guns do you have? Weapons you're willing to lose to save the herd?"

81

"Huh? None!" barked the stunned lawman. "They aren't making firearms anymore, son!"

"Seriously, Sheriff. I admired your armory during my escape … err … previous visit. Sure looked like there was quite the stash of weapons in that room." When the sheriff didn't immediately respond, Cisco continued. "Look, I get your concern. And you are right. No one *is* making weapons any more. But consider this … your sanctuary of survivors will starve without food. You can't eat an M16 either."

Hewitt exchanged looks with several of the men he referred to as the elders. Staring down at the stone floor, he responded, "In an emergency, we could probably come up with 5 or 6 guns. Some of the weapons in our inventory aren't actually in working condition."

Smiling, Jack replied, "That's okay. I know where we can get more. Now, either tell me to go to hell or feed me some of that great steak. Like I said, I'm in 100%. I believe we can do this and save the herd … and your community."

The commander was asked to give the citizens of the rock sanctuary time to debate his proposal. While waiting for the outcome, Jack was shown to a lesser room where a large chunk of steaming meat was waiting, complete with real knife, fork, and spoon.

An hour later, Hewitt, Carlos, and Prichard appeared in the doorway. "We're in, Commander. Finish up that grub, and let's get started."

Chapter 21

"We need an alternator out of somebody's car," Jack announced while examining Hewitt's radios. "Preferably one made in the USA and not a heavy-duty model. Just a plain, old 12-volt alternator. If you have a charger that plugs into the cigarette lighter, that would be even better."

"Okay," the sheriff responded with a skeptical eye. "And how are we going to spin this alternator to make electrical power?"

Smiling, Jack responded, "We're going to use my bicycle. The rear hub just happens to be a half inch, and so is the bolt holding the front pully on most domestic alternators. I'm going to replace the belt with my chain and pedal until we have enough charge in the radios for the mission."

"How do you connect that to the radios? How do you know it's the right amount of juice?"

Nodding, Jack answered, "For low voltage DC equipment, it really doesn't matter. Within reasonable limits, as long as the current going into your radios is higher than the charge stored in the batteries, they will charge. Your radios run off of 3 volts. I won't even have to pedal very fast."

Rubbing his chin, Hewitt still wasn't sure. "How do you know all this, Commander?"

"Submarines are electrically-powered machines, Sheriff. The Navy teaches its officers and techs a lot about electricity, rotational mechanical energy, and other boring-as-hell subjects. If you're 500 feet underwater and something critical breaks, you've got to know how to fix it."

Finally sold, Hewitt called over two men and said, "Take Henry's tools. Then grab my keys and take the alternator and charger out of my patrol car. It's parked behind Carlos's diner."

"While they're gone, I'm going to build a frame to hold the bike and generator," Jack continued. "I spotted a pile of scrap lumber yesterday. You have a saw, hammer, and nails, I assume?"

Nodding, the sheriff responded, "Yes. I'll get the tools and be back in a minute. I've got to see this contraption."

Three hours later, Jack's bicycle was minus its back wheel, suspended above a wooden stand.

Hewitt's greasy alternator arrived a few minutes later, along with the charger from his cigarette lighter.

Jack went right to work, measuring and cutting. Just before dark, he mounted the bicycle and gingerly began pedaling.

After the initial test of his device, Jack studied the batteries from Sheriff Langdon's police radios. "Those have a range of just over 10 miles," stated the lawman proudly. "They are the new digital models – the last major purchase the county allowed me to make."

"Money well spent," Jack said, grabbing a roll of duct tape and delicately connecting the alternator's output to the positive and negative posts on the charger. "Always glad to see tax dollars at work for the people," he concluded, smiling at his host.

Jack then hopped back on his bike and pedaled for five minutes. A small crowd was gathered now, the activity a novelty in the normally-mundane routine of the Cliff House.

Again dismounting, Jack shrugged, "Here goes nothing." The commander grimaced and hit the radio's power button.

Smiling broadly, Jack held up the device for all to see, a glowing, orange light illuminating the dial. "We'll need to ride the bike about an hour to charge each unit. Still, to have the radios when we go into Tucson is a big plus."

The water jug was right where Sarah and Justin had left it.

Jack noted that someone had replaced the basketball-boulder high on the embankment.

Sauntering nonchalantly down I-8, Jack paused at the predetermined spot. "I'm the weary, thirsty traveler. What's that? Oh my! It's water!" he whispered, the words dripping in sarcasm.

Jack noted that the men he'd killed here just a few days before had been moved. "I wonder if they eat their own?" he theorized in a hush.

Under the old, threadbare blanket hanging from his shoulders, Jack's grip tightened on the M4. Looking left and then right, he approached the jug.

As he got closer, he could understand why Sarah and Justin had struggled to lift the bait. The container was full of broken glass, probably from a nearby windshield. In the grey light, the sparkle resembled water.

Taking a knee beside the fake treasure, Jack took a deep breath and tugged.

He watched the line tighten, and then the rock dropped onto the gong-metal. Jack didn't run, didn't hide, and didn't flinch. The commander's only reaction to the loud alarm was to disengage the safety on his rifle.

It took a minute before the hornets reacted to Jack kicking their nest.

First, the commander spied faces staring down at him from the hilltop … and then the carnivorous barbarians charged, boiling over the ridge like a herd of spooked buffalo, whooping like an Indian war party.

There were at least a dozen of the ambushers, and none of them seemed to wonder why Jack wasn't running. Just as they approached the steepest part of the knoll, all hell broke loose at the westbound rest area.

Jack dove for the ground, the move more from a distrust of the Cliff House marksmens' skills than any threat from the cannibals. His weapon was just coming up as a wall of lead slammed into the descending bushwhackers.

Round after hot round tore into their ranks, a sweltering wall of bullets tearing and slicing flesh and bone. There was little the human predators could do to escape, their footing already questionable due to the ash and steepness of the rise.

One crazed savage managed to make it to the bottom, raising a lever-action rifle as if he genuinely thought shooting back would help. Jack's shell hit the man just in front of the ear, and then the rest area fell silent again.

Cisco waited for five minutes, making sure that a second wave didn't initiate another attack and spill over the ridge. When no reinforcements arrived, the commander waved to the eastbound cluster of buildings, and then watched as Hewitt and 10 of his team rose from their positions and began hustling to the west lanes.

Sheriff Langdon quickly assigned a runner, a younger guy, who took off jogging to retrieve Puff. Hewitt then pointed to two others, "Collect all their weapons and ammo, and anything else of value. If you find any meat on them, I wouldn't eat it."

"I think we better check their camp," Jack offered. "If you could spare a few guys, I just want to make sure we have eliminated the entire colony."

Up the knoll they trekked, Jack and six of Hewitt's men.

They found that the commander's initial guess regarding the location of the cannibals' shelter had been correct. All the rest area's buildings showed signs of occupation. They found no one home, no one hiding, and no sign of a bugout. It appeared that when the alarm sounded, the response had been all hands on deck.

One of the men from Ventura did make a grisly discovery, however. At the rear of the rest area, behind the maintenance shed, a steep cliff dropped to the valley below. At the bottom of the sheer, 50-foot drop, a large pile of bones had collected. Human skulls and rib cages were easy to discern among the remains.

Ignoring the vomiting man, Jack shook his head and walked away. He felt an undeniable sense of righting a wrong and was going to leave it at that.

Puff arrived 20 minutes later, Hewitt and his men giddy from their victory.

As Jack helped load the collected weapons onto the trailer, he hoped this first engagement wouldn't embolden his companions to the point of recklessness.

"That was easy," Hewitt said in a low voice. "I hope these guys realize it's going to get a lot harder from here on out."

"I was just thinking the same thing," Jack nodded. "Still, we didn't lose anybody or waste a lot of ammo. The confidence can't hurt, I suppose."

Someone yelled, "All aboard," and then the men scrambled for a position on Puff's wagon.

Jack took his assigned place, toward the front near his bike. Out of habit, he double-checked his pack and found nothing had been disturbed.

With a jolt and clank, Puff starting rolling down I-8, quickly achieving her maximum speed of five miles per hour. After riding his bike for days, the pace seemed slow to the commander.

It was over 14 hours travel time to the edge of Tucson, and that didn't count having to stop and refill Puff's supply of wood and water or camping for the night. If Jack's timetable were accurate, they would enter the big city just after dusk in two days.

When the road sign stated the next exit was located a half mile ahead, Puff's driver stopped the noisy tractor.

While Hewitt's crew began refueling the past-its-prime machine with bundles of wood and plastic jugs of water from the trailer, Jack and four others dismounted and prepared the gear.

"This exit has two gas stations, and that's it," Billy announced. "I used to deliver candy and potato chips to the convenience store located on this side of the interstate. I don't remember any houses or other structures in the area, so there shouldn't be any reason for anybody to be holed up here."

"You never know," Jack replied, checking that his rifle was supplied with a round in the chamber.

Having the local knowledge as a delivery driver was a big help, and Jack hoped Billy's attachment to the community wouldn't be an issue once they were closer to his home and friends. Hewitt was convinced the guy was rock solid.

While Puff ate and drank, the commander and his team pushed off, heading toward the exit and hoping to find their campsite for the night.

The light was already fading by the time they arrived, but they could still read two signs high in the murky air, both advertising regular and diesel fuel. "Truckers welcome," claimed one of the advertisements.

It was clear from a distance that one of the stations had burned. Jack had no way to tell if lightning or man had caused the blaze. They headed for the better structure.

Approaching on a wide lane, the men from the Cliff House were on edge. "Look for tracks in the ash," Jack cooed, trying to calm jittery nerves. "Be alert for paths of packed pumice. Use your nose and ears. If you smell something cooking or hear voices, then we know we have company."

By the time they reached the edge of the lot, Jack sensed the place was abandoned. Two of the front, glass panels were missing, a low dike of glass obscuring any potential footprints near the entrance.

The hoses on the gas pumps were lying on the ground, probably discarded there by frustrated motorists. A handful of cars were parked along one border, one of them having accidently backed into a pole. The driver had left it right there, evidently not caring about the late model, luxury sedan.

Jack was the first to peer inside what had been a nice convenience store and snack shop. Bare shelves stared back at the commander, the entire interior in complete disarray.

Papers, drink cups, food wrappers, and displays were strewn everywhere, most now covered by a thin coating of charcoal grit. It was obvious the store had been picked clean, but that was just fine with Jack. They weren't here to scavenge or loot. They just wanted shelter for the night.

Kicking a beef jerky rack out of the way, Jack ventured inside. With his rifle swinging back and forth in quick motions, the commander headed for the back room, Sheriff Langdon's men in tow.

The station didn't have much of a storage room, and it was in no better shape than the public areas. Jack almost twisted his ankle when he accidently stepped into the now-open floor safe. It was empty as well. "You can't eat money," he whispered to the empty spaces.

"There's no one here," Jack stated. "Billy, run back and tell Hewitt to bring Puff on up. This is home for the night."

As he watched Billy hustle toward the interstate, Jack brushed off a stool that had at one time hosted the cashier's butt. Setting the seat back behind the counter, the commander glanced at his new friends, and said, "Next? Can I help you, sir?"

The humor helped a little, but Jack still recognized anxious, searching eyes under their masks. "Relax guys. I'm pretty sure we'll be safe in this building. No one has any reason to come here."

Puff's obnoxious clanking announced the tractor's arrival a short time later, Commander Cisco and his remaining teammates doing their best to clean out the store's interior enough so that they could take turns catching some shuteye. It was no easy task.

After the steamer was pulled around the back of the building and out of sight, Billy started a fire while the others continued to move display racks and trash out of the way. Hewitt found a broom in the rubble, and soon there were clear places to position the bedrolls for the night.

"We'll work in shifts," Hewitt announced. "If I catch anybody sleeping on guard duty, I'm going to make them go back to the rest area and dig a grave for all those bones. Understand?"

Two hours after taking over the gas station, Jack was chewing on some reheated steak and eating Mrs. Morgan's canned corn from her garden. "The pay sucks, but like the Navy, you can't beat the food," he said, glancing around at the others. "The sleeping arrangements definitely need improvement though. For sure, these are no 5-Star accommodations. We should have checked the online reviews before booking," he joked in an attempt to lessen the apprehension of the men.

After everyone had eaten, the sheriff asked Jack to review the plans for the morning one more time.

Nodding, Jack stood in front of the men, the interior illuminated by two small candles. "We'll be in Tucson tomorrow, guys. I know we've drilled this a dozen times, but let's go over it again."

Watching as all heads nodded north and south, Jack began. "Billy, what is your jump off point after we enter the city?"

On and on they continued the review, Jack firing question after question at the team. "Where do we rendezvous? What do you do if we get separated? Who is supposed to be covering that area?"

After two hours, Jack noticed a lot of yawning and red eyes. "Alright guys, you've got this down as good as any military team I've ever worked with. Let's get some rest, and we'll finish this tomorrow."

Chapter 22

The western suburbs of Tucson ushered a new round of doubts into Jack's head.

Unfortunately for the commander's team, the Mirage Resort was only a few streets away from the university and their objective.

The initial concept had been to up-armor Puff and convert Prichard's trailer into a war wagon. Jack had visions of creating a mobile fortress, reinforced with thick lumber and sandbags, accompanied by a dozen gun barrels sticking out to discourage any resistance. Jack had noted the effectiveness of such a primitive device in San Diego when the Eagles had attacked the church complex.

That manually-powered battle tank would have succeeded if Jack and the church defenders hadn't gotten lucky.

The problem was Puff. While the torque-heavy steam engine could easily pull the weight of additional armor, building a protective box around the tractor would be a daunting task. It had been Carlos who observed, "If the tractor gets shot out from under us, aren't the cattle dead anyway? There would be no way to haul up enough hay or to get the Coccidiostat back from Tucson."

The next strategy had been to simply sneak into Tucson under cover of night, load up the bags of chemicals, and skedaddle out of town.

Geography made that option difficult, as did the noise generated by Puff's large, single piston. Reaching the university required passing by the enemy stronghold. The risk was too high that the local headhunters would detect either the Cliff House men or their tractor. Getting caught out in the open with 50-pound bags of chemicals on their backs would almost certainly lead to a lot of dead bodies.

Given all that, Jack had arrived at the age-old, traditional, military tactic of a distraction. They had to draw the local gangbangers away or keep them occupied long enough to load the medications onto Puff's trailer and get the hell out of dodge.

There was also the possibility that the university no longer contained any stock of Coccidiostat. "Hell, given what you've told us, Commander, the entire school might have burned down. If they have resorted to eating people in Tucson, who knows what else might have gone on over there?" Henry had asked.

As the team entered the edge of Tucson, Jack wondered if their scheme wasn't too complicated. For the last hour, while they chugged along a surface street, the commander had compiled a substantial list of things that could go wrong.

Yet, they had to try. There had been too much work and sweat equity invested. And what other choice did they have anyway? Momentum and desperation overrode the Cisco's desire to call off the raid.

Billy's local knowledge again played a key role. "We can hide the tractor at my employer's warehouse. It's less than a mile from there to both the university and the resort. There's a big, indoor space that will keep Puff from being observed by prying eyes."

Sure enough, they found a good spot to hide the tractor before its clanking engine alerted everyone in central Arizona to their presence.

After pulling Puff into the warehouse, Jack and Hewitt dispatched a ring of sentries to the outside. "Make sure no one wanders by and starts nosing around. Come back here if you see anything moving."

Now confident that they had managed to get close to their objective without being detected, Jack remained vigilant as the men from Ventura began unpacking gear and double-checking their weapons.

For the next hour, the warehouse was a beehive of activity. Jack studied them while the team prepared for the mission. More doubt crept into his mind.

Sure, they were all scared. Who wouldn't be? Capture or injury most likely translated into the worst possible suffering and horrific death. Even if killed on the battlefield, being eaten afterward was enough to give even the bravest man second thoughts.

It was more than just fear that gave Jack pause.

While it was completely rational for men facing danger to suffer from a wide range of debilitating reactions, the commander had always been surrounded by individuals with military training when embarking on a hazardous mission. Now, with few exceptions, the men around Jack had no such experience or schooling.

The armed services had learned the value of repetition long ago. As far back as the Civil War, the Army had discovered that a significant percentage of its soldiers didn't fire their weapons during battle. Others, it was proven, purposely aimed high or wide to avoid killing.

After Gettysburg, a post-action analysis found one man's muzzle loader with ten balls stuffed into the barrel. He had been pretending to fire, then reloading upon command. All this, despite taking growing, lethal fire from the Confederate troops attacking his unit and slaughtering several of his comrades.

The commander knew that taking another human's life wasn't a natural act, even if that man was trying to kill you.

The Army had determined that the problem was a lack of training, or more accurately, mental conditioning solidified by repetition. During his time at the Academy, Jack had come to think of the drills and perpetual replication of identical exercises as "brainwashing."

Over the years, the military refined its techniques. This is one of the reasons why drill sergeants are often so harsh, screaming at the top of their lungs and subjecting recruits to enormous amounts of stress. The other branches of the service implemented the same basic methods, whether it was mounting missiles onto a combat aircraft, charging a machine gun nest, or reloading a torpedo tube in the hope that rookie soldiers would perform well under combat conditions.

Jack knew the men around him didn't have the benefit of such training, and he, like so many who had led troops into battle, wondered how they would react to the stress of taking fire.

No doubt that Sheriff Langdon could handle whatever happened; three decades of law enforcement were enough to steady any man or woman walking into harm's way.

Jack also noted a difference in the older men though. The more seasoned of the crew possessed a spark in their eyes that the younger generation didn't seem to have. An indicator of a bit more confidence? Maybe they didn't have as much to lose? Or they had a better grasp for what was on the line? Perhaps the experience of life was enough to shore up their resolve?

The commander continued his visual assessment of the volunteers and realized that it was the fresh-faced recruits that troubled him the most. Each of them betrayed a weakness that made predicting his behavior impossible. The guy behind Puff's tire showed just a bit too much bravado for Cisco's comfort. The other man, on the far side of the wagon, was a pale shade of green and looked like he was going to toss his cookies at any moment. The third man put Jack in mind of his own grandfather who had battled Parkinson's Disease, so pronounced were the young man's hand tremors. The commander watched the recruit as he attempted to load his weapon and hoped he wouldn't cause any friendly fire casualties.

Shaking off his apprehensions, Jack went to work on his gear. He was concerned about a possibility that might never materialize anyway. Keeping busy would slow down his mind and keep him on track. How silly would it be if he worried himself to death before even leaving the warehouse?

The commander watched as Billy wrestled with a large satchel in an attempt to load it onto his bike. They had acquired the second two-wheeler from the antique mall during one of their hunting and gathering excursions. While it didn't have the fancy gears and do-dads of Jack's modern machine, it was still the best way for a man to quietly haul a heavy load.

Helping Billy secure the duffle onto the rear frame, Jack said, "I know this sucks. Just keep in mind what a nasty surprise we're going to deliver to our flesh-eating friends."

Soon it was time, darkness finally falling around the city.

Nodding to Hewitt, Jack and Billy pushed their bikes onto the concrete drive, waved, and began pedaling toward the Tucson Mirage. "Good luck," several of the men called.

Jack soon found himself pedaling through what appeared to be the set of a Hollywood disaster movie. Old newspapers and plastic trash were scattered on the streets, some of the blown garbage gathering in mounting piles when pinned against a home or caught under the bumper of a car.

Other than the crunch of their tires rolling through the ash, there wasn't a single noise or odor. Just abandoned, dark buildings stretching into the distance.

Jack and Billy had memorized the route, the commander knowing that getting lost was almost as bad as getting killed. Stopping at the corner gas station to ask directions was simply out of the question.

Still, in the dark, it was difficult. Both struggled not to gawk at the surreal scenery that they passed by. Rather than paying attention to street signs, or counting blocks, Jack found his eyes drifting from burned out shells of homes to collapsed commercial buildings, his brain trying to make sense of what he was seeing.

Most of the cars along the street had been looted. Trunk lids were raised, gas caps and doors open, and often the interior contents were strewn around the vehicle. It reminded the commander of his departure from San Diego and the chaos that had been Interstate 8.

It was also easy to tell which homes had been ransacked. Clothing, dresser drawers, pots, and even large pieces of furniture cluttered the front yards.

The ash here was haphazard as well, some areas sporting over an inch of grit, while others seemed to have been wiped clean by the wind. More than once, Jack spotted a mound that he was sure was evidence of a body covered in the grey spew.

It was a billboard that caught Jack's attention next. "The Tucson Mirage Resort. Next Right," read the large letters. Underneath, the advertisement boasted, "Central Arizona's Premier Luxury Resort. Over 450 Acres. Four Pools and 36 Holes of Championship Golf!"

"Want to get in a quick 18 holes before we kick these guys' asses, Billy?" Jack asked, nodding at the sign.

"My short game's been hurting lately. I'll need some handicap strokes, sir," he smirked.

"Just what this outfit needs, *another* smartass," Jack teased back.

They found a good spot to hide their bikes, less than two blocks from the resort's perimeter. "Stay here," Jack ordered. "I want to see what kind of security they have posted. If I'm not back in 15 minutes, radio Hewitt and call the whole thing off."

"Yes, sir. I remember the plan. Be safe, Commander."

Jack checked his rifle for the Nth time, then patted the magazine pouches attached to his vest. Like previous times he'd been about to enter a fight, the body armor no longer felt heavy on his shoulders.

Jack approached slowly, clinging to the shadows, hugging the few buildings and homes along the route. He finally identified a good scouting spot next to a dry cleaner's sign.

His first observation was that the Mirage was a massive complex. With an adobe exterior and red tile roof, the commander counted at least six different buildings. No one had thought to draw up a map of the resort.

Top to bottom, left to right, Jack thoroughly scrutinized the area. Examining the landscape for any indication of a sentry, guard, or wandering body-snatcher, he studied the ground, windows, and even the roofline. He noticed nothing.

The only sign of occupation was the front steps. While it was difficult to be sure in the low light, it appeared to Jack as if the ash there had been packed down by a stampede of footsteps. He couldn't be sure.

Initially, Jack was troubled by the lack of security, wondering if Justin's story had been true. It then occurred to the commander that the cannibals were probably the dominant force in the city. Why would anyone chance venturing near their headquarters?

"Did you hear the one about the cannibal who ran into his mother-in-law in the jungle?" Jack whispered the old joke as his optic scanned the building again.

"I'd like to have you over for dinner tonight," he continued with the jest.

The humor did little to settle his nerves, so the commander returned to plotting the next, logical moves for Billy and him.

The Mirage's main building, complete with ash-packed front steps, was out of the question. Becoming embroiled in a gunfight out in the open was one thing, close quarters combat inside an unknown structure was quite another.

Jack spotted a walkway between two of the lesser buildings and focused there. He noticed no tracks in the ash, and there was a good escape route if they were discovered.

A minute later, he was jogging back to Billy, who was relieved to see him to say the least.

"What does it look like? Did you see them? Can we get in?" flew the series of rapid-fire inquiries out of the nervous man's throat.

"Be cool. Yes, I think I found a good way to sneak onto the grounds, but I'm not sure of the layout. That place is huge."

"Would this help?" Billy responded, holding up a crumpled brochure from the Mirage. "I saw it lying on the street and picked it up to refresh my memory of the place."

Jack opened the folder and grinned. There, inside the leaflet, was a high-level map of the facilities. It wasn't detailed, or to scale, but at least he had a better picture in his mind. Refolding the advertisement and stuffing it in his pocket, he said, "Come on. We can get the bikes closer. I didn't see any guards."

When they approached the street, Jack whispered, "Walk across one at a time. You cover me from back here and wait until I'm ready on the far side. Stoll casually. No hurry, just another cannibal coming back from a hunt. We're friendly, on the same side. Got it?"

Billy nodded, leaning his bike against the dry cleaners and readying his rifle.

"See you in a minute," Jack said, and pushed off.

He'd never felt so naked and exposed, rambling across the pavement toward the body-snatcher's nest. It was all Jack could do to keep the speed out of his step as he pushed the bike. Even then, he tried to maintain the heavy satchel between him and the rows of dark windows overlooking his approach.

A minute later, he rolled on the resort's property, pushing his load between the two buildings, trying to act like he belonged. The M4 was in his free hand, ready to come up and work in an instant.

They stashed the bikes between two dead bushes. It wasn't much cover, but the best available. Jack maintained his slow and deliberate jaunt, exiting the corridor into a large, open area riddled with paths, trails, and several smaller buildings. A sign indicated that "Swimming, Sauna and Spa" were located to the right.

The sound of music drifted across the property. While it was hard to tell the exact direction of the source, Jack thought the tunes were coming from the right as well. "Assholes. They've started the party without us," the commander hissed, "and this surely complicates things."

Billy's head tilted to the side, a clear demonstration of his confusion. "How does that complicate things?" he asked.

"Now, Billy, everyone knows that if you arrive late to a cannibal's dinner party, you are likely to get the cold shoulder," Jack teased.

The inexperienced recruit stared at the commander for a second before finally smirking and slapping his teammate on the back. For an instant, the rookie relaxed. Jack hoped it would calm his colleague enough to steady his nerves a bit and take off the anxious edge. They were, after all, about to create a war zone.

The duo huddled next to a wall. "The pools are that way," Jack said, pointing to the sign. "I think that's where the music is coming from. I'm guessing that's where most of our new friends are gathered."

"Do we take the bikes or haul in our goodies on our backs?" Billy asked.

It was a legit question and served to reassure Jack that his cohort was thinking clearly. "Let's not chance the bikes," he replied. "I don't think our objective is that far away."

The canvas duffels were very heavy and cumbersome, the contents rattling as the two men helped each other adjust the loads. To Jack's ears, it seemed like everyone between here and Phoenix should have heard the racket they were making.

A few minutes later, with the sacks on their shoulders and rifles ready, the two trudged into the maze of the complex's interior.

Jack followed the melody, chords and drum beats his guide. As the approached closer to the swimming area, an occasional bout of laughter drifted between the buildings. Soon, they could identify individual voices.

A sign indicated the resort's villas were to the left. Tapping Jack on the shoulder, Billy then pointed at the directional, "If I were crashing somewhere for free, I'd being sleeping in those. They're supposed to be the best digs in the whole place."

Nodding, Jack agreed that the assumption was probably accurate. "Our first job is to find the prisoners. We just need to keep in mind the savages probably have reinforcements in the villas."

They smelled the pools before they saw them, but it wasn't the familiar odor of chlorine they had come to expect from a 5-Star resort's aquatic amenity. Jack grimaced at the rank mixture of feces, human body odor, urine, and decay.

Approaching a corner, Jack peeked around and spotted three massive concrete holes, the diving platform and blue paint announcing they had finally arrived at the objective. There, reclining in the lifeguard tower, was the commander's first sighting of a sentry.

While he couldn't glimpse the pools' contents, the stench told Jack that people were being held inside the gunite lockup. That overwhelmingly pungent stink coupled with the hack of sporadic coughing was all the commander needed to be convinced he and Billy were in the right place.

The watchman, barely old enough to lifeguard before Yellowstone's eruption, was balanced on the edge of the chair, an AK47 resting in his lap. He yawned, then shifted slightly in his seat, his hand reaching to scratch the skin under his mask. The guy looked bored.

Commander Cisco admired the tactical foresight of his rivals. They had the perfect setup for a makeshift prison, including the guard's elevated perch, which had been intentionally designed and sited to allow an unimpeded view of the entire area.

It would be relatively easy to corral the condemned at the deep end. Anyone attempting to escape would have a tough time climbing out of the swimming hole from such a depth. The prisoners' waste, or at least some of it, was probably washed down the drain.

The lifeguard also posed a significant tactical problem for Jack. There was no way to approach the over watch without being detected, and his plan hadn't accounted for that.

Billy realized the snag quickly. "I wish I had my crossbow," he whispered. "I could take him out without a sound from here."

Commander Cisco nodded in agreement, his mind contemplating their alternatives. "We need to know how many people are in each pit,"

Jack mused, "and then … somehow, I've got to lure that sentry down from his ivory tower and take him out."

Time seemed to be slipping away from them as Jack pondered every imaginable option. "We could throw a rock like they do in the cowboy movies," Billy offered. "When he went to check on what made the noise, we could jump him."

Shaking his head, Jack quickly dismissed the idea. "What if he called for backup instead of coming down? Twenty guys might respond, and then we're fucked. Besides, what you see in the movies never works."

Jack finally decided that he would take the same approach he'd used to enter the grounds. He would emerge from the shadows like he was a member of the cannibal gang and simply stroll up to the guard and then yank him off the tower.

There were so many things wrong with the idea, Jack couldn't force his legs to stand and begin the walk. There had to be a better way.

"Did you know that in the Roman Empire, there were only two crimes that warranted crucifixion as a punishment?" the commander advised in a barely audible voice.

Billy shook his head, clearly puzzled by where Jack was going with the trivia.

"Those two unpardonable crimes were high treason and participating in a slave revolt," the commander continued, glancing at his team member. "I'm pretty sure we can't expect any mercy either if we are caught. So … let's get this uprising started."

Jack rose, ready to execute his risky plan to disable the guard. Before the commander could take the first step, sobbing sounds drifted out of the closest pool. Then a weak voice whimpered from below the diving board, "Sir? Sir? I think she's dead. She won't move."

Mumbling a clearly audible curse, the sentry snapped upright and leaned toward the direction of the voice, trying to see if the complaint were genuine or some sort of ruse. "Damn it!" he barked, turning around to dismount the ladder.

Before his feet had hit the second rung down, Jack was up and moving.

"Why do they always have to die on my fucking shift," the guard grumbled as Jack closed the distance.

Just as the sentry's sneaker hit the concrete deck, Jack was drawing his knife. The guard never saw the commander's blade, even after it was buried to the hilt in his throat.

Crouching, ready for action, Jack waited for an alarm to sound. After a long pause, ready to fight or run, the commander then peered down into the pools. It was the most pitiful, horrific image his brain had ever processed.

Dozens and dozens of eyes stared back at him, filthy, hollow faces that seemed to be shocked and terrified at the same time. Jack was initially reminded of old, black and white photographs of the Nazi death camps.

Most of those kidnapped had been stripped naked, a few with rags as loin cloths. The closest swimming pool was nearly full of men, the other pool containing the female captives. The odor emanating from the concrete jail was nothing short of nausea-inducing, but nothing compared to the horror of the vacant expressions of the lost souls that gazed back at him.

Jack waved Billy over, his teammate struggling to carry both duffle bags as he bounced past the lounge chairs and tables lining the area.

Rushing to help, Jack grabbed one of the bags and headed for the men's pool. Waving Billy to the other swimming hole, he instructed, "Take the others to the women."

On the way, the commander stopped and scooped up the guard's Kalashnikov, carrying the assault weapon to the edge of the deep end. "Do you want to live?" he hissed at the sea of faces staring back at him. "Will you fight to live? Here, take this and destroy the men who put you here. Take control of your own destinies. Take back your city!"

Jack tossed the battle rifle to the closest man. In a flash, Cisco's hands were in the duffle, pulling out the weapons salvaged from the rest area's dead, as well as the few spares Hewitt had surrendered. "They're all loaded," the commander continued, "Go, and fight for your lives!"

The captive men at the bottom began crowding closer to the pool's edge, anxious, eager hands reaching for each gun. One by one, Jack passed out the weapons, the recipients mumbling, "Thank God," and "Bless you," and "Thank you."

All the while, Billy was doing the same with the women.

The commander had counted on some sort of hierarchy of command already being in place. He knew from his training that prisons, work camps, and even gulags always had some social structure, no matter how dire the circumstances. The Mirage's pools proved no exception.

A middle-aged man gathered the armed prisoners near the shallow end. "Wait here until that guy gives us all a weapon. We'll rush those son-of-a-bitches as a group and kill every last one of those bastards," Jack heard the local leader say.

In less than two minutes, Jack had handed out all the weapons.

Still, the commander had his doubts about the execution of his plan. The captives were certainly motivated, but they were all rail thin and weak, some of them struggling to hold up the rifles or handguns as Jack passed them down. A few of the detainees remained in the pool, lying or sitting next to the wall, too weak or scared to climb out of their aqua-blue cell.

Billy distributed the remainder of his weapons and joined the commander. They watched as the two, newly minted armies gathered next to the lifeguard stand. Finally, the male leader turned and asked, "Are you going with us?"

"No," Jack replied. "But we are going to help. I want you all to wait here until you hear my signal."

"Signal?" the man questioned.

"You'll know. When you attack, hit them hard, with everything you've got."

The man seemed to accept the commander's words, and then was waving his troops forward. If the situation hadn't been so dangerous, Jack would have sworn he was watching some sort of sick comedy on television.

The gaggle of naked, streaked-dirty bodies waddled across the pool deck, some of the stick figures not much larger than the rifle barrels in their arms.

"Come on," Jack said, motioning for Billy to follow. "Let's soften up the resistance a little for them."

Following the sound of the music, Jack and Billy rushed through the pool complex and down the path toward the villas. On the way, Jack pulled Hewitt's radio from his belt and keyed the talk button. "Unit one, unit one, go! Go! Go!"

It seemed like an eternity before Hewitt's voice crackled over the airwaves. "Roger that. Godspeed. See you at the warehouse."

Again, Jack and Billy sought cover against a wall. Ahead, around a slight bend in the path, the two men could see a sweltering inferno blazing in a fire pit, the outline of several men visible in the light.

A handful of women gathered there as well, but mostly Jack noted several younger thugs, all of them with rifles handy. They had made a circle of lounge chairs, and two people were even dancing to the music.

Tapping Jack on the shoulder, Billy pointed to a small mountain of car batteries piled against a neighboring structure. "That's how they're powering the boom box," he said.

"Damn, and I was hoping for live entertainment for this evening's festivities," Jack joked.

The commander dug around in his almost empty bag, pulling out two glass bottles, each with a length of white cloth acting as a plug. The smell of gasoline quickly permeated the air.

Handing one of the Molotov cocktails to Billy, Jack pointed and said, "Let's circle around there. We can get close enough to heave these in and get this little shindig really hopping."

Nodding, Billy stood to follow, holding the gas bomb away from his body like it was a snake about to strike.

They backtracked past one row of villas, moving with caution just in case a stray cannibal were lurking in the shadows.

Emerging between two of the luxury units, Jack's stomach rolled as the smell of grilling meat waffled past his nose. He realized what kind of feast was being prepared, the barbaric act inciting his rage almost to the point of boiling over.

"Ready?" Jack asked, producing a disposable lighter from his pocket.

Billy merely nodded.

Jack ignited Billy's cocktail first, then his own. The cloth caught fire quickly, the petrol having plenty of time to wick through the material.

"Now!" Jack hissed, raising the bomb and doing his best imitation of a baseball pitcher.

As the two flaming objects streaked through the air, the commander's carbine was up and at his shoulder. His thumb found the selector switch and clicked the weapon to full automatic.

The cocktails exploded with a "whoosh," at the same moment as a maelstrom of lead tore into the gathering. Jack heard a woman scream, another male voice yelling, "Shit!" at the top of his lungs.

A man stumbled from the wall of flames, his entire body engulfed in fire. Jack watched the human torch desperately swipe and claw at the blaze that consumed him, his wail of agony so intense it could be heard over the muzzle reports of the commander's carbine. It was a vision he would never forget.

Billy's weapon was now firing, both attackers working their rounds in and out, up and down.

Jack noted movement at the edge of the kill zone and centered his dot on a brute with a shotgun.

The commander's shots tore into the ruffian's chest, causing the staggering flesh-eater to spin just as he fired, sending the 12-gauge's pattern ripping through a huddled mass of his friends.

In less than a minute, the shock and awe passed. Jack and Billy reloaded, both men trying to maximize the advantage of surprise.

More of the gang members were responding now, Jack spotting the door of a neighboring villa fly open and a rifle barrel flashing white as a stream of bullets smacked into the wall next to his head.

The opening now had Jack's attention, his carbine spraying a blizzard of hot lead into the doorway.

As the seconds passed, more and more return fire struck near the attackers, the body-snatchers recovering much faster than Jack had anticipated.

"We have to go now!" Jack yelled over the battle's din.

"Where are the pool people?" Billy shouted back.

It was an important question, Jack realizing that if he and Billy simply ran, there was a good chance that the cannibals would chase them down within minutes. What troubled Cisco even more were his partner's eyes.

Billy's reaction was the opposite of Jack's initial fears. Instead of being a cowering, ineffective companion, the guy seemed unwilling to stop until every last cannibal had been massacred.

Over and over again, Billy shouted and screamed insults at the same time. "Take that, fucker!" "Eat this, bitch!" "Come on chicken shit; come and get some more!"

"We have to get back to the bikes and ride out of here!" Jack finally screamed, firing a burst at a group of counter-attacking thugs. "We need to get out, now!"

"Not yet," Billy yelled back. "We need to kill them all!"

The pace and rhythm of the firefight then changed, the commander hearing several other guns joining the fray. "I believe our reinforcements have finally arrived!" Jack exclaimed, relieved that he and Billy weren't carrying the load alone.

The two instigators retreated, using the same route that had gotten them close. Ahead, Jack spotted several men running toward the fire pit, and he wasn't sure if they were revolting prisoners or more gang members coming to the aid of their friends.

Pulling Billy into the dead bushes, Jack pointed and then motioned for his friend to be quiet.

Just as the new arrivals approached the duo's hiding place, another gun fight erupted. Lying prone and trying to dig deeper into the ground, the commander realized that he and Billy were caught between the two groups.

A minute passed, the opposing sides exchanging several shots while Jack and Billy cowered in the middle. The whole complex, it seemed, was now embroiled in a running, confused firefight.

Finally, one side had enough and withdrew, allowing the two masterminds to again make for their bikes.

As they rounded a corner, several bullets ripped through the air, sending both men scrambling for the earth.

Again and again, bullets tore into the ground next to Jack and his charge, the aim inaccurate but still thick enough to pin them down.

The commander sensed the shooters, whoever they were, were finding the range, one of the incoming lead pills tugging at his shirt sleeve. "We have to move!" he shouted at his recoiling partner. "Get ready when they reload."

Finally, the incoming fire paused. Jack was up in a second, screaming for Billy to run.

The commander made it two steps before he sensed that his man wasn't beside him. Thinking Billy was hit, Jack pivoted and found his comrade staring at something in the distance.

Jack followed Billy's gaze to a grisly, nightmarish scene. There, hanging upside down from some sort of rack was a naked, dead man. The poor fellow's throat had been slit, probably to drain the blood in preparation for butchering.

"Come on!" Jack screamed at his friend. "No time for sightseeing now."

"Mr. Goodyear," Billy mumbled, unable to peel his eyes away. "He was always, so … so … nice to us."

Another barrage of rounds tore through the air, sending Jack plunging to escape the zipping, hissing death. As he dove down, the commander jerked Billy with him.

Even then, lying exposed on the sidewalk with bullets whizzing over their heads, Billy couldn't seem to take his eyes off Mr. Goodyear. "What a horrible way to die!" Jack heard him shout. "You bastards! You animals! You all should die!"

With a surge of super-human strength, Billy leapt to his feet. Mindless of the incoming fire following his move, he charged, screaming like a madman, firing his weapon at random shadows and shapes.

Jack dove from his knees, trying to tackle his partner, but missed.

In a heartbeat, Billy was out of reach and darting away at full speed.

The shooters shooting at Jack now had a clearer target, their aim tracking Billy as he raced through the darkness. Jack hesitated, thinking he should go after his teammate, but also knowing that his chances of escape were decreasing with every passing second.

Sighing, Jack stood and rushed for his bike. Maybe Billy would come to his senses. Maybe he would meet them back at the warehouse.

One last time, Commander Cisco scanned behind him, hoping to see Sarah's husband emerge from the darkness. The battle was now rampant throughout the Mirage's once-manicured compound, two new columns of flame reaching for the night sky while sporadic gunfire still echoed through the air.

Shaking his head in disappointment, Jack mounted his bike and began pedaling hard.

Chapter 23

Jack was several blocks away from the resort before he stopped to wipe the sweat from his eyes. He wanted to vomit, lie down in the middle of the road, curl up in a ball, and die.

The haunting images wouldn't vacate his ethically and morally challenged brain, the faces from the pool, the scorching man, Billy's crazed eyes. Jack's hand moved to the pistol on his belt, motivated by the thought of having to face Sarah and Justin and tell them he'd left their father and husband behind ... and challenged further still by the awareness that he had abandoned the emaciated captives to face their cannibalistic abductors alone.

"I've had enough of this world," he whispered, thinking to pull the weapon and end it right then and there. He couldn't save them all. This would be easier. This was a way out of the madness.

Hewitt's voice drifted through the radio on the commander's belt, the tiny speaker carrying the sheriff's excitement. "We've got the goods! Meet you back at the warehouse."

Jack blinked, not able to believe what he'd just heard. Lifting the radio, he broadcast, "Come again? Please repeat?"

"We've found the chemical. Plenty of it. We're on our way to the warehouse. Are you okay?"

The commander didn't have the heart to ruin the moment. In the short time he'd known the man, Jack had never heard Sheriff Langdon sound so happy. "On the way," he replied.

Jack rode on, knowing that he should be excited ... or at least satisfied that they had won the day and saved the herd. "Everyone knew there might be causalities," he said, trying to pull himself away from the abyss. "We all knew the risks going in."

His words sounded hollow to the commander's own ear. Still, he somehow kept on pedaling. He didn't know what else to do.

Jack arrived back at the warehouse at the same time as Hewitt's men were plodding into the large building, substantial bags on their shoulders. Before Cisco dismounted, he could sense the giddy atmosphere of success surging through the lawman's team.

The sheriff, wise from years of assessing people in an instant, knew something was wrong the moment he laid eyes on the commander. "Billy didn't make it?" he asked.

"No," Jack replied, shaking his head but not offering any details, not sure of how he could explain what had happened.

Everyone left Jack alone as they loaded their booty onto Puff's trailer, the commander standing off to the side and completely unapproachable.

Once their treasure was secured, they all climbed aboard.

After lifting Jack's bike onto the trailer, Hewitt advanced toward him and said, "Come on, Commander. Let's go home."

For three days, Jack watched Sarah and Justin.

Each morning, they would climb to the highest point above the Cliff House and stand vigil, scouring the eastern skyline for movement ... to see if Billy was anywhere to be found.

Jack had told them the truth, explaining as best he could what they had encountered at the Mirage. "Your dad was a brave man," the commander told Justin. "You should be proud of what he did."

It was the not-knowing that was the worst of it for the young wife and son. Over and again, Jack cursed himself for leaving before he knew the final chapter of Billy's story.

On the fourth day after their return, Jack again watched Sarah and her son climb the steep trail. From that angle, the distraught wife resembled his own Mylie.

"I wonder if she ever looks for me?" Jack pondered. "I wonder if the girls ever scan the horizon and wish they knew whether their dad was dead or alive?"

The sound of Hewitt's boots drew the commander back to the present, Jack turning to see the sheriff watching the mother and son ascend the trail.

"You know you did the right thing," the lawman offered. "Billy always was the high-strung sort. Hell, for all we know, he's organizing those pool inmates and taking over all of Tucson."

Jack grunted at the vision, appreciating Hewitt's effort to pull him out of his funk.

"It's the uncertainty of what happened that is the worst," Jack repeated.

It then dawned on the commander that he was describing his own dilemma as well as that of Sarah and Justin. Not knowing about Mylie and his daughters was the worst. That's why he had left *Utah* and her crew. That's what kept him going.

Standing, Jack turned to face his new friend. "I'll be leaving in the morning, Sheriff. It's time I headed to Texas."

"Are you sure? You are welcome to stay here and help us rebuild when this all passes," Hewitt offered in a soft, friendly voice.

"Yes, I'm sure," Jack nodded. "Besides, I'm putting on weight from all that beef you're feeding me. I need to start pedaling again, or I'm going to need to renew my gym membership."

"El Paso or bust?" Hewitt grunted, secretly glad to see Jack climbing back into the saddle, but sad to see a good man go.

"No. I've learned my lesson with Tucson. I'm going to avoid the big cities from here on. There's no room left in my head for the nightmares."

Episode 5 Prologue
The day of the eruption ...

Keith watched his employee shoulder the rifle. Following the barrel's trajectory with his eye, he could barely identify the prey, so effective was the wild animal's natural camouflage. An impressive thick and tangled chestnut brown coat covered the hefty figure, blending it with the surrounding terrain. It was the cocky, black eyes framed by the oversized, curled horns that betrayed the quarry's position as they arrogantly returned the hunter's gaze from nearly 400 yards away. Certain that the rookie's bullet would miss the ram, Keith braced for the shot and the spirited mocking that would surely result.

Before for the thunderous muzzle blast had finished rolling through the New Mexico valley, the remaining three men in their party were already snickering.

As expected, the prey bolted rather than slumping to the ground, its snow-white tail bobbing up the steep hillside as it bounded for salvation.

"Glad I am safely behind you, man. You couldn't hit the broad side of a barn with both hands," one of the seasoned sportsmen chuckled.

"Don't pay any attention to him, dude," another began, "at least that bullet dropped close enough that you scared him away."

"An improvement for sure," the third spectator feigned encouragement. "That first buck this morning just sneered at us and continued to graze before stomping off."

Feeling sorry for his employee, Keith stepped to the shooter and patted him on the back. "It's okay, Joe. You're the best hang and tape drywall man this side of Scottsdale and the scariest dude with a blade I've ever seen. No one should expect you to be able to shoot too."

Following the boss's lead, three of the other members of Meyers's Construction Inc. stepped forward and expressed their condolences as well. "You almost had 'em," one commiserated, followed by, "Better luck next time, man."

Keith caught a quick glance of the face of his watch, and the boss's focus immediately shifted, much to the relief of Joe the shooter. "We need to get going back to the job site anyway, guys. We'll come back tomorrow and get that big buck."

Ten minutes later, the hunting party had returned to their pickup; the conversation now centered on the hotel renovation that was their real reason for being in Southeastern New Mexico. "How much longer you think we're going to be on this job, boss?"

"At least another three weeks. The manager has even asked me to quote remodeling the lobby. Sounds like we've got a satisfied customer on our hands," Keith beamed.

Just like that, the men had unloaded their hunting rifles and were piling into the company truck. No one seemed to notice the fiery, red line that was the sunrise to the east.

As they bounced toward Carlsbad, Keith felt a wave of satisfaction concerning his investment in the hunting lease. It was good for the guys to reestablish old bonds, to rebuild the comradery that had seen them through tough times. If he could keep this crew together for another six months, it would establish a foundation that would take his fledgling company to the next level.

Less than a mile toward the job site, a pair of headlights brought Keith back to the here and now, the bright beams combining with the sun to nearly blind him.

Braking and swerving with the same reaction, one of the men in the backseat barked, "Shit!" right as the Chevy's rear wheels careened off the pavement and began slipping across the sandy, New Mexico desert.

Keith's brawny arms fought the wheel as a stream of curses exploded from his throat. Finally, after a nearly 360-degree slide, the pickup came to a rocking stop.

"What the hell was that idiot thinking?" the boss snapped, reaching for the door handle. "That asshole is probably drunk or was texting or some shit."

A quick glance in the mirror showed the offending vehicle skidded to a stop less than 100 feet away.

"Go kick his ass, boss," encouraged another shaken member of the construction team.

In a flash, Keith was out of his truck and stomping toward the reckless driver, working up a full head of steam as his size 14 boots kicked up puffs of grit. The first thing he noticed was the park ranger emblem on the side of the government-issued pickup; the object of his second observation was a guy equal to his height and weight moving out the driver's side door.

"You okay?" a voice boomed from behind the uniform.

"Well, we're alive, if that's what you mean, but no thanks to you," Keith snapped. Then offering his best Yogi the Bear imitation, he continued mockingly, "Let me guess? Some emergency at Jellystone Park? You missing a pic-a-nic basket, Mr. Park Ranger, *sir*?"

The ranger frowned, but he ignored the verbal jab, his words tumbling out in a rush. "Sorry about the mishap. My name is Norval Pickett. I oversee the park at Carlsbad Caverns, and like everyone else, I am seeking shelter from this oncoming shit storm." Keith's questioning glare let the park official know that his adversary was unaware of the larger issue at hand, so he continued, "Haven't you heard about what's going on?"

Keith could tell the man was flustered by far more than their near collision and seemed to be privy to information that he needed. "Heard what? We've been up in the mountains hunting this morning. What could possibly be going on here in Bumfuck, New Mexico that could justify driving like your ass is on fire?"

"I thought everyone knew by now. It's been all over the radio this morning – Yellowstone has exploded, and I was hurrying into town to see if I could catch a television broadscast."

"What? Are you sure? I don't know a thing about that. We were just heading back to our job site. My crew and I are removing the asbestos from the old Simpson hotel and haven't been had much time for the boob tube."

Norval nodded, "So *you* are the guys doing that renovation. I am just on my way there, as a matter of fact. I heard old man Simpson bought one of those top of the line, fancy-schmansy, oversized, flat screen TVs for the lobby. Ordinarily, we don't have much use for such extravagances at the park office, but today, I want to get the best possible information about this eruption. Anyway, if you men are all okay, I need to get going. From what I heard on the radio broadcast, this is serious stuff, and I have to see the news reports on this blast for myself. Guess I'll see you gents later."

Then, without another word, the ranger pivoted and made for his own truck, leaving Keith standing beside the road with nothing more than an open mouth. In his haste, the government honcho spun his wheels on the asphalt, leaving a fresh, black rubber mark as evidence of his hurried departure.

Processing the information shared with him, Keith slowly turned toward his own truck, his neurons firing in rapid succession as they assimilated the ranger's demeanor and words. Could all the doomsday predictions about Yellowstone's caldera have been set in motion while he and the boys had been blowing off a little steam? Keith's brain swirled with best and worst case scenarios. *How is all of this going to affect us and when? Do we need to shelter in place or head for home?* Still mentally running his options, the boss glanced up at the men who trusted him for their livelihoods. Would they once again be trusting him with their lives like they had in the Army so many years before?

The business owner's somber mood was immediately interrupted by the comical scene before him. "Damn! Looks like I'm watching *The Three Stooges Head West*, he snorted. Disenchanted by the obvious de-escalation of events, and still hyped up from the adrenaline dump of the near collision, his own crew was clearly engrossed in a verbal altercation. Brimming with bloodlust, the co-workers were quarrelling among themselves, each man with his own theory why the jackass who had run them off the road wasn't writhing on the ground with a busted nose and swollen lips.

"That was the head ranger over at the caverns," the construction manager explained. "He's all in a huff… something about Yellowstone blowing its top this morning."

"Yellowstone? You mean that super volcano finally is letting loose?" Joe asked, his normally lighthearted expression now veiled with worry.

Keith opened the driver's door and climbed inside the cab. "Yeah," he sighed, "that's what the man said."

Joe let out a low wolf whistle before commenting on the turn of events. "That can be some serious shit. I saw one of those TV documentaries a while back. They said there is enough lava under that park to bury half of the good ol' USA."

"Really?" asked another of the men. "There's a volcano at Yellowstone? I never heard of such a thing."

"Really," Joe confirmed. "We'd better find out what's going on too, boss. If that lava dome has cut loose and is really kicking ass, we might all want to think about getting home to our families."

"Okay, let's follow the ranger and get the skinny," Keith agreed, apparently considering Joe's words seriously. A few seconds later, they were racing off to catch up with Pickett.

Ten minutes of well-over-the-limit driving brought the Meyer crew rolling up beside the same pickup that had threatened their lives before.

The men piled out of the pickup and poured into the lobby. Clearly mesmerized by the 70-inch screen, Ranger Pickett stood alongside the hotel clerk and a handful of guests, each one rivetted by the reporter's words and silently gawking at the television. Before Keith ever viewed the first images of the disaster, he knew the news was going to be bad from the expression of horror fixed on every face.

"Reports are coming in of poisonous gas in the northern suburbs of Denver," the announcer stated. "Colorado State Police are ordering an immediate evacuation of all citizens residing north of Interstate 70."

"That must be at least two million people," someone in the lobby hissed. "Where in the hell are they supposed to go?"

"Not our problem," the head ranger muttered.

Next, the reports buzzed with recounts of earthquakes and a tsunami along the Western Seaboard. Another journalist, broadcasting live from Seattle, simply vanished mid-sentence.

"Like I said," Joe chimed in. "That volcano is a monster. We better start making some plans, boss."

"What sort of plans are you talking about?" demanded Keith. "Hell, how to you *plan* for something like this?"

"We can expect very drastic weather changes from now on," Joe began explaining. "The atmosphere is going to be filled with dust and dirt. Breathing will become decidedly unhealthy. Locating drinkable water will probably be a problem. Hell, if this goes on long enough, food sources will dry up. If even half of what that documentary predicted happens, we are in serious trouble."

Stressful situations weren't anything new to Keith and his team. In fact, he and his current employees had initially met years ago, all members of the 82nd Airborne Division that parachuted into Panama. Pulling a friend's gonads out of the fire had been all in a day's work to them.

They all knew that Joe was about as far from a "Chicken Little and the Falling Sky" guy as they got. While there wasn't a wild animal within miles that feared the man's shooting skills, Joe did command the respect of his buddies when it came to logic and common sense. He was a man known for his integrity, who cut to the chase and didn't fall prey to exaggeration.

The developing occurrence raised a hundred critical issues in Keith's mind, each demanding immediate attention. *How long before the dust turns the fresh breeze into poison? How much time before airborne venom reaches us? Can we outrun this catastrophe? If escape isn't in the cards, where is the best haven to ride out Armageddon itself?*

Fortunately, his questions ran parallel to the cable company's news coverage.

For hours, the construction crew stood with the locals … all equally awed by the disaster unfolding on the television. Experts, scientists, government officials, and academics were paraded in front of the cameras, all of them touting the same underlying message that Joe's documentary had predicted. Carlsbad, New Mexico, the United States, and the world were in serious trouble.

It was Norval who offered the first positive idea as the drama played on. "I'm going to close the park," the head ranger mumbled. "I'm going to have my people bring their families inside."

"What good would that do?" Keith asked.

"There are hundreds of tons of fresh water inside the caves," Pickett stated with confidence. "The air inside should remain ash free, and we have several weeks' worth of food stored for the park's restaurants. There are plenty of recourses there for us to keep our people alive."

Something in the government official's tone rubbed Keith the wrong way. "And what about the people stuck outside?" he asked. "What about the hundreds of vacationers trapped at all of these hotels?"

Pickett merely shrugged, "They had better be heading home, I suppose."

Chapter 24

Jack couldn't make spit, and yet somehow found his parched state amusing. "I'm so thirsty, even my sense of humor is dry," he croaked to the empty New Mexico desert, trying to work up a mouthful of moisture.

The effort led to more distress, the commander's lips cracked and charred under the ever-present mask. "Got to find water. Should be just over this ridge."

"It's been two days since you've had a drink," he reminded himself. And then shaking his head to clear the mental cobwebs, he asked himself, "Or is today the third day?"

Worse than his throat and mouth, the pounding inside his skull was like a jack hammer beating against his entire cranium. His joints ached, and his stomach burned. "Signs of dehydration," he reasoned.

For the Nth time, he was second-guessing his decision to avoid populated areas. "Which is worse? Being eaten by cannibals or shriveling up and dying out here in the middle of nowhere?"

The highway sign several miles back advertised a park called Rattlesnake Springs. According to the ash-spotted billboard, the place contained a campground and recreational facilities. But it was the word "spring," that had drawn the commander's attention.

He struggled up a slight rise, the two-lane, New Mexico highway not engineered nearly as level as the interstates that had ushered him most of the way from San Diego. Still, I-10 led directly into El Paso, and after encountering the flesh-eaters in the Tucson rest stop, Jack wasn't about to venture near a large, urban center like the West Texas city.

He couldn't be faulted for his priorities.

He could still smell the Cliff House's fresh stream as he had taken a knee and filled his plastic bottles. It had been his final step of preparation before leaving. And that act had contributed the most critical component of his kit.

He had carefully closed every lid, double-checked every cap. Water was precious, and the commander knew he was about to journey through one of the most arid stretches of North America.

For the first two days after leaving Hewitt and his clan, Jack had managed his supply judicially. Not a drop had been wasted.

Then, the largest jug in his pack, the 1-liter soda bottle, had failed.

Jack wasn't sure if he had over-tightened the top, or if the plastic had just become brittle with age. Whatever the reason, he had found the damn thing empty, the bottom of his pack soaked with its contents.

That was at least two days of water. Gone. Vanished. Wasted. Dripping into the ash as he pedaled, darkening the pumice as he crossed the desert. After all you have survived, Commander, looks like you are doomed because of a faulty liter of cola. *Wonder if the local Walmart will exchange this for me?* he mused, desperate to keep his spirits up.

Commander Cisco knew the value of keeping his mood light. Continuously being on the lookout for food, water, and shelter was nearly as exhausting as pedaling through the carpet of ash. That, combined with the constant need to maintain a heightened state of alert left Jack completely stressed out with no opportunity to relax and enjoy life. The emotional drain took its toll, as it would on anyone, and left the commander vulnerable to depression.

As the miles passed, Jack found it increasingly difficult to deal with the reality that Yellowstone had created.

The commander had always looked forward during troubling times. Years ago, as a young teen, he'd found that forcing himself to focus on the future was the best way to cope. An unproductive week at school was overcome by the approaching weekend. A bad day at the Academy could be offset by daydreaming of his own command. He and Mylie's worst quarrel was counterbalanced by one of their daughters doing something amazing.

Now, in the pewter and charcoal void, about the only way he could continue to motivate the bike's pedals toward the east was to think of the future, and that was where the problem truly resided.

What if he did find Mylie and the girls alive and well? How would he feed them if Texas looked like Arizona and New Mexico? What was the point? What was their future?

Shelly and the people at Mud Lake were eventually going to run out of chili. Hewitt's herd was fragile at best. At any time, a lightning storm or contagious blight could wipe out Archie's greenhouse. Who knew how the men back at Utah had fared?

No, the problem Jack soon began to realize, was how he could possibly create a long-term future for his family.

Now, none of that would matter without a water source. His previous concerns seemed trivial given the death sentence that his dry throat predicted.

The commander knew a few survival tricks, distant memories from childhood television shows and old black and white movie reruns. He decided against eating, knowing that digesting food required water. He also avoided pedaling to the point of perspiring.

There was no need to avoid the sun as cobalt skies had gone the way of buttercup daffodils, iridescent peacocks, and bay mares. *Well, at least I won't have to stock up on sunscreen for a while,* he mused.

Then, out of the pewter haze that was the sky after Yellowstone's eruption, Jack spotted the second road sign.

It wasn't much of an announcement, just a small, green rectangle with a white arrow and letters. "Rattlesnake Springs – 1 Mile," it advised.

The mere thought of cool, clean water rolling down the back of his throat empowered Jack with energy he no longer believed existed. The bike seemed lighter now, the pedals no longer fighting their way through the ash cover that incessantly challenged the tires' advance.

Rattlesnake Springs wasn't much as far as parks go, or at least the handful Jack had visited before joining the Navy. It was outfitted with the pre-requisite booth to collect the traveler's fee, a paved parking area, and two cinderblock buildings that housed restrooms.

It took the commander another few minutes to determine the location of the creek – or at least the posted map that showed visitors which path to follow. "Shit! Are you kidding me? I have to hike into the wilderness now?" At least the trail was level. No more inclines to negotiate … for a while.

Still, water was water, and with his empty plastic bottles and dry CamelBak in tow, Jack began the trek to the oasis purportedly 1.2 miles from the trailhead.

As his legs protested the additional exercise, the commander briefly considered the effect of fallen ash on the local serpent population. He had always heard that cockroaches were considered the most likely survivors of any catastrophe. He didn't know about the likelihood of rattlesnakes enduring volcanic slag but decided to watch his step and keep his weapon handy just in case. *Be just my luck those reptiles would shelter under a rock and slither out for a meal once I step close,* he mused. *And it's not like anyone is answering 9-1-1 calls anymore*.

The M4 carbine hanging from his shoulder weighed a ton, as did his boots. His pants and shirt felt like they were plastered to his body, cemented down with what seemed to be every ounce of ash blowing across the desolate stretch of highway.

The path had been engineered using several switchbacks as it meandered through the desert terrain. The commander realized steep inclines had been avoided since climbing them presented a hazard to elderly tourists with compromised vision, balance issues, and arthritic knees. "Hell, I should have shown my AARP card at the gate and received a discount," he croaked in a hoarse whisper.

For just a brief moment, Jack considered leaving the trail, the lesson from the rest areas still fresh in his mind. "Water can be used as bait," he remembered, picturing the trap he had narrowly avoided outside of Tucson.

Given the state of his body and mind, Jack quickly dismissed the concern. The harsh reality was that he was out of options and faced certain death if he didn't hydrate his failing body. Scouting and climbing over the surrounding rocks just wasn't in the cards. Post-apocalyptic caution was thrown into the ash-filled wind.

He smelled the stream before he saw it, the scent of the water emboldening the commander and lengthening his stride. Another bend, and there it was, a stone lined pond that would have been right at home on any Midwestern farm.

Jack had hoped for some sort of cover or shelter to protect the precious liquid from the ash, but nothing of the sort initially met his eye. Fighting the nearly overwhelming urge to rush to the edge and begin slurping mouthfuls of the goodness, he forced himself to pace along the shoreline in search of the spring that must be feeding the miniature pond. "I wonder just how much tainted water could I swallow before I would jeopardize my health?" he whispered to the clean-looking pool. "Have the hazardous contaminants dissipated enough that I could chance a sip?"

Forcing caution back into his thoughts, the commander barely avoided a rash act. His gaze moved to the tangled, skeletal undergrowth at the far end of the basin. That's where the most water would be. Plants like to drink. "You're not without your wits after all, Commander Cisco," he noted. "At least not yet."

As he stepped toward the leafless shrubbery, Jack could tell this had certainly been a green oasis before the eruption. Now, only barren, brown stalks and lifeless foliage met his eye.

Finally, he approached what appeared to be a manhole cover embedded in the bank. Its heavy, metal lid was a struggle, but after several grunts and groans, the commander managed to roll away the iron cap.

There it was, powerfully gushing from the sand – the spring!

With the speed of a lightning strike, Jack's hand shot into the shallow flow of cool water. The first swallow was unlike anything he had ever tasted on his lips. No cold beer had ever been as satisfying, no frozen treat providing as much euphoria.

"And you were paranoid about being ambushed," he started to say between gulps.

A geyser of water exploded skyward before the words could form in Jack's throat, stinging bits of rock and soil following a nanosecond later.

Stunned, Jack was slower than he should have been, but his instincts kicked in. He rolled into the pond just as the crack and zip of rifle rounds split the air that his body had just vacated.

The shooters, whoever they were, adjusted quickly, but the manmade shoreline of limestone offered the commander just enough cover as Jack tried frantically to rally his terrified and confused mind.

He was too scared to move and didn't know which direction to go even if he could force his legs to respond. He didn't even notice the icy water, nor did he spot the men sneaking up behind him from the far side of the stream.

Hot lead slammed into the mud and stone bank, Jack pressing his body lower until he was completely submerged except for his eyes and nose. He could feel the baritone compression of large caliber lead as it ripped past his ears.

Just as he was sure the men trying to kill him were going to zero in on his skull, the tempo and sound of the gunfire changed. Now, bullets were flying in both directions. Now, the report of rifles blasted at his back.

Assuming that the men behind him were allied with the shooters that had driven him into the pond, Jack thought the clash had subsided. *Commander Cisco, Military Strategist,* he chided himself. *Here you hide in the bog, surrounded by the 'Water Police.' So much for the theory that asking forgiveness is better than asking permission.*

His assessment of the situation, however, proved to be flawed.

Thirty feet from the shoreline, Jack spied a man rise with a shotgun pointing directly at the commander's forehead. Before the assaulter could even shoulder the scattergun, three bullets tore into the aggressor's chest with devastating effect.

A blizzard of lead was now whizzing over Jack's head, the two parties obviously well-armed and intent on eliminating each other.

Given little attention was now being paid to his mud-immersed body, Jack began inching his way along the shoreline, hoping to remove his carcass from no man's land as soon as possible.

Bit by bit, he pushed his way through the mire and silt at the bottom of Rattlesnake's pit, slowly trudging through the sludge, keeping low, and praying neither side noticed his progress.

While the gunfight still raged behind him, Jack approached a slight trench where natural drainage from the desert had created a shallow gully. Taking a deep breath, the commander lunged out of the water on his hands and knees and scrambled like a madman for the slight depression.

When the air above him didn't fill with buzzing, snapping lead death, the commander felt reinvigorated and began crawling on hands and knees as fast as his limbs could move.

It seemed like the longest 20 yards Jack had ever attempted to negotiate, his eyes remaining fixed on a series of waist-high rocks and cactus that would offer salvation. If he could make that cover, he might even have a reasonable chance of escape.

Finally reaching the stone bastion, Jack managed to rise to his feet and then stood, drinking in deep gulps of oxygen.

A few moments had passed before he felt strong enough to move again. Hefting his rifle and concentrating on the continuing firefight behind him, he attempted to draw a mental map of the conflict. He had hostiles to the east and west, the pond to the north. The southern side of the spring appeared to be unoccupied.

Tightly gripping his rifle, the commander began moving bent at the waist, scurrying from crag to pillar and then pausing to listen again. On the third such maneuver, he sensed that the skirmish was now mobile. Either that, or the stone formations surrounding him were playing tricks on his ears.

The next cycle of movement proved problematic. To the south, there was no cover, the flat, barren landscape offering zero places to hide and nothing that would stop a bullet. More importantly, the gunfire to his rear now sounded even closer than before.

Jack decided to cut to his left, spotting a bulky outcropping of boulders that would provide an excellent place to hide.

Rushing to the stone formation, Jack rounded a corner and froze to prevent discovery. Three men were scuffling not more than 10 feet away from his position. The commander pressed his body into the rock crevice with the skill of a contortionist while struggling to pace his labored breathing.

Within a second, it became apparent that the struggle dynamic was two against one. The burliest fellow was backing away from the other two, one of the attackers pulling a blade while the other advanced with balled fists. Everyone, it seemed, had run out of ammunition.

Jack had no dog in this fight. He had no way of knowing who had been in charge of his welcoming committee and who had just been in the neighborhood when he moved in. There was no way to tell which of them had sighted his skull and let loose a bullet intended to create a new hole in his head and who heard the gunshot and decided to get in a little target practice. What he did notice was that the outnumbered dude was wearing a uniform.

"I'm going to slice you up like a Christmas turkey," growled the attacker with the hunting knife, holding the edge low and moving in on the balls of his feet. "You and them other rangers aren't going to deny us anymore."

"Kill 'im, Joe! Cut 'im up," the other assaulter snarled, letting his armed friend go first.

At the same time, the outnumbered fellow spotted Jack creeping up behind the assailants and mouthed one word – "Help."

Something about the uniform engendered trust in Jack's mind. He too had served his country as did most men who donned such garb. With no other facts to complete his analysis, the commander's logic compelled him down the path of helping the cornered ranger.

Seeing the eye contact from their prey, the unarmed fellow pivoted sharply and peered right into the commander's face. "He's the fucker that was in the spring!" the man barked.

Jack's carbine was at his shoulder in a flash, the muzzle now pointed directly at the knife wielder's head. "Back off," the commander hissed. "Just back the hell out of here."

At that moment, another man burst around a nearby stone slab. He had ammunition. He was shooting.

Jack felt a tug at his shoulder before the burning, stinging bolts of pain shot up his upper arm and shoulder. Without conscious thought or effort, his trigger finger was working hard, the M4 singing its deadly song as the commander poured lead from his sweeping barrel. One stream of thought directed Jack's reaction – put down the shooter.

Joe-the-knife-man somehow avoided Jack's burst, as did the hefty ranger. The other two men involved in the fray, however, were not so fortunate.

Before Jack could even digest what had just happened, the ranger was moving. Surprisingly quick for a guy with such a sizeable profile, Cisco watched as the previously cornered man rushed over and yanked the rifle from one of the men that the commander had just killed. Then, in another flash of movement, the uniform was towering over Jack.

"You're hurt," the burly dude assessed, nodding toward the expanding, red stain on Jack's sleeve. "Hey, thanks for saving my ass, man. Come on..... Come with me."

The pain was now beginning to impact Jack's reasoning and common sense. He hadn't managed to secure any water, and this plot of earth was obviously hotly contested. He could hear gunshots and voices nearby. With his legs already growing weak, the commander didn't feel like he had any choice.

"Lead the way," Jack replied.

A hundred questions dashed through the commander's mind. What had he stumbled into? Who were these guys? Why were they fighting amongst themselves? Which side wore the white hats? Jack's post-apocalyptic cynicism presumed there was most likely a right and wrong side. *How pessimistic*, he thought. *Have things devolved to the point where you always assume that one group is driven to save the species, another with much more self-centered interests*? Once complex choices had seemingly devolved into a rudimentary analysis of the world as black or white, good or evil.

Jack followed the big fellow over a series of squatty, rolling hills toward some unknown objective. As they left the stream behind, he began to observe occasional sentries along the route, all of them wearing the same uniform as the man leading him into the unknown. Jack struggled to keep up, his throbbing deltoid a constant reminder of his injury as he continued to move. His mud soaked clothing was an additional drag, his hands and lips quivering from the cold. He prayed this journey was short – his legs were shaking and wobbly now, either from the pain, loss of blood, or both.

Eventually, the men approached what Jack realized was one of the main entrances to the famous Carlsbad Caverns, his guide finally slowing his long stride and drawing alongside the struggling commander.

Has everybody moved below the surface? Jack thought. *First the Marines at the air station, then Hewitt's stone mansion?*

It made sense, he supposed, his mind traveling to places like New Your City and Washington with their extensive subway systems. Then there were Houston and Atlanta with their sprawling subterranean developments. He was wondering how many thousands of people had sought shelter in those protected spaces? How long could they survive without outside support? Just then, his host spoke, bringing the commander back to New Mexico.

"We're safe now. My name is Norval Pickett, and I'm the head ranger here at the park. I want to thank you again for saving my life back there. Let's rest for just a minute and let you catch your breath," the host said, gesturing toward a low group of rocks suitable for a rest stop.

Still off his game from the blood loss and adrenaline surge, Jack displayed uncharacteristically bad manners, ignoring the man's thanks. Still breathing hard and not sure who he had joined ranks with, the commander demanded, "Who were those guys you were fighting? What's this all about anyway?"

"We can talk about that a bit later," came the gentle, but guarded, response. "Right now, let's get someone to take a look at that shoulder."

They continued their journey at a more manageable pace, and Ranger Pickett then asked the obvious question. "And who might you be?"

Jack provided his host his most basic information, including name and rank, and a brief history of his cross-country adventure.

"So … California really did fall into the sea?" the ranger asked.

"No, at least not the southern end. I did hear from reliable sources that the northern coast suffered far, far worse."

Norval switched gears to continue narrating the tour. "The men you see around you were all staff here at the park. Their families bunked in once the pumice threat became imminent," Pickett explained, sweeping his beefy arm in a wide arch. "When Yellowstone blew, I closed the gates and had all my people move into the caverns. We've been holed up inside ever since."

They continued further into the underground chambers, Jack's head on a pivot as he tried to absorb the changes in air temperature and light. He had hiked through caves before with Miley and the girls, but nothing like Norval was now leading him through.

While the rocks and crystalline formations were breathtaking, what really drew the commander's eye were the electric lights installed here and there along the otherwise ever-darkening path.

"You have electrical power?" Jack asked, amazed to see evidence of technology.

"The park has its own primary power plant," Norval bragged. "In order to keep the noise from disturbing the environment, the original designers installed the generators and diesel fuel tanks inside of one of the less-spectacular caves, well away from the public areas."

"There's more than one cave?" Jack asked.

"Oh, my, yes," Norval responded. "There are over 110 known caves and grottos with new ones being discovered all the time."

"Where do you get fuel for the diesels? How do you keep them from clogging up like every other internal combustion engine on the planet?"

Norval waved off the questions, "I'm not sure how they keep running. When the government contracted for the generators to be installed, there were a lot of environmental concerns. As far as fuel goes … well … there are lots of sources of diesel around. Let's just say that we've mounted a few scouting expeditions into the neighboring towns."

The ranger's words and tone sent additional chills down Jack's spine, his reaction having little to do with the cool air or his waterlogged duds. *Scouting expeditions?* Jack thought. *More like looting excursions, I'd wager. Armed to the teeth no doubt. Maybe the guys shooting at me in the spring were pissed about this guy making off with their goodies. That would explain a lot.*

While scavenging for diesel fuel wasn't the worst thing the commander could imagine, Pickett's words served to not only put Jack on higher alert but they instantly tainted the commander's impression of the man beside him. *So much for the honorable Dudley-Do-Right wearing the ranger uniform.*

I'm sure a lot of survivors have done worse, he quickly reconciled. *Stealing fuel is petty theft in the grand scheme of the post-apocalyptic world. Hell, more like a parking ticket.*

Still, as they stepped deeper into the bowels of the cave, Jack couldn't help but develop a sense of foreboding. What was it the guy about to kill his host had said? "I'm going to slice you up like a Christmas turkey," and, "You and them other rangers aren't going to deny us anymore."

What exactly does "deny" mean, Jack wondered. It was an odd choice of words.

For a moment, Jack considered turning around and heading out. He still had his rifle and knew where the sentries were stationed. That would be the safe, smart thing to do, right? The realization that he had no water, a bleeding arm, and wasn't exactly sure of his location halted that line of thought. And in truth, he had no real evidence that Ranger Pickett was on the wrong side of the morality scale.

Before Jack could plow any deeper into his analysis, a woman appeared beside them, her kind eyes and leather bag full of bandages making her purpose clear.

"This is Carmen," Norval announced. "She is our resident medical expert and my second in command."

Jack nodded to the woman, noting her shiny, black hair and fresh scent. Probably in her early 30's with shoulder-length tresses and chestnut brown eyes, she was one of the most attractive women the commander had ever seen. Jack also noted her understated, but seductive swagger, her hips casually swinging atop a pair of legs so impeccably shaped they looked like a sculptor had chiseled them from the finest stone.

Norval and his people evidently had access to enough water that attending to personal hygiene was not an issue, Jack concluded. Considering that virtually every decision he had made to survive had been driven by water conservation, Jack's realization was even more astonishing than Carmen's striking appearance. Still, he couldn't help the testosterone charged, mental image of Ms. Legs drawing him a bath.

As the scissors sliced away the damaged cloth, Jack snapped back to reality. Without a word, Carmen began cutting away Jack's sleeve just above his wound. "I was a nurse back in Mexico City," she reported with a thick accent. "You are lucky. Your wound isn't life-threatening as long as it doesn't get infected."

A convulsive shiver chose that moment to rack Jack's frame. Feeling his skin tremble, Carmen hesitated her triage and shot him an apologetic look, thinking she had caused him pain. When she began again, her touch was extremely gentle.

All the while, Jack couldn't help but notice that the way her thick lashes perfectly framed her eyes made them appear even more provocatively feminine.

Little Ms. Florence Nightingale then ran her fingers across the top buttons on his shirt and announced, "You're soaked! And filthy! Talk about a breeding ground for all types of infection in that open wound. Quick, get out of those wet things. The temperature inside the cave is always very cool. You'll eventually get accustomed to it – but not if you are wearing damp clothes. I'll grab you a blanket, and we'll get you cleaned up."

Despite a healthy dose of modesty, Jack didn't hesitate to undress in front of the two strangers. Carmen, true to her word, returned with a heavy, green wool cover that reminded the commander of the scratchy, government-issued bedding he'd first received at the Academy.

Whether it was to take advantage of his being distracted, or an honest attempt to divert Jack's attention from the pain and discomfort, Norval took the opportunity to fire a series of questions at the commander.

Wincing as his wound was cleaned, Jack answered honestly, but was cautious and stingy with the details. The last thing the people at the Cliff House needed was a bunch of vagabonds raiding their beef supply. Pinemont could provide enough eggs to sustain its own population, but not enough to supply large groups like Cisco had observed in this subterranean community. And there was no doubt in the commander's mind that Archie's veggie garden wouldn't last a week with Picketts' mouths to feed.

Still, the commander knew he couldn't appear completely uncooperative. That tactic might generate suspicion or mistrust, and he was in no position to insult his hosts.

So, Cisco did his best to provide just the right amount of information to establish rapport without compromising the other fledgling societies. Yes, he'd encountered survivors. No, there was zero government authority as far as Jack knew. There were no living plants or animals that he'd seen.

Jack found it odd that Norval's interrogation seemed more focused on law enforcement and surviving government structure that any sources of food or pockets of survivors. The head ranger pressed his guest hard when Jack mentioned the absence of military communications and command structure that *Utah* had encountered. Twice he asked if Jack had spotted any sign of state or local police. Pickett seemed almost relieved that the United States of America no longer existed, at least west of the Rocky Mountains.

As Carmen finished wrapping his arm, she produced two white capsules. "Here, take these for the pain. They will make you drowsy, so don't operate any heavy machinery," she teased.

"What are they?" Jack inquired.

His question prompted an unspoken exchange between Norval and Carmen. Finally, after an uncomfortable pause, she responded, "They are some pain meds I brought with me from Mexico."

Jack frowned, the offer of ultra-valuable medications as shocking as the fact that these people bathed regularly. "Thanks, but no thanks," the commander replied, pushing back her hand. "You should save those for more serious wounds and for your own people. I'll be fine. I *would* appreciate some water, though."

Carmen shrugged and returned the pills to her bag. "Suit yourself."

A man appeared just then, the look on the fellow's face making it obvious that he needed Norval's immediate and undivided attention. As Ranger Pickett took his leave, he motioned for Carmen to take care of their guest.

"Come on," she cooed. "I'll show you where you can get something to drink after we find you some clothes that fit. We have the purest water in the world, and you can drink until your heart is content. After that, I'll take you to a cot where you can get some rest. Later, Norval will complete your tour of our underground palace," she promised.

Chapter 25

After a short walk that involved several turns, twists, and cutbacks, Jack followed Ms. Legs into a larger than normal chamber of the interior. Once inside, the commander found himself staring down at what could only be described as several small ponds of water. Each was slightly larger than a resort's hot tub and appeared to be relatively shallow, at most only a few feet deep.

Smooth, rock walls lined each reservoir and provided enough separation to allow a series of paths and walkways between the individual repositories. A couple of large watering troughs, like the kind used to hydrate livestock, lined the rear wall of the cavern. "The two tubs in the back are for bathing," Carmen explained. "Our fearless leader is uptight about polluting the water, but you can drink from any of these other ponds," she continued with a sweep of her hand.

Jack moved quickly to the nearest pool's side, taking a knee and reaching into the crystal-clear liquid. Scooping a handful, he found the water was somewhat tepid and was accompanied by a slight mineral odor. Cautiously swallowing a mouthful, he then turned and beamed at Carmen. "I'd give it 5 stars … Absolutely unbelievable," he burbled before plunging both hands back for a refill.

It was even more satisfying than the spring outside, refreshing, clean, and delivering an overwhelming sensation of pureness. After emptying several hand-cups into his mouth, Jack wiped his lips with a sleeve and paused to breathe. Glancing around the spacious cavern, he couldn't help but admire the liquid asset that Norval and his group controlled. *You could keep an entire army hydrated with this water supply*, thought Jack.

As he continued to drink, another unsettling thought popped into Jack's mind. *I wonder what their source of food is? So far, no one in here appears to have missed many meals. Maybe Ranger Pickett has found a way to grow something down here?*

The commander remembered visiting La Cave Des Roches during a deployment. On shore leave, Jack and a group of shipmates had explored a series of grottos in France. Translated roughly into "caves that grow mushrooms," those caverns had been used to produce food. The group had toured what was essentially a 75-mile network of underground caverns where tons of vegetables were harvested each season. The humid air, combined with a year-round, constant temperature, resulted in the perfect environment for growing delicious fungi. It was an amazing underground agri-business.

The conditions here were nearly the same as the caves in France. Had Norval created a subterranean farm of some sort?

Taking a break from his rehydration, Jack decided to lightly ply Carmen for information. "This is quite the little underground paradise you guys have here," the commander stated warmly. "Quite an abundance of water, I see. But do you grow anything in the caves to help feed your people?"

"Yes, as a matter of fact, we do," she responded, her eyebrows rising with surprise at his question. "As soon as you're finished drinking, I will show you."

Jack pushed himself away from the water buffet, forcing himself to quit slurping the life-giving liquid. Partly because he knew consuming too much too quickly might make him sick, but mostly out of embarrassment over his aqua-gluttony.

Again, with Carmen leading the way, Jack was guided further into the depths of the tunnel system. After several minutes of walking, they entered an exceptionally well-lit cavern that was also especially roomy.

Jack estimated the high canopy spanned a good 75 feet wide with ceilings soaring 100 feet above the stone floor. Someone had strung electric lights alongside the path, the bright bulbs illuminating walls that were nearly solid green with some sort of algae or moss.

"We have gotten rather good at cultivation," Carmen beamed. "According to Norval, this species isn't native this far into the dark sections of the caves. When the Parks Department installed the first electric lights several years ago, this gunk started growing deeper and deeper into the formations. The rangers even struggled to keep the spread under control for years, all in the name of preserving the natural ecosystem of the caverns. Now, everyone is glad it is here."

Jack stepped over and gently touched a patch of the green carpet. "What does it taste like?"

"Kelp," she giggled. "Bitter kelp. One of the rangers' wives was a biology major, and she claims it is rich in some nutrients, but I still struggle to get used to the taste. We also are trying to farm snails for protein, but Norval says getting enough of them to feed everybody is going to take several months."

"Amazing," Jack replied, scanning the green walls. "I've met a lot of people who would give anything to have a renewable food source of any kind, palatable or not."

His statement seemed to change Carmen's previously welcoming demeanor. "We should be getting back," she announced in a chilled tone, almost as if his words had reminded her of some pending unpleasantness. "I'm sure Norval has a thousand questions for you. You're the first stranger he's allowed inside the caverns since the eruption."

Keith and his ragtag army withdrew from the encounter at Rattlesnake Springs, their faces dark masks of anger and frustration.

Their goal had been to engage Norval's men at the back entrance to the caverns, fight their way inside and finally end this conflict. Instead, the Myers construction team had suffered three killed and another man seriously wounded. More causalities. More death. More pain.

The former construction manager paused for a moment, his eyes scanning his force as they plodded along the desert trail.

The core members of his fledgling business, Hamilton, Joe, and the others, had been together for many years. They were no strangers to stress, hard times, or combat.

As Keith watched his column pass, he made eye contact with Hamilton, or Ham. The two simply exchanged knowing nods. "Still breathing," was the non-verbal communication.

Myers's mind reverted back to the first time he'd seen his friend broadcast that basic but critical message. The year had been 1989, the location Panama City, Panama.

Keith had been a young lieutenant, full of vigor and convinced the 504th Parachute Infantry Regiment of the 82nd Airborne Division was the most bad ass group of fighting men ever produced by the US military.

They had parachuted into the Central American nation, using the most dangerous of all deployment methods – a nighttime combat jump.

Throughout the night and well into the next day, Keith and his men had exchanged heavy fire with the Panamanian Defense Forces in an operation named "*Just Cause.*"

It had been a short but intense affair, a quick and overwhelming victory that received little airplay back in the States. Still, the brotherhood of combat had been formed between Keith and his men. Years later, when he saw an opportunity to start his own construction company, the first people he called were his old buddies from five-oh-four.

His men called him "the strategist," but after today's botched operation, Keith wasn't feeling very strategic. At 6'5" and topping out at 230 pounds, Myers had never had to rely on his size to maintain a leadership role. He, like so many young officers in the military, used his brainpower and logic to gain the respect of his men. It was a bond that often persisted for a lifetime, and Myers Construction, Inc was a prime example of that perpetual tie.

In Keith's case, however, intellect didn't translate into a lack of fighting skills or capability. Trained in all facets of combat by the military schools at Fort Bragg, he could hold his own in virtually any physical confrontation. Even more legendary was his temper, as the beefy LT was known to get mad or mean at the drop of a hat. Word quickly spread that incompetence among the ranks wouldn't be tolerated.

Ham was the team's small arms expert, qualified with just about anything that had a barrel and could spit lead. Almost as tall as Keith but sporting a slighter build, he had always been the unit's second in command. The duo seemed to be on the same page all the time. In fact, they were even known to finish sentences for each other.

Joe came next, his thick torso supported by big bones and oversized hands. He had been with the team since the beginning and was a quiet individual. The last place on earth any man wanted to be was in a hand-to-hand contest with Joe.

Keith again made eye contact with his more pensive comrade, the disappointment and worry clear in his friend's gaze.

Bringing up the rear of their shot-up group was James, the comedian who seemed to be able to find humor in any situation. Seldom serious, Jimmy preferred the lighter side of life, especially when it came to finding fault with his teammates, and jokingly pointing out any shortcoming or failure. Keith often wondered which was sharper, Jim's wit or Joe's fighting knife.

"So much for being a backdoor man, eh, boss?" Jimmy said as he passed.

The remainder of Keith's assault force trailed behind, including those carrying the fallen.

With sad eyes, Keith watched the limp bodies bounce and jolt as their pallbearers managed the uneven terrain. He'd seen so much death since the eruption. He wondered if it was possible to become immune to the work of the Grim Reaper.

For the first time he could recall, Keith questioned the wisdom of asking his old Army buddies to join his new company.

In reality, he had made those initial phone calls because of a chance meeting with Ham a few short weeks before. "I was working as a scab electrician in Scottsdale," his old buddy had explained. "When the housing bust kicked in a few years back, they laid everyone off, and I've been living on unemployment ever since."

A bit more research informed the former officer that his other friends weren't doing much better. Joe had re-enlisted for another tour and fought heroically in the first Gulf War, only to come home with a bad case of PTSD. He had struggled to hold a job ever since.

Jimmy could only find work as a bartender in Las Vegas. "If you ain't a bombshell or don't have a college sheepskin, finding steady work can sure be a struggle. There's not much work for worn out paratroopers these days, LT," the joker had reported with a jaded voice.

Even Keith himself had floundered, his efforts to build a good life for his family always seeming to hit an impenetrable and unforgiving wall. Despite a degree in finance, promotion and advancement in the corporate world were challenging at best. In the cutthroat environment of ever-changing computer software, internet based business, and off-shore service providers, the brawny fellow was always struggling to hold his own.

Deeply troubled by how veterans were being treated, Keith had taken the plunge and started his own construction company. He would hire those who had served their country. He would give as many as possible a home, and most importantly, hope.

"What have I led you into?" he whispered, watching his defeated group pass by. "Would you have been better off if I hadn't called?"

Keith's mind traveled back to that day when Norval's green pickup had run him off the road. That had been the first he'd ever heard of any sort of active volcano bubbling under Yellowstone. It had been a day that he would never forget.

While the whirlwind of events that followed was now a cloudy kaleidoscope of dim and hazy memories, Keith could recall that first afternoon in The Simpson lobby with exacting detail. Ranger Pickett's words would forever remain fresh in his mind.

"They had better be heading home, I suppose," the ranger had spouted when questioned on what the local vacationers and residents should do as a result of the eruption.

That one sentence had summed up an attitude that had led to countless deaths and unimaginable suffering.

Shaking his head in disgust, Keith fell in line behind the last of the ragtag unit, his mind racing through the ever-present doubt and second-guessing that came with any setback.

Just as the park ranger had suggested, Keith and his men had left Carlsbad the day of the eruption, driving toward Phoenix and their eager, frightened families. What they had encountered could only be described as chaos.

The two Myers Construction trucks seemed to be the only people trying to get into Arizona's largest city. Not even Jimmy could manage a joke about the outgoing lanes packed with citizens attempting the mass exodus.

By the second morning of the eruption, widespread looting plagued every retail outlet that offered foodstuffs. From organic bananas to breath mints, anything that could provide calories was in exceedingly high demand. Violence spread like wildfire throughout the city. Pandemonium ruled from the bustling, downtown skyscrapers to the normally calmer suburbs and every point in between.

By the third day, Keith and his guys had gathered at the boss's modest home. "We can't stay here," Ham noted. "My wife and kids are scared shitless. Less than four hours ago, I watched a gunfight on my street that rivaled any skirmish I ever saw in Panama."

"My family is in the same, tight spot," Keith nodded. "There's not a can of soup left in the city, and that damn volcano is still spewing tons of garbage into the sky. But where can we go?"

"I think we ought to head back to Carlsbad," Ham had suggested. "There are a lot fewer mouths to feed down there. A lot less competition for resources. We could hunt in the mountains and get water from the springs."

For two hours, the team had hashed through a rough plan. Unfortunately, none of them had any idea how dire things were about to become. None of them were prepared for the scope of the disaster and its long-term impact on the environment.

Now, looking back, Keith realized he'd been naïve. "Once they understand that people in the urban areas are condemned to certain death, the rangers will let us live in the caves," he'd suggested. "That ranger said there were tons of water and food down there. We'll go back and ride this out under the ground."

They had poured into the park, a convoy of company pickups and family vehicles, all filled to the brim with weapons, ammo, camping equipment, and as much food and water as they could gather. Their escape from the anarchy that was Phoenix had been an epic adventure of its own, but their numbers had worked in their favor, allowing them to complete the journey.

Given their military background and the supplies they had brought, Keith had expected Norval to welcome them with open arms.

Instead, the head ranger had ordered them off the premises at gunpoint and sternly warned them never to set foot in "his" park again. The encounter had come within a hair's width of breaking out into a pitched battle.

Quickly recovering from the shock of being denied sanctuary, Keith and his crew had returned to the only local place they knew – The Simpson Hotel.

Keith instinctively knew they needed to "up-armor" the facility to survive. Foul air had already slain tens of thousands downwind of the volcano. The television and radio broadcasts were a constant stream of warnings, every government agency advising residents to remain inside, not to breathe the ash that was falling like snow along the Eastern Seaboard, and to beware of the risk of roofs collapsing under the weight of the pumice.

Fortunately for the refugees, Myers Construction already had stashed a considerable amount of equipment at the old inn. What had started off as a basic remodeling job had turned into a major project when asbestos had been discovered in the structure. The owner's misfortune had turned into Keith's salvation.

His men were outfitted with air filters, masks, breathing systems, and all the equipment required for a large-scale hazardous materials removal. Truckloads of drywall, lumber, new windows and doors, and even plumbing supplies were stored in the barn.

"This hotel is going to become our Fort Apache," Keith announced to his disheartened followers. "We need to filter the air as best as we can, shore up the roof, and make this place defendable. The swimming pool will serve as our water reservoir, and its cover will protect it from the ash. Let's get going guys. If the talking heads on television are correct, we only have a few days before hell rains down from the sky."

It had been three days before the first heavy ash fall. In that time, he and his men had worked around the clock trying to prepare for what they all hoped would be a limited period spent hunkering down at the at the old lodge.

The Simpson Hotel had been constructed shortly after World War II, the facility located much closer to the actual Carlsbad Park than the town that bore the same name. Because of the desert location and the flatness of the landscape, the original builders had planted dense vegetation and tree lines to enhance the isolated locale. This combination of landscaping and camouflage, Keith hoped, would serve to protect his people from both the elements and any passersby that might have ill intent.

That assumption proved to be far from reality.

Within hours of their beginning construction, panicked locals and stranded tourists began driving into The Simpson's lot and seeking shelter where they could find it. The town of Carlsbad, it seemed, was chockfull of vacationers who didn't know where to go, yet didn't believe they could make it home. Many reported being chased away from the park by hostile employees.

Keith's team was nearly unanimous in their view that strangers shouldn't be welcomed into their fold. "We've only got so much food and water," Joe had stated. "There's not enough to go around."

Pulling the retractable, steel ruler out of his tool belt, Jimmy had playfully offered his assistance. "No worries, guys. I got this. Only the ones that measure up can stay. I am thinking 36-24-36."

Keith, always the strategist, did the real math.

Despite his intention of removing emotion from the equation, his effort proved ineffective. Too many variables made any prophetic models ineffective. How long would the ash fall? What was the government's planned response? How long did the storm's refugees need to hold out before they could expect assistance? What type of help could they expect?

"We aren't going to be like those asshole rangers," he eventually proclaimed. "We're not going to turn people away. That's not how Americans roll."

In the matter of a few short days, the men of Myers Construction transformed The Simpson's second floor into what could be described as a hybrid between a medical isolation facility and a bed and breakfast inn.

Their asbestos removal gear was repurposed into an air filtration system for the entire floor. Windows were sealed, vents and ducts closed off, and entrances converted into safe passages with double doorways. None of the team had any real experience with toxic elements; they simply relied on common sense, what little they had garnered from the non-stop newscasts, and Joe's memory of the long ago broadcast documentary.

Still, some of the military training was helpful. All of them had passed through the required courses on fighting with what the Army called "NBC" suits, or Nuclear, Biological, Chemical. By the time Keith was shepherding his flock of more than 50 frightened people into The Simpson, he was sure their preparations would survive the impending threat.

Less than four weeks after the ash began to fall, the first signs of respiratory illness began to rear its ugly head. Tempers had grown short well before that.

Food rationing was one thing, water conservation another. No one felt like they were getting their fair share. Fights broke out, arguments and frenzied rages flared.

Throughout it all, Keith and his old Army buddies grew closer and began to assert more and more control. Even then, it was clear that their supplies weren't going to last nearly long enough.

The first death occurred in what he and his men began referring to as eruption plus five, or the fifth week since Yellowstone had changed all of their lives. An elderly lady, on vacation from Seattle, succumbed to the ash.

A family from Iowa lost a 3-year old child next, the toddler showing flu-like symptoms and coughing up mouthfuls of blood for a few days before finally crossing to the other side.

By the end of eruption plus seven, they had buried over a dozen people, with almost that many more showing signs of illness and despair.

It soon dawned on Keith that things were not going to get better without some significant changes. While food and water were always a concern, their makeshift filtration system was failing miserably, resulting in their demise. They needed clean air at a minimum.

In his mind, the options were limited to one potential solution. He had to get his people into the caverns.

As he trailed behind his men, Keith remembered the first time he'd approached Ranger Pickett about sharing the underground space. The man's hostile attitude and overt threats had seemed so out of place and unreasonable.

"No, you can't move into the caverns. Understand that we will shoot you if you try. We have very limited resources in here, and our job is to protect this national treasure for future generations. Sorry, but you are on your own," Norval had preached.

"What future generations?" Keith had argued. "There aren't going to be any tourists hiking through your damn park if we don't save the people who are here right now. We know you have practically unlimited water supplies, and you've admitted none of your folks have had lung issues. For the love of God, Ranger, let us move inside. You won't even have to share your food, just access to clean air and water will save dozens of lives."

Norval would have none of it, and Keith's famous temper began to boil over. Three days later, the first gunshots were exchanged.

As the dispute escalated, it became apparent to Keith and his men that the only way they were going to gain entrance to the caverns was to force their way in. Norval and his crew were determined to keep them out, and the result was a full-blown shooting war.

Pickett and his rangers weren't stupid, nor were they without military skills. The entrances to the caverns were fortified, blocked, or heavily defended.

It was just yesterday that one of Keith's scouts had discovered yet another opening to the system of caves. This one was behind Rattlesnake Springs, and his man had found the area unguarded.

That bit of intel, it seemed, wasn't accurate.

Keith's invasion force had slammed into a strong defense at the rear door, including the stranger at the spring.

According to Joe, the new guy was equipped with a military issue M4 and plenty of ammo. Had Norval somehow managed to rally reinforcements? Where had this stranger come from? Why was he siding with the enemy inside the caves?

Shaking his head in disgust over their failure and the fresh complexity to the dilemma posed by the newcomer, Keith's mind returned to the primary issue at hand. He had to get his people inside the cave, one way or the other. Their filters were failing, and more and more of their group were showing signs of respiratory issues. The pool water was almost gone, and while they could get fresh water at Rattlesnake Springs, carrying enough of the heavy liquid back to The Simpson was logistically an impossibility.

Keith felt a growing source of desperation building, yet tried to keep his rage in check. Time was running out, the situation made worse because their salvation was almost within reach … but not quite so.

As he watched the column ahead, his attention moved to the limp, lifeless bodies being hauled back to the hotel. "I think we're all better offing dying quickly with weapons in our hands," he whispered. "I've watched enough people struggle to breathe and finally succumb. That's no way to go," he continued.

Then the brawny contractor's thoughts turned down a different path. He began wondering just how far his mind would go to justify the causalities suffered today. Was death by a bullet really better than coughing up a lung? Was he just trying to give his soul an escape route? To clear his heavily burdened conscience?

"One thing's for certain," he hissed. "That monster Pickett and his merry band of murderers would be happy to put all of us out of our misery."

Chapter 26

Despite the exhausting combat and days of pedaling, sleep eluded Jack. The pain in his arm and shoulder had escalated from a dull ache to throbbing misery, the commander now second-guessing his refusal of the meds Ms. Legs had offered.

But his injury was not the only challenge that prevented Jack from succumbing to the sandman. His adrenaline was in overdrive, and his heart raced a little faster since he'd ventured underground. He was keyed up from being immersed in an unfamiliar environment, around people he neither knew nor trusted. While he wanted to believe he had discovered another group of like-minded survivors, the little voice in the back of his head just would not be quiet.

Sure, Jack shared the same stereotypical respect for park rangers as most Americans. The general image projected by the National Park Service was of a group of honest, trustworthy individuals who not only cared about the country's natural resources but also worked hard to ensure that visitors were kept safe and could enjoy the "purple mountain majesties and amber waves of grain."

Rising to sit on the edge of his assigned cot, Jack scanned the dimly lit interior of the room where he'd been resting. The crags and rough stone walls were reassuring in a way, but not enough to slow his racing mind.

While he still hadn't been given the official tour of the caverns by the head man, Jack had seen enough to send his thoughts in a dozen different directions.

One of the unforeseen issues with traveling at a snail's pace across the doomsday landscape was that Jack now had more time on his hands to think than during any other period in his life. Sometimes, that had worked against him, as there had been incidents when he fell victim to the paralysis of analysis. He had found himself hesitant to act because he had no basis for making a decision. After all, there just wasn't a lot of hard data available about the best way to survive the eruption of a super volcano or how to journey half way across the continent in its wake.

Often times, like this particular night, Cisco found his neurons firing when his body cried out for rest. Fighting the insomnia was futile. Until his mind could answer its questions, it refused to be still. Jack realized his best recourse was to recline on the bed, close his eyes, and let his mind run amuck.

Almost every evening, the commander contemplated whether to turn back, stay put, or continue to the Lone Star State. Archie's gardens, as much as the Cliff House's herd, were inviting oases of calm and order in what was otherwise a world of swirling insanity. Maybe his voyage to reunite with his family was a pipe dream. Maybe his best chance at survival and happiness meant sheltering in place. If only he could pick up a cell phone and call the girls, hear their voices, know that they were alive and wanted him back … but long distance communication was ancient history now. If he needed answers to those questions, he would have to venture further east. And in the meantime, he would just have to make the best decisions he could based on the limited information he had, and those parameters were tough for Commander Cisco.

Gingerly flexing his arm to test both its strength and the level of pain associated with movement, thoughts of Mylie entered Jack's mind.

Theirs, like so many, had been a chance meeting.

Jack had been in his last year at Annapolis and a brigade commander of midshipmen. Right before Christmas break rolled around, his mom called him about family holiday plans. As luck would have it, Aunt Grace required emergency surgery for her hernia, and the commander's mother had been called to care for her. Jack was not known for his bedside manner, and Mama Cisco recommended that her son might want to go home with a classmate over the Christmas break. "Jack," she had suggested, "you know I love you, but Grace needs complete rest to recuperate. That smart-ass sense of humor of yours would tear out every surgical stitch for sure. Santa's just going to have to come a bit later."

That holiday detour had taken the young Cisco to central Texas Hill Country and a town he'd never heard of called Fredericksburg.

There in the arid Lone Star State's midsection, about as far away from the open ocean as the first-class midshipman could imagine, Jack discovered that Fredericksburg had been the home of another famous sailor – Admiral Chester Nimitz.

After hiking Enchanted Rock and consuming a healthy amount of beer and brats, Cisco seemed to even speak German. Breaking away from the festivities, Jack was excited to discover that the town had a museum dedicated to the Admiral and the Pacific War, and that's where he'd met Mylie.

He could still remember walking through the front door of the place, wide-eyed and impressed that a small, landlocked burg could host such an extensive facility. Ten seconds later, after seeing the smiling, gorgeous, young woman working at the reception desk, Jack had forgotten all about Admiral Nimitz and the war with Japan.

It took Midshipman Cisco another five minutes to build up enough courage to approach her.

Despite the clumsiest conversation Jack had ever attempted, he somehow managed a dinner date for that very evening.

Over a cheeseburger and fries, Jack quickly learned that Mylie lived on a small ranch just outside of town, her father raising breeding stock that was well-known throughout the region. Her mother was a professor at the local community college, teaching political science.

Mylie claimed that both sides of her family could trace their German roots back at least 300 years. Given her silk-like, blonde hair and jade green eyes, Jack believed her.

Two nights later, with a polka band playing in the background at a local watering hole, Mylie disclosed that she was about to leave her childhood home and venture off to Texas A&M. The museum was just a summer job. She wasn't even sure who Chester Nimitz was, or why he was so popular with all the nice, old men who came in wearing hats that sparkled with pins and were embroidered with "Navy," "Veteran," and ship names from World War Two.

Unlike Jack, her family life was quiet, secure, and well-structured. The commander had often wondered if part of his wife's struggling with his extended deployments was due to the "Leave It To Beaver," environment in which she had been raised.

They had kept in touch throughout his final year, somehow managing to carry out a long-distance romance. Finally, more than two years later, they were married at the Fredericksburg First Baptist Church.

She left Texas with a strong belief in the family unit and the traditional roles each partner played. Life married to a career Naval officer, especially a submariner, quickly changed all that.

Her freshman and sophomore years in college had represented the first time she had left home for any extended period. Married to Jack, she had been forced to pack up and move to three different bases in less than 24 months. Not exactly the best lifestyle for finishing her degree. In the midst of what was a whirlwind of new places, faces, quarters and friends, Mylie became pregnant. Her husband was at sea when the labor pains began.

Sitting on his cot, Jack shook his head at the memories. "If I could just take a few moments back," he whispered, frowning deeply. "If I had just handled that differently … if I could have just shown a bit more understanding when … this would have turned out so differently."

Standing while still manipulating his swollen arm, it dawned on Jack that Carlsbad and its caverns might be his salvation.

Here, for the first time since he'd begun this crazy adventure, Jack saw long-term hope. The cave was safe, had the opportunity for a renewable food source, and possessed the infrastructure that would allow for the rebuilding of society.

Here, inside this subterranean community, you could raise a family. You could breathe down here without a mask. You could walk around without a rifle. You could drink without fear and even take a bath.

Glancing around at the stone façade, the commander had to admit it wasn't Los Angeles or Atlanta or even Terre Haute. Yet, it was far and above any place else he'd encountered. Carmen had mentioned that there were hundreds of miles of caves and trails. In Jack's mind, that translated into enough space for hundreds, if not thousands of people.

Here was a solution. A fix. An answer to his most nagging issue, other than wondering if Mylie and the girls were still alive.

That thought made him turn to what he believed was the east, and Texas. "I'm coming," he whispered.

It then occurred to Jack that he'd left his bike and the precious contents of his pack at the trailhead. Ignoring the shot of hot pain jolting through his frame, the commander rose and went to look for Norval or one of his brood.

He didn't have to go far.

A lanky ranger appeared at the room's opening before Jack had made it three steps. "Can I help you, sir?" the man asked, adjusting the rifle resting in the crook of his arm.

Jack got the sense that the guy was a guard who been assigned to watch the prisoner. Was he a captive?

"I just remembered that I left some extremely valuable equipment at the trailhead leading to the spring," Jack responded honestly. "I was going to see if someone would help me find my way to retrieve it."

"Are you talking about your bicycle and pack?" the young ranger asked.

"Yes," replied Jack, slightly surprised by the man's knowledge. "Those items are all I own, and they are critical to my journey."

"We brought them back here to the caves. They are safe."

The first feeling that entered into the commander's head was curiosity. How had they found his bike so quickly? What were they doing in the open air? The answer was obvious after a time – the rangers had been making sure their enemy wasn't going to come back. His tools had been a surprise discovery.

"Well, given the perilous conditions outside, I am sure there is someone's hand I should shake for the neighborly assistance," Jack began plying the sentry with kindness before making his request. "But you know," he continued, "one of the tires was riding oddly, and I have a repair kit stashed in my pack. I would sure like to check that out now if it wouldn't be too much trouble," Jack suggested.

A flash of puzzlement passed across the sentry's eyes, but then he shrugged. "Follow me, please."

Jack was led through a series of formations, some of the underground passages narrow and tight, others sporting soaring ceilings and ornate crystal formations. It was evident this section of the caverns had been part of the public area, the smooth, poured concrete paths easy to negotiate.

After only a few twists and turns, Jack became disoriented, the state troubling the commander even further. How in the hell would he get out of this place if bad came to worse? It was a labyrinth with few landmarks and without any sky to provide a sense of direction; he could envision himself wandering down here forever. *At least a mouse can smell his way through the maze*, the commander mused, wishing he had a pocket full of breadcrumbs to mark his way.

Around another turn, Jack heard voices and within moments was standing beside Norval. There, resting against a rock wall, was his bike. The backpack was on an oversized, mahogany table that the head ranger was using as a desk.

"Oh, hello," Norval greeted with a cheery voice. "Couldn't rest?"

"No, I'm too tense after that gunfight," Jack stated with a nod. "Then I realized I'd left my only worldly possessions at the trail head. Thank you for retrieving them."

Stepping to his pack, Jack realized instantly someone had rifled through the contents. He always closed the pouches the same, specific way, and the buckles had clearly been disturbed.

It then dawned on the commander that he, in Ranger Pickett's shoes, would have done the exact same thing. Trust would have to be earned by both sides.

Norval interrupted Jack's examination with an offer, "Would you like a tour of one of our most amazing national treasures, Commander?"

Again, Jack found himself at a loss for words. Slightly embarrassed over his paranoia regarding his hosts, Cisco nodded and answered, "That would be interesting. Thank you."

As the two sauntered away from Cisco's belongings, Pickett began his spiel with a tone worthy of a professional tour guide. Obviously, the man had done this before, probably entertaining countless vacationers who had flocked to the park for decades.

Jack was shown several breathtaking formations, numerous passages, and even an underground stream flowing across the rock floor. His biggest surprise, however, was an elevator! The damn thing was even working!

"Come on," Norval waved, "I'll take you down to the basement."

The two men stepped into the lift, and a few moments later Jack felt his weight being raised off the floor as the car rushed downward. "How deep are we going?"

Nodding at the frequently asked question, Norval answered, "This elevator is the equivalent of an above-ground unit servicing a 78-story skyscraper."

"I haven't felt that same tickle in my gut since I was strapped to the Goliath at Magic Mountain," the commander teased. Downward they dropped, Jack finding himself fascinated by the recessed electric lights on the car's roof. He was constantly amazed at the first electricity he'd seen since leaving *Utah*.

At Norval's behest, Jack stepped off the elevator after it had slowed and finally settled at the bottom. He was amazed at the sight that met his eyes.

The Grand Room was enormous, the ceiling so high it was barely visible in the dim, manmade light. The place reminded the commander of the one time he'd visited the domed football stadium in New Orleans. "This reminds me of the Superdome," he whispered.

"Actually, this room is a bit larger," Ranger Pickett stated with pride. "We are over 600 feet below the surface here."

The tour continued, Jack astonished by the next feature his guide pointed out. "We have a fully equipped restaurant, and quite frankly, it saved our bacon when Yellowstone exploded. There are over 400 square feet of freezer space right here, and another huge area of supply rooms is positioned at the back of the cafeteria. We used to carry quite the frozen food inventory," he paused to change direction in his tour. "Several hundred tourists dined with us daily. And because of our unique location, it's not like we could just snap our fingers for more brisket or fries. Our suppliers struggled with the time involved in delivering product underground, so we just added more coolers and storage."

Sure enough, Jack was shown into a large, glass-fronted sub-building that seemed to come right out of the grotto's rock walls. Inside were rows of tables, complete with napkin holders and salt and pepper shakers. He noted the menu board offered a cheeseburger value meal for $8.99, complete with soft drink. "Wow," he mumbled. "What's the special today?"

Norval chuckled at the attempt to lighten the mood. "We've had to ration the supplies," he admitted. "While we have virtually unlimited water, there are only so many calories down here."

"How much do you have left?" Jack inquired, more to make conversation than anything else.

"That's not discussed," Pickett curtly replied.

Jack found the ranger's answer odd, the hairs on the back of his neck stretching taunt at Norval's tone. Before he could formulate a response, the head ranger was leading the way down another walkway.

The manmade path soon morphed into a bridge of sorts, the walkway meandering between two bodies of water. "How deep do you think those pools are?" Norval asked, producing a flashlight and illuminating the bottom.

"Umm… about two feet I'd guess," Jack answered, not sure what point his host was trying to make.

With a laugh, Norval said, "This one is over 12 feet deep. The water is so clear and pure, it's difficult to judge the depth."

Indeed, Jack would have never conceived the pools were so large. Like the ones he'd been shown before, it looked like he could have easily reached in and touched the stone he saw through the clear basin.

They continued the tour, Norval pointing out various formations while terms like speleothems, stalactites, soda straws, and draperies rolled off his tongue with ease.

The two men paused a bit later, the tour guide indicating a stunning crystal created by dripping water and stating something about the formation being over 50,000 years old. Jack, mildly interested, soon let his focus drift to a nearby opening in the rock wall.

Without asking or waiting, the commander stepped toward the hidden crevice, and noticed the sign that indicated, "Park Personnel Only," above the entrance. This area was obviously "behind the curtains," the lighting chosen for utility and function rather than esthetics ... and the floor less worn than that of the main trail. A bit further in, he spied a large steel door with a heavy padlock in place.

"That area is off limits," Norval's harsh voice boomed from behind. "You shouldn't venture off the main paths."

This time, Jack was ready and pushed back. "Why?"

Pickett blinked once, then again. His mouth moved but no words came out. It was as if the man was completely shocked that Jack would question his authority.

"Because ... well ... because I said it's off limits," sounded the now-angry ranger.

Before Jack could challenge the logic of the man's statement, Norval recovered, "There is dangerous equipment in our system. Sometimes the electrical wiring gets corroded, and we wouldn't want any of our guests getting a nasty jolt."

The answer was bullshit, and Jack knew it. He'd been around high voltage conduits most of his professional career and knew no government installation would install such an apparatus without a plethora of warning signs and fail safes.

Before the commander could push back, Carmen appeared out of the shadows. "Oh, there you are," her soft voice soothed. "I've been looking all over. We're going to be shutting down the generator an hour early this evening. One of the engineers wants to perform some service on the machinery."

Again, Jack found himself not understanding. Ranger Pickett, apparently satisfied with the distraction her warning had provided, answered Jack's unasked question. "We've found it is better for everyone's attitude if we have a day and night cycle, just like life on the surface. Sunset is evidently coming an hour early this evening."

Grunting, the commander responded, "That's pretty interesting. We do the exact same thing on submarines. The Silent Service discovered that people perform better if the boats mimic the shifts of night and day."

With a broad smile, Norval turned to his second in command and announced, "See, I told you it was a good idea. Besides, it will make our supply of diesel fuel last twice as long."

Jack thought he must have counted a million sheep before slumber overtook him. A gentle snore indicated he was finally sleeping soundly despite being in a strange place surrounded by unknown people. Suddenly, he snapped wide awake, a scraping sound yanking him back to full awareness.

He rolled over on his side ready to defend himself in an instant, but the noise never came again. He held his breath hoping to draw in more sound. There it was! Someone was approaching, moving with soft steps and trying to be stealthy.

He smelled Ms. Legs's scent before Carmen's dim outline came into view, a curvaceous, hourglass form that left no doubt in his mind regarding the identity of the nocturnal visitor. "Oh," she cooed. "You're awake, Commander."

Before Jack could respond, she stood beside the cot, gently touching his limb where the bandages bulged. "I thought I would come and check on you … make sure you weren't developing a fever," she lied.

"Thank you for the concern," he whispered back, wondering why they were conversing at such a low level.

She continued to touch him, her finger tracing across his shoulder, down his arm, resting on the back of his hand. She lingered there, for a bit, finally adding, "Of course, if you did have *any* sort of fever, I could probably provide an effective treatment."

To say that Jack was taken aback by the approach would have been an understatement. Still, she smelled wonderful and was an extremely attractive woman. Just in time to thwart temptation, a vision of Mylie entered his mind, instantly popping the lust balloon.

Carmen seemed to sense his mental withdrawal and backed off. "Seriously, Commander, I am glad you're awake. I wanted to talk with you for a moment … while prying ears enjoyed a few Zs."

Cisco didn't know which bothered him more, the seduction or the conspiracy. Both were shifting his mind into overdrive. "Sure," he finally managed. "Always good to share information, I suppose."

"Is it true," she whispered in a rush. "Is it true that society has disappeared out there?"

Not having the slightest clue where the conversation was going, Jack answered with a shrug. "I guess you could say that the world as we knew it is gone. And 'society' isn't the word I would use to describe the few groups of people I've encountered. For sure, the government isn't functioning in any capacity … at least not that I've seen. The outside world is largely empty, void of life."

She stood quickly, pacing two rapid steps away and then performing a hasty turn as if deep in anxious thought. "So, what is it like out there, then? Are all the people just gone? No cars? No lights? Is it really like you were telling Norval?"

"Yes, my account was entirely accurate," Jack said with a touch of defensiveness. If the park ranger wanted to verify his story, he didn't need to send in his seductive second in command.

"So, there's no reason why we should …," she began, but then abruptly stopped as if she was about to divulge a secret and had changed her mind.

"No reason why we should, what?" Jack said, trying to get her to finish.

"Oh, never mind. It doesn't matter. What is important is that when you leave in a few days, I want you to take me with you."

Jack was stunned. "Excuse me? What did you just say?"

"I want out of here, Commander Cisco. As soon as possible. I can secure enough supplies and water for both of us."

"Why? I know this is going to be difficult for you to imagine, but your underground community … living here in the cavern has the best quality of life I've discovered since the disaster. You've got water, food, and electricity and above all else, fresh air. I really don't think now is the best time for a young lady to be hitting the road."

Shaking her head, Carmen fired back, "You don't understand what it's like here, Jack. Things aren't as they appear…."

She stopped short, her head tilting as if she had heard someone approaching in the darkness. Jack listened with her for a moment and then prompted her for details, "Go on.... You were saying?"

When she turned back toward his face, Jack noticed her expression was unmistakably colored with fear. "I'm sorry," she said. "I have to go. It wouldn't be pleasant for either of us if Norval found me down here."

In a rush of denim scented in perfume, she was gone, padding silently across the cave floor and leaving Jack more puzzled than ever.

He sat in silence for several minutes after her departure, his brain trying desperately to reconcile the few facts he knew about Pickett and his outfit. The effort soon proved to be a waste of time and energy. He didn't know squat, the jigsaw missing too many pieces to clarify the picture.

Still, there was no way he was going to be able to get back into dreamland. Intrigue drove his thoughts at light speed, curiosity and suspicion doing their part to power his overactive imagination.

"What could Pickett possibly be doing to her that would drive Carmen out of this sanctuary? Was the old ranger kinky or something? Was he physically abusing her? There weren't any obvious signs, no bruises or welts. Still, why would a sane person choose the chaos outside instead of this communal haven?"

Jack paced beside his cot for a bit, making laps across the cool cave floor beneath his feet. Finally deciding that sleep was hopeless, he decided to dress and explore. Of all the things he'd seen and heard in the last 24 hours, it was Norval's reaction to the locked door that bothered the commander the most.

"Maybe that is where I will find my answers. What could he be hiding?"

Chapter 27

The discouraged column of Myer's men finally arrived back at The Simpson, the extended walk doing little to resolve their leader's nagging issues.

Darkness hung over the structure, the dim light adding to the melancholy appearance of what had been a building designed to provide enjoyment and relaxation to vacationing families.

Over and again, Keith tried to rationalize what the hell had gone wrong. He replayed every scenario, explored every possibility. Something out of his control had caused them to lose today's battle, and he was determined to understand what had happened.

In the end, he kept arriving back at the same conclusion – the rangers had someone spying on them, perhaps even a mole inside the hotel. That was the only reasonable explanation. Those fuckers had been waiting on his men before they even made it close to the cavern's back door.

As he set down his rifle and gear next to the threshold, a soft rap sounded on the door frame. He could tell by the expression staring back at him that the news was not good. "We've lost another child, today, Keith," announced one of the community's women, her words dripping with grief.

"Who?"

"The little Thomas girl," the woman choked back hard sobs as hot tears streamed down her cheeks. "She was only four years old."

"Shit!" the man of muscle barked, "Her lungs?"

"Yes."

Keith nodded, his soul unable to offer more emotion. There had been so many, and the kids were always the worst.

The incident caused him to remember his own little boy, his son succumbing to the ash in the ninth week. Bryce had only been 11 years old and so full of life and energy. Keith had held him tight for the last few hours, feeling every cough and convulsion that had racked the youth's frame.

Before he could push aside that horrible memory, another visitor knocked on Keith's door. This time he looked up to see Ham standing in the entryway, his friend's expression announcing he had even more bad news.

"The pool is down to just three days' worth of water," Ham declared in a solemn tone. "And given the distance to Rattlesnake, I'm not sure we can carry enough water back and forth to keep everyone here alive."

"Well, we've got one less to worry about," Keith countered, rubbing the bottom of his sore feet. "The Thomas girl passed away while we were gone."

Ham merely shook his head, seemingly hardened to the constant parade of bodies they had already buried. Finally, he added, "We're running out of time, boss. Bad air is one thing; a lack of water is another. Any ideas?"

Keith began repeating his analysis, ending with the same result. "The rangers won because they were waiting for us. Somehow, they knew we were coming. We have to get the guys together and solve this problem."

Ham again nodded his agreement. "Want me to call an all-hands-on-deck?"

"Ham, listen to me. They must have someone spying on us. That's the only possible answer. Either that, or we have a traitor in our midst."

The second in command had trouble with his friend's last statement. "No way any of these people are helping Pickett and his henchmen," he stated with confidence. "Every family here has lost someone. Why would any of them help that asshole kill more of us?"

"Then it's got to be a pair of eyes and ears up in the hills. That's the only possibility I can come up with."

Ham finally agreed. "Sounds reasonable to me. The question is, how do we catch them? This is big country. There must be a million places to hide within visual range of 'Fort Simpson.'"

"I've got an idea," Keith said, brightening noticeably as the thought matured in his mind. "Call the men together, and let's make *Norval's* life a little more difficult for a change."

Jack knew that the sandman wasn't coming back that night. Carmen's visit and the day's other events formed an endless parade of questions, secrets, and mysteries in his head.

After pulling on his boots, he rose from the edge of the cot with his face fixed in determination.

The commander's weapon was still leaning against the rock wall, exactly where he'd left it. When he started to reach for the carbine, he noticed the magazine had been removed. "Shit," he hissed, wondering what other pieces of his gear had been pilfered.

Memories of the locked room and Norval's reaction dominated his thinking. It was the first time he'd seen the head ranger flash angry. There was more to the restricted area than any loose electrical wires or dangerous equipment. He needed to know what was being done behind that door.

The commander had been a resident of the cavern for several hours and hadn't noticed any sentries inside, even at key intersections and strategic points throughout the compound. Other than the tall ranger posted outside his sleeping area, there hadn't been any obvious examples of security. Some sixth sense told Jack that guards were present, and if he was going to go snooping around, caution would have to be a priority.

Using his pillow and a wad of bedding, Jack did his best to create the fake outline of a man sleeping in his cot. The ruse wouldn't pass any but the most casual inspection, yet it was better than just leaving behind a clearly empty bunk.

"I'm just looking for the bathroom," he whispered, rehearsing his excuse if discovered.

Wanting to avoid the man who was plainly posted outside his sleeping quarters, Jack chose the opposite direction, treading carefully and creating no noise. He soon found himself in a lesser corridor, the route Ms. Legs had sashayed down just a short time ago.

Getting lost was still a major concern, but Jack had been paying more attention as Pickett's tour progressed. There were numbered markers along most of the walkways, the numeric landmarks probably used by the rangers and tourists to keep their bearings. The commander was now confident he'd figured out the system.

Moving slowly and being stealthy took time. At each intersection, Jack stopped to listen, projecting his senses in the hope of detecting any human presence. He eventually found the ponds and crossed the bridge in a rush to avoid exposure.

He exhaled with relief once inside the hidden nook, happy to be in a less-visible space. Ahead of him was the door with its heavy padlock that had raised Norval's ire.

It was an easy decision not to attempt picking the lock. Jack didn't have any skills in committing petty larceny. Busting open the latch was out of the question as well, as he didn't want to leave any evidence of breaking and entering.

Down the narrow rock hall he continued, glad the dim, battery powered emergency lights were functioning well enough for him to see the way.

Soon he approached a second metal door, its green, government-issued paint an identical shade to the first opening. There was an identical latch for a padlock, Jack's finger finding the surface worn from use. This chamber had been secured at one point in time. Twisting the knob slowly, the commander was surprised to find the door was unlocked.

He opened the door less than an inch, leaning in with his ear and listening intently for any sign of human occupation. A minute passed without any sound emitted from the interior.

Stepping inside, the first thing Jack noticed was the odor. It took him a moment to identify the chemical fragrance that landed somewhere between a disinfectant and floor wax. "A porta potty?" he whispered to the dim room. "A portable toilet 78 stories underground?"

As his eyes adjusted to the lower light inside the chamber, Jack began to notice an odd collection of objects.

The room was a good 30 by 30 feet, with rock walls on three sides and single emergency bulb somewhere high above. The stone floor was nearly covered in mattresses, most of the bedding aligned in neat rows with enough space to walk between.

As he stepped further into the grotto, Jack's toe made contact with something on the floor, sending an empty plastic milk jug rattling across the stone and making one hell of a loud racket.

Inhaling sharply at the startling noise, Jack cursed his stupidity and then listened intently for any reaction to his failed attempt at stealth. When a platoon of armed rangers didn't come crashing through the door, his pounding heart began to slow.

Now paying more attention to where his steps landed, Jack noticed a significant amount of trash had collected in the area. He spotted candy wrappers, empty soup cans, energy bar wrappers, and even a few toilet paper tubes.

Bending to pick up a piece of the garbage, Jack found himself holding a box of feminine napkins. Aside from his general unfamiliarity with the product, the packaging itself seemed odd. Further investigation in better light revealed that all of the labels on the litter were written in Spanish. Even the plastic, green restroom-box featured a sign that read, "El Baño."

"So, Norval had people locked up inside here," he whispered to the stone walls. "A lot of people, and from the amount of garbage strewn around, they were captive here for quite a while. Is this the park's jail? Why would he feel the need to retain this many inmates?"

A noise outside interrupted Jack's analysis, the commander rushing to hide behind the portable toilet. A moment later, the beam of a flashlight streamed through the door.

Jack held his breath, sure that his clumsy encounter with the milk jug had been heard. He watched as the circle of light traveled the room, praying that the sentry wasn't all that diligent.

It seemed like the guy searched the room for an hour, Jack's lungs beginning to ache from his lack of breathing. In reality, it was only a minute before the room again went dark, and the commander heard the metal clank of the door being closed. "Please don't lock it," he hissed, his mind instantly visualizing being trapped. Jack decided to wait at least five minutes before trying the door to give the guard time to move some distance away.

"One thousand one," he counted, his voice barely above a whisper. "One thousand two …" the sense of panic began to swell up inside of the commander. As the seconds ticked by, that discomfort expanded into overwhelming anxiety. While being a submariner and having claustrophobia were mutually exclusive events, he had no desire to be locked inside of a rock cell for some unknown period of time.

"One thousand one hundred fifty," he continued, focusing on the sequential numbers in hope of reducing his fear. While there had been no sound of a padlock being applied, visions of his dehydrated, shriveled body began to flash through Jack's mind. He could see himself prone on the rock floor, the agony of hunger and thirst building with each passing hour.

"One thousand two hundred ten, one thousand two hundred eleven …." Then, realizing that he might already be a captive in this room, he considered, *Those park rangers will think I just left. They won't ever even bother to look for me – here or anywhere else,* and his pulse rate jumped yet again.

"One thousand two hundred forty-five…." *Almost time to open the door. Hang in there, man. Don't let this situation mess with your head,* he told himself. Then trying to steady his increasing blood pressure, he reminded himself of a joke. *What's the difference between a politician and a porta-potty? One's full of shit and the other is used at a construction site*, he mused.

"One thousand two hundred eighty, one thousand two hundred eighty-one …" As he got closer to the five-minute mark, the fear of turning the knob loomed even larger. What would he do if the handle didn't turn? He was screwed. Even if he did manage to pound on the door and draw someone's attention, Norval would probably have him executed for venturing back into the restricted areas.

"One thousand three hundred!" A moment later, Jack slipped out from the back of the stinky booth and hastily moved to exit the potential death trap. His hand grasped the cold steel and rotated the knob. Relief flooded his soul when the door opened smoothly. He inhaled deeply, flooding his lungs with fresh air and encouraging his heart to slow a bit before stepping outside the secret room.

Peeking out of the threshold, Jack spotted the sentry's flashlight beam traveling along the path the commander had used to reach the hidden rooms. He would have to find a different route back to his cot. That realization, despite his knowing about the marker system, forced more stress into his core. The caverns were extensive, and it wouldn't be impossible to get lost for days … maybe forever.

He maneuvered through a seemingly endless matrix of trails, rooms, and stone corridors. More than once, Jack worried about vanishing completely off the face of the earth or perhaps bumbling into a patrolling ranger. Each time, a numbered marker at an intersection or along the path allowed him to gradually negotiate back toward his assigned sleeping quarters.

Rounding a corner, Jack froze when the distant sound of voices softly echoed through the stone hallway. It was nearly impossible to tell how far away the conversation was taking place, nor could he discern who was speaking.

Ducking low, he began to advance toward the source of the words, each few steps allowing him to make out more and more of what was being said.

He spied an opening ahead, the trail broadening into what everyone down here called a room. A few paces more, and Jack was certain he was listening to Ranger Pickett and Carmen. He found a notch in the rock wall and settled in to listen.

"Why did you visit the stranger in the middle of the night?" boomed Norval's voice.

"You asked me to care for his wound," came her defiant response. "I wanted to verify infection wasn't taking hold."

"I don't want you seeing him alone," he responded with an easier tone. "We don't know anything about that man. He might be dangerous or prone to violence. You are a very desirable woman. He might try to hurt you."

Jack heard Ms. Legs grunt and then chuckle sarcastically. "Your concern for my safety is touching."

"Look," the ranger continued, "I know we've had our differences. I'm well-aware that our circumstances have forced me to take action that you find repulsive. I had hoped that by now, you would see the necessity and reason behind my acts."

There was a pause, Carmen trying to choose her next words carefully. "I don't know that I can ever accept what you've done, or what you are asking our people to do. You've changed, Norval. You're not the same man I've done business with all these years, and quite frankly, you scare the hell out of me."

What came next shocked Jack. Exploding into an angry rage, Norval's vocal eruption caused even Jack to wince. "*My* actions! *Change!* You're damn right I'm not the same man I used to be! Who could stay the same with the world falling apart? I've kept our people alive, and I'll be damned if I'm going to let some second-class smuggler from south of the border tell me how to shepherd my flock!"

"You didn't think I was a second-class smuggler all those years we were making loads of money. You didn't doubt my judgement as the illegals and narcotics flowed through your precious bit of Americana," she pushed back.

Jack waited, anticipating another explosion from the burly ranger. Instead, Norval's voice became low and frosty.

"Look, we have a unique opportunity here, a chance to build a new society from scratch. God's wisdom has provided us with the circumstances to recreate civilization a second time, and I'm not going to waste it. For the hundredth time, I ask you ... I beg you ... give me your allegiance, and join me. You can sit at my side and help guide me through the troubled times that loom on the horizon."

Carmen grunted, "You still want me to be your queen? Is that it? You still have this vision of repopulating the earth in your image?"

"We have all the tools. You heard Cisco; we have electrical power, unlimited water, and the most advanced community he's encountered. Why not? Why can't we start from these humble beginnings and spread life across the world ... with our values ... with our vision of what humankind should really be? We can correct all the mistakes of the past! You and I, together, can mold and shape our race into what it should have been from the beginning. We can instill our principles, our morals, and our ethics."

From his hidden perch, Jack stood stunned, Pickett's words sending ice cold chills down the commander's spine. The man was obviously deranged, suffering from some form of megalomania.

"What are you going to do with Commander Cisco?" Carmen asked, trying to change the subject.

"That depends. If he will pledge his loyalty and gun to me, then he can join our ranks. If not, then we'll dispose of him just like the others."

"The others," spat Carmen. "Those poor, innocent souls. No one deserves to die like that."

"I did not kill them," defended Norval. "I left them in God's hands."

"You hauled them out into the desert with only water," she protested, the emotion rising in her voice. "You knew the ash would kill them. You knew they didn't have a chance."

Angry again, Norval bellowed, "They had their chance! They had an option. What did you expect me to do? Allow those disloyal, faithless wretches to stay here and consume our precious supplies?"

"*A choice?* Sure, you gave them a choice. They could have agreed to become your breeding stock. They could use their wombs to produce your soldiers and spread your insane vision of how the world should be. That wasn't really much of a choice if you ask me."

"I offered them a future," Ranger Pickett countered. "For a bunch of young, lawbreaking women who were sneaking into our country illegally anyway, was it really so much of a stretch for them to partner up with my rangers and began raising families? We are going to need soldiers for our cause, Carmen. Why can't you understand that?"

Then, like a switch had been flipped, Norval's tone changed again. "Please, I ask again, join me. I need you, Carmen. I want you beside me."

He's in love with her, Jack understood. *That's how she's managed to survive so long.*

Ms. Legs was obviously way ahead of the commander in understanding her own mortality. As if she could hear Jack's thoughts, her tone changed, and she became flirtatious. "We have accomplished great things together," she said softly. "And I have to admit, you've kept us all alive. Give me some time, Norval. Please, give me a chance to digest everything that has happened."

Jack sensed the conversation was over, and when no more words were exchanged, he carefully backed out from his hide and retreated to the last intersection. Twenty minutes later, he was crawling into his cot, his mind reeling from everything he'd learned.

Yet again, sleep eluded him.

Over and again, Jack mentally replayed the overheard conversation, and its contents troubled him deeply.

It wasn't the ranger's master plan … or even Carmen's role that bothered Jack the most. It was the fact that Norval, given the assets of the cavern, might actually be able to pull off his crazy scheme.

How hard would it be to recruit the likes of the Tucson cannibals and other desperados? How long could the good people at Mud Lake hold out against even a moderately sized army moving against them? When the food ran out at the Marine air station, would the men with families to feed join forces with the mentally imbalanced ranger?

Visions of cloned "Pickett Armies" entered Jack's mind, the brawny ranger leading his hordes as they spread across the land. If Norval was smart and cautious, he could conquer the entire Southwest bit by bit, growing stronger with each victory. Stranger military campaigns had been successful.

And what about Carmen's obvious connection to Mexico? Jack knew the mysterious woman had her own cadre of men inside the caves. Did she have access and connections that would bolster Norval's ranks with additional manpower?

There was another exasperating angle as well. Sighing with frustration, Jack realized that it wasn't the threat of some marauding warlord that bothered him the most. No, it was the bursting of his salvation bubble that cut the deepest.

There was little he could do to stop Norval's march to regional control, and quite frankly, Jack didn't care. What really bothered the commander was the lost opportunity to provide a safe place for his family – should he find them alive and well.

"I was going to bring you back here," he mumbled, again glancing toward the east. "I was going to save you and the girls by bringing you back to this paradise, Mylie. I had it all worked out. I am so sorry. I've failed you yet again."

For nearly an hour, Jack vacillated from one negative thought to the next. With exhaustion finally kicking in and no place to go but up, he returned to his cot and stretched out.

Forcing himself to grasp the positive aspects of the situation, he focused on counting the "good sheep."

"You didn't die of thirst in the desert," he began, desperately seeking a silver lining. "You didn't get killed at the spring. You found this place by accident – maybe there are more islands of surviving, good people out there. Maybe you just need to keep looking."

"One thing is for certain, Commander," he whispered to the night. "You have to find a way out of this madhouse."

Chapter 28

There was a sense of comfort in their comradery, Keith especially pleased with how quickly his team fell back into their old military roles as they sat discussing the potential of a mission.

"We need to set a trap," Ham had stated with confidence. "The only way we're going to find the spy is to force them into showing themselves."

"He's right," Joe had added. "It would take a battalion to search these hills and still they might not find a well-hidden man."

Jimmy had come up with the best solution, Keith and the men agreeing on a simplistic approach.

Two hours before dawn, Keith and his team had loaded up with their fighting rigs and without light or sound, had fanned out from The Simpson into the inky darkness.

Their objective was to form a picket line between the hotel and the nearest entrance to Carlsbad Caverns, hoping to catch the enemy observer as he rushed back to report what he had seen.

And Keith intended to provide quite the spectacle.

At dawn, every able-bodied man at The Simpson was to make a grand show of gearing up for a major assault. Meyer even ordered some of the women to don rifles and packs. He wanted Norval to think that his foe was mounting an invasion. If that didn't flush the observer from the hills, nothing would.

It was a ruse, but one Keith hoped would sell. With any luck, he and his core team would catch a spy in their snare.

The strapping man found the perfect hide, nestled into a small cut, worn away by thousands of years of erosion. From his perch, Keith could observe a wide section of open ground below. If his strategy flushed Ranger Pickett's eyes and ears out of the hills, the informant would most likely have to cross here, and Meyer would be ready.

An hour after sunrise, Keith thought their plan had failed. By now, The Simpson's courtyard and parking lot was a beehive of activity, giving all appearances of an invasion being mounted. Yet, there had been no sign of any observer rushing back to report what he had seen.

"Maybe they are using a radio?" he questioned, watching the still and silent rocks. "Do they have some other method of signaling?"

Since The Simpson couldn't sustain electrical power, radios that required charging weren't a tool he and his men could use. Advantage to Norval and the rangers.

Still, Keith didn't think his foe was that sophisticated. The units he'd seen on the rangers' belts before the collapse hadn't been military grade and no doubt were capable of only a limited range.

Just as he was considering rising to return in defeat, Keith spotted the slightest movement in the rocks. There were no more jack rabbits or javelin, and no one had seen a bird in weeks. The motion had to be human.

Now focused with laser-like intensity, Keith soon identified the outline of a man. A moment later, the spy bolted across the open area, his olive-green ranger uniform announcing that their plan had worked.

The observer made it four steps before a single shot split the morning air. Keith watched the ranger stumble, try to stand, and then fall back into a puff of ash. Ham's aim was as good as ever.

The ex-paratroopers streamed out of their hiding places, weapons up and ready to engage if the prone ranger was playing possum. By the time they had him surrounded, the pewter ash under the fallen man's chest was running with streaks of crimson.

Keith stood for a moment, watching as Jimmy kicked the ranger's rifle away. Then, his gaze switched to the injured man's torso, seeming to study the wound as his chest rose in fell in heaving breaths.

"You're gut-shot," Keith stated coldly, peering into the ranger's wide eyes. "There's nothing I can do for you, even if I wanted."

"We should put him out of his misery," Joe stated, nodding toward the downed man's mid-section. "That's got to hurt like a bitch."

Finally, the ranger spoke, managing to groan a single word. "Water."

Keith knew that the human body went into overdrive after lead invaded it. The ranger's systems would be trying to replace blood loss, fight infection, and repair damaged tissue at the same time.

All of those activities required water, and more than one veteran soldier had commented that they had "never been so thirsty," as when they had been wounded.

Taking a knee next to the dying man, Keith produced his canteen. "We both know you're not going to make it. I'll be glad to give you a drink, but I want information in return."

"Please," came the weak response as the ranger tried to reach for Keith's water.

When Keith didn't produce the canteen, the dying man became belligerent. "Asshole."

Keith laughed at the rebuke. "Me the asshole? Now ain't that the pot calling the kettle black? You are the bastards who are keeping innocent men and women out of the caves. You are the ones willing to let dozens of people, including children die in this ash wasteland. And you know what troubles me the most? I still have no fucking clue why!"

"Norval is protecting his own ass," pushed back the ranger. "He has been running Mexican girls and smuggling dope through the park for years."

Despite being shocked by his enemy's admission, Keith managed a friendly smile. Happy that the dying ranger had come to his senses and was starting to talk, Myers held out the canteen and pressed it to the fellow's lips, providing a few sips of cool relief. The act wasn't based on any sense of compassion, but to allow the interrogator a chance to digest what he'd just been told.

"That doesn't make any sense," Keith finally retorted, pulling back the canteen. "Why would Ranger Pickett give a flying flip about his past sins? There's no law anymore. Given the current state of things, who the hell would give a rat's ass about his previous moonlighting infractions?"

"He's turned into some sort of control freak," the ranger managed between coughs and grimaces. "It's like he's morphed into a dictator or something. Weeks after the catastrophe the stress started to get to him, and I think he just cracked. Anyone who disagrees with him is given a one-way ticket to the Mojave. He's never going to let you in. You would challenge his absolute authority, and that's just not going to happen."

"So why are all you guys following his crazy ass? Why hasn't someone busted some lead into his insane skull and ended this nightmare?"

The injured man took another sip from the canteen before responding. "How would we organize a mutiny without risking our own lives? How would we know who was still loyal to Pickett and who realized our leader had lost more than a few marbles? That, and no one has had the balls to challenge Norval's rule."

Again, the container tilted, this time Keith allowing the fading ranger several deep swallows. "Now that is the first thing I've heard since Yellowstone puked that makes a bit of sense," he mumbled.

The gut shot ranger lasted another five minutes, Keith managing a barrage of tactical questions. "Where is the weakest part of Pickett's defenses? How many men does he have? How much ammunition?"

By the time the ranger had drawn his final breath, Keith's canteen was empty. It had been a small price to pay for the information he'd gathered.

Rising to address his men, Keith announced, "For the first time since we fell into this cluster fuck, I feel like we finally have the upper hand. Let's head back to the hotel – I've got some thinking to do."

"Are we going in, boss?" asked Ham.

"Yes. We're going to take those bastards down, and then I'm going to enjoy washing Norval's blood off my hands."

Jack was shown back to his bicycle, the two-wheeled contraption bringing a much-needed smile to the commander's lips.

While he'd cursed and struggled at having to push the damn thing through the ash and wind, in reality, he fully understood that his ride was as important to his survival as his rifle or pack.

Stepping over and rubbing the frame, Cisco was reminded of a happy reunion that had occurred years before.

He had been on an extended deployment, his Ohio-class "Boomer" submarine ordered to remain at sea for an extra month. Not the kind of news that tended to endear a Naval officer to his spouse. As anticipated, Mylie's attitude was a bit frosty upon his return.

His daughters, none the wiser, had rushed to his open arms with squeals of delight and joy. The commander remembered the sweet scent of youth and clean hair as he'd squeezed them in a tight embrace and marveling at how much they had changed since his last trip home. After exchanging a less-than-passionate kiss with his wife, Jack had then made for the backyard to find Kilroy.

The black lab had always been the family's problem child. A rescue dog, caring for the lanky animal had put a serious dent in the family's discretionary budget. There had been heartworm, ticks, and of course, the shelter's demand that Kilroy be neutered.

Still, the friendly pooch had quickly become part of the family. Mylie, despite her vigorous dissension about acquiring a pet, had eventually fallen in love with the retriever's dreamy, sable eyes.

As usual, Kilroy welcomed Jack home with an unconditional loyalty and gushing love that can only come from a mutt. A few minutes later, Callie and Sierra had joined their father and pet, rollicking on the green grass and cackling with sheer bliss.

After a bit, Jack glanced up to see Mylie standing at the edge of the yard, intent to fight the smile that was spreading across her face. "Come on, Mrs. Cisco, you're missing out on a great tickle fight," Jack had called out.

On that day, Kilroy had helped bring Jack and his wife together. Now, deep inside the bowels of a dark cavern, Jack looked at his bike and prayed it would one day play a similar role.

"You're a lot like Kilroy," Jack whispered to the rubber and metal machine. "You're a pain in the ass and a lot of trouble, but you're loyal, and I need you in so many ways. Maybe one day you will help mend a marital fence or two."

Jack filed the memory and got down to the business at hand. His first task was to inventory his pack. For the next 20 minutes, he unzipped compartments, spreading the contents on the cool, cave floor. Everything was there, except for his ammunition. Norval had stated early on that he couldn't allow an armed stranger roaming around the cavern, and Cisco couldn't find fault with the ranger's logic.

The scrape of a boot against stone distracted Jack from re-stuffing his pack. The commander glanced up to see Carmen observing him from the edge of the room.

"Planning on going somewhere?" she asked.

Jack rubbed the wound on his upper arm while responding, "Well, you are responsible for that, ma'am," the commander responded. "You did an excellent job patching me up. There's no sign of infection, and I don't need my arms to pedal."

She stepped toward him, her eyes soft and friendly. When she was closer, she said, "You realize Norval isn't going to let you just stroll out of here, don't you?"

Ignoring the question, Jack asked one of his own. "How did you get hooked up with a guy like that?"

Carmen's eyes dropped to the cave floor, partly out of embarrassment, mostly to avoid his gaze while she decided how much to tell. "I was a nurse in Mexico City for several years. I witnessed the corruption and graft destroy my country and felt helpless to do anything about it. I did my job, caring for the sick and providing kindness to those at the end of their days. Over time, I grew tired of seeing the wealthy receive the best medical care available, while the poor died in droves because they were unable to afford even the most basic treatments and medications. After a while, I decided to take action. It all started innocent enough; I would pocket an occasional bottle of narcotics or high-end antibiotics, sell them on the black market, and then use the proceeds to help those who needed a hand."

"Robin Hood?" Jack asked.

She smiled and nodded, "I suppose that is a fair comparison. At least at first."

"So, what happened?" Jack continued. "How did you end up here?"

"It wasn't long before the local cartel took notice of my activities. They weren't happy that I was competing within their home turf, but I was lucky. The men running my part of Mexico City were more businessmen than gangsters. They realized I could be a valuable asset, and asked me to become associated with their operation. I agreed."

Jack grunted, "Let me guess, you worked your way up the ladder and eventually graduated to human trafficking?"

A grimace crossed Carmen's face, her lips pulling tight. "What you call human trafficking, Commander Cisco, might be described as an employment broker. A nurse in Mexico earns less than half of what a teenager flipping burgers in Phoenix brings home. I offered a placement service for the brightest nursing students from the poorest families. We farmed them out to wealthy American clients as nannies or for elderly care.

Many of my girls sent significant portions of their paychecks back home to help their siblings and parents."

"And the narcotics?"

She peered down again, obviously feeling guilty about that aspect of her arrangement. "I needed the cartel connection and Norval as well. My knowledge of pharmaceuticals proved helpful, and in the end, I rationalized that we were doing a lot more good than bad."

Jack acknowledged her story with a neutral, "I see," and then turned back to packing his gear.

"You never answered my question," she said. "Do you really expect Norval to let you walk out of here?"

Shrugging, Jack said, "I saved the man's life. Why not let me leave? What purpose would it serve to hold me prisoner or kill me?"

Shaking her head, Carmen said, "I don't think you know who you're dealing with, Jack. Norval's mind has been working in … well… bizarre ways lately. That's why I'm so desperate to get out of here."

"And what are going to do once you're out?"

The simple, logical, question seemed to take Carmen by surprise. "I'm going to make my way back to Mexico," she eventually stated. "I have friends in Juarez."

The innocence of her plan made Jack laugh out loud.

"What?" she protested, seemingly insulted by his reaction. "I can take care of myself … have been for years."

"You have no idea what it's like out there," Jack responded. "I have no doubt you're one tough lady, but seriously, the world that exists beyond these stone walls bears no resemblance to what you knew. I've encountered everything from painted tribes of high school students carrying AKs to cannibals who use sophisticated booby traps to lure human quarry. There is no food, no water, and damn few people left. Most of those who still walk the earth survive by preying on others."

"Then why are *you* so anxious to leave this underground paradise if the planet has evolved into this hellish world you describe?" she countered.

"Because I am determined to find my family and see this through together with them. I am going to make it to Texas or die trying."

She studied him for a moment, Jack fighting the urge to squirm given the intensity of her scrutiny. "Those are noble words, Commander Cisco. Your loyalty to your family is touching, but shortsighted, I fear."

She then stepped toward him, drawing uncomfortably close and gently draping a hand on his shoulder. "I came here with six, tough cartel men, and they remain loyal to me," she continued in a seductive tone. "With your leadership and experience, combined with my men and a few of the others, we could remove Norval from the picture. You could stay here and help us survive this ordeal. Later, perhaps, you could take some of the men and retrieve your family if they are still alive. Didn't you say we had the best survival environment you'd encountered? Don't you think your wife and daughters would find the confines of these caverns more comfortable than some Texas ranch that is knee deep in ash?"

Her offer wasn't unexpected.

After eavesdropping on her conversation with Norval, Jack had spent a considerable amount of time contemplating Carlsbad's future.

The electric lights, something he'd always taken for granted, were an amazing luxury in this day and time. Being able to saunter around the subterranean community without carrying a weapon or wearing a mask was a huge bonus, as were unlimited drinkable water and the safety of the rock walls. It would be difficult to imagine a better situation to raise and protect his daughters given the challenges of a post-Yellowstone world.

As Jack contemplated his response to her offer, Carmen sweetened the deal. He sensed her hand reaching for his, and then was shocked when she slid the cold grip of a pistol into his palm. "You must trust me," she whispered.

Not sure how closely they were being watched by the constantly hovering rangers, Jack tried to be smooth as he casually tucked the weapon into his belt. "Thank you," he mouthed. "Any idea where Norval has stashed my ammo?"

She nodded, whispering, "Your 'supplies' are in the cabinet behind his desk. It is locked, but the key is hidden behind the lamp to the right."

Jack had to laugh, somewhat relieved that Ms. Legs had apparently been planning her escape for some time. It engendered a level of trust, but the commander still wasn't ready to put his life entirely in her dainty, but obviously manipulative hands.

"Ranger Pickett will be coming for me soon," Jack whispered. "Find me after he and I have had our little powwow. I will have made my decision by then."

"Sir, Ranger O'Brian has been killed," reported one of Norval's men.

The news seemed to take Pickett by surprise. "What? How do you know this? What happened?"

"When he didn't report back in, we waited two hours and then sent out a search party. We discovered his body three miles outside the entrance to White's Cave. He had been shot, sir."

Rather than concern over his fallen man and the family he left behind, Norval's mind went to Keith and his pesky followers. "So now he knows we've been watching them." Then, almost as an afterthought, he asked, "Any sign that O'Brian had been tortured?"

"No, sir, but his weapon and ammunition were missing. His pockets had been searched."

Norval rubbed his chin for a short time and then barked, "Move every man to the north entrance. Now!"

"What? Sir? You want us to leave the other openings unguarded?"

"Why are my orders constantly being second-guessed around here?" the head ranger exploded in a furious rage. With his arms flaying in wild, swinging motions, he screamed, "I'm getting sick and tired of my every decision being questioned, despite the fact that I've kept all of your sorry asses alive!"

Before the stunned subordinate could blink away his shock over the outburst, Norval reverted back to a calm and collected demeanor. "Of course I want all the men assigned to the north

197

entrance. That was the weakest point in our defenses, and Keith now knows that. That is exactly where he will attack. Now, please execute my command."

Confused and wanting not to provoke Norval further, the ranger left in a rush to implement the boss's orders.

Satisfied that he had yet again outsmarted his opponent, Pickett pivoted and strolled with confidence from his office mumbling, "Now, to address our new commander."

Norval found Jack sitting on his cot and studying a map. "I wish to have a word with you, Commander Cisco. I apologize for the short notice, but there is an impending battle ready to shift into high gear, and I haven't much time."

Jack sensed instantly that something was off with the head ranger. Norval's behavior and tone were broadcasting warning signals that made the commander's blood run cold. Somehow, he managed to keep his cool. "Sure, Ranger Pickett. You've been such a gracious host. Whatever I can do to help."

Norval led the way back to his office, offering Jack a seat and then heading to the metal cabinet where the commander knew his ammunition was stored. He couldn't help but try to sneak a glance at the contents, just to be sure.

Producing a bottle and two shot glasses, Pickett was all smiles. "We are going to have a great victory today, Commander. While I'm a practical man who doesn't generally count his chickens until they hatch, I'm confident in our ultimate success."

"Congratulations," Jack said, lifting the small glass of amber liquid in a toast.

Answering with a nearly identical gesture, Norval continued. "Now, on to a subject that has been on my mind since your arrival, Commander."

"How can I be of service, sir?" Jack asked, hoping to simply placate the unbalanced man standing before him.

"You see, Jack, we here at Carlsbad find ourselves blessed with a unique opportunity. I believe strongly that we hold the future of mankind in our hands, and I fully intend to lead our species in the right direction."

Norval paused to sip his whiskey, his expression indicating that he was also giving Jack time to digest the magnitude of his words. The commander struggled to keep a deadpan face, his brain a swirl of activity. Mental alarm bells were clamoring at the sound of the ranger's words. Cisco had studied men like this when he was in the Academy – leaders who felt duty-bound to create a master race, justifying ethnic cleansing and genocide as a means to an end. But in all his dealings with the head park ranger, Jack had never envisioned him as the new Adam, the new father of humankind. It was all the commander could do to keep from laughing in his host's face. Instead, he offered, "Please go on, Ranger Pickett. You certainly have my attention."

Jack expected more of the man's unhinged manifesto, or perhaps an indulgent recounting of why Norval was qualified to be the new and omnipotent ruler of the known civilized world. The head ranger offered neither.

"You see, Commander, you are the first person I have allowed to join us here in our little community. Many have sought shelter here, some even resorting to violence in an attempt to gain entry. But God granted *me* his wisdom and guidance, and because of that divine gift, we have managed to prevail. I had been praying for a sign to begin the next phase of our recovery. When you saved my life back at the spring, I realized you were the man who could help me to accomplish our goals. Your heroic actions convinced me to bring you into our fold."

"Thank you," Jack answered, now completely baffled about where Norval was going, thinking that this unbalanced man might self-destruct before his eyes. Could such a fellow be a real threat? *Hitler was able to grab power during the chaos of an economic depression in Germany, and many very good people ignored their instincts and followed him,* he reminded himself. *Better to keep my friends close and the deranged megalomaniacs closer,* Jack determined, committed to intently listening if for no better reason than to keep an eye on Pickett.

"You're an experiment, Jack, a lab rat of sorts. I know good and well that eventually I am going to have to recruit others to my cause. The scope of my ambitions, combined with the pure logistics of the situation, will eventually require more manpower than my small group of followers could possibly hope to produce. That means we need talented, brave men like yourself if we are to further my agenda. I have selected you to be my test case, Commander."

Not knowing what to say, Jack merely nodded and mumbled a weak, "I see."

Taking the response as an endorsement, the disturbed ranger continued without hesitation. "For years, I have watched the dredge of mankind visit our park. We explain to visitors why they shouldn't smoke inside of these ancient formations, go into great detail about how the crystals won't grow if coated in tar. Yet, time after time we catch them sneaking a cigarette or lighting up a pipe. I can't tell you how many times we've found some tourist from Toledo chipping off a hunk of a 100,000-year-old stone straw to take back to their miserable condo as a souvenir. We have evolved into a self-centered, uncaring virus on this planet, and for one, I'm glad mother nature has finally extracted her revenge via Yellowstone's eruption."

"So, you believe people are the problem?" Jack asked, now curious how far this power-hungry leader would go to purge the earth of those who did not meet his standard.

"Absolutely!" Ranger Pickett answered without pause. "There are too many of us! We have bred and multiplied to the point where our existence is unsustainable! God has seen fit to take the first steps in clearing the slate, and has bestowed me with the tools necessary to finish the job and begin rebuilding society as it should have been!"

When Jack didn't respond right away, Norval took it as a sign that he should continue. "We have raped the earth of its resources. We have ignored global warming and its impact on our ecosystem. We have waged war on our world's natural resources. Now the planet has struck back and extracted her revenge. Now is the opportunity for those of us with a superior mindset to rebuild and not repeat the mistakes of the past."

Norval's rant was so repulsive, Jack felt his stomach begin to hurt. Only the comfort of Carmen's pistol, still tucked into the small of his back, allowed the commander to sit calmly and listen.

"Eventually, the air will clear," Pickett stated. "Eventually the earth will begin to heal. When it does, I want to be ready. I want our people to start repossessing the empty cities and towns. I want our forces to spread out and bring our way of life to an ever-expanding sphere of control. We will do it the right way, this time, Commander. We won't allow human beings to ruin things a second time."

"So, if you need people, why not welcome in the group I saved you from?" Jack asked in innocence.

Noval's hand sliced through the air in a dismissive wave. "Keith Meyer and his followers aren't qualified to survive. They are nothing more than a microcosm of what went wrong before. They are weak, old, and tired. Their leaders are narrowminded and intent on only saving their own asses. They can see nothing of my vision or the future that I demand."

Jack understood. The men outside the cave had strong leadership that would challenge Norval's megalomania, and that just wouldn't do. The commander's confirmation of that fact did prompt another question into his mind. "So why are you interested in having me join your ranks?" he asked, reaching slowly for the pistol.

"Because I believe military men understand serving the greater good. You have spent your adult life protecting others and have sworn loyalty to a cause that you believe is larger than your own petty existence. Those are the values I seek in recruiting new followers. Men who will put aside their own insignificant egos and strive for the advancement of our kind."

"So, you're just going to let the others die?" Jack asked, his hand now having casually worked its way to his hip without Norval taking notice.

The head ranger grunted and then broke out into an evil grin. "Yes, they deserve it. *They* are the problem, Commander, and I believe we will continue to encounter others like them as we expand. For that, I am going to need men like you. We will only accept the best and brightest, those survivors who see the wisdom of our vision for society. The rest will be left for God to judge."

You mean those survivors who agree with your bullshit will be allowed to live, and the rest will be killed, Jack thought. He was quickly growing tired of Norval's raving words and reached for the gun.

Before Jack could close his hand around the pistol's grip, two new rangers came rushing into Norval's office. They stopped, panting, just behind the commander's chair.

"Sir, our apologies for barging in, but we have just had a report that the men at The Simpson are forming up. It looks like they're going all out this time, bringing every available weapon, and even the women and children are armed."

Norval nodded calmly, his response then taking Jack completely by surprise. "I anticipated as much," he stated with a nonchalant tone. "Take our friend the commander down to the immigrant room, and make sure he's locked inside. I don't need any distractions until this business is finished."

Then Pickett turned to Jack and said, "We'll finish our conversation later, Jack. Until then, wish me luck."

Chapter 29

Keith watched the bustle of activity, his heart soaring with pride at how the people were reacting.

Not since they had been preparing The Simpson for the avalanche of death that was about to fall from the skies had he seen such energy and drive from the team.

More and more, he was beginning to include all of the survivors at the hotel as part of his inner group. They had earned it.

He and his men had the benefit of military combat under their belts, that experience helping Joe, Ham, and Jimmy prepare for what might be the last day of their lives. The others, however, were all civilians, many of them having been stranded in New Mexico and having no hope of ever returning to their homes or families.

Together they had endured all the hardships – food rationing, restricted freedoms, and the pain of seeing their loved ones taken one by one. They all knew the future would be bleak; they were all well aware that the world would probably not return to normal, in their lifetimes.

Yet, they kept on going. Scrambling, fighting, clawing, and contesting every obstacle and bit of bad luck the world could throw at them. "Yellowstone has provided the most grueling boot camp the world has ever seen," he'd once told Ham. "These people, if they survive, are going to be as tough as iron spikes."

It wasn't lost on Keith how his own attitude had changed as well.

Since capturing the spy, he self-confidence had rebounded nicely. Still stinging from the last battle and the people he had lost at Rattlesnake Springs, it had been difficult for him to accept that he'd been outmaneuvered. Things were going to be better this time. The playing field had been leveled, and he was assured that he had the upper hand.

His lieutenants had agreed.

Calling them together, the plan had been simple to hatch. "How many people do we have that are fit to fight?" he'd asked Hamilton.

"About thirty including a couple of the women," responded his second.

"Good," Keith had sighed. "Let's go after his weak point in two waves. Joe, you lead team one. Jimmy, you take the second. It's all or nothing. No reserves, no second chances, no retreat. Either we sleep inside the cavern tonight, or I'll see you all in hell."

They could feel the electricity of survival in the air. Every man and woman … every resident of the hotel understood what was on the line. The pool was nearly dry. Their food reserves were dwindling, and the air filters were failing. It was now or never, do or die.

People were flying down the hallways preparing themselves for that battle that what was to come. Rifles were pouring out of closets, ammo was being stuffed into magazines and packs, and the last of the water being dispensed into any container that would hold the precious liquid.

Keith spotted one group doing their best to assemble medical kits, tearing hotel linens into usable strips for wound care. What food was left was being gathered and dumped into plastic bins.

"Everyone is going, even the elderly women and younger children," Ham reported a short time later.

"I didn't order that," Keith stated. "What's going on?"

"They all know, boss. Everyone realizes that the choices are simple. Either we move into the caves or die trying. The alternative is a slow, painful death here at the hotel. No one wants that. Everyone understands how important this fight has become. I've never seen these people so motivated."

Keith nodded his understanding, and while the thought of children and the elderly marching out into the desert into a gunfight didn't sit well with him, he had to respect their "do or die bravado."

Twenty minutes later, Ham reported that everyone was ready.

As Keith scanned the two columns now formed at The Simpson parking lot, he realized that most military commanders would have to seriously question the sanity of taking such a ragtag looking force into battle.

Keith, however, knew better. He didn't fixate on the hodgepodge collection of weapons and clothing, nor did his mind fret over the lack of ammunition his troops carried. "George Washington saw worse," he whispered as he inspected the lines. "Most of his guys didn't even have boots."

What Keith saw were heads held high and confidence behind even the most worried mother's eyes.

Finally assured they were ready, he marched to the front of the formation where he found Jimmy patiently waiting. "Let's get this done, boss. I need a bath tonight."

Laughing, Keith waved his hand forward. "Let's go people. Tonight, we drink our fill and breathe clean air."

The two sentries escorting Jack through the maze of cavern trails were both armed. One of them sported at least 20 pounds of muscle on the commander's lanky frame, the other wiry fellow looked like he needed a gym membership.

Were it not for the pistol securely tucked in the back of Jack's pants, he would have been approaching desperation. Both that weapon and its implied element of surprise served to keep his heart rate in check.

The commander knew where they were going, his unauthorized scouting of the cave system having already discovered the room full of mattresses. Cisco had no intention of being locked inside with the stinking porta-potties and the other debris from the human trafficking operation.

He also had the advantage of knowing the route the two guards were taking. Despite being created for the public at large, the manmade path was still uneven in places. As they continued to wind down into the bowels of Carlsbad, Jack's mind was busy anticipating each bend, turn, and dip.

For their part, the two men assigned to deny Jack freedom were not professionals.

The commander noticed that they didn't always maintain proper spacing, and the man behind him had even accidently bumped into Jack at one point.

Coiling at every sharp turn and blind spot, Jack waited for his chance. At each opportunity, whether by luck or circumstance, there seemed to be some reason why "now" wasn't the right time. Before long, the commander realized he was quickly running out of options.

The three men had almost reached the hidden passage leading to the padlocked rooms when Jack spotted the perfect location. One of the trail lights had evidently burned out up ahead, plunging the narrow passage into nearly complete darkness.

Deliberately slowing his pace, Jack allowed the man behind him to catch up slowly. The commander's ears were tuned on the guard's footfalls while his eyes bored into the leader's back. He needed the guy behind him close, the man in front a comfortable distance away.

Jack pretended to trip over a stone and at the same moment barked a painful sounding, "Shit!"

As the ranger behind him stepped forward to help what he thought was an injured prisoner, Jack's leg shot out in the darkness, kicking the guard directly in the Achilles tendon with considerable force.

The blow caused the trailing ranger to stumble, and by the time he recovered, Jack was behind him and shoving Carmen's pistol in his ear.

"Drop the weapon, or your friend loses considerable grey matter," Jack hissed at the lead sentry. "I just want to get my bike and get out of here. No need for anybody to die today."

Jack sensed hesitation in the lead ranger's eyes, the pistol pointing in the commander's direction far from steady. Cisco kept talking.

"Seriously, dude, I don't want to hurt anybody. I just don't want to join a fight that I don't believe in. Just put down that pea shooter and let me go. You have my word as an officer and gentlemen of the United States military that I won't harm a hair on your heads."

"Do it, Steve," added the man who felt Jack's barrel up against his temple. "It ain't worth either one of us getting killed."

Common sense finally registered with the younger ranger. With a heavy sigh, he pointed his firearm skyward and then slowly bent and placed the weapon on the path.

Jack waited until the man had risen with his hands in the classic 'don't shoot,' position before shoving his captive forward. In a swift movement, the commander bent and scooped up the surrendered weapon before motioning his two prisoners to continue down the path.

Less than a minute later, Jack and his captives entered the secret passage. The commander knew one of his escorts had a padlock in his pocket, and before long the guards were locked up tight in the porta-potty cell. "It's not the Ritz, but it does feature indoor plumbing … of a sort," he quipped, double-checking the lock with a tug.

As he walked past the first room that had been secured on his first visit, Jack noted that the lock was no longer in place. With his pistol pointed up in the air, Cisco pushed open the heavy, steel door and cautiously peered inside. It was empty. Eerily vacant.

"What the hell?" Jack whispered, fully expecting to have encountered rows of mattresses or piles of illegal narcotics. "What did Norval store in this room? What did he move out of here? Why?"

Having neither the time nor the inclination to solve this mystery, Jack shrugged and hustled off. While Carlsbad Caverns contained the perfect backdrop for survival, her inhabitants made the location far less desirable. Time to shake the dirt off his boots and head on his way. He was looking forward to seeing his bike, and while he couldn't scratch behind its ears, the commander thought he might pet the frame.

The north entrance was a narrow, seldom-used split in the surrounding desert rocks. Other than a slightly packed path of sand, there wasn't a single hint that the opening led to one of the largest cave systems in the world.

Again, Keith felt that luck was with his camp. All the other attempts he and his men had made to breach the rangers' defenses had required the attackers to cross a broad, open section of ground. This unfriendly terrain had enabled Norval's henchmen to detect their presence and as well as provide lethal fields of fire.

The north entrance was a different story. Crags, boulders, and outcroppings rose nearby from the desert floor and provided excellent cover.

Lowering his binoculars, Keith smiled at Ham. "About the only problem I can see is the actual mouth of the cave. It's less than a dozen feet across – a fatal funnel if we don't execute this correctly."

"That's how I'd defend it," Ham replied. "Let us get close, bunch us up in the narrow spot, and then turn on the buzz saw."

Grunting at his friend's description, Keith then smiled. "Fortunately for us, we've brought along our secret weapon."

Ham scanned the surrounding stones before answering, "Yup, and the wind is just right. Ready, boss?"

"Let's do this."

From behind their perch, Ham waved first to the left and then to the right, his signal anticipated by over a dozen pairs of eyes.

Rifle barrels appeared from several nooks and gaps in the rocks. In unison, they began firing into the opening.

No sooner had the first volley slammed into the stone façade, than dense, dark smoke began to spiral skyward from behind a nearby formation of boulders.

As bullets continued to pepper the cave opening, two men with ropes scurried from behind the hefty rock formation towing what appeared to be a king-sized tumbleweed behind them. The huge, twisted ball of dry mesquite and oak scrub was ablaze, the red flames and thick haze forming a tail behind the sprinters.

Ten feet from the north entrance, both men suddenly stopped, flinging the flaming sphere of firewood toward the opening.

The scorching orb crackled and spit fire as it bounced along the stone path entrance, momentum coupled with the wind pushing it into the cave just as Ham had predicted.

Using the cover of the smoke to approach, two groups of armed then rushed toward the entrance, their faces covered by the plastic masks Keith and his construction crew had used to remove asbestos from the hotel.

With weapons held high, they stormed in behind the flaming ball and began firing.

"Time for us to go earn our pay," Ham said, chambering a round into his rifle.

"Let's do it. Let's show these people why we make the big dollars," Keith agreed, working the action on his 12-gauge pump.

Commander Cisco chose his escape route carefully and purposefully. No need to rush. After all, Norval would be distracted and his captors would be enjoying the human trafficking way station accommodations for a bit. Jack figured his bicycle would be exactly where he'd last seen it. On the way, he needed to stop by Norval's office and retrieve his ammunition and magazines before making his escape.

As he made his way to the upper levels, sounds of the battle began to drift through the caves. While he couldn't be sure of exactly where the fight was occurring, Jack was sure he could find an exit that wasn't embroiled in a firefight.

Twice the commander had to duck into a nearby crevice or nook, alerted to the presence of approaching rangers by the heavy pounding of scurrying boots.

Jack was given the impression that the passing men weren't looking for him. Given the urgency of their pace, they seemed to be rushing toward the distant skirmish.

He found Norval's office empty and experienced a brief moment of disappointment. *I've always heard there is nothing as expensive as a missed opportunity,* he mused. *Had I acted sooner, I might have simplified everyone's lives and rid the world of a criminally insane despot in training.*

The key to the metal storage cabinet was right where Carmen had said it would be, and for a moment, Jack wondered where the temptress was. "She's a survivor," Jack whispered, opening the lock. "She'll be just fine."

Jack located his ammo and quickly began stuffing his pockets with his gear. After all of his belongings were removed, he decided Norval owed him for saving his worthless hide and grabbed a box of .556 as compensation. It was still a long way to Texas, and a man just never knew.

Loaded down with ammo, Jack hustled out and made a beeline for the chamber where his bike and pack were stored.

Jogging along the stone path, the commander noted the clamor of the battle growing louder. As he passed the last intersection, the sound of shouting voices drove the commander to cover.

Diving prone behind a relatively flat section of rock, Jack held his breath as several men converged at the crossroads less than 15 feet away. Norval's booming voice effortlessly overrode the rumbling firefight beyond. "Everything ready?" the tin pan dictator bellowed.

"I believe so, sir. We just finished setting the charges per your instructions," the novice ammunitions handler answered excitedly.

Charges? Jake thought. *What the hell are they talking about? Explosives?*

"Is there something else? Do you have a *question for me*?" Ranger Pickett snapped, sensing some hesitancy among his ranks.

"Well, sir ... it's just ... I have never set a charge that large before," the nervous fellow began. "What if I didn't construct it just right? That's quite a big bomb, sir. And I am just concerned it might take down the entire cavern, sir."

Norval pivoted sharply and stared directly into his recruit's eyes. "Are you saying," he began, "that you question the safety of this operation, young man?"

So intense was the head ranger's glare that that the bomb maker shrank in fear. "Oh, no sir! Not at all, sir! My only concern is in my own ability to execute your directive correctly, sir."

"Good!" Norval acknowledged.

"Tell the men to prepare to fall back to the secondary position. We'll let them into the main chamber and then detonate the explosives. Let's see how Mr. Meyer and his cutthroats like being buried under a couple thousand tons of rock."

Ranger Pickett's other soldier wasn't so sure. "Sir, are you aware they have their women and children right behind their shooters? If we let them in and then collapse the cave's roof, they will be crushed, too."

"That's not our issue," Norval countered. "They were going to die anyway. We'll be saving them a lot of pain and trauma."

Jack stayed still as Pickett and his men moved away, their voices fading into the din of the distant battle. The commander was stunned over what he had just heard, the cold, cruel logic of Norval's plan shaking Cisco to his core.

Finally thinking it might be safe to stand and continue to this bike, Jack vacillated, trying to make sense of it all. "Why can't people understand we all need to pull together, now more than ever?" he whispered to the dark cavern. "Why do we keep on killing each other in droves? Didn't Yellowstone teach us anything about the value of life?"

It took him a moment to realize that he was troubled by something far deeper than the questions of humanity and good versus evil. It dawned on Jack that what was really eating at his insides was the survival of the species, and what the future would bring if people like Norval were allowed to thrive.

"You've been struggling with this since you left San Diego," he admitted. "The vicious tribes of the youth and the war at the church … the lumberjacks in Pinemont … the cannibals in Prescott. What will our world be like if these dark forces win? They bring no hope. The offer no future. It is a much bigger issue than simple scruples, ethics, or morality … right versus wrong."

With those words echoing through his mind, Jack stopped and inhaled deeply. He had to put a stop to this. It might be a small example in an unimportant part of the world, but somebody had to step up. Wasn't that what he had always been about? Wasn't that why he had joined the military and sworn to serve his country?

Jack continued on, increasing his pace to a fast jog. He was still heading for his equipment, but his bike was no longer at the forefront of his thought. The commander wanted his rifle.

For the first time since the eruption, Keith was winning.

The information they had gathered from the spy was proving to be accurate, his forces moving into the north entrance with less resistance than had been anticipated. That, and their little trick with the rolling ball of fire seemed to be achieving results.

Joe and Ham's teams had taken the entrance, and now it was Keith and Jimmy's job to exploit the opening. They had punched a hole in Norval's seemingly impenetrable fortress. It was time to pour through and expand the beachhead.

With his 12-gauge high against his shoulder, Keith rushed past the first line of assaulters. He noted Ham's men looked dirty and tired, but their heads were high, and their eyes were clear.

"We're winning," they all wanted to say, but it wasn't time to celebrate just yet.

With eight men in a line behind him, Keith darted to the next cover, an outcropping of stone that led into what appeared to be a massive chamber.

At the edge of his vision, the brawny man spotted movement, the flash of a green uniform. Keith's shotgun was there a nanosecond later, sending 11 pellets at 1700 feet per second screaming at the target.

Before the recoil had faded, Keith racked another shell into the chamber, the scattergun's muzzle sweeping ahead for more work. Despite his size, Meyer stayed on the balls of his feet, took small steps, and constantly kept his head turning as if it was on a swivel.

Three steps from his goal, a bullet whizzed past his head, the sound like a vicious dog's jaws snapping shut. Without thought or command, Keith's body instantly calculated the angle and split the air with another load of buckshot. This time there was feedback, a scream of agony telling the former paratrooper he had hit his mark.

A wall of gunfire now rained from the big room, Keith and his team scrambling and diving the last few feet to the salvation of their cover.

The air was thick with cordite and rock chips, as a blizzard of lead flew back and forth. *This is going to be tough*, Keith thought, estimating the number of defending rifles and the width of the opening he and his men would have to pass.

Jimmy was 20 feet away, on the opposite side of the secondary opening. The two leaders made eye contact, exchanging an unspoken message. "This is going to suck," they both said, followed by Jimmy's sly grin and mouthing the words, "Did you expect to live forever?"

With that, Keith watched him rise and loose several shots with his AR15 as he dashed into the open. Without hesitation, the eight men behind him did the same, charging into the dragon's mouth without pause.

"Up and at them!" Meyer screamed, rising to follow Jimmy into what could only be described as hell's very gate.

A hailstorm of lead zipped past Keith, impacting the stone walls with a chorus of thunks and whacks.

Over and again, flame blazed from his shotgun's barrel as his finger and hands worked in unison to produce a maelstrom of lead pellets. The other men were firing now, aiming at the vague shadows and muzzle flashes of the defenders.

Keith spotted Jimmy go down, a round striking his friend's left leg and spinning his body in a pirouette.

Changing course with a sharp dart, the strapping man rushed to his friend, scooping toward the ground and grasping a handful of Jimmy's shirt.

Despite the weight of his wounded pal, Keith lost little momentum as he dragged Jimmy to the edge of the opening. There wasn't much cover there, their new position offering only a slightly better angle to avoid the incoming fire.

"How bad?" Keith yelled to his friend over the thunderous echo of gunshots reverberating off the stone walls.

"I'll live, but I am gonna have to bow out of next week's 5K marathon," he responded.

Taking the opportunity to reload his scattergun, Keith shoved brightly colored shells into the tub as he assessed the battle. While the rangers were putting up a serious defense, the return fire aimed at his men was withering. Only Jimmy and one other man had been wounded. He would have expected three times that number by now. "This is too easy," he whispered.

An old proverb popped into Meyers's thoughts, an insight he'd first heard from the instructors at Fort Benning's celebrated airborne school. "If it's going too well, you're probably walking into an ambush," one of the savvy, old black hats had stated. "No gunfight ever goes as planned. No firefight ever goes well."

Before he could analyze the situation further, movement drew the brawny adversary's attention. Three of the women were sneaking up behind him, running bent at the waist to avoid the deadly lead.

They were after Jimmy, surrounding the wounded warrior and then pulling him back to safety despite the rounds impacting all around them. Keith's chest swelled with pride at their bravery and dedication. They deserved to live. They had earned it. We have to finish this for them.

Motivated by his people, he rose with a ferocious battle cry, working the pump as fast as his forearm could slide the mechanism, pouring clouds of 30-caliber pellets into the retreating rangers. Keith charged into the mayhem, blistering patterns of death into the defenders.

Before he realized his weapon was empty, Keith had reached the back of the big room. His men were right behind him.

They had taken one side of the room, he realized, fingers working in a blur as he reloaded. Shouting to his second, "In another few minutes, we will hold this vast chamber. Don't give them a chance to regroup. Don't let them breathe. When

Jimmy's team cleans up the far side, we will spread out and take this complex once and for all."

A group of nodding heads acknowledged his orders, his team wide-eyed and scared, but more than willing to continue the fight. Another swell of pride rose in Keith's chest. The men beside him weren't professional soldiers or gung-ho warriors. They were auto mechanics, farmers, shopkeepers, and salesmen. Yet, they were fighting as well as any man walking the earth.

We're winning, he thought. The end was in sight, and for Keith, it couldn't come soon enough.

Chapter 30

The body armor bolstered Jack's confidence, as did the load vest, sidearm, and six full magazines he quickly shoved into pouches.

There was something about preparing for combat, some sense of comfort garnered from strapping on tools and weapons that a man knew he could trust. The M4 carbine felt reassuring in his hands as he slammed home a full box of pills and then pulled the sling tight against his chest.

His decision to stop Norval needed little moral support.

He wouldn't be able to live with himself if he didn't act on what he'd overheard. He needed to stop this madman and his strategy to annihilate his enemies.

A moment later, after one last check of his kit, Jack moved off in the same direction as Norval and his men. It wasn't a difficult trail to follow – he only headed for the increasing sounds of battle.

While he remained steadfast in the choice he'd made, Jack hesitated as he crossed an intersection that led to one of the non-contested entrances to the cavern. He only paused for a second, peering longingly at freedom's path and trying to push aside the fact that he could be on his bicycle and out of the area in a matter of minutes.

In that moment, another thought occurred to him. While Carmen had suggested it originally, Jack had been unable to even consider her concept at the time. He could kill Pickett and take over.

That reasoning shortened Jack's stride, his mind working through the ramifications of the situation and his surroundings. It was evident that most of the rangers, as well as the people outside, knew Norval was as crazy as a jaybird. Wouldn't they welcome sane leadership?

All in all, Norval wasn't completely off his rocker. Mankind would have to rebuild. Someone was going to have to step up and be a leader. Why not Commander Jack Cisco?

"What makes you think you're the right man for the job, Jack?" he questioned as he moved toward the ensuing firefight. "Who died and left you in charge?"

Yet, the commander was confident in his moral compass. He knew right from wrong. He understood human freedom and dignity. He would be a far better leader than any criminalized park employee.

Jack could approach Mud Lake, the Marines, and the people of the Cliff House with an open mind and a friendly embrace. He had proven himself to those communities. They would welcome the chance to join his efforts in rebuilding.

Not only could he steer humanity along the right path, but he could also increase his chances of making it to Texas alive. Surely, he could find a dozen healthy and physically capable recruits to make the trip with him. Wouldn't it be better to cross the wilderness in strength?

"Hi, Mylie. I brought along the cavalry. Hope you don't mind," he whispered with a grin.

All the elements were there. Archie had seeds, Pinemont had eggs, and Hewitt had cattle. They could all join him in the caves and wait for the earth to heal.

He fantasized about emerging into the sunlight, Shelly and Hewitt at his side as trusted lieutenants. He pictured expanding circles of influence, expeditions to the major cities, and the life he could provide for his daughters.

They would put down the wicked and ruthless people encountered along the way while offering the decent folks protection and opportunity.

"But who will be the judge, Commander Cisco?" Jack asked himself, pulling up short. "Who makes the decision on good versus evil? Were all of the cannibals actually malevolent degenerates, or just desperate, starving souls that took a turn down the wrong path?"

What about the lumberjacks? Jack wondered how he would view them if he had encountered them before the people in Pinemont. Would they still fall on the wrong side of his moral fence, or were they merely hungry men driven by desperation? Hadn't both sides of that conflict tried to kill him?

"And that's the problem," he finally concluded. "I'm not qualified to be anyone's judge or jury. Neither is Norval Pickett, or anyone else. I might end up just like him – a power hungry lunatic who is no longer playing with a full deck. We have to come up with a better way."

It was all too much for the moment, the sound of the skirmish pulling Jack back from his delusions of grandeur. Still, he felt a sense of relief in overcoming the temptation and allure of grabbing power and seizing control. The rock under his feet felt like the high road as he began jogging again.

As he advanced, the report of gunfire became louder, rolling and bouncing off the stone facade with little to absorb its energy. Jack couldn't imagine how thunderous it must be in the middle of the actual fight.

Movement up ahead caused him to slow. There was a slight widening of the walls on each side of the path, an oblong, egg-shaped room. Jack could see people there … green uniforms … huddled over some sort of device.

The commander knew he'd found his target when the group of men stood. There was Norval, his head rising several inches above the other fellow. The head ranger held wires in his hands. The detonator!

For the first time since he'd overheard Pickett's sinister plot, Jack hesitated. He now knew that other rangers were merely following orders. Carmen had suggested many of them wanted to bolt with her, but couldn't figure out a way to escape his clutches. If the commander fired at Norval now, he would surely kill some of the others around him.

Deciding the gamble of moving in for a higher percentage shot was worth it, Jack hugged the rock wall and advanced. He was within 70 yards when a voice from behind him shouted, "Look out!"

Bullets slammed into the stone next to Jack's head, sending stinging bits of rock into the commander's neck. Jack pivoted, snap-firing three rounds at the ranger who had somehow managed to sneak up behind him.

Fortune was with the Cisco, his third round catching the ambusher low on his right side and taking him down.

Warned of the threat's presence, Norval and his group opened up, leveling a steady stream of hot lead in Jack's direction. Diving for cover, the commander realized he was in big trouble. Outgunned, he could only keep his head down while a storm of bullets forced him against the rock floor.

"I need to be a gopher with steel teeth right about now," Jack cringed.

Instinctively, Cisco knew that he needed to move in order to live. A quick glance told him that Norval and his rangers were already one step ahead of him, skirting along the wall and trying to outflank his position.

Keeping against the ground, Jack belly-crawled backward, the rough stone surface cutting into his stomach and chest. He reached a smooth area that had been bowled out by water over the millennium. The geological nuance was deep enough to protect his body below the ground's surface, and so provided reasonable cover.

Up came his carbine, a surge of relief racing through the commander's body. It felt good to be throwing death back at his foe. Again and again, the M4 pushed against his shoulder. Now it was Norval's exposed rangers who were scrambling for their lives.

For over a minute, the two sides seemed at an impasse, the stalemate doing little more than expending ammunition as both sides fired round after round but accomplished little other than keeping their foes pinned down.

As Jack fed his third mag into his rifle, it dawned on the commander that he was almost halfway through his ammunition. "God, it goes fast," he hissed, sending a spread of six rounds pinging off the walls above Norval's crew. "Something has got to change, or we're going to be throwing rocks at each other in a few minutes."

Norval evidently came to the same conclusion at about the same moment.

Jack heard shouting from the other side, his ringing ears unable to decipher the words. The intent, however, soon became clear as two of the rangers stood and charged.

The commander had no choice, exposing himself as his weapon spit at the two assaulters. The lead ranger slumped to the ground in a heap, his already dead body bouncing at an unnatural angle across the cave floor. The second fellow dove for cover, barely avoiding Jack's follow-on volley.

Just as he was wondering what possible motive Norval's men might have for exposing themselves in such a stupid, suicidal move, a line of bullets slammed into Jack's position from the left. "Fuck!" he yelled, rolling out of his cover. While he'd been busy with the first two, the others had moved!

The incoming fire pushed him back, Jack unable to sneak even a wildly aimed shot. Ranger Pickett's men had him now, advancing behind a deadly barrage of fire.

The commander's retreat was halted a few moments later, his boots backing into an unmovable wall of solid rock. The rounds were coming closer now, snapping and popping into the stone floor just inches from Jack's face.

There was no place to go, no room to egress, no ridge or outcropping to hide behind. Jack felt a chip of rock shrapnel smack into his forehead, the numbing impact causing him to jerk with pain. "It's over," he whispered. "I'm sorry, Mylie. I tried. I really did. I love you. I love the girls."

With eyes ratcheted shut, Jack waited for the searing bolt of agony that would end it all. In that instant, his mind screamed with a million questions, regrets, and memories. Would it hurt? Would Mylie ever know what he had tried to do? Who would stop the Pickett now?

Jack was so focused, waiting for that last and final bullet, that he didn't notice the change in the battle's rhythm.

Chancing a quick peek through squinting eyes, Jack saw and heard a new presence in the cave. There were new weapons firing, new shouts and cries in the air.

Now willing to chance raising his head for a better look, Jack spotted the park rangers firing in the opposite direction, their attention no longer focused on ventilating the Navy commander's hide.

The survivors from the hotel have made it! They have broken through! Jack thought.

Cisco pulled his rifle close, thinking to join the fight. He would show Norval Pickett that he didn't have the right to choose who lived and died in this world.

But it was Ms. Legs's words that rose above the din. "Are you okay, Jack?" the melodic voice called out, followed by several commands in Spanish.

The commander noticed two men who were not wearing uniforms appear from a hidden nook, their weapons spraying at Norval's retreating crew. Carmen's head poked around the corner, her eyes immediately seeking the commander.

Reinvigorated by his new lease on life, Jack was up, slamming home a fresh mag and determined to get back into the fight.

He crawled forward, pulling his weapon along the floor, seeking an angle. It didn't take long.

For the next five minutes, the battle ebbed and flowed. Carmen's men had surprised Norval's crew, but could little more than even the odds.

Norval's men had had the advantage of cover, falling back into an area that featured several man-sized columns of rocks that made digging them out next to impossible.

Again, Pickett's voice boomed through the cavern, issuing commands and trying to rally his men. This time, Jack was ready.

Like before, two of the pinned down rangers rose, firing wildly at Carmen's men. Jack ignored them, focusing the red dot of his optic where the rest of Norval's crew were positioned.

Sure enough, three of them scampered from the rocks. Jack's finger began working the trigger.

One fell immediately, two of Jack's shots tearing into the man's chest.

The other two continued with their maneuver, now hustling for a spot where they would have the angle on Carmen's helpers.

Jack hit the second man, stitching a short burst just above the knees and taking another out of the fight. He had just centered his dot on the third when his carbine locked back empty.

Jack reached for another mag, then experienced an immediate wave of panic. He was out of ammo.

Seeing the commander's vulnerability, the final attacker willed every iota of energy to his body and surged toward his enemy for the kill shot.

Cisco saw the hatred in the ranger's eye, the muzzle of his rifle now looking like a huge, black dinner plate and it zeroed in on Jack's head. Just as the commander saw the assailant's finger tighten, large chunks of his head exploded into a crimson mist as Carmen's men found their target.

Pulling his pistol, Jack aimed a few quick shots at the last two of Norval's gang. Whistling pings sounded as the shots ricocheted off the surrounding stone, all missing the mark.

Now aware that the rangers were protected by impenetrable cover, the commander realized it was going to cost a lot of lives to dig them out from behind the rocks. *They didn't say anything about having a firefight in a cave at Annapolis*, Jack lamented.

At the edge of his vision, Commander Cisco spotted another figure rise and run. Realizing it was Pickett, he loosed a string of .45-caliber slugs at the scampering shadow.

"He's going for the detonator!" Carmen shouted out an urgent warning.

Her men were in no position to interfere, pinned down by the now-desperate rangers. In a heartbeat, Jack understood what was on the line.

He came out from behind his cover, legs pumping with every ounce of strength he could muster. He could observe his nemesis clearly now, the commander's eyes boring into Norval's back as the beefy ranger made for the exposed wires that would detonate several pounds of explosives.

Ranger Pickett's head start was significant, and for several steps, the commander didn't think he could catch up. "Push it!" Jack hissed. "Give it everything you've got, Commander. It's now or never!"

Norval stopped, bent down, lifted one wire and then scooped up a second.

Jack could see the exposed copper ends now, Norval lowering them to what appeared to be an automobile battery. The commander wasn't going to make it.

Looking up from his murderous device, Pickett's eyes bore into Jack's soul, his lips pursing in a taunting leer. "I've beaten you, asshole. Nothing can stop me now!"

Every fiber of Jack's being focused on his stride, his knees and ankles protesting as his legs pumped like pistons to close the gap.

Norval touched one of the leads to the battery as Jack closed to within five steps.

At four steps, the head ranger's meaty hand positioned the second wire.

At three, Norval was moving the last connection to the battery's terminal.

At two, Pickett heard Jack's boots slamming into the stone and looked up. An evil smirk crossed the madman's lips before his focus returned to killing Keith's invaders.

At one, Jack launched into a headfirst dive that would have made any baseball player proud.

Jack's shoulder slammed into Pickett's chest with the exposed wire less than an inch from making its deadly connection, both men rolling hard across the rock floor. The commander's pistol, jarred from his hand, rattled over the rough stone and out of reach.

Norval was up first, his size 15 shoe lashing out at Cisco's ribs. The blow landed, but not squarely. Still, it was enough to knock the commander off balance and tumble him back against the rock.

"You traitor," Norval hissed, stepping in with his massive fists balled into tight knots. "I gave you a chance to join our master race and achieve true greatness. Your children could have led entire nations, and this is how you repay me!"

Jack's boot lashed out, catching the advancing giant just above the knee and causing Norval to grimace in pain. Before the brawnier man could recover, the commander was up and backing away.

The ranger came in, swinging hard and taking advantage of his longer reach. Jack ducked one, then a second blow. Norval's third attempt landed, the punishing blow nailing Jack in the jaw and sending white lines of ringing pain through the commander's head.

Staggering, Jack again withdrew, using his feet to keep out of Ranger Pickett's reach.

I'm not going to win this going toe to toe, Jack realized, drawing deep breaths and fighting off the pain. *I have to outsmart this pompous sphincter wart, or he's going to kick my ass.*

For the next minute, the commander avoided the oversized fellow, using his feet and staying just out of reach. "You're a chicken shit, Navy man!" Norval barked, trying to lure Jack to come closer. "Come on, sailor boy. Surely you're not scared of an old man like me?"

He's big and smart, Jack thought. *He's also crazy. Think, Commander. Damn it, think!*

"I don't have to beat your ass, Pickett. The Simpson survivors are going to break through any second now. I'm sure they'll finish you off for me," Jack taunted back.

There was truth in Jack's words, and Norval's expression changed visibly as he realized the commander was just buying time for the cavalry to arrive. With a deep, bear-like growl, the ranger tucked his head and charged.

Jack was ready, sidestepping the slower man's thrust and landing two hard rabbit punches on Norval's temple.

The strikes stunned Pickett, causing him to momentarily lose his footing as he fought to regain his balance.

Jack leaped onto the burly man's back, his right arm encircling Norval's thick neck. The commander held on like a cowboy riding a rodeo bull, the ranger spinning and bucking in an effort to throw him off.

With his still-healing arm and shoulder screaming from the effort, Jack gritted his teeth and strained to tighten his grip. Every cell of the commander's frame was focused on crushing his opponent's windpipe and ending the fight. The head ranger had other ideas.

Norval now realized two things. First, he needed a different approach to dislodge the commander from his back. Second, he could no longer breathe.

Changing tactics, Norval began backing up as fast as his straining legs would allow. A few steps later, Jack's back was slammed into the stone wall, the impact knocking the air from his lungs in a whoosh. The commander barely held on, struggling to draw fresh air into his body.

Norval staggered two steps forward and then reversed direction. Again, Jack was slammed into the unyielding rock with rib crushing force.

No matter what, don't let up on his neck, Commander Cisco thought, fighting through the fog of agony that racked his body. *Don't let go!*

Staggering forward as if to prepare for another backward charge, Norval's purple face was covered in veins as he pulled with all his remaining strength against the arm that was choking the life from his body.

Every tendon and ligament in Jack's body howled from the strain, his tortured muscles feeling as if they were being shredded in a meat grinder. He too was having trouble breathing, sure that at least two of his ribs had been splintered against the rocks.

Just as he was about to lose his grip, Jack felt the beast under him stagger, and then the stone trail was rushing up at the commander's face.

Norval's dying throes were violent but short, the beefy man's body heaving in convulsions as his tortured carcass made once last effort to survive.

Lying on top of the ranger's back, Jack never loosed his grip, waiting twice as long as he thought necessary before relaxing his hold on Norval's throat.

For several seconds, Jack remained on his knees next to the dead man, drawing oxygen into his lungs and trying to rub some sense of feeling back into his arm.

Only then did it dawn on Commander Cisco that there was still a battle raging behind him. Keith and his people were still dying in the cave, as well as the surviving rangers and Carmen's men.

Struggling to reach his feet, Jack staggered back toward the main corridor where Ms. Legs and the rangers were still locked in a stalemate. "It's over!" Jack shouted through cupped hands. "Noval's dead! Stop this craziness!"

Exchanging puzzled looks, the two defending rangers didn't seem to know how to react. "It's over," Jack repeated. "Norval is lying dead back there. I've disabled the detonator. End this, right now. Nobody else needs to die!"

Still unwilling to budge from behind their cover, the two rangers didn't discharge their weapons but weren't willing to surrender either. It was Carmen's voice that finally got their attention.

"This is Carmen; you men know me well. I am Norval's second in command. I make this promise to you. Come out, and you won't be harmed."

Jack was relieved to hear the safeties engage on the rangers' weapons. Moments later, the secreted shooters stood with their guns pointed skyward. Upon seeing the situation de-escalate, Carmen rushed to Commander Cisco, his legs now barely able to hold him upright. "Are you all right?" Carmen asked, her voice thick with concern.

"Yeah, I'm okay. Just weak is all. Go … go stop the others and end this stupidity. Go pull rank on the rangers still fighting in the cave."

She nodded, pivoting to rush off, face full of hope that she could stop the still-raging battle. Jack found a place to sit, his shaky legs and spent body thankful for the perch.

Jack watched as Keith and one of his crew lowered the last of the explosives, the two men handling the hazardous object with extreme caution.

The sound of soft footfalls caused him to turn, a glowing Ms. Legs coming to see what progress was being made.

"I just finished assigning the last person sleeping quarters," she beamed. "Keith and I decided it was best to keep the surviving rangers separate from the newcomers for a while, even though both groups understand that Ranger Pickett was the catalyst for all of the bad blood of the last few months. They are ready to start the healing process, and I hope one day we are one, seamless community."

Keith joined them just then, the ex-paratrooper obviously pleased to have removed the last of Norval's treachery. "The bomb has been disarmed. We can let people come and go through here without fear of setting off our own Carlsbad Cavern eruption," he announced. "I'll let everyone know it's clear."

The two leaders of the new underground society turned, motioning Jack to join them as they headed for the lower levels of the cavern. "We just finished inventorying the remaining food supplies," Carmen explained to Keith. "There is just over six months' worth if we are careful."

"Any luck with figuring out how to grow more of the cave moss … or to make it a little more palatable?" Keith asked. "That might buy us a bit more time."

Shaking her head, Carmen replied, "No. One of your people was a chef in a previous life, and she's trying out a few recipes to see if we can make it a bit more tasty. She also said that it would take a while to figure out if there were any medical uses. Given our unsophisticated medical equipment and our lack of spices to work with, it might be a while before we know what the real value of our 'cave moss' is."

"One of the rangers told me there is an underground pond that still has living frogs," Keith interjected. "Maybe we can start raising them as a food source. I remember eating some pretty tasty frog legs in New Orleans years ago. Tastes like chicken."

"Ewww," Carmen protested, "I'm going to have to be pretty desperate to eat frog," she said with a grimace. "Still, I suppose it beats starvation."

"One thing is for certain. When things start growing again outside, we'll have plenty of bat guano to use as fertilizer. I saw a cave yesterday where it was at least waist deep," Keith said.

"Why does the apocalypse have to be so gross?" Carmen teased. "Bat poop? Frog legs? Moss? Next thing you know, you guys will be trying to serve me cave crickets as a valuable source of protein."

"Hey," Keith brightened, "That's not a bad idea. Maybe…."

"Stop!" Carmen laughed. "I was only teasing. Will you men eat anything?"

Ham arrived just then, interrupting the banter. "Keith, we're ready to hold the first meeting regarding the elections. Are you still planning on stopping by to give your two cents worth?"

Nodding, Keith turned to Jack and Carmen. "No rest for the wicked. If you folks will excuse me?"

Jack stood next to her, watching in silence as Keith hustled off with his friend. "So, you've chosen the democracy route as opposed to Norval's fascist leanings?" Jack teased.

She nodded, "Yeah. We thought given recent history, that democracy was an effort that was best started sooner rather than later."

"I'm glad to see it. To be honest, I think you and Keith are both a little tired of running the show and making all the decisions."

"Oh, and that's not all," she continued. "Keith and I have agreed on a more peaceable lifestyle for our community. We have had enough bloodshed; we don't want any part of conquering our neighbors so that we can harness their resources for ourselves. In fact, we had a meeting this morning to brainstorm ideas for self-sustainment. Turns out one of the tourists who is part of the Simpson Hotel refugees is a botanist by trade. Apparently, when Yellowstone erupted, he was here studying some edible mushrooms that have colonized in one of the more remote chambers."

"I remember Ranger Pickett talking about how there were more than 100 caves in the park. No telling what you would find in them all. I guess it doesn't surprise me that you found mushrooms," Jack pondered.

"Exactly," Carmen continued excitedly. "They are an excellent source of protein; they are easy to grow, and they are bound to taste better than bat livers," she giggled.

Carmen paused, her tone growing more serious now. "You know, Commander Cisco, I am a better leader …," she bumbled, struggling to choose the right words for the man to whom she owed so much. "Heck, I'm a better person … for having met you," she admitted. "You were the grain that tipped the scale … that led us to rebel against Norval…. Everyone here owes you so much."

Their eyes met, both of them well aware of what was coming next. Jack came right out with it, "You know it's time for me to hit the road."

"I know," she replied, staring down at the cavern floor, blinking away hot tears that threatened to breach her bottom eyelids. "Are you sure there's nothing I can say or do to change your mind? You really do bring out the best in me," she added.

Gently placing his palms on her shoulders, Jack again found himself hesitating. Carmen was not only strikingly attractive, but she had proved herself a brilliant, brave woman. It was so tempting to grant Mylie her divorce in abstention and remain here to help the good people of Carlsbad rebuild.

Yet, the commander knew he would never forgive himself if he took the easy way out. He still loved Mylie and could think of little else but his girls.

"No," he finally responded. "I have to go to Texas. I have to see this through."

Stepping close, she reached up and toyed with the collar of his shirt. Again, she flashed the most seductive eyes Jack had ever seen. "Are you sure? *Really* sure?"

"Yes," he replied. "You are a stunning woman, and my head is screaming for me to stay. But my heart still belongs to my family. I have to go to Texas. I have to see this through."

She nodded a reluctant acceptance of his words and stepped back to restore the space between their bodies. "I understand," she murmured. "But please … promise me you'll come back if things don't work out. Will you do that?"

"Yes," he replied with a smile.

"Oh, hey, I had one of the guys drop in a few extra medical supplies just in case you needed a little something for that boo-boo on your shoulder," she teased, trying to raise the melancholy cloud that lingered over them both. A few seconds passed before Carmen's attention returned to business. "Do you have everything you need for your trip, Commander Cisco?"

"Yes," Jack nodded. "Keith was a little hesitant to let me restock my ammo but finally gave in, and I am well supplied now. My pack is full of food and water, and my bike is ready to go. I plan on heading east in the morning."

"How much further do you have to go?" she asked.

"I'm halfway home," he replied. "And if the second half of this journey is as eventful as the first, I am going to have one hell of a story to tell my kids."

Carmen smiled as she watched him leave, wishing she could be a fly on the wall when he opened his pack.

Episode 6 Prologue
The Day of the Eruption ...

Heather Lanier glanced at the sun in the rearview mirror, squinting in pain as the bright orb consumed the horizon behind her. She whispered a curse, but it was only half-hearted. Her mother's health was failing. All too soon, these cross-Texas jaunts wouldn't be necessary. That realization, combined with the early hour and her road-weary bum, pushed her in a melancholy funk.

For a fleeting moment, she considered broaching the subject of relocation with Mom – again. The daughter's analytical mind had no problem compiling a series of logical arguments for why living anywhere but the west Texas town of Drews was a viable idea... more importantly, how moving closer to Houston would be the best option for the aging parent and busy child alike.

"Better health care," she began. "The Houston Medical Center represents the most impressive collection of hospitals in the country, practically bulletproofing the population from germs, viruses and any other conceivable malady. And, let's not forget that I could drop in to see you at lunch or after work every day. And then there are the folks who move to H-town strictly for the retail therapy. The metro area offers shopping malls bigger than the entire town of Drews where anything you want or need can be purchased at a moment's notice. Tasty restaurants tempt citizens from The Woodlands to Sugarland... from Katy to Baytown. You can relax at Lake Conroe or stroll along the beach at Galveston and feed the seagulls," she reasoned to the empty car.

Mom loved seagulls, her home brimming with paintings, figurines, and even a snow globe collection of seaside landscapes featuring the gangly birds. Yet, as far as Heather knew, her mother had only traveled to the ocean a handful of times.

Ahead, a slow-moving pickup distracted Heather, the other inhabitant of Texas 176 apparently not in any rush to reach his destination. Accustomed to maneuvering through Houston's dog-eat-dog traffic, she double-checked her mirror and then signaled to change lanes and pass. The old rancher, his arm hanging out the open window, threw a casual, friendly wave as she maneuvered around him.

That simple, innocent gesture immediately deflated Heather's mounting arguments. "The people out here are friendly," she stated with a reasonable imitation of her mother's voice and Western twang. "I know all my neighbors and their children. I can name everyone who attends my church. The folks at the corner cafe have my order ready before I can even tell them what I want. If I had a problem with my plumbing or my car or anything, there are fifty people I could dial to help me. Drews, Texas offers a real sense of community. I would be lost and confused in the big city."

"But, Mom, I would be in the city with you. We could spend quality time together. You could make new friends, and we could see more of each other," Heather countered.

"You've got your job, and hopefully one of these days, a nice young man to occupy your life. Maybe even grandchildren one fine day. I was born in the country, and I'll die here," Heather continued, again doing her best to mimic her parent's tone.

There it was, the same old, tired reasoning that always seemed to dominate her visits to Drews. A husband. Grandchildren. The woman's proper role. Inevitably, the conversation would end up back in Heather's lap. *Apparently, I, the single, workaholic daughter need make changes to my life, not the other way around,* the beleaguered child mused.

Passing a sign that announced it was exactly 37 miles to Drews, Heather let out a sigh that signaled more frustration than contempt. She was a woman who was out of step with her upbringing, out of sync with the reality that surrounded her. She was a foreigner in her own hometown, a stranger to her only surviving family.

In this barren, arid landscape dotted with cattle sheds and oil pumps, a girl earning a degree in engineering was akin to her having purple hair and three eyes. Landing a job at NASA's Johnson Space Center was as alien and farfetched as the stars she and her colleagues hoped to reach someday. Her accomplishments meant nothing here because they were beyond the scale and scope of local values. In Drews, wedding anniversaries were respected almost as much as the number of healthy offspring pushed from a woman's womb. Here, the rushing yards accumulated by the local high school halfback were more important than how far the Mars Rover had managed to travel.

The outskirts of Drews interrupted her thoughts, a large sign on the edge of town reminding her that she had left Houston in such a rush that she hadn't stopped and bought her mom a gift. "I'll stop in Wally World and pick something up," she whispered, flicking her turn signal to change lanes.

Given the early hour, the chain store's lot was nearly empty. In fact, she had to wait several minutes before a sleepy-looking manager hefted a substantial keyring to unlock the doors.

"Good morning, ma'am," the man greeted.

"Good morning," she replied, choking back the sarcastic comment that formed in her throat. Then, after she had passed, "I hate friendly people at 7AM. It's sick… just not right. Damn the town of Drews, Texas and its *neighborly* people!"

Thirty steps in, she realized she had no idea what to purchase her mother. "Nothing big," she mumbled, glancing up and down the multitude of aisles. "Just a thought. That's what counts."

Her mind drifted back to her mother's love of the sea. "I need to find a clerk. Maybe they will know if there are any ocean-based knickknacks."

Pausing at one of the main intersections, she scanned the nearly-empty store, looking for anyone with a corporate logo on their shirt. Her search proved fruitless.

Strolling toward the rear, she finally spotted what seemed like the entire workforce congregated by the towering wall of televisions.

At first, Heather was annoyed when none of the employees would even peek her way. Curiosity soon replaced her frustration as all the clerks seemed glued to the nearest television. "What is so mesmerizing on the boob tube at this obnoxious hour?"

Within a minute, she spotted a report that Yellowstone was erupting.

For a half hour, Heather stood dumbfounded with the rest of the store's staff as they watched the cable news feed.

"That damn explosion isn't close enough to hurt us, is it?" someone asked.

"Naw. It's too far away. We'll be fine," answered a supervisor.

Heather knew better.

She had read enough in school to grasp the scope of what was occurring nearly a thousand miles to the northwest. More importantly, her department at NASA included atmospheric studies. She recognized that mankind was in serious trouble. She estimated that she had two, maybe three days depending on the upper-level currents in the ocean of air that surrounded the planet to batten down the hatches and get ready to ride out one hell of a storm.

Breaking away from the ever-growing gaggle of employees and curious customers, Heather began compiling a mental list while she moved through the store. Her first stop was in the home improvement department, more specifically the paint section. In a rush, she grabbed every mask available.

Finding an empty cart, she then purchased as many furnace filters as the buggy would hold. She almost sprinted to the grocery section, now worried that word of the disaster would spread quickly. Four cases of bottled water weighed down the cart next, that limited number all that she could manage to fit inside the already overloaded buggy.

Her mind raced with a list of necessities. How much food did Mom have? Was the pantry filled with shelf-stable supplies? Should she stock up on vitamins or canned goods? Was Dad's old shotgun in the closet? How much ammunition was left behind? What would need to be done before that weapon could be used again?

She paid for her selections, growing angry as the cheerful clerk seemed more interested in gossiping than scanning Heather's purchases. In a flash, she was out the door and jogging the cart to her car. As soon as the contents were secured in her trunk, she pivoted smartly and returned for another load.

She purchased four boxes of 12-gauge shells, 400 rounds of .22 ammunition, three large rolls of plastic, a tarp, and 10 rolls of duct tape. Again, her cart was topped off with additional cases of water.

Five times Heather returned to the store. On the fifth trip, it was evident word had finally reached the sleepy town of Drews as more and more citizens crowded the aisles, worried expressions evident on the faces peering at her over various staple items.

As she stood in line to buy her fifth full load of the morning, she took a moment to scan the other customers' carts. *Six packs of beer? Five bags of potato chips? Ten cartons of cigarettes?*

Gone were the friendly, smiling expressions of the locals, replaced by gnarled lips and alarmed eyes. A sea of carts streamed both in front and behind her... each buggy stuffed with potential purchases. The checkout queue now reached halfway to the back of the store.

"This place will be down to bare metal shelves by lunch," she whispered, observing the steady influx of patrons entering the front door.

Again, she crossed the now-full parking lot at a swift pace, wondering if there were room for another load – if anything were left to buy.

Punching the remote to unlock the doors of her SUV, Heather began stacking more water and canned food into the back.

"Now lookie there, Martin. This lady is just being downright greedy it looks like to me," the voice behind her snarled.

Heather turned to find two scamps looming beside her car, their eyes having trouble deciding whether to stare at her breasts or the load of treasures in the SUV's cargo area.

"She's a pretty thing, too," continued the talkative one. "Not too shabby from where I'm standing."

"Move on," Heather countered. "Not interested. I like my men with teeth."

It took a moment for the insult to sink in, the man's face twisting into a grimace beneath his scraggly beard.

He was what her co-workers would have called scruffy, sporting an untucked, dirty, long-sleeve shirt, worn jeans, and a baseball cap that was so soiled she couldn't make out the logo. Her remark about his teeth hadn't been entirely in jest.

His partner was a bit more put-together, but it was clear neither of them was working on his physics thesis or a captain of industry.

"Now that wasn't a nice thing to say, Missy," Mr. Aggressive finally managed. "Why don't you hand over those car keys and then get in the back seat like a good girl. We just want your groceries... and maybe a little fun."

He stepped toward her, meaning to grab her arm.

Twisting away and just out of reach, Heather held up her key ring and said, "You want these?"

With eyes darting between the late model SUV full of critical goods, and the key ring dangling in her hand, he hesitated only a moment. "Yes," he growled, stepping closer.

Heather was ready, snapping the ring around into a tight grip and slashing across his eyes in a lightning-fast move.

A high-pitched scream sounded from Mr. Badteeth's throat, his hands flying to his burning face. Almost in the same motion, his knees gave out from the pain, kneeling to the blacktop while howling in agony.

The silent one seemed in shock at the bang-bang sequence, hesitating long enough for Heather to square up and make it clear she was ready to fight.

"What's going on here?" another male voice boomed, two older men drawn to the scene by the still-whimpering man on his knees.

"They're trying to hijack my car," Heather answered never diverting her attention from the second attacker.

With blood on his hands, the first rascal struggled to rise, eventually helped by his associate. "It's just a misunderstanding," the quiet rogue finally managed. "We were just flirting with her," he added.

"Looks like she's not interested," one of the older gents grinned. "Why don't you boys move on.... Be about your business."

The ne'er-do-wells didn't like it, but the small crowd now gathering around Heather's car was more than enough to deter two wannabe highwaymen.

"Are you okay, young lady?" asked another middle-aged man who was readying for a skirmish.

"Yes," Heather panted, watching as her two attackers slinked away. "They did scare me a little, but your timely arrival helped to keep them in check. I shudder to think what might have happened. Thank you so much for your assistance."

"This Yellowstone thing has everybody acting crazy," commented yet another fellow, glancing at the back of her car with a smirk.

"Thanks, guys. I better be going," she nodded, the man's mention of the volcano helping her regain both composure and focus.

She accelerated out of the parking lot, mumbling to herself about her encounter with the welcoming committee in Drews, Texas.

Chapter 31

Crossing into Texas was a non-event for the commander.

Jack didn't know what he had expected, but the ash-covered sign heralding the entrance to the Lone Star State seemed to be a letdown. No brass bands. No fanfare. No cowboys on horseback or BBQ grills. Hell, there wasn't a single pickup truck in sight.

Braking the bike in the middle of the two-lane highway, Jack dismounted and stood for a minute, giving his saddle-weary butt a break. "Texas looks like New Mexico... only flatter. Great. More wind, more ash, more grit in my clothes."

Scanning his surroundings, he decided it was safe to relax. For as far as he could see in any direction, there was nothing but level, starkly barren land occasionally dotted by a dead, waist-high patch of scrub oak. Only the telephone poles broke the spell of the mundane, stretching off to the east until disappearing into the grey sky that had been his backdrop since leaving San Diego.

The good news was it would be almost impossible to sneak up on him or set an ambush. The bad news was that the overcast environment dampened his spirit, threatening his sanity.

Food and water were quickly becoming an issue as well.

After encountering cannibals, megalomaniacs, nomadic vagrants, and lumberjacks with battle rifles, he had decided to avoid the major cities. El Paso, coupled with neighboring Juárez, was the largest metropolitan area along his route. It had been an easy decision to bypass that region despite knowing it would add over a hundred miles to his journey.

He had understood heading north and following a rural route would make securing food and water more difficult. What he hadn't expected was the side effects of the brain-numbing, morale-crushing setting.

"Mind over matter," he whispered to the desolate world around him. "Your mind is breaking down, and your body isn't far behind. Better pull yourself together, Commander."

Since leaving Carlsbad, each morning had proven more difficult to roll out of his sleeping bag and face the day. More than once, he'd considered turning back. At the lowest points, pulling his pistol and tasting the barrel seemed like a reasonable solution, especially when he considered the possible foolishness of his harrowing journey. *What are you doing anyway?* he wondered. *Mylie is more likely to spit in your face than take you in her arms. Let's not forget those divorce papers – not the best reason to be on this suicide mission.*

No doubt physical exhaustion played a role in his substantially depressed spirit. He was undertaking a bicycle ride that would have given even a professional peddler pause. Pushing his two-wheel plow through the ash and pumice was difficult enough without the additional weight of his weapons, food, water, and pack. His knees and back now throbbed steadily, his calves and ankles in a constant state of protest.

"You've been through Hell's backyard just to see that sign," Jack mumbled, staring at the highway marker, the colors of the Texas flag barely visible beneath the thick layer of Yellowstone's exhaust. "You can't stop now."

Shaking off his downhearted mood, he reached for his pack and the maps he had stuffed in one of the outside pockets. Scouting ahead with his gas station mini road atlas reminded the commander of summertime trips of days gone by. The whole exercise reminded him of life before the catastrophe and helped protect his sanity.

"There's a town ahead," he announced to no one. "Drews, Texas. Doesn't look like a metro area for sure… should be easy to bypass."

He then began scanning the map for the most critical word in his post-apocalyptic vocabulary, "spring."

He'd never considered it before the eruption, probably passing by a hundred different towns with that magical word embedded in their names. Big Spring, Desert Springs, Hot Springs, Cold Springs… the list went on and on.

Now that potable water was the most vital resource on the planet, that word took on a whole new meaning. If a community or park had "spring," in its name, chances were that it had earned the handle for a reason. And right now, Jack needed water more than anything else.

The two blue spots in the vicinity were surprising, especially given the arid landscape he'd been riding through. The existence of lakes in the desert was unexpected, but they would not solve Cisco's problem. He'd looked through Dr. Reagan's microscope at the tiny shards of glass that permeated the ash. He accepted her explanation that they would slice his stomach and intestines into tender, hemorrhaging meat.

He was convinced that there wasn't a safe drop of surface water anywhere. And as people had begun to realize the scope of Yellowstone's devastation, they cleaned out the local stores of staples. *No use stopping by Kroger's,* he reminded himself. *No bottled water there.* The source had to be a spring that bubbled from the earth's core or liquid that had been stored in a sealed container.

Another glance at the blank map deepened Jack's funk. Other than Drews, there wasn't a major highway, interstate, or modest hamlet within two days' ride. Even beyond that, the pickings looked slim. A tiny speck labeled Hudson Springs was at least four days away and would add over 150 miles to his journey.

Like dozens of times before, Jack was faced with a difficult decision. Civilization meant danger, and his gut was screaming a loud warning. "Your luck isn't going to hold out forever, Commander!" A carousel of images swirled through his mind, the Grimm Reaper having visited his vicinity far too many times.

Yet, replenishing his water supply wasn't negotiable. He'd been conserving to the point of discomfort. He hadn't wasted a drop as best he could recall, but there was only so much he could carry. These days, he only appropriated this precious liquid for hydrating his body. "Let's face it, Cisco. That body odor could easily be classified as a bio-weapon," Jack chided. "And worse yet, your enemies will smell you before they see you."

He pivoted, turning to stare back at his narrow, lonely tracks in the ash. The temptation to return to Carlsbad was a siren's melody enticing him with its sweet notes. Water and food were back there. People. Shelter. Carmine. A bath. A future.

For the hundredth time, Jack wondered if risking his life on this journey was all worth it. Given what he'd encountered, the chances of Mylie and the girls being alive were diminishing with each rotation of his tires. Was he enduring all this tedium, risk, and physical punishment for no reason other than to erase a nagging sense of fault? Was his self-imposed guilt even deserved?

"You're lonely, worn down, and scared," he admitted. "You want to take the easy way out. You're making excuses. Suck it up, Commander."

His thoughts drifted to central Texas, picturing his father-in-law's ranch. What if he made it, and they all were dead? How many years was he taking off his life to find a woman who didn't even want him around? What if he had to bury his family? He couldn't imagine anything more devastating. His body couldn't endure much more, his mind just as fragile. And if that did happen, would he have the strength to turn around and head back to a survivor community?

In the end, it was the loneliness of his surroundings that cinched Jack's decision. He would enter town and hope to locate a supply of water and perhaps even restock his dwindling food supply. He might even get to sleep under a roof – or Heaven forbid, in a bed. He would take a break, recharge his batteries, and repair his attitude. It was a long way to the Texas Hill Country and his father-in-law's home. *Sure would be nice to hole up in the local bread and breakfast before beginning the next leg of this trip,* the commander mused.

He remounted the bike and began peddling, satisfied with his decision. Drews, Texas probably didn't have that many residents before Yellowstone spewed death into the atmosphere. It was a tiny dot on the map with a smallish font. "The likelihood of encountering survivors is low," he mumbled, trying hard to reassure the butterflies in his gut.

A few miles later, Jack checked the firmament above him and noted the slightly brighter hue in the overcast sky. The sun was going down, the days getting shorter. He wasn't going to make it to Drews before dark. He began scanning for some sort of shelter.

The highway made a slight bend to the south, and after riding another few miles, he discerned the outline of some sort of structure in the distance. His hand instantly reached for the M4 carbine resting on the handlebars.

As the road passed beneath his tires, the image became clearer. He spotted oil tanks, a complex of pipe, and a small outbuilding.

The facility was surrounded by a fence, a thick, electrical wire dropping into the compound from the lines running parallel to the road. "Not much chance anyone would be living there," he assumed.

A few more minutes passed before he was within scouting range. Dismounting, he pulled the rifle from the bike and stepped to the closest utility pole. Using the thick wood as a brace, he began examining the tanks and building for any sign of human activity.

The magnification on his optic allowed a more precise view, and within a minute Jack ascertained the place was uninhabited. He could spy no disturbance in the ash, nor was there any reason why people would gravitate to this location. It had probably been a sub-station of some design, the tanks used to store the product pumped from the few wells he noticed scattered across this section of desert.

Still, he'd been fooled, ambushed, and suckered before. His sense of caution and high alert permeated the chilly atmosphere.

Slinging the rifle, he began pushing the bike the last half mile, eventually stopping at the gated, gravel drive that led to the storage tanks.

"Midland Petro Development," he read, glancing at the faded sign wired to the gate. "No Trespassing!"

There was a phone number, but Jack doubted anyone would answer. "Customer service sucks these days," he smirked. "And if the police come, well, I'm guilty as charged. Take me to jail. Feed me. Let me take a crap in a real toilet."

There wasn't even a padlock on the gate.

The driveway was undisturbed, as was all the ash surrounding the small outpost. Jack found himself walking among three medium-sized metal tanks, each about 20 feet high and almost as big around.

The small building was constructed of metal and not much larger than a double-wide outhouse.

Brushing the pumice off the tiny window, Jack peered inside to see that most of its interior was consumed by a large pump and a small shelf full of valves and other spare parts. "Shit. No room at the inn," he mumbled.

The site smelled of raw oil, but the odor wasn't overwhelming. "If I pull out that shelf, there's probably room inside to lay down," he observed. "That's better than pitching a tent... especially if a storm whips up."

He walked the facility's perimeter twice, keeping a careful eye on the ground and the surrounding desert. There wasn't evidence of a single footprint, track, or disturbance. "Obviously not a 4-star property. Not popular with the locals."

Finally satisfied with the complex's security, he returned to the road and pushed his bicycle to the shed. With his bike's chain lock and a small handful of scrub branches pulled from the fence, he returned to the entrance a second time.

He began erasing his tracks, brushing softly back and forth for a few hundred feet along the path he'd just created. The ruse would not fool a skilled tracker, but the trail wouldn't be so apparent in poor light. *You just never know when company might come to call*, he thought.

Continuing his sweeping motion up the drive, Jack paused at the gate and secured it with his bicycle lock. The primitive security tool wasn't as desirable as a trip wire, but he hoped a little advance notice of any surprise visitors might increase his life span. He recognized the gadget wouldn't stop a determined assault, but he believed removing the lock from the metal entrance would be almost impossible to accomplish without making noise. And after all, he *was* a light sleeper these days.

Cisco then set about removing the heavy, metal shelves and spare parts, careful to stack them on the far side of the shed where his activity wouldn't be visible from the road.

There was less than an inch to spare when he tested his new nest. Still, the rough, wooden planks of the floor would provide some insulation against the cold earth. The thin tin walls would keep the wind at bay... a little.

Returning to his bike, the commander unhooked and hefted his pack. The breeze kicked up just then, sending a chill across his back. "It's going to be a cold one tonight," he complained. "Think I'll chance a fire."

Again, he returned to the fence line, being careful to step where his tracks couldn't be easily identified from the road. A few minutes later, he'd gathered an armload of scraggly oak branches, a smattering of mesquite kindling mixed in.

His first thought was to build his fire outside of the shed, but then an idea occurred. With a few grunts of exertion, he loosened one of the metal shelves and trekked it into his new abode. Setting the thick steel in the corner, he stood and observed his "fire plate," quickly ascertaining that it would be a workable deterrent... preventing the hot embers access to the wooden planks.

He was down to three cans of food – pinto beans, creamed corn, and the last tin of Shelly's chili. He hated all of the choices. He had consumed the last of his precious salt and pepper but still had three bouillon cubes carefully stashed in a rescalable sandwich bag.

"I'll splurge," he whispered. "Tomorrow might be a busy day. I might need the energy."

He opened the beans and corn, pouring them into his steel camping pot, careful not to spill a smidge. He then unwrapped the small foil and crumbled a cube of the tasty bouillon into the mix. A quick sniff told him the "flavor du jour" was chicken.

He started the fire easily with his disposable lighter, soon sitting back to admire the slight blaze and wondering about the sense of security that always seemed to accompany a flame. "Some primordial satisfaction stemming from man's dominance over the environment, I suppose," Jack speculated.

He watched the campfire swell, careful to meter its growth, making sure he didn't burn his new digs to the ground. Not only would it suck to have to sleep in the tent tonight, but a column of smoke on the horizon might also bring unwanted guests to the feast.

Soon enough, his pot was over the fire, subject to the constant and vigorous stirring of his camping "spork." After all, Cisco couldn't afford to singe a single kernel of corn. Every calorie helped ensure his very survival.

The hobo stew eventually began to bubble and boil, Jack setting the hot pot aside to cool. While waiting, he grabbed his rifle and stepped outside to check the surroundings. Securing the area had become his second nature.

The glow from the blaze wasn't visible outside the shed, and the desert was growing dark and quiet. He reached beyond the fence with his senses, another silly, ridiculous habit that did nothing but make him feel better. "If I die tonight, at least I used every resource at my disposal to establish my safety," he mused. He neither detected nor sensed any threat.

Turning to reenter the shed, he stubbed his foot on one of the weighty valves he stacked beside the wall. Cisco could feel the blood rushing to his big toe and knew he'd have a nice bruise there by morning. He reached down to adjust the position of the offending device. The stout, bronze unit was the size of a basketball, and moving it prompted another idea.

Hefting a couple of them back inside, he situated them as close to the blaze as possible. "Once they get all nice and toasty warm, they should make useful space heaters for the night," Jack beamed.

He ate quickly, the salty brine and mixture of vegetables far tastier than he'd anticipated. He was careful to stop when the pot was half empty. The remainder would be his breakfast in the morning.

He refueled the fire with the last of his thin branches, sitting cross-legged on the floor and gently prodding the hypnotic flames with a stick.

His thoughts were of Mylie and the girls, his mind drifting back through both good times and bad. "I'm coming," he promised the flames. "I'm unstoppable."

A yawn brought the commander back to reality, his body seeming to need more and more rest as his journey progressed. Exhaustion was a constant companion, as were hunger and thirst. He wondered for a moment how much he weighed, his clothes baggy and loose.

Shaking his head to clear the fog of negativity, he wrapped his hands in cloth and carefully lifted the metal shelf full of glowing embers.

Each of the bronze and steel valves had two openings, four inches in diameter. After verifying the internal gate was closed, Jack began pouring the hot the red-hot embers into his makeshift metal stoves. With any luck, they would radiate heat for most of the night.

A few minutes later, the commander crawled into his sleeping bag, minus his boots. Between the warmth of a mostly-full stomach and the hot coals, he felt as comfortable as at any time since he left the security of *Utah* and his shipmates. He wiggled his toes, testing their newfound freedom before settling in for some shuteye. It was luxurious.

The next morning, Jack awoke well after daylight. Squirming out of his bag, he stretched and twisted, trying to work the kinks from his back and legs. Still, evidenced by his late rising, it had been a pretty good night.

His first task was to reignite the fire. After a quick change of socks, he put his boots back on and then stepped outside to gather more kindling.

Somehow, the stew didn't taste as good this morning. Regardless, he didn't waste a single crumb, drinking the broth while opining for a steaming cup of coffee.

Within an hour, he'd broken camp and was riding toward Drews, Texas. The sky seemed just a bit brighter than normal this morning, surely a good sign. The commander wondered how long it would be before enough sunlight pressed through the overcast murkiness to create a shadow. "The ash has got to settle at some point," he proclaimed to the empty road. "It just has to."

The first sign of civilization was the Drews Baptist Church, a massive metal building, probably raised on the outskirts of town where land was cheap. A sizeable, gravel lot flanked the front and sides of the structure.

The sign by the road advertised Sunday services beginning at 9:30AM. Glancing at his watch, Jack realized he was just a bit early. Still, it wouldn't hurt to check the building out. He'd found refuge in a house of worship before.

Again, he dismounted, feeling zero guilt for toting his rifle onto holy ground. He fully planned to enter the building with the carbine firmly in his grip. He wondered if the baptismal pool would contain water that was safe to drink. "You could bathe and save your soul at the same time," he chuckled, before ducking in anticipation of the impending lightning strike that would surely accompany his bad joke transgression.

He walked the bike entirely around the sizable structure, not finding any sign of occupation or recent activity. Still, it was difficult to tell for certain. The wind had swept the concrete sidewalks clear of Yellowstone's wrath, and the ash naturally puddled around the gravel, making the surface uneven.

He decided to enter the front door. It was no surprise that the entrance was unlocked.

Instantly, he realized that the church had already been looted.

While the pews remained in orderly fashion, the contents of a small closet beside the entrance were scattered across the center aisle. Jack spied hymnals, a few choir robes, a child's jacket, and a shopping bag that contained several small Bibles.

Working slowly, he rounded the oak benches, making his way around the outside edge of the sanctuary. The commander's head was on a swivel, the barrel of his shouldered rifle continually sweeping right and left. He had learned so much since leaving San Diego, gained so many skills crucial to his survival.

Reaching the front of the meeting room, he ascended the three steps to the raised podium, then stepped to inspect the lectern. The pulpit had been stripped of all its religious fittings. Nothing of interest there, not even a vial of Holy Water.

Jack spotted a door on each side of the stage, one behind the choir box, the other slightly hidden by a velour drape attached to the ceiling. "Ignore the man behind the curtain," he mumbled, choosing the more sequestered option.

It opened to a small hallway leading to a series of what appeared to be the church administration area. All the doors had been forced open, the contents of each room strewn up and down the hall.

Gradually, he made his way to a mounted nameplate announcing he was entering the "Minister's Office." Inside the uninspiring space, he found a desk, several metal filing cabinets, and a modest credenza. Every drawer was open; the floor was littered with manila folders, church bulletins, religious paperbacks, and even a couple of bowling trophies.

Another door led to a series of Sunday School rooms, Cisco finding each of them having been thoroughly ransacked as well. There wasn't a single package of crackers or stick of gum to be found anywhere.

Discouraged, he trekked back out to his bike and continued peddling toward Drews. If every building in this small town had been as thoroughly searched, it was going to be a long, thirsty ride to the next stop.

As he traveled closer to the center of the village, Jack began to pass more and more buildings. A used car lot, a machine shop, a collision repair business, and even a funeral parlor lined the street. Obviously, all of them had been looted, everything from chairs to a lined mahogany coffin lying near the wide-open doors.

"And I was hoping for a hot bath," he mumbled, wondering now if he'd made the right decision not to bypass the hamlet.

Cisco's comment, however, brought about an idea. Didn't most homes have hot water heaters? Would the liquid in those tanks be safe?

At the next intersection, he decided to cut off the main drag and test his theory. While the thought of entering a private residence made his stomach tense, water and food are becoming critical. At some point in time, he would have to chance breaking into some upstanding citizen's "home sweet home."

He came to the first residential street, several one-story ranch homes lining both sides of the pavement. It appeared to be a quiet neighborhood, Jack estimating most of the houses having been built in the late 1960s, early 70s.

After passing the first few dwellings, his heart again dropped. These too had been plundered, their contents scattered across the yards and driveways. Jack's mind returned to the water heaters. Would they still have drinkable liquid? Would he find them empty, bone dry? At worst, he hoped to give himself a sponge bath.

He realized that his procrastination was costing him calories in his search for sustenance – calories he could not spare. He would enter the next home. Continuing to pedal, Jack cut sharply into the following driveway and stopped.

The residence was a comfortable ranch, red brick with dark brown shutters bracketing a bowed picture window. The front door was ajar;

the entrance was partially blocked by a lamp leaning at an odd angle. Jack spied various items of clothing scattered around the front porch.

He decided to circle the house, dismounting slowly and lifting his rifle from the handlebars in a deliberate motion. As unlikely as it was that someone was living inside, he didn't want them to start shooting over a misunderstanding.

With an intentionally powerful voice, he announced, "Hello there! Anyone inside? I don't want trouble. If you're in there, just yell out, and I'll leave."

There was no answer.

After slinging the rifle, he began pushing the bike further up the driveway. Finally reaching the rear edge of the home, he scanned the backyard carefully.

He guided the bike a small distance into the yard, just enough so that it wouldn't be visible from the street. Jack then began walking around the house, repeating his warning as he stepped gingerly across the dead grass.

He was almost to the yard's boundary when something odd met his eye. There, along the far side of the home, was a path.

For a moment, Jack thought it was the light playing some trick with a drift of ash, but as he approached closer, he could detect a well-worn trail of some sort. A quick glance left and right showed the thoroughfare was void of traffic… for the moment.

With his rifle now at ready, the commander followed the path for 100 yards to the north. There were footprints in the mud, the lifeless foliage clearly having been worn down after the ash had settled.

The route also seemed to be a well-traveled course, Jack able to identify at least four unique patterns of shoe soles. There were at least that many different sizes as well.

"You've stumbled onto the community walking trail, Commander," he whispered, now curious where the path led.

Turning around, he followed the route for an equal distance in the opposite direction, ready to run or fight on a moment's notice. He lost the trail on Main Street, the sidewalks and blacktop erasing any evidence or sign. Jack was puzzled.

There were survivors of the apocalypse here, which given what he'd encountered since Yellowstone's temper fit, wasn't a surprise. Those people had taken to walking the same direction on a regular basis, traveling from or to the downtown to some unknown destination at the other end of the trail. Why?

"Has to be either food or water," he decided, his whisper carrying louder than he had expected in the dead-quiet streets.

Jack returned to the location where his bicycle rested on its kickstand in the backyard, his eyes not leaving the local thoroughfare for long. The last thing he needed was to be caught unaware if the citizens of Drews, Texas showed their faces, particularly if they were armed and outfitted in Kevlar. Not exactly the welcome wagon.

With a grunt, he made a determination. He needed to know what was at the other end of that well-worn pathway. He would scout on foot.

Like the home's front door, the garage's entrance had been violently breached as well. "Somebody probably after lawnmower gas," he mumbled. After a quick scan of the mess inside, he decided it was the perfect place to hide his two-wheeler.

An old box of clothing provided the bike with quick camouflage, Jack positioning his chariot on its side and then covering it with an armful of shirts and slacks that smelled musty and stale.

With one last glance over his shoulder, he left the entire inventory of his worldly possessions behind.

His plan was to step on one side or the other of the path, hoping to spy any travelers before they caught a glimpse of him. That soon proved difficult, however, the trail veering off in a narrow, straight line to the north, slicing through three blocks of the neighborhood.

And then the houses ran out, the trail leading into an empty tract of brown, dead, waist-high weeds, eventually disappearing into a slight depression.

Jack suddenly felt nervous.

Here, he had little visibility and even less cover. The surroundings offered multiple opportunities for an ambush or for Cisco to simply bumble into a hostile party.

Beyond the pitfalls of the terrain, he also felt a disconnect between where he expected the path to lead and where it actually wound. After following the path toward the edge of town, he had fully expected it to end at a warehouse, spring, or some other resource that would sustain Drew's survivors. An empty field of weeds wasn't what he had in mind.

He strolled left, and then right, his footfalls making new tracks as he tried to examine the route in front of him from every possible angle to give him an idea of what lay ahead. Despite having succumbed to Yellowstone's fury long ago, the undergrowth was just too thick to observe any distance.

"You've got no choice, Commander," he grunted. "You have to know if there is any food or water at the end of this path. Your very life may depend on that information. If you turn around now, you'll wonder what was out here for the rest of the trip… or until you surrender to dehydration and starvation."

In he went, rifle high, no longer concerned about appearances or misunderstandings. Five steps in, the safety clicked off his weapon.

Down the grade he plodded, eyes darting right and left, barrel sweeping both directions. Within 30 yards, he bottomed out into what was nothing more than a drainage ditch. He paused at the far bank, knowing he was vulnerable as he climbed out of the gully.

Within a dozen steps, Jack could see where the footpath ended. Here, on the northern edge of Drews, a mobile home park marked the border of the community. "You've wandered onto the wrong side of the tracks, Cisco," he chided.

It made sense, he supposed. Like so many settlements and cities across America, the lower income families often settled on the outskirts of town. It seemed that land along the municipality's fringe was almost always less expensive due to several factors. Folks generally had extra ground to cover to pick up a gallon of milk or to commute to work. But affordable housing frequently offset the price of convenience.

"The locals who survived have been using the trail to raid the village," he guessed. "They've worn out a path going to gather whatever is left. Hell, I'd be doing the same thing."

The crack of a branch sent Jack's pulse sky high, the commander rushing off to his left and into a deep thicket. Sliding into the brush like a baseball player stealing second base, Jack rolled hard and brought his weapon to bear on the trail.

It seemed like an eternity before a flash of color showed through the long-departed weeds. The center of the commander's crosshairs followed without wavering.

A single human shape appeared, Jack somewhat relieved that any fight would be one-on-one. The figure moved a few steps closer, and he pulled away from his optic. The hiker was a woman, alone, and he hadn't expected that.

"This town is just full of surprises," he mouthed without a sound.

Chapter 32

He watched as she meandered nonchalantly along the path, an empty, plastic, milk jug and a red bucket in her hands.

"She's after water," he observed, again using a silent voice.

She passed without incident, Jack noting the shotgun slung across her back. He also realized that despite the mask covering her face, she was damn pretty. He estimated her to be in her late 20s, with shiny hair and bright eyes that signaled she was far from malnourished.

Ten minutes passed before he heard her making the return trip, now struggling with the weight of the full containers.

Still, she seemed at ease, and that reduced the commander's natural tendency to remain hidden. He had to take a chance.

Standing slowly and lowering his weapon, Jack offered, "I can help you with those."

He was surprised at how quickly she moved, the 12-gauge in her hands almost before the bucket and jug hit the ground. In response, he held the carbine out to his side, both hands spread wide. "I mean no harm. I'm Commander Jack Cisco, United States Navy, ma'am."

She blinked once, finger tightening on the scattergun's trigger. For a moment, Jack thought he had made a deadly mistake.

"Please don't shoot me," he implored in the calmest tone he could manage. "I'm only passing through and need food and water. I'm on my way to the Hill Country to find my wife and daughters."

"Do you make it a habit of scaring the shit out of women, Commander?" she challenged, not lowering the shotgun one inch.

"If I meant to harm you, I could have shot you without warning," he reasoned. "I was over here when you wandered by the first time, scared to death that *I* was about to be ambushed."

That logic seemed to resonate with her, yet she didn't lower the gun. "What do you want?" she finally asked.

"Water. Food, if possible. That's all. Unless somebody tries to kill me, I'm harmless. I mean that."

"So, you're *walking* to central Texas? From where?"

"My sub docked in San Diego several weeks ago. After we figured out what had happened, my captain gave me leave to try and locate my wife and daughters. And I'm actually riding a bicycle, not walking."

It took her a bit to digest his words, her gun slowly drifting toward the ground. "Okay, Mr. Navy Man, I suppose that if you really wanted to do me in, you could have, just like you said. Now that you've made me spill my water, you can follow me. I'll show you where you can get all the water you want."

"So that's what the path is all about. A source of water. I had guessed as much, but was losing faith," Jack sighed, slinging his rifle and taking a step toward her.

Leaving the heavier bucket on the ground, she backed up a few steps. "My name is Heather Lanier," she declared. "Pleasure to meet you, Commander."

"Please, call me Jack," he replied, smiling for the first time in a long while.

"Okay, Jack. Still, I don't know you from Adam the ax murderer, so I'm going to let you carry the bucket in front of me. Please don't get cute; I haven't had to shoot anybody for weeks."

He laughed, nodding his understanding. "I suppose I don't blame you."

As they began walking, she started talking, her words rattling out like she hadn't spoken to anyone in months. "The home we're going to visit belonged to the Campos family. They were never what you would call prominent in the hierarchy of Drews society, at least not until the volcano blew. In fact, they were a quiet, Hispanic clan that hardly anybody noticed."

She paused for a moment, apparently gathering her thoughts before proceeding.

"The folks up here on the north side were quite poor, living in double-wide house trailers, campers, past-their-prime recreational vehicles, and beat up old shacks. Most of them were blue-collar workers… slaves to their daily routines, with little variety in their lives. Take Mr. Juan Campos, for example. He always wore his sweat-stained, 10-gallon hat and drove the same, old beat-up Chevy pickup. He had a job out on the drilling rigs, and left for work every morning while the rest of the neighborhood snoozed away. Once in a great while, you might also see him buying a six-pack at the corner convenience store, but that was about it."

She seemed eager to talk, launching right into her narrative without hesitation. Jack didn't comment, again sensing that it had been a while since his guide had spoken to another human being. Besides, her voice was like a symphony to a man who had been alone in the desert for days.

"His wife, Mrs. Anna Campos, on the other hand, was a slightly pudgy woman with an enormous smile and was often seen about town because she worked as the cleaning lady at the local elementary school. While she struggled with the English language, she took pride in her work and never complained. Her thoroughness with a broom and dust cloth was legendary. On the weekends, she taught the kindergarten Sunday School class at the Catholic church."

Finally breaking his silence, Jack stopped walking and turned to face the young woman behind him. "So, you were raised in this community?"

"Yes, born and raised. I had to leave for college, of course. And then after I graduated, I moved away to start my career. I'm an engineer… or *was* an engineer… at NASA before everything went to hell."

"Understood. Now please, continue. I'm fascinated."

Without waiting for a reply, Jack pivoted and returned to his stroll along the path. He stopped a few steps later, a house trailer coming into view.

Stepping forward to stand beside him, Heather nodded toward the homestead and pointed to the random toys peeking out from the carpet of ash. "The yard around the Campos homestead was always like that – always full of children and their baubles, as I recall. There were plastic cars, trucks, doll parts, and a rusty swing set. The clothesline that always seemed to be billowing with rainbow-colored laundry created a backdrop for the makeshift playground."

She then gestured toward the side yard, "But here was the main attraction… a second-hand, above ground pool that Mr. Campos had managed to haul home."

Jack followed her finger, nodding at the feature. Although the blue dolphins and mermaids imprinted on its plastic surface had faded long ago, he could almost hear the squeals of delight as the neighborhood kids splashed and played.

"Throughout most of my childhood, the hot summer months of West Texas were made just a little more tolerable for us kids because of that swimming hole. I spent many an afternoon in that old, sun-bleached pool. It was a luxury, really, enjoyed by children from all over Drews."

"Does it still hold water?" Jack questioned, wondering how the locals kept the ash from contaminating the source.

"No, of course not. It is, however, the reason why a handful of us have survived," Heather chuckled, her mind flooded with happy memories of her youth. "You see, during the brutal Texas summers, wind-blown debris and dirt from dozens of bare feet would make the pool less inviting. Every few days, Mrs. Anna would pull the plug, draining the dirty water into the yard. We would all stand around and wait while she began the tedious process of refilling the pool with a garden hose."

Jack still didn't get it but figured his answers were coming. He didn't have to wait long.

"That refilling soon proved to be a problem. The Campos's were not wealthy people, and when Mr. Juan began seeing spikes in their already outrageous water bill, he threatened to disassemble the whole thing and drag it to the landfill."

Frowning, Jack shook his head. He estimated the pool held several hundred gallons, which probably put a severe dent in a poor man's beer budget.

"Mrs. Anna was a strong woman, though. She wasn't about to let that happen. She enjoyed the children and appreciated the gratitude the pool garnered from her friends. I guess she thought it made their home special. One day, the two of them got into an argument that everyone in the neighborhood could hear. I remember the missus digging in and telling her husband that he had better come up with another solution if he wanted to sleep inside the house again."

Heather smiled at the recollection. Then, without warning, she resumed her trek, making for the modular home's backyard. After a few steps, she continued, "Mr. Campos stomped around back here that whole day, trying to decide what to do. I think he was scheming for a way to keep his wife happy and still be able to put meat on their table. As a girl, I was a little scared of him and had been keeping a close vigil over the side of the pool when he finally had his 'Eureka!' moment."

"And?" Jack asked, urging her to continue. He was captivated by her story-telling skills, the details resurrecting his own memories of life before the collapse of society.

"I couldn't miss the broad smile that spread across his face. He had managed to figure out a way to fill the watering hole without breaking the bank. Later, I learned the details. It seems that Mr. Campos's father had purchased this land well before the town's water system had made it this far north. When Grandpa Campos had bought the property, there had been a well, covered long ago when Drews' utilities spread to this section. Mr. Juan found the sand-covered concrete slab that topped the well's casing. A few minutes later, he lowered a plastic cup secured by a kite string into the depths. Sure enough, there was water down there. The following weekend, he bought a rusty, but functional, cast iron, pitcher pump. With the help of a couple of oil field co-workers, several lengths of scrap pipe, and numerous six-packs of beer, they had cool, clean liquid flowing by the time Mrs. Anna returned from church on Sunday afternoon. The pool was back in business, us kids fighting to take a turn at working the handle to fill it."

Jack noticed it now, the faded red paint of the pitcher pump. He smiled, finally understanding why Heather had gone into such detail.

With a sweep of her hand, she offered, "Be my guest."

Balancing the bucket under the spout, Jack began thrusting the handle. After two strokes, a robust stream of water spurted from the spigot.

After filling the container, he dipped a hand into the liquid and then smelled the water. It carried a fresh, unpolluted scent and was crystal clear.

Heather took her turn, adding water to the bucket first. She was far more careful with her milk jug, placing what appeared to be a coffee filter on the container's mouth to ensure none of Yellowstone's junk made it inside. "Always fill the bucket first," she explained. "Then make sure the spout is good and clean for the drinking water."

"Let me guess," Jack smiled. "The bucket is for the toilet and washing?"

"Yes, it is," she nodded. "I'm lucky that Mom's house has its own septic system. I know a few people who live closer to town that had some very smelly issues. As long as I feed it water, the bad stuff still flushes away," she giggled at the euphemism. Jack couldn't help but notice that her eyes smiled in the process and how charming she was in her speech. She continued her narrative in a more matter-of-fact tone, "I use half of this bucket to fill the john, the other half to wash dishes and to bathe. Once a week, I make two trips and fill the bathtub. Once a month, I even heat the water. That is my favorite day... it gives me something to look forward to."

Nodding, Jack was a bit envious at her mention of neighbors. "How many people have survived in Drews?"

Her demeanor changed immediately and she became gloomy, shaking her head at the remembrance and making Jack instantly regret the insensitive inquiry. "I'm sorry," he quickly apologized. "I didn't mean to intrude."

"No, no, it's alright," she finally replied. "It's just so hard to think about. There are only about 10 people left alive as far as I know."

"Really? That's amazing. I would have never guessed that in a community this size so many would have made it."

With her jug of water now full, Heather carefully screwed on the cap and then stood. "The ash killed those who didn't stay indoors and filter their air. Within two weeks, the water was tainted, and that finished off another percentage of the population. By this time, the folks who were left started scavenging additional provisions from those who didn't make it. After that, when food supplies got low, survival of the fittest kicked in. Those strong enough to take provisions from the weak did," Heather sighed and paused before continuing her story. "Unfortunately, most of the 'taking' involved the business end of a weapon. In short, we killed each other for several weeks."

It took her answer a moment to sink in. When it finally did, Jack's head snapped up and began searching the area while his hand reached for the carbine.

His reaction caused her to laugh again. "It's okay here... and along the trail. There's a truce in effect now. I don't know if we all wised up, or if we just got tired of the butchery, but as long as we stay on the path, no one from Drews will bother us."

"A truce?"

"Yes... a peace treaty of sorts," she nodded. Heather then noticed the sky in the west, a scowl knotting her brow when she realized the heavens were growing dark and angry. "We better be heading back. That looks like a storm might be brewing, and believe me, we don't want to be caught outside if it's one of the bad ones."

"Oh, I believe you," Jack replied, his eyes now following her gaze. "If it's anything like the lightning storms I've passed through, they can really put a damper on a good apocalypse," he teased in an attempt to cut the tension prompted by the life-threatening squall.

"We haven't had one of those in over two months now, but I'm aware of what you're talking about. Nor have I seen any of the acid rain since right after the eruption. Lately, they just kick up a lot of wind and stir around the ash. It makes it really hard to see, and I'm worried this cheap mask won't protect my lungs."

Wasting no time, Jack hefted the bucket and picked up the pace, heading back toward town. He could hear Heather's footfalls behind him.

Approaching the gully, they worked their way carefully down the steep embankment so as not to spill the sloshing water. With painstaking care, the commander reached the crest, pausing briefly for Heather to catch up. She had just inhaled after climbing out of the ditch when a bullet kicked up a spike of dirt next to Cisco's boot.

The precious liquid now forgotten, Jack dove to the ground, landing badly as another round whizzed over his head. He couldn't make out the shooter but had a pretty good idea where the culprit was hiding.

Rolling hard toward a small mound of dirt, the commander managed to bring his carbine up and began scanning for a target.

"What the hell," Heather's breathless voice sounded from a few feet behind him. "Hey!" she then yelled to the attacker, "We're on the damn water trail! Why are you shooting at us?"

Another shot rang out, this one aimed at Heather's voice. It found its mark.

With a yelp of pain, she grabbed her side and went down, a burning, red-hot stripe of agony now streaking across her midsection. "I'm hit," she growled, scooting away to examine her wound.

Jack spied a patch of cloth through the underbrush, his barrel moving to the right as he snapped three shots. He then lowered his aim to knee level, and let go four more rounds of 5.56 NATO pain.

A scream let the commander know he'd ruined someone's day, but he felt no regret. Before he could adjust to finish the job, a volley of shots sounded from his front.

Bullets were flying everywhere, some passing harmlessly overhead, others slapping into the sandy soil uncomfortably close to Cisco's prone frame. Jack's mind quickly realized the safety of the gully. He knew that in their current position, they were outnumbered and desperately needed cover.

"We can't stay here," he shouted, figuring there were at least five shooters. "We have to get back to the ditch. Can you move?"

Before she could answer, another barrage pummeled the ground around them, Jack's hand stinging as a near miss drove chips of stone shrapnel into his flesh. The attacker's aim was getting better with each exchange – it wouldn't be long before they were killed, or overrun.

Rolling once left, he sent a spread into the underbrush, his sights picking lanes more from instinct than any visible target. He'd learned to trust the deeper parts his brain when the action was moving faster than his conscious mind could register. He fired from gut feel, not visibility.

The expenditure of ammunition wasn't intended to connect with any specific target, but to keep the attackers down, scared, and away. He desperately needed to buy time and distance and was more than willing to use bullets to pay the bill.

Five shots here, six over there, another four up the middle, the carbine pushing insistently against his shoulder as hot lead split the West Texas air. He rolled right, switched magazines, and then began working the trigger again.

Another salvo roared from the underbrush, most of the rounds impacting where Cisco had been lying just a moment before. They had to get to the gully; there just wasn't enough protection from the growing skirmish. Whoever was trying to kill them had some skills and would probably rush them any time now. That would be the end.

He chanced a backward glance at Heather, pleased to find she was back-crawling toward the ditch, dragging her shotgun after each painful movement. "Go! Hurry!" he snapped before re-welding his cheek to the rifle's stock. "Move!"

Six more rounds ripped blindly through the brush, and then Jack began imitating his new friend. Back he pushed, his hands digging into the loose soil while cradling the carbine in the nook of his arms. His eyes never left the weed line to his front, waiting for the enemy to rise and charge.

He hadn't made it four feet before the return fire bellowed in, this time from two directions. The foe had split its forces. Now, they were trying to flank him from both the right and left. Smart. Very smart.

Jack didn't bother countering the salvo, instead choosing to focus on making it to the gully. It was going to be close.

Now the bad guys began a steady stream of incoming rounds, the bullets sizzling past Jack's head like a swarm of angry insects. He felt something tug at the load vest across his back, and hot lead nicked the sole of his boot.

And then the earth disappeared from under his feet, followed a second later by Heather's surprisingly firm grip pulling him backward down the bank.

"Thanks," Jack barked, regaining his composure and hefting the rifle back to his shoulder. "Keep your eyes to the right; I'll take the left. I think they're coming in from both directions."

With the wall of dirt to his front and only the very top of his head exposed, Jack's entire outlook suddenly improved. Now he waited with the eye of a predator, no longer the prey. "Come on in," he hissed. "The party's just getting started."

Despite his ears ringing from the carbine's bark and his heart hammering in his chest, Jack could now distinguish voices in the distance. He couldn't understand the faint words, nor could he pinpoint their position, yet he was confident someone was issuing orders. Such an organized attack couldn't be good.

Heather's shotgun signaled the next round of the bout was on, the 12-gauge's throaty roar initially giving the commander a start. Two human forms simultaneously popped up less than 50 yards to their front. Both men fired one shot each and then dove for the ground before Jack could center on either target.

Then a third aggressor rose, more to the left. Jack swung his barrel as the man fired his own scattergun, the pellets sending up a geyser of soil less than a foot in front of the commander's face. Heather shot again, then again. Her arms worked the pump action in a blur of familiarity and speed.

The first duo then reappeared, this time 10 yards closer. Jack was onto the game now and didn't bother adjusting his aim. He stayed left, waiting for the man with the 12-gauge.

Up number three popped, this time much closer, the shotgun's barrel like a deep, black hole as it steadied on Jack's head. Cisco snuffed the man before he could pull the trigger, three lead pills tearing into the shooter's chest at 3260 feet per second. The shotgun fired skyward as its owner fell.

Swinging his weapon back right, Jack was almost too late to engage the counter-acting pair as they rose. He hit one of them, the impact of his bullets knocking the fellow's leg outward into an odd spiral.

The rogue's partner dove for cover before firing a single round.

More voices now, someone from Heather's side of the firefight conversing with another on Jack's side of the equation.

"Can you hear them?" Jack asked, his ears ringing like he was inside of a bell.

"No, but I can tell you they're speaking Spanish," she panted.

He glanced over at her waist, sure the bushwhackers wouldn't attack again while in the middle of a conversation. A large circle of red now covered most of her blue jeans from just above her right thigh to her midsection. "How bad?" he asked.

"It hurts like hell," she grunted, loading two more shot shells into her weapon. "I think the bullet just grazed me. Nothing vital is hit; I'm sure of that."

He thought it was a lot of blood for a flesh wound, but he didn't voice his opinion. He needed her in the fight, or they would both be bleeding a lot more.

Realizing that it had been quiet now for several seconds, Jack returned to his optic, ready for the second assault. Instead, a single voice sounded over the empty field. "We only want the woman. Let her go free, and we'll let you live!"

Exchanging puzzled glances, Jack and Heather were both confused. "Do they think I've kidnapped you?" he asked.

"Who knows," she whispered. "Maybe they want a sex toy or some other sick shit."

"He used the words, 'Go free,'" Jack countered. "That typically relates to a prisoner. Are they friends of yours? Did they see me and think I have shanghaied you?"

Shrugging, she yelled back at the shooters, "What? What the hell are you talking about? We were just out getting water, and you people tried to murder us. What do you want?"

"Heather?" the distant, questioning voice queried, its tone almost hopeful.

Jack glanced at his new friend, now completely confused. She was apparently just as perplexed.

After a few seconds, she brightened and then in a hesitant voice, shouted, "Miguel?"

"Yes, it's me. I heard you were back."

Anger now shrouded her face, "You almost killed me, you stupid jerk! Why did you start firing at us? What in the hell are you doing?"

"We only meant to take out the man!" he angrily retorted.

His answer was like throwing gasoline on an already white-hot fire. The screaming, raw neurons in her bleeding torso were momentarily drowned out by her intense fury. Before Jack could react, Heather crawled out of the gully, her body fueled by pure rage.

Now at the top of the ditch, Heather wobbled slightly, her legs weak and beginning to fail under her weight. Her stumble seemed to infuriate her even more, catapulting her ire to new heights.

"What are you doing?" Jack shouted, "Get back down here!"

He thought she was insane, exposing herself to a group of cutthroat killers who had just done their best to aerate their hides. She was bleeding, in pain, and obviously out of control. *She has a pair*, Jack had to admit. Perhaps it was bravery to a fault, but he had to respect the iron that obviously ran through her core. "Heather, don't. Wait!" he tried again.

She ignored him, now marching through the sand as she made for the sound of Miguel's voice.

Awestruck, he had a front-row seat for her tirade. She was a vision, her hair blowing back in the breeze, shoulders straight and wide, head held high in defiance. The shotgun never wavered, an icon of impressive strength and undeniable will. Jack was mesmerized. He'd never seen a woman quite like Heather Lanier.

As Jack watched helplessly, a figure appeared from the weeds, a tall, thin, young man wearing a mask across the lower half of his face.

"You! You… Cerdo estúpido!" Heather shouted as the masked man approached. "You just shot me, you stupid pig! Look! I am bleeding! What were you thinking?"

Miguel, for his part, evidently decided that silence was the best strategy, at least for the moment. A few seconds later, they were face to face.

"Well? Did the Marine Corps make you a mute?"

The man did not respond to her brazen query, at least not at first. "I'm sorry," he eventually mumbled. "We didn't mean for you to get hurt. We saw you leave your Mom's house alone, and then that man over there came out of the brush. We thought he was trying to hurt you."

Heather was so frustrated that she couldn't find any words to express her exasperation. Pointing an angry finger, her lips moved, but nothing came out. Her arms flew wide, but again, only silence filled the air. Finally regrouping, she managed, "What are you doing back in Drews?"

Before he could answer, a gust of wind blew, kicking up a cloud of ash and sand. "Shit," Jack cursed; they had forgotten about the storm.

He couldn't hear if Miguel answered, another blow buffeting the area, generating a stinging blizzard of powdery ash. Before the wind settled down, a rolling clap of thunder sounded to the west.

With her adrenaline dump now burning off, Heather tried again to shout at the man standing before her. The effort was drowned out by the howling atmosphere.

Just as frustrated and not wanting to be caught out in the elements, Miguel dismissed the angry woman with a wave of his hand and then motioned for his men to join him. Both Heather and Jack watched as four others rose and turned toward town in retreat.

One of the shooters, his face obscured by a skull mask, turned and flipped Jack a middle finger before darting off. "La venganza le visitará, Señor," he shouted. Revenge will visit you, sir.

Just like that, they disappeared into the weeds and swirling ash. Another boom shook the ground as Jack began climbing out of the ditch. "We have to get inside," he yelled at Heather. "Now!"

She was already scampering toward shelter, her legs weak from the pain and loss of blood. She did manage to wave Jack forward, as if he needed direction.

By the time they passed the house where the commander's bicycle was hidden, the storm was raging with all its fury. Both Jack and Heather had to trudge along, bent forward, to keep from being bowled over by the wind, the biting ash stinging their eyes and any exposed skin.

Lightning split the sky as they approached the Lanier residence, Jack flinching as a third and then fourth bolt struck nearby in rapid succession. "We haven't had one this intense in a while," the local yelled as another strike streaked through the darkening clouds.

The skies succumbed to inky blackness as Heather led the commander to a small stoop. Fumbling with a key in the dark, she flung open the door and hastily dashed inside. Jack's eyes searched the murky landscape but were only able to detect the brick veneer of a modest home. "Let's get downstairs, just in case," Heather shouted with far too much force, her brain still in fighting-the-wind's-volume mode.

The commander was led down a series of narrow steps, the duo pausing to rest in an area not much larger than the average bathroom. The flash of a lit match illuminated the tiny room, Heather then applying the flame to a single candle.

Jack knew instantly they were in the home's root cellar, several nearby shelves full of mason jars brimming with carrots, potatoes, corn, and other delicacies. "My mom planted a garden every summer," Heather explained, noting his gaze. "When the crops started producing, she was always in the kitchen tending her pressure cooker, getting ready to can what she had harvested that day."

"Wow," Jack said with wonder in his eyes. "I didn't think anybody did that anymore."

"She was pretty old fashioned when it came to a lot of things. For years, I thought the habit was completely silly, but I didn't say anything because I figured it was good for her to have a hobby. Now… well… now, it's keeping me alive."

Jack realized his host was talking about her mother in the past tense. "What happened?" he asked in a somber tone. Before she could answer, he spotted her bleeding side. There was a fresh, wet, expanding area of crimson soaking her through her pants and shirt at her waistline. "Here. Let me take a look at that wound."

The commander spied an antique daybed in the corner and gently guided her to recline. "Now, I need you to relax as much as possible. And just so you know, in order to get a good look at this, I need to unbutton your jeans and raise your shirt." His eyes connected with hers, nonverbally seeking her permission before proceeding. She inhaled deeply and rested her head on the pillow as if she had made the decision to trust him. Her apparent logic and ability to make a sound decision under pressure impressed him.

Noting the queue, he gently unzipped her jeans and folded the cloth to one side to expose the injury. In so doing, he revealed the top of a very sheer pink thong covering her flat midsection. A micro-second later, his mind flashed hot with the image of the bikini-clad girl splashing in the ocean. *Damned hormones!* he chided, shaking his head to clear the mind movie and force his mind back to the present. *Get back to work, Commander!*

Once again, he focused on the critical triage. The steel of his knife glistened in the candlelight as he began carefully cutting away the surrounding cotton of her blouse, the sticky, dried blood requiring a delicate touch.

Initially, Heather was apprehensive, a strange man wielding a substantial knife so close to her body. A moment later, that anxiety eased, and she began talking. "In the weeks following Yellowstone's eruption, mom and I struggled. Using rolls of plastic I bought at Wally World that very morning, I taped and sealed every window except one. I used expanding foam around the front door."

Jack realized Heather was now traveling back in time, the pain in her voice building with every word. "Smart," he mumbled, still working on her waist and welcoming her distraction at the telling.

"Well, actually, I got the idea from a work project. During my NASA days, I was involved in an upgrade to the atmospheric control system on the International Space Station. So, I used a series of furnace filters and a double seal to keep the ash at bay while still allowing for enough airflow to keep our oxygen levels nice and fresh. I used the success of that study when I closed the house. I even left a single window and the back door accessible."

"What did your mom think of that?" he asked, imagining Heather running around with plastic wrap and handfuls of filters.

Heather's chuckle was warm, but short. "She thought I was crazy… thought I had gone completely off my rocker."

"I bet," Jack snickered, joining in on the light-hearted moment with a big grin, silently admiring her ingenuity and survival inclination.

In the flickering glow, Jack noticed her expression return to a frown. "Mom thought I had gone mad, but in fact, it was my precious mother who was having issues. I tried to warn her, tried a dozen times to get through that thick skull of hers. I kept telling her that she couldn't go outside. Somehow, she just couldn't accept that the air and water would kill her."

"That's too bad," Jack agreed, shaking his head. "From what I've heard, there were a lot of people who just couldn't accept that Mother Nature had turned against us."

"'But what about my garden?' Mom kept asking. She was disoriented and not thinking clearly. I explained a hundred times that Yellowstone had launched billions of tons of rock, soil, ash, and poisonous gasses into the air. I explained that we were going to have to survive the most brutal winter ever, that we couldn't go outside, that everything exposed to the ash was going to die."

"How old was she?" Jack asked, knowing where the story was going.

"She was 67," Heather responded, sniffing and then wiping away the tear that had streamed down her cheek.

For the next 20 minutes, she continued to share her story, explaining how the cruel tentacles of Alzheimer's had already burrowed their way into Mrs. Lanier's mind.

Despite the situation, regardless of their surroundings, Jack couldn't help but notice Heather's beauty. She had just been shot, welcomed a hobo into her home, and yet maintained an angelic face, clear eyes, and a steady voice.

Somehow, the woman sitting by him possessed an inner strength that fueled her glowing countenance. She wasn't movie-star gorgeous, but oozed both confidence and grace in her actions. Sure, her hourglass shape was notable, and when combined with radiant skin and fresh hair, was easy on the eye. There was more, however. She projected a wholesome, intelligent balance that Jack couldn't help but find attractive.

It's amazing how doomsday can alter a man's vision of a desirable female companion, he thought, mentally reviewing her impressive intellect, intense willpower, and unwavering resolve. Glamour girls weren't so much in demand, besides no one was producing fancy foundations and eyelash-curling mascaras anymore. No, surface beauty held little value and didn't matter as much as being healthy these days. Delicate wasn't as sexy as solid and robust. Skinny super models wouldn't last long in these times. They would be a burden, unable to carry their own water. The young lady beside him was down-to-earth, fit, vigorous, capable, and yet completely feminine.

She was an incarnation of pioneer women who had been ready to fight or work beside their men during the worst of it.

Still, now is not the time to be a sailor on leave, he reflected. *Down, boy. You're an officer and a gentleman in addition to being a married man. Don't forget that.*

Working with the softest touch possible, Jack tugged away the strips of her clothing, inhaling sharply at the deep trench of raw, bleeding flesh right at the beltline. "That's going to need some work," he whispered. "And it's going to hurt a little. Keep talking while I take care of it. It will help distract both of us."

She didn't say anything for a bit, watching with those deep green eyes as Jack extracted a roll of bandages from the medical kit on his vest. Next, he removed a small pump bottle of topical antibiotic spray and a package of gauze squares.

She gulped abruptly when he shot a mist of the antibiotic onto the open wound, her reaction causing him to mumble a sincere, "Sorry, but if that gets infected, you're in a lot of trouble."

"No problem," she replied, quickly regaining control. Then, with another deep breath, she resumed her narrative again. "That first morning when the ash had begun to fall, I climbed out of bed to find Mom singing 'Frosty the Snowman' in the backyard. She thought the whole thing was like one of those old black and white Christmas movies, spinning in circles with her hands spread wide."

Not knowing how to respond, Jack just nodded as he continued to treat her injury. Heather, after wincing at his touch, kept on going.

"Three nights later, I almost shot my own mother. She decided, before sunrise, to head outside, intending to check on a dear friend. Mom couldn't get the sealed front door to cooperate, so she proceeded to use a hammer to open it. I woke up, thinking someone was trying to break in."

The storyteller and medic were interrupted, a close-by lightning strike shaking the cellar's roof. After listening to the thunder roll off across the desert, she returned to her tale. "We spent the first week playing board games, laughing over old family photographs, and trying to be creative with the canned food stored down here. The electrical power and water failed in the first few days, but the natural gas for the cooking stove lasted for almost two weeks. After that, I hooked up a propane tank Dad used for the grill."

"And you guys stayed inside the entire time?"

"Yes," she nodded. "But by the end of the second week, I was starting to experience some pretty intense bouts of cabin fever. I even caught myself in some bizarre behavior, like checking and double-checking the window seals, paranoid that there was a leak somewhere in the house. A minute later, I would be positive that the ash had settled enough to go outside. I craved a salad, would give anything to smell fresh air, and was sure that the walls were closing in around me. It took every ounce of my willpower to keep my sanity." Heather paused and sighed, before continuing, "Mom had been diagnosed with dementia several years ago, and that disease put her in no condition to survive these conditions."

"I can actually relate to cabin fever," Jack acknowledged, shaking his head at the painful memory. "Having spent months at a time on a submarine, I've had similar experiences. Hell, I almost sank our boat on my first patrol."

"Again and again, Mom's diseased mind faltered," the patient reported. "She almost burned down the house by mishandling the candles. In the first month, I found her wandering aimlessly outside, without a mask, over a half-dozen times."

"The ash took her, didn't it?"

Heather began sobbing, wiping her nose on a sleeve. "It was the fourth week when she started coughing. The next day, there was blood in the old lace handkerchief she always used to cover her mouth. I knew then it wouldn't be long before I would be alone."

Pulling her close, Jack wrapped his arms around her, feeling the emotion as the sobs racked the woman's body. Between sniffles, she managed, "The next day, Mom couldn't get out of bed. The following night, she stopped breathing. She drowned in her own blood."

Jack embraced her tightly, his own mind wondering how many others had suffered a similar fate.

"For some reason, I couldn't cry that day," Heather confessed. "It was almost as if I was relieved by Mom's passing away. Now, I'd give anything to talk to her again. It took me two days to dig a deep enough hole to bury her, and even then, I was afraid the shallow grave would be scavenged by wild dogs or other animals."

Heather then surprised Jack, a sharp laugh resonating from her throat. "It never occurred to me that I hadn't seen another animal or person for over a week. Even the birds and houseflies had disappeared. I was grieving so deeply I obviously wasn't thinking clearly myself."

"You're lucky you didn't get sick," Jack observed.

"Burying Mom did prove one thing, that wearing the paint masks worked. Yeah, all that huffing and puffing over the shovel left a wet grey spot, but I didn't get sick. I felt like the shackles had been taken off. I could leave the house if I was careful."

Her voice then dropped low, the painful memories flowing again. "I wanted to be as gentle as possible, but I was not strong enough to lift her. I wrapped my mother in a clean, white sheet and dragged her to the edge of the garden. After a short prayer and goodbye, I just automatically began shoveling the dirt to cover her body."

"You've been through so much," Jack said, admiring the lady beside him even more. "That damn volcano has caused so much death and pain. I sometimes wonder if we're really the lucky ones."

She ignored his cynicism, somehow needing to chat about her recent past, "The following week I cracked open the last case of bottled water. Mom and I had filled the bathtubs to flush the toilets, drinking and cooking with the pure water as carefully as possible. I remembered thinking that the end of that case would be the end of my life. I tried to concoct some sort of filter. I found a half bag of BBQ charcoal in the garage and tried to configure a strainer. I knew that NASA had been recycling liquids on various spacecraft since the Apollo program, so I realized there had to be a way."

"Did your plan work?" Jack asked, now curious about the knowledge she had gained. A million times he had considered how critical some sort of filter could be in the future survival of his family... and of all mankind.

"The technical issues kept me up at night. I toyed with a myriad of configurations of pots, pans, and other kitchen utensils. I cut up the garden hose and incorporated some spare pipe out in the garage. One troubling question kept popping up – how could I test the results without risking my own life?"

Now that her mind was beyond the tragic death of her mother, Jack answered with humor. "Capture a prisoner and make him drink the water?"

She laughed, but it was thin. "Funny," she weakly responded.

"So, where did your experiments get you? Since you're walking back and forth to the well, I assume you gave up?"

"Just like school and work," she exhaled. "I resorted to solving one problem at a time. About that time, it dawned on me, I didn't have any water to test my device."

Rubbing his chin, Jack guessed, "So you went exploring and found the well?"

"I'd had my father's shotgun beside my bed since arriving home. I filled a pocket full of shells, donned a white mask, wrapped a cotton scarf around my mouth for good measure, and set off on a grand adventure."

He began wrapping her with a bandage, careful with the tension. Each orbit of her waist resulted in a light whimper emitting from her throat. "That's going to hurt a lot for a while. You've lost a little tissue, but I don't think there's any permanent damage."

"So much for next year's bikini season," she grunted, staring at the wound.

He stood, sipping a drink of water while glancing around the cellar for a second look. Working on her injury reminded him of the most crucial question of the day. "Who were those guys?" he wondered aloud.

Ignoring his question, she continued talking about her first trip into what was essentially a new world. "It was so strange that day, hiking away from the front yard, the yellow and browns of my childhood now replaced by the greys and silvers of Yellowstone's ash. Everything was covered in at least two inches of the stuff. Mailboxes, fence posts, and even the utility lines looked like they had just endured a heavy blizzard of snow. The pumice was heavier than water... many of the lines snapping under the weight. The ash crunched under my sneakers, but that was the only noise I heard. At first, I thought the covering was deadening all sound, but then I realized there was nothing left alive to make any racket. It was the most lonely, isolated feeling I've ever had.

For a long time, I wondered if I were the only living being left on the planet."

"I bet that was depressing," Jack observed, now questioning why Heather wouldn't address the white elephant in the room. He was determined to press. "Who were those guys?"

With a deep sigh, she looked down at the floor and frowned. "An old flame... his name is Miguel. I thought he was still in the Marine Corps. We were an item in high school."

"I thought as much," Jack nodded. "Let me guess, after graduation, you went to college, and he left to serve in the military."

Now, she was in another place. "Actually, it was over before graduation. He was the school's star quarterback... tall, handsome, and cocky. He was so full of himself. He thought life meant getting a job in the oil patch, buying a double-wide, and popping out as many kids as possible before his wife's womb gave out. He was the hometown hero who thought that life began and ended right here in Drews. I believed there was a great big world out there and wanted to see all of it. I guess after Yellowstone was finished, we were both wrong."

"You mentioned that there was a truce along the path to the well, but Miguel didn't seem to know about it," Jack paused, watching her expression as he probed. "So... you didn't know Miguel was back in Drews?"

"No," she responded. "I've only run into a handful of people, most of them surviving in the hospital's basement. I guess the ventilation system there was designed for infection control and was a little more robust than most. Anyway, I had no idea Miguel, or those other men, were in the area."

"Maybe he came back to find his family?"

Shaking her head, Heather answered, "I doubt it. After he left for the Marines, Mom told me his family packed up and moved during the last recession. I think she said they went down to Midland, hoping to find work."

"So, what is he doing here?"

"No idea," she responded, her voice soft and distant. "There's no reason why he would have come back that I know of."

Jack thought he had a pretty good idea about Miguel's motive for returning, but didn't say anything. The Marine wanted his old girlfriend back, and for some reason that the commander couldn't quite fathom, the thought of Heather with such a man made Cisco's stomach hurt.

Chapter 33

An hour passed before Jack and Heather realized that the storm had finally passed. The commander was anxious to retrieve his bicycle.

Climbing the stairs, Jack was impressed as his host gave him a tour, showing off her efforts to secure her mother's home. It was also the first time he had used a proper toilet in weeks.

As Jack strolled from room to room, he noted every detail. An eclectic collection of seaside snow globes adorned the tops of all the living room furniture and mantel. One large wall was devoted to a pictorial history of Heather's life and achievements, from her hospital footprints to her Summa Cum Laude sheepskin. The opposite wall displayed an assortment of photographs of an older couple enjoying their middle-class life, grilling in the backyard, attending the church picnic, and watching the local Christmas parade together.

"Your dad?" Jack asked, pointing at a picture of a beaming man showing off a large, just-landed fish.

"Yes. He died about five years ago from heart failure. At least he lived long enough to see me graduate from college."

"It looks like they had a good life together," he replied, eyes dropping to the floor.

"Mom was never the same after he passed away. She lost dad and me about the same time. I graduated and moved to Houston, and less than a year later, I got the phone call that he had collapsed while helping her in the garden. He lasted long enough for me to kiss him and say goodbye."

They continued the tour mostly in silence, Jack noting that Heather skipped her own bedroom.

She seemed to brighten when they returned to the kitchen. "I have enough food downstairs to last several more months if I'm careful," she bragged. "With the water from the well, I almost have a normal life, albeit a lonely one."

"There *are* people out there," Jack reassured. "I've run into the good, the bad, and the ugly. I suppose it's just like it was before the volcano blew, an equal mix of holy and evil."

"Are there a lot of folks still alive?" she asked, her face hopeful.

"No," Jack replied. "Not many at all, at least compared to before. Let me retrieve my bike, and I'll bore you with my story while we eat."

She struggled to the kitchen and then remembered, "We didn't manage to get any water! I have enough for now, but eventually, we'll have to finish what we started."

After watching even basic movements cause her pain, Jack shook his head. "I'll bring my wheels back and then go on a water run. You need to rest."

Stepping outside brought back the reality of Jack's world, the melancholy grey environment seeming so harsh and bleak compared to the soft, warm, inviting interior of Mrs. Lanier's home.

For the first time in his life, Jack appreciated the trappings, the faded couch in the living room, the doilies adorning the end tables, and the assortment of seaside knickknacks. He had always overlooked such trimmings, more interested in the size of the television or the quality of the pool table's felt. His perspective had shifted.

Behind him, the Laniers had created more than a structure of brick, drywall, paint, and carpet. In there was a home, a humble place that welcomed the heart and radiated comfort. He paused, contemplating if he would ever dwell in such a place again. Mylie had tried, but the constant transfers and reassignments made it difficult to set down roots. The always seemed to be loading their lives into cardboard boxes.

His bike was right where he'd left it, hidden under the scattered clothing two streets over. Other than a downed tree, no doubt a victim of the storm, nothing appeared to have been disturbed.

He pushed his ride back to Heather's home, deciding to stash it inside if his new friend didn't mind. "Care if I keep my only earthly possession under your roof?" he asked, finding her working in the kitchen despite the doctor's order to rest.

"Why do you say that? You can have practically anything on the planet. It's all sitting out there, just waiting for a survivor to walk over and pick it up."

Jack frowned, trying to come up with the words. "My brain doesn't work that way. I don't like taking things that aren't mine."

"Mr. Borden, right across the street, was quite a cyclist. He was as old as my mom and rode at least 20 miles a day. I think he had about ten bikes in his garage, including one of those fat-tire models. He didn't survive the ash, and now his house has been looted at least three times. If you needed one of those bikes… had to have it to survive, who would it hurt if you took what you needed? Who do those bikes belong to? Mr. Borden doesn't care anymore. Neither does his family because they're all dead, too."

Shaking his head, Jack replied, "But they're not mine."

"So, you are telling me that you carried around this bicycle on your submarine, Commander?"

Knowing he'd been had, Jack's lips turned into a scowl. Yes, he had pilfered the bike. "I see your point," he said. "The line between scavenging resources for survival and selfishly looting can be a fine one, and no doubt folks would disagree which is which," he acknowledged.

"I would imagine that anyone who has survived has taken liberties with ethics to do so," she responded. Then, with a dismissive wave, she continued, "No time for philosophical arguments about apocalyptic morality. You better go and get some water before we run out. You need a bath; I need water to cook breakfast. How do beans and corn sound?"

Jack started to protest, tempted to tell her that his last two meals had been beans and corn. He held his tongue. "Sounds great," he answered, not wanting to spoil her creative spirit.

Taking a milk jug and bucket, he prepared to exit by wrapping his mouth and nose. The carbine was strapped tightly against his chest.

He didn't see any new or old tracks along the path, the storm's wind having blown clear any obvious signs of usage. That all changed as he arrived at the edge of the empty lot.

The freshly drifted ash was covered in multiple boot prints. Jack dropped low, replacing his grip on the containers with the cold metal and plastic of his rifle. "They came back for the bodies," he whispered after seeing what appeared to be drag marks. "Miguel has more leadership skills than I gave him credit for. Men will fight harder if their officers honor the fallen."

He strayed off the path, moving on his hands and knees to keep his profile lower than the surrounding brush. He paused often, listening, trying again to extend his senses.

"You're an idiot, Commander," he chided after not receiving any input, normal or otherwise.

Making his way to the location where he was sure he'd dropped one of Miguel's soldiers, Jack found blood stains and more drag marks in the ash. "He didn't waste any time after the storm was over. This is a man who has ambitions."

Satisfied that the rogues had vacated the area, Jack returned to retrieve his containers and complete his mission. It had been a busy day, and even beans with a side of corn sounded good.

He approached the gully, still alert, but confident there was no threat. He trekked down the bank and was halfway up the other side when the sand next to his head exploded in a fountain.

He fell instantly back down the embankment, his weapon coming up as the safety clicked off. The shot had originated in front of him... from the trailer between him and the well. "Did Mr. Campos come back from the dead?" he pondered.

"You! In the ditch! The well is now closed! This is my family's land and water. Leave or die!" someone to his front demanded. He had heard this voice before; the shooter was none other than Miguel.

"Why are you doing this?" Jack challenged. "These people will die without water."

"This is my well," Miguel answered with a sneer. "I don't want to share the water with anyone. Either find other water, or leave."

Before Jack could respond, he heard movement to his right. Two seconds later, there was a footfall to his left. *Miguel is getting frisky*, the commander thought. *Pretty brave considering I killed two of his boys just a few hours ago.*

Cisco's heart told him to stay and fight it out. According to Heather, a handful of people still lived in the town, and they would need that

289

water. Besides, Jack was tired of tin-pan dictators and power-hungry thugs.

Jack's gut quickly overrode the urge to take a stand. He was grossly outnumbered, alone, and had gotten lucky before. This wasn't his fight. He began to back away.

Returning to Heather without water was far more troubling than Jack anticipated. As he entered the back door, she read his expression instantly. "What's wrong?"

He explained Miguel's warning and subsequent statements, Heather's eyes losing their spark as she backed away and slumped into a nearby chair. "Oh, no. I was afraid of that."

"Is Miguel's last name Campos by any chance?"

She nodded, then answered. "Yes. It was his parents who had the pool."

"So, technically, it *is* his land?"

"Yes, I guess it is. But I still don't understand. If he cuts off everyone's water, what does he hope to accomplish? Does he want to oversee the graveyard? Be the king of the dead?"

Jack didn't bother speculating on another man's unknown motives. "I've seen some pretty strange behavior since everything went to hell. Nothing surprises me anymore," he responded while rubbing his chin as if deep in thought. "By the way, is there another source of water?"

She shook her head. "No, not that I know of. Everybody in town was using the well."

"There's not another working pump?"

"I'm sure most homes had their own wells back in the old days. According to what my parents said, there were a lot of small towns in the west that were trying to attract new residents, and expanding the city's water accessibility was an important consideration to expansion. Drews was no exception. When the city expanded its water system during the 1970s, those wells were filled in or capped off."

She started to stand and nearly fell, a brief grimace of pain crossing her face. Jack was beside her instantly. "What's wrong? The wound?"

She nodded, wiping away the water forming in her eye. "It started throbbing while you were gone."

Jack helped her sit back down and then began unwrapping the bandage. "I was worried about that," he said, looking at the puffy, red flesh surrounding the injury. "The spray I used is only a topical treatment. You need a proper antibiotic. Do you have anything here at the house?"

After thinking for a moment, Heather shook her head. "No, other than her mind, Mom was pretty healthy. She didn't have any meds here. How much trouble am I in?"

Reexamining her gash, he replied, "It's not bad yet, but it is infected. We need some pills."

He rose, pulling open two nearby drawers until he found a clean dishtowel. After tearing the cloth into a few strips, he sprayed the wound again and then reapplied the dressing.

"All of the residences around here were looted in the first month, most of them multiple times. I'm willing to bet the ranch that antibiotics and pain medications were high on everyone's shopping list."

"I wouldn't take that bet," he nodded. "A lot of people believe antibiotics will cure anything. They would have eaten them like candy when they started getting sick."

"The drug stores would have been cleaned out as well," she said. "Meds were probably second on the list after liquor."

Jack agreed, his mind taking a physical inventory of every small town he'd ever visited, trying to figure out where there might be a forgotten stash of lifesaving drugs. "What about the hospital? Didn't you say there were people living there? Would they have kept the looters away?"

Frowning, Heather responded, "It's possible, I suppose. I somehow managed to keep them out of here."

He was getting to the painful stage of dressing her torso and thought keeping her distracted would help. "I've been meaning to ask about that; I'm curious about how you kept the wolves at bay?"

Her eyes glazed over as she went back in time again, her voice becoming a monotone as she revisited those disparaging days after the apocalypse. "I shot one of them on the front porch and left his body there for all to see," she replied without a hint of emotion. "By the time there were three corpses spread around the yard, the mischief-makers moved on. I am not sure if it was the stench or the skeletal remains that made us a less desirable target, but I surely slept better after the bodies stacked up."

Jack wanted to ask more questions but decided now wasn't the time. He could read her pretty well and understood she had pushed back the images of those awful days to some backdoor compartment of her mind. More than once since surfacing off the San Diego coast, he'd done the same.

Still, he was impressed. Here was a stunning woman, down-to-earth and smart, who had somehow managed to survive when practically everyone else had not. She had endured tragedy, horrors beyond imagination, and watched helplessly as the world around her had collapsed. She was alone, uncertain of the future, and without any hope of relief. Yet she still carried on, head held high, and somehow capable of helping a stranger while sharing what little she had left.

While he could use most of those same words to describe his own circumstances, he had additional assets. Being a male had one basic advantage, upper body strength critical to survival in this violent world. In addition, he had military training, access to weapons designed for combat, and the benefit of being a professional war fighter. He suddenly found himself wanting nothing more than to save the young woman at his side.

"Let's eat," she suggested, being more careful this time as she took her feet. "Maybe we'll strategize better on a full stomach."

The meal was hot, fresher than anything from a tin can, and seasoned with both salt *and* pepper. Jack managed to swallow every morsel, despite monopolizing the conversation during dinner. He told her his story, including the people of the Cliff House, Mud Lake, and the battle at Carlsbad. Heather seemed enthralled by the news of his journey and the fact that so many people had survived. Her reaction made him realize just how isolated the woman beside must have felt.

From the beginning, he'd had the company of the men on *Utah*, working together as a team to survive. She had been alone, caring for a sick parent. While he'd been underwater, blissfully ignorant of the developing threat to mankind and thousands of miles away from the eruption, she had watched the world collapse with a front row seat. It made Jack appreciate her even more.

"That was excellent," he ended, pushing away his plate.

"Thank you," she answered. "You know, it's getting dark outside. We need to do the dishes and then extinguish the candles. I've found it best not to let anyone know I'm up and about. I have my bedroom windows blacked out, so we can move in there. Besides, I also have something important I need to show you."

"Later. Right now, I've got dish duty," he insisted. "You need to stay off your feet."

There was enough water in the kitchen bucket to scrub the plates, Jack finding the smell of the dish soap stronger than he'd remembered. He also wondered if Heather would mind his using some of the thick liquid on his body once they had secured more water.

He then plodded to the side of the house where her bedroom was located, managing to maneuver through the unfamiliar layout by the last, remaining natural light leaking in from outdoors.

Rapping lightly on the closed door, he heard her say, "Come on in, but don't get any ideas, Commander. I'm not a girl who has a habit of inviting strange men into my bedroom."

"For survival purposes only," he kidded back.

"Your surprise is in there," she nodded, indicating the attached bathroom.

Hesitating, he peered inside the white-tiled facility, finding a bucket of water, washcloth, and bar of soap sitting beside the tub. "I have an emergency supply of water – just in case," she explained. "Mom bought soap in bulk at the warehouse store. I'm sorry I couldn't heat the water, but that should make you feel a little more human. I'll leave you to your bath."

She closed the door behind him, leaving Jack to wonder just how offensive was his man-odor was. Shrugging, he decided she'd handled the hygiene topic as delicately as possible and began to undress.

He had just wetted the wash rag when she knocked again and then handed him a bundle of clothing through the narrow opening of the door. "Pass me out your dirty clothes, and I'll see if I can freshen them up a bit. These were my dad's. They should fit you well enough."

He found a pair of worn blue jeans, flannel shirt, boxer shorts, and a pair of socks. They smelled freshly laundered. "Thank you."

Plugging the sink's drain, he poured half the water into the basin and began washing every inch of his body. The tepid water was chilly at first, but the combination of soap and wet washcloth felt wonderful on his skin.

The sink was bordered by a dark ring of grime by the time he'd finished.

The commander then dipped his hands in the bucket and wetted his hair. He took his time massaging the soap bubbles into his scalp, and then poured the remaining water over his head to rinse.

The clothes were a loose fit, but no worse than the Marine Corps fatigues he'd acquired in San Diego. These days, everything seemed a bit baggy, but he'd manage. The clean garments and lack of grit made him feel almost human again.

He exited to find Heather sitting in a bedside chair, a paperback book in her hands, a small candle burning on a nearby table. "You can sleep on the couch is that's okay. I'm sorry, but I'm not prepared to go in my Mom's room, and the guest room is full of storage boxes."

"No problem," he smiled. "I've been sleeping on the ground for days. The couch will be paradise."

She watched him leave her room, blocking the candle's light with her palm as he exited. "Nite."

"Good night, Heather, and thank you for everything," he said with all sincerity. "Tomorrow, we'll find you some medicine to help that leg."

"I'm counting on it, Commander."

Chapter 34

The following morning, Heather's gunshot was worse, just as Jack had dreaded. "How do I get to the hospital?" he asked after examining her wound.

"In the dining room, the top drawer of the china cabinet, there is a map of Drews. It shows all the businesses in town. I'm not good with directions."

He retrieved the chart, a plastic piece about the size of a placemat. In addition to the standard overhead view of the street grid, several businesses were notated, along with a short description. "This is pretty good," he commented, holding it up to signal his success. "Where did this little gem come from?"

"I think it was some sort of promotion by the chamber of commerce. When everything first fell apart, I found it while searching the house for useful items. Although I'd come back to visit Mom at least once a month, a lot had changed around here since I was a kid, so I found it helpful after I worked up enough nerve to explore town."

Scanning the map, Jack quickly located his chosen destination. "It's not that far," he declared.

"You shouldn't run into anyone on the way there," Heather added. "But when you approach the hospital, avoid the main entrance. Instead, go around to the back, by the loading dock. There is a green metal door there. Knock three times, then once, then another three times. That's the signal I worked out with Dr. Spencer. He's the leader of the survivors there."

"Okay, so you are friends with these people?"

"Our relationship is a little complicated. You see, they are the only other survivors in town, and the doc has suggested strongly that I move in with them. On one hand, I can see the value of community in a situation like this, but I don't really know those people that well." She paused as if deliberating about how much to say before continuing, "And I just have a creepy feeling when I am around Dr. Spencer. I think he is interested in more than the contents of my root cellar."

Jack grinned at her choice of words. "I see… I think."

"I am curious about how he receives you though. So, go downstairs and pick four or five jars of food to barter. I carried pickles the last time, so choose something different. You can tell Dr. Spencer I'm hurt, but no one else. It will help with your negotiations... I think he's a little sweet on me. They invited me to move in with them, but I really don't trust some of his friends."

"Understood," Jack nodded, thinking the doc had good taste. "I'll be back soon."

He decided to walk, his backside still not wholly comfortable being reintroduced to the bike's saddle.

With his magazines topped-off and the map in his hand, Jack left via the back door. A few minutes later, he was working his way toward Main Street.

Heather's scouting report proved to be entirely accurate. The commander didn't note a single sign of human occupation along the route. After a few more blocks of empty buildings and complete silence, he relaxed just enough to truly notice the charm of the town, rather than simply watching for an ambush around every corner.

Cars and pickups still lined the road, most of them covered with a thin coating of ash. He passed a barber shop, family grocery, and then strolled by the public library. "I wonder what the fine is for an overdue book these days," he joked.

He crossed a couple of intersections, finally taking a left turn onto a wide avenue. He spied the hospital's sign a short time later.

It wasn't a large building, only two stories in height and less than a city block long. Still, given the small population and rural environment, Jack supposed that most of the town's residents were proud of the facility.

He had just reached the main driveway when the commander's senses alerted him. An odor waffled through the air, and not a pleasant one at that. A few steps later, Jack recognized the stench of decaying flesh. The carbine came up, the click of its safety breaking the silence.

As he worked his way to the rear of the hospital, the stink became stronger.

He approached the corner, chancing a quick glance toward the loading dock that Heather had promised was there. The area appeared deserted. Nothing was moving.

Twice more, Jack popped his head around the thick limestone wall, taking longer to scan the area with each glance. His finally located the green metal door. Alarm bells sounded in his brain when he realized the rear entrance was standing wide open.

Moving at a jog, Jack made for the loading dock, his eyes constantly seeking the nearest cover should a firefight break out. No one shot at him.

He spotted the bodies a moment later, dumped in a heap outside the green door and partially obstructing it. "Oh, no," he sighed.

He could tell the corpses were fresh, the dead decomposing quickly in the wake of Yellowstone's eruption. After a closer examination, he found that all of them had been shot. He counted nine bodies in the cadaver mound.

"Shit," Jack grunted, scanning the area for any tracks or signs while making double sure that no one was sneaking up on him. "Now I'm going to have to search the hospital for some sort of antibiotic without anyone's help or expertise. And keep an eye out for the other pharmacy shoppers in the process. So much for a quick trip to the ER."

He discovered one last corpse just inside the door. Like the others, the deceased had taken a bullet. As Cisco started to walk off, he noticed a name embroidered on the man's shirt. "Spencer," Jack read, "Nice to meet you, Doc."

"I guess the peace treaty didn't work out," the commander continued, hustling to enter a long hallway.

The building was surprisingly dark inside, Jack having to pull his flashlight and use precious battery power that he wouldn't be able to replace.

He roamed throughout the central area, passing nurses' stations, the check-in desk, a chapel, and several administrative offices. There was no sign of any medications or a pharmacy.

"This looks like it was an orderly evacuation," he observed. All the beds were made, the desks clear, and all paperwork apparently filed neatly away. "I haven't seen anything this tidy since I left *Utah*."

He continued, hoping to find the stairs and search the second floor. On the way, a doorway with a sign caught his attention. "Physician's Lounge," it read.

"I wonder if they left any coffee or doughnuts behind," Jack wondered, pushing open the door with his rifle's barrel.

Just like the rest of the place, the breakroom had been thoroughly sanitized. There wasn't even a sugar packet or creamer beside the coffeemaker. Jack imagined that the facility's survivors had taken the time to scour each floor for supplies while preparing to hunker down and ride out Yellowstone's wrath.

As he spun to return to his search, another plaque on the wall caught Jack's attention. "Fire Escape Route," was printed in bold letters across the top, a diagram of the hospital below. There was a red circle indicating, "You are here."

Now this is what I have been looking for ever since I noticed the unmanned help desk, he mused. Each of the main areas was labeled, including Administration, Maintenance, Surgery, Maternity, Intensive Care, and finally, Pharmacy.

"Eureka!" Jack grinned, now learning exactly where he was headed.

He should have known it was in the basement, the fact that Heather had mentioned that's where the survivors had lived having escaped his memory.

Down the stairs he stepped, feeling like he was finally making some progress.

That enthusiasm quickly evaporated once he was below ground, the hall at the bottom of the stairs full of clutter and debris. "Someone should call housekeeping," he whispered, scanning the mess with his flashlight.

Stepping through overturned chairs, boxes of files, and stacks of bedding, Jack eventually worked his way to a sturdy, steel door marked as the pharmacy. The destruction inside was even more intense.

Every cabinet, drawer, container, and box had been opened, the looters tossing aside anything that didn't hold their interest. Jack bent and picked up a bottle, shining his light on a label that read, "Gelatin Suppositories."

"What a pain in the ass," Jack quipped, continuing his search. Within an hour, he deemed the effort a waste of time and energy. Anything of value, either to cure or treat pain, had been scavenged.

Anger began to swell in Jack's core as he worked his way out of the hospital. Whoever had raided the place had killed the only medical personnel within a hundred miles, and one of the few surviving groups in the region. And then, while the victims bled out, the attackers had scavenged their retreat for food, water, and medical supplies. Why didn't the interlopers simply join forces with Dr. Spencer's group? After all, Heather had been invited to move in with the community. There was plenty or room at the hospital, even if the basement was the only habitable floor. What possible logic could have justified such violence?

Cisco exited the way he had come in, wrinkling his nose at the disgusting stink. The dead did serve one purpose, however. Jack was reminded of Heather and her increasing need for a cure. If he didn't find some antibiotics soon, she would be joining the ranks of the deceased.

He moved out of the odor's range, finding a quiet spot just over a block away. There, he pulled the map of Drews from his pocket, hoping it would inspire a Plan B.

He started at the hospital, looking for something, anything, in the general area that might contain what Heather so desperately needed. He didn't have to look far.

According to the chamber of commerce, there was a complex of doctor's offices on the next block. "Makes sense," Jack mumbled, peering up from the map. "Docs always want to be close to the hospital."

Returning the map to his pocket, Cisco hefted his rifle and began walking. "Doctors have samples. I bet no one thought to look there."

To say Jack was disappointed would have been an understatement. As he approached the row of offices, it was evident that someone had already vandalized the entire area. Chairs, old travel magazines, and artificial plants littered the area near the front, making entering the first door difficult. The reception area was trashed entirely, as were the two examination rooms and the physician's private office. There were pry marks where locked cabinets had been forced open. Other than a few tongue depressors, he didn't notice anything of value.

In the second office, he discovered a small refrigerator full of vials. For just a moment, Jack's heart raced with success when he read the label. "Amoxicillin! That has to be an antibiotic!"

The next line of print, however, deflated his balloon of hope. "Keep refrigerated," he read before slamming the bottle against the wall in frustration. "Shit! This stuff's no good."

"You need to find pills, Commander," Jack whispered, continuing his search. "That narrows it down even more. This is like looking for a needle in the looter's haystack."

The next two physician's offices proved just as fruitless.

Again, he pulled out the map and began scanning. If someone had gone so far as to search medical offices, there was little chance the nearby pharmacy would be anything short of rubble. Still, he had to check. Heather's life was on the line.

He thought of dentists, but didn't believe they ever kept anything but nitrous oxide machines and gum-numbing injections at their locations. He consulted the map and turned to walk toward the local drug store.

As he moved down the empty sidewalk, Jack thought about Sheriff Langdon and the people of the Cliff House. "I sure do seem to be spending a lot of time trying to save people or animals," he whispered, recalling the mission to salvage the herd.

That thought sparked another. "Veterinarians! Animal antibiotics! Aren't they the same? Close enough? Would anybody have thought to scour a vet's office?"

Ducking into the entranceway of a nearby building for cover, Jack pulled his map and began searching for a vet, again optimistic. Sure enough, about eight blocks away, the Drews' Animal Shelter advertised a "full line of veterinary services."

He changed directions, certain the odds were better. *When Fluffy and Rover became sick from the ash, did their owners think to loot the vet for medicine?* he wondered.

He passed a gas station that had burned to the ground, the bones of three bodies protruding from the charred ruins like zombies trying to dig their way out of a grave. Beside it was the shell of a once-thriving hardware store, all of its oversized windows having been shattered in the panic that followed Yellowstone's eruption… its shelves bare and aisles almost empty.

Perhaps it was the ominous scene; maybe it was the abandoned silence of a ghost town. For whatever the reason, the hairs were standing up on the back of his neck. Jack suddenly felt like he was being watched.

He stopped, carefully studying the surroundings, peering in every nook and window. He spotted nothing, but that did little to put him at ease. "Reach out with your senses," he silently reminded himself. "Feel your surroundings. Is there anybody there?"

Impatience quickly set in, Jack feeling like a fool standing in the middle of an empty street while trying to exercise some mystical sixth sense. Pivoting to continue his journey, he was determined to stay even more alert than normal.

The next street showed signs of a firefight, two police cars wrecked in the intersection, both doors open and riddled with bullet holes. Jack observed several body-sized lumps lying under the ash. He left the dead undisturbed.

There it was again, that eerie premonition that told him he wasn't alone. "It's all the dead," he whispered, staring at what was now essentially the town graveyard. "They're spooking you."

Finally arriving at the front of the animal shelter, Jack was initially disappointed. There was a broken window in the door just below a sign that announced, "Closed."

"You have to check," he mumbled.

He tested the door, pushing on it lightly with the barrel of his weapon. The frame had been splintered by forced entry, a finding that caused his heart to sink even further.

Yet, the waiting room appeared undisturbed. A row of chairs, separated by small end tables, remained neat and orderly.

A display of fur-baby brushes, leashes, and collars flanked one wall, none of which appeared to have been touched. The same could be said of the receptionist's desk, a dusty message pad, appointment book, and phone, all sitting where they belonged.

He started for the interior, but then he paused. Getting trapped inside of a building wouldn't do, and he had zero idea if there were another exit. Fire codes aside, the commander couldn't assume there was a back door.

Glancing around the reception area, his eyes settled on the display of doggie accessories. The sighting of a leather collar made him smile. "Alarm bells."

He removed the choker from the packaging and gently jingled the bells.

Moving further inside, Jack pushed on and began his search in earnest. He encountered a hallway that offered several doors. The central area still smelled of antiseptic floor cleaner tempered by a tinge of wet doggie odor. "I bet Spot didn't like this place very much," Cisco noted.

He turned, placing the canine collar on the inside doorknob. If anybody came in behind him, he would know.

The first room was apparently used for storage, and that's where Jack detected the first evidence of looters. A sturdy shelf that covered the entire far wall now stood completely empty. Each rung, however, was labeled with a small tag describing the brand of dog food, weight, and price. "That's why they broke in here. They were after the puppy chow. Must have been pretty hungry. I would have never thought of that."

He continued his exploration, checking a series of examination rooms, a grooming parlor, and a janitor's closet. The final doorway was labeled, "Dr. Broncoski."

Jack found the entrance locked, and that actually was good news. Looters typically didn't relock doors after they were finished. It took three strong kicks from his boot to gain entry. Inside he spotted a desk, a metal locker, two filing cabinets, and a small refrigerator that was nearly identical to the one where he'd found the liquid antibiotics.

The tall, metal locker seized his attention first. The door was securely locked, and that was a problem. Not having any tools, Jack pondered blasting the damn thing open, but then reconsidered. The noise might attract whomever had killed the hospital staff, or the bullet could damage the contents inside. "That would just be your luck, Commander," he quipped. "Your gun-happy ass would probably start a fire. Or worse yet, the round would ricochet, and then we would have two wounded patients."

Remembering a toolbox in the janitor's closet, Jack hustled back to see what might be of use. He returned with a long-handled screwdriver, claw hammer, and the intent to break and enter.

Lacking criminal expertise, the venture took longer than he expected, prying, punching, bending, and kicking. A fair amount of cursing accompanied the physical effort. Finally, the door surrendered, and Jack smiled for the first time that day. Inside were several shelves, all laden with various pet medications.

He began reading the labels, looking for some sort of description that would help determine which was right for Heather's situation. That, he quickly realized, was going to take a long time. Given there were gunmen loose in Drews, he thought it prudent to get home as soon as possible. His new friend was alone. Plus, he didn't know the territory, and being caught outside after sunset didn't seem like a wise strategy.

He returned to the grooming room where he'd noticed a large, industrial-sized wastebasket containing a thick, plastic garbage bag. A few moments later, Jack swept all of the meds from the shelves into what would be Santa Claus's bag of presents for Heather.

After finishing with the cabinet, Jack decided to continue his search of the virgin room. He found crackers, breath mints, and even two packets of instant coffee in the vet's desk. "A goldmine," he beamed, stuffing the java into his pocket.

About the only disappointment with the vet's office were the contents of the bottom desk drawers. Neither held the prerequisite bottle of bourbon and two glasses. "Didn't anybody watch those old movies?" Jack complained. "Doctors, sheriffs, and businessmen always kept liquor stashed there." Since the apocalypse, he'd searched a half-dozen desks and not a one had produced a stiff drink. What was the world coming to?

He was about to leave when he noticed a three-ring binder sitting on the desktop. "Weights and doses," it was marked. After a quick browse, Jack threw the book into his bag. It was full of reference guides from the drug manufacturers. He would be able to not only treat Heather's infection, but he would do so far more safely once he could take his time and read the instructions.

A minute later, he was at the door, a hefty bag of tablets and pills draped over his shoulder. Reaching for the knob, he froze when the dog bells jingled. Someone else was in the building, and he was willing to wager his next payday that they weren't bringing in Muffin for her rabies shot.

Jack set the bag down gently, his grip on the carbine tightening as he listened intently. If these were the same butchers that had murdered the hospital dwellers, chances were there was an unfriendly entourage waiting for him. Jack didn't know if it was Miguel or some roving band of strangers, and it didn't matter.

He heard the scrape of a boot on the floor; then someone whispered a curse. Jack couldn't hear well enough through the closed door to make out the words or recognize the voices.

He quickly glanced around the room, knowing from experience that the thin sheets of gypsum board and paneling wouldn't stop bullets. Once the ne'er-do-wells figured out where he was hiding, they could easily stand out in the hall and spray death without even bothering with the door.

The now-empty pharmacy locker was constructed of sheet metal, but too heavy for him to move. However, the filing cabinets were constructed of hardwood, and with their drawers crammed full of paper, they could stop lead. The castors on the bottom of each made them relatively mobile.

He could hear the visitors now, about three doors down, moving in his direction. They knew he was in here somewhere. Eventually, the process of elimination would lead them to Dr. Broncoski's door.

Working as quietly as possible, he rolled the filing cabinets together in front of the desk. Ducking behind his makeshift bulwark, he waited for the inevitable firefight. The thin walls were a two-way street, and Jack was determined to give as much lead as he received.

The seconds turned into minutes as he waited, his fingers growing stiff from gripping the M4 carbine so tightly. After a period, his ears began playing tricks on him while he waited for the assault.

It felt like an hour passed before an odd aroma wafted into the vet's office. Jack's eyes flew wide when he realized the smell was emitted from some sort of burning chemical. "What the hell are they doing out there?"

Whiffs of burning wood made their way to him, Jack rising from behind his fortress of file folders to move toward the door. "They're trying to burn me out," he hissed. "Cowards!"

Deep inside, Jack knew the people he was dealing with were actually tactic savvy. Why waste ammo in a world where they weren't making bullets anymore? If they wanted him dead, smoke inhalation by arson would do the trick just as well.

Jack unlocked the vet's door and chanced a glance into the hall. That effort was met with a thick cloud of choking smoke billowing into the room. At the far end, next to the janitor's closet, he noticed head-high flames blocking the way out.

Remembering the Navy's fire training, the commander dropped low. Heat, as well as the toxins of the fire, would rise, and he needed every lungful of clean air he could get.

Through the flames, Jack spied movement. Squinting to avoid the smoke, the commander watched as a figure moved on the other side of the fire. A second later, the face of a skull appeared behind the red and yellow waves of sizzling heat.

"Miguel's henchmen," Jack whispered. "Come to extract his revenge. I bet it was his crew that killed the people at the hospital, too."

In addition to teaching Jack to stay low during a fire, the Navy had shown him a few other things about dealing with flames. The commander wasn't nearly as worried as most men would be. In fact, he welcomed the overconfidence his foe was demonstrating.

Ducking back inside the door, Jack took a moment to plan his escape. The hall was narrow, the fire spreading fast. If he was going to make a run for it, it had to be now.

He was hampered by the bag of meds. While it wasn't overly burdensome, it was bulky. Yet, there was no way he was leaving it behind.

"Offense is the best defense," he whispered, gathering his courage and mentally walking through his next steps.

Then he was up, hefting the trash bag over his shoulder, inhaling a series of deep breaths, and readying for the charge.

Flying around the doorframe, Jack rushed at the blazing blockade, scurrying while bent at the waist, his carbine held at the hip and ready to fire. Just before he reached the edge of the inferno, he measured his steps and then bounded using a motion like a track star running the hurdles.

To the three men on the other side of the scorching bonfire, it must have looked like hell had released its hounds, the image of a deranged, sprinting, leaping figure breaking through the flames prompting them to freeze momentarily.

Jack landed in the middle of the fire but kept on going. The heat was sweltering, singeing the hair on the back of his hands, but he knew there was no choice.

He burst through the other side, weapon firing into their midst. One man went down instantly, the other two trying to maneuver their rifles into the fight. Proximity was the problem.

The three arsonists were standing far closer to the blaze than Jack had expected, his final leap and forward momentum landing him within arm's reach.

Weapons were firing on all sides, the three remaining men a furball of swinging barrels, grunted curses, and white-flashing muzzle blasts.

Jack lost his footing, tripping over the man he'd just shot. He dropped the bag on the way down, forced to use his arm to brace against the impact.

More shots rang out as Jack kicked hard at a shadow of movement, his boot impacting with tremendous force on a knee. A bullet hit the commander's body armor, the sledgehammer strike knocking the air from his lungs.

Rifle slings tangled with clothing as the dead man's blood turned the floor into an ice rink. Shadows from the spreading fire, combined with the smoke now curling over and around the combatants, made the fight a nightmare. Somehow, Jack lost his grip on the M4.

The commander spied a pair of legs to his front and grabbed for the man's ankle. Just as he caught the foe's limb and twisted with all his might, a rifle barrel crashed into his shoulder. Both men howled in pain, both of them grappling to find a throat, eye, or any other soft target.

In the confusion, one of Miguel's men began pulling the trigger, randomly sending blistering lead through the narrow hall. Jack felt his wrestling partner jerk as the friendly fire tore into his body, and then the injured attacker went limp.

A pair of hands found Jack's throat, another man's face suddenly filling the commander's limited field of vision. Pushing hard against the attacker's arms, Cisco strained to break the grip that was crushing his windpipe and cutting off the circulation to his brain.

The rogue intent on strangling Jack was powerful, his position providing enough leverage that the commander's superior strength was rendered worthless.

I'm not going to die here, Jack thought, black, fuzzy circles clouding the edge of his vision.

With the superhuman effort of a man convinced he was about to die, Jack managed to twist just enough to bring his leg into the struggle. Working his boot between them, he felt the sole now flat against the attacker's chest. He pushed with all the strength he had left, propelling his foe backward into the fire.

A shriek of agony followed a moment later, Jack able to see as the strangler tried to extract himself from the boiling inferno, arms thrashing at the flames that consumed him.

The commander rolled hard against the opposite wall, his lungs screaming for air, every muscle in his body feeling like it had been pulled from the bone. The smoke was so thick he couldn't see anything but whirling shapes of muted colors.

He had lost his rifle early in the melee, his hand now filled with the grip of his sidearm. He heard a weak voice call out, "Jose? Jose? Help me."

The .45 automatic bucked in Jack's hand, the massive, slow, 230-grain lead bullets delivering kinetic devastation to anything in their path. A man screeched in pain and then fell with a thump.

Jack began patting the floor around him. He needed his rifle. He had to locate the bag full of meds. The blaze was getting hotter now, spreading faster as it overtook the building.

He touched his carbine first, then a body, then a pool of blood. Perspiration was dripping into his eyes, reducing the already poor visibility in the hall.

Finally, he sensed the plastic bag, wadded it into his fist, and began dragging the medicine in the direction where he remembered the door. Jack crawled low, embers now whirling down around him. His body ached, his shoulder throbbed, his legs were nearly numb from exertion.

He approached the door leading to the receptionist's area, the dog collar ringing as he twisted the knob. The air was clearer here, his lungs trying to feed his blood.

Jack coughed, inhaled, and then coughed again as he continued to crawl toward the exit. His next prayer was that Jose and the boys hadn't left any friends outside. He was spent and wouldn't be able to put up much of a fight.

He successfully crept to the main entrance, the cool air rushing across his face so welcoming. He paused there for a moment, rubbing the soot from his eyes as he drank in lungfuls of fresh oxygen.

Finally, his vision cleared, the commander first checking the street outside for any movement and then making a quick inspection of his weapon.

After three minutes, Jack felt he could stand. Another five passed before he deemed walking was a possibility. The fire was now eating into the reception area, the smoke rolling high into the grey sky. He needed distance, both from the failing structure, and the attention it might draw.

He didn't have the strength to carry both the rifle and the bag. Dragging Heather's cure along behind him was the only option. "So much for Santa Claus carrying home the presents," he croaked. "I do smell like I just came down the chimney though."

Step after difficult step, Jack trudged, his body slowly recovering as he moved away from the vet's now engulfed office. No fire trucks came,

309

no curious crowd of onlookers gathered. Only the ghosts seemed interested, but the commander didn't care about them.

Chapter 35

Opening the back door to Heather's home, Jack's hopes of finding his new friend bustling around the kitchen were quickly dashed. Everything was exactly as he had left it that morning. She had spent the entire day resting.

Still, he held out hope as he moved for her bedroom. She was there, struggling for breath, her body glistening in a feverish sweat.

Dropping to a knee beside her, his touch caused her eyes to flicker. "Hey," he greeted. "How are you feeling?"

Her eyes now open, she tried to rise but stopped just a few inches off her pillow. "I feel like shit," she pronounced. "My head is throbbing. It feels like it's a hundred degrees in here. Guess I forgot to pay the electric bill," she feebly joked.

"Well, I'm not much of an A/C expert, but I will take a look at that wound," he answered, gently brushing her hair from her face.

He pulled back the covers and started removing the bandage. He could see immediately that her injury was thoroughly infected.

"The bad news is that your wound is not healing. In fact, the infection has spread. The good news is that I found some antibiotics. We will set you on the path of recovery in short order."

Her response was a mere nod, another indication that the lady of the house was extremely ill.

He made her drink some water and then worked to rewrap the gunshot with a clean bandage. After that, he left, closing the door behind him with a gentle, silent touch. He had some reading to do.

The 3-ring binder from the vet's office proved invaluable. In a few minutes, he learned that not any old antibiotic could be used on every ailment. The meds were somehow specialized, some working well on respiratory issues, others intended for specific types of bacteria.

After a half-hour of research, Jack settled on a drug named Cephalexin, which was recommended for bites and other varieties of open skin wounds. Now, he had to figure out how to administer it.

He estimated Heather was about 120 pounds, having gathered that vets prescribed dosages by the weight of the patient. The chart, intended for canines, topped out at 100 pounds. "Guess they don't have any really big dogs around here," he quipped. Still, it was close enough.

He poured the trash bag's contents out on the living room floor and began digging through the multi-colored boxes of medications, mining for Cephalexin-gold.

He found a bottle, then another. Both were unopened. A quick calculation and double-check of the chart indicated Heather should consume two of the capsules every eight hours.

He hustled to the kitchen, found the emergency water ration, and poured her a glass.

"Here, take these," he instructed after waking her again.

"Now, this wouldn't be one of those date-rape mickeys?" she teased, smiling through the discomfort.

"No, but they should help you get through this," he smiled.

He stayed beside her, using a bit of the water to moisten a cloth and cool her forehead. He knew it would be at least a day before the medicine took effect.

As the seconds slipped by, she slept, and Jack passed the time engaged in deep thought. If these antibiotics didn't work, should he try and drain the wound? Did he even know how? He devoted a lot of thought on how to ask her opinion on the subject.

He peered down at her, amazed at the woman's strength and character. Even under duress, she was lovely. He replayed their many conversations in his head as he did his best to keep her cool.

"You're falling in love with her," he finally admitted. "What about Mylie? What about the girls?"

Sitting there, next to a young woman who needed him so badly, Jack found it was easy to justify ending his foolish journey and hanging his hat right there in the Lanier household. *Any idiot would admit your wife and children probably didn't survive*, he thought.

There was a lot to be said for Drews, Texas and one Miss Heather Lanier. She was smart, even brilliant, and undoubtedly possessed the guts and determination to survive when so few still lived.

Jack also liked her. She was practical, operated with common sense, and yet maintained an aura of grace and control that the commander found attractive.

"Wait a minute," he whispered. "I thought the patient was supposed to fall in love with the nurse?"

Shaking his head to clear those thoughts, Jack rose and made for the kitchen. They needed water, and it was almost dark. He would make something to eat and then see how well Miguel and his boys could guard the well after the sun went down.

There was something comforting about reloading his magazines. While Jack hadn't expended many rounds in that afternoon's fight, he still went through the process of unloading and reloading each of them.

Next, he cleaned the barrel of both pistol and rifle, field stripping each to make sure none of Yellowstone's exhaust was going to cause him a problem. The M4 received two drops of oil on what his instructor back in San Diego had called the "Bolt Carrier Group."

After a quick meal of canned potatoes and the best pickles he'd ever eaten, Jack heated a cup of water for the coffee he'd discovered at the vet's office. "For tomorrow you may die," he recanted, stirring the instant java until his brew turned mud-brown.

He then sorted the next few doses for Heather, leaving the handful of pills on her bedside table with a note. "If I don't come back, I want you to know that I'm grateful for everything you've done for me. Kindness to a stranger is one of the finest qualities in any human being. You are a great lady."

Strapping on his body armor generated almost as much confidence as the warm coffee sliding down his throat. Almost.

Next came the load vest, its ladders securing pouches containing ammunition, a medical kit, his fighting knife, and a small set of gun-cleaning tools. He had four 30-round mags on the vest, two more stuffed into his back pockets. Counting the one in his rifle, the commander was humping over 200 rounds.

On the advice of his instructor, Jack also acquired a flat blade screwdriver. "Occasionally, in a gritty environment, the M4 will jam hard enough that you either have to slam the stock into the ground, or pry loose the bolt with a tool. It's rare, but when it happens, you will be out of the fight. With all this ash, I'd highly recommend that you carry something to get your weapon up and running as soon as possible."

So far, his rifle had functioned flawlessly, but that could change. Tonight wasn't the night to be gunned down due to equipment failure. Heather needed him.

He checked in on her again, peeking in through a crack in the door. He found her resting peacefully, at least as peacefully as someone fighting a life-threatening infection could sleep.

A thought occurred, a brief flash that he should wake her up to say goodbye. That concept was quickly dismissed. She would protest and then worry. He was confident there was no need.

Heather had mentioned that at one point, she had considered moving out of her mother's home to a location that offered more post-apocalyptic resources. "A few years ago, some the successful businessmen from town developed a master-planned community on the east side. It is about a mile outside of Drews, features impressive estate-style homes with spacious, well-groomed yards and generous swimming pools. I was tempted to pull up stakes since an oversized, inground pool meant flushing and bathing water would be handy. I could take more hot bubble baths. In the end, though, I decided to just stay here." Jack had little doubt Miguel knew about those high-end residences. If the commander was reading the young man correctly, he had most likely commandeered a mansion with a in-ground water source and was sleeping there.

The ex-Marine had come to town with at least seven soldiers – Jack having seen that many himself. The double-wide trailers by the well would be tight, uncomfortable quarters for that many men. In addition to the lack of space, Jack was sure no one would like being inside such a flimsy shelter when the storms hit. No, Miguel was probably kicking back in the lap of someone else's luxury.

That equated to Miguel's people having to post guards at the well, if the tyrant still intended to hold the critical resource hostage. Jack knew that he had already killed at least five of the man's followers. Even if Miguel's entire headcount hadn't been present during yesterday's encounter, the commander knew it would be a drain to secure any location 24x7.

A single sentry would require at least three men, each taking an eight-hour shift. Even if Miguel only used two guys per day, that commitment of resources would still put a significant damper on his other activities.

Jack assumed they were patrolling, probably searching the entire area for scavenge-worthy treasures. He'd no doubt run into one such posse today at the vet's clinic. It was probably one of these patrols that had followed Heather from her home.

No, they probably weren't guarding the pump at night. In the worst-case scenario, Miguel might be able to spare one or two men for the job. If there were more, Jack would simply turn around and come home and put their hopes on a Plan B.

Exiting the back door, Cisco had thought about another wrinkle to throw at the want-to-be dictator. In the garage where he'd initially hidden his bicycle, the commander had spied a wheelbarrow. He would use that to haul back a substantial supply of water and thus reduce their exposure to Miguel and his henchmen. He hoped eventually the little Nazi would come to his senses. With the hospital's residents dead, there wouldn't be anybody else to protect the water source from.

Gathering himself, Jack reached for the door and then stepped out into the cold, dark world.

If Miguel were smart, he'd be watching the path. Jack had no intention of taking the commonly-used trail. In his previous trips to the well, he'd noticed a gravel road that fed the area. It would mean a longer, bumpier excursion, but would be the safer route.

He found the wheelbarrow right where he had seen it last. He loaded it with four milk jugs and five buckets before securing the all-important coffee machine filter. He figured that much water should last the Lanier household at least four or five days, guest included.

Gripping the two wooden handles, he began pushing the cart toward the street.

The journey was longer than taking the trail's shortcut, but Jack didn't mind. He knew from his training that it took the human eye up to 30 minutes to adjust to its most accurate night vision setting. He could use the extra half hour's walk to allow his peepers to adapt to the inky surroundings. Now was not the time to scrimp on tactical advantages; he would need every bit of leverage he could muster.

Three hundred yards from the Campos driveway, Jack pushed his hauler to the side of the road and secreted it behind a slight brush pile.

With his rifle now occupying his hands, he set off across the open desert, intending to scout the Campos lot from all directions in the hope that he would spot any sentry before being detected.

He took his time, confident that the later the hour, the less alert any lookout would be. He approached the Campos property from the back, disappointed in the lack of cover the terrain afforded him. He stayed low, inched along very slowly, and paused every few steps to listen.

When the back of the modular home was in clear view, Jack stopped his forward progress and withdrew.

He moved 30 degrees on the compass and repeated the same approach. Again, no one was home.

On the third avenue in, he was less than 100 yards from the old pool when a bright spark appeared ahead. Jack went prone, his weapon coming up and ready.

Seconds later, he understood the context of the flicker. Someone was lighting a pipe. He watched as the match was whipped through the air and extinguished. Next, the bowl of tobacco, or whatever it was, glowed red. He could detect the eyes of the man through his optic, shining in the night above his mask.

Jack could have shot the man easily, but that would have generated noise, perhaps brought additional guns into play. While he felt confident the fellow was pulling solo guard duty, he couldn't take the chance. Besides, at this point, he only suspected the lookout of having malevolent intentions toward the general citizenry.

Withdrawing yet again, Jack decided to approach the trailer from one more angle to get a better view and make sure the sentry was alone. If he had to circumvent a guard to shore up the water supply, the commander hoped the fellow was working solo.

Aware that the pipe-smoker might be lurking around the perimeter, Jack was cautious. Once Cisco smelled the pipe, so he paused for a careful examination of the area, but didn't discern the guard's presence.

The commander retreated again, making a wide circle and then returning to the spot where he'd last observed the man. It took him a while, scanning in the darkness, but he eventually located Miguel's henchman.

He was reclining in a lawn chair, less than 20 feet from the old pool. *I don't blame him*, Jack thought. *It's cold as hell, boring, and probably the worst job anyone could be assigned.*

The sentry seemed fixated on the path, his chair pointed at an angle where he would be able to detect anyone rising from the gully. Perfectly situated for his assignment, he was able to guard both the swimming area and the pitcher pump. And were it not for his mistake with the pipe, Jack would have had trouble identifying his position.

With a deep breath, Jack began approaching the guard directly from behind. He chose his steps carefully, eyes darting between the masked head and the ground directly to his front. Cisco paid particular attention to his own balance, gently planting a toe and then gradually rolling his weight to the heel. If he felt any twig, branch, or resistance, he would withdraw the foot and try another spot. The entire process was tedious, time-consuming, and exhausting.

Jack was still 15 feet from the sentry when his legs began to cramp. The temperature outside was close to freezing, and the commander was more used to bike riding than stalking an amateur night watchman.

Another four steps, and Jack was ready to move in. His hand reached for the knife on his vest, his mind rehearsing the thrust, point of impact, and the amount of force that would be required to kill the guard.

Just then, the sentry stood, stretching his arms above his head and then scratching his ass. Jack was close enough to realize he was about to strike a young boy, probably no older than 15 or 16 years old. His hand moved away from the blade.

The kid sat back down, yawned, and then reached for his pocket. Jack charged.

The guard didn't even manage his feet before Jack's rifle butt struck his head. The blow was vicious, but measured, sending the young thug rolling across the desert floor and ash.

Jack didn't give him a chance to breathe or shout for help. Rushing forward, he stepped on the sentry's rifle while shoving the barrel of his carbine into the sentinel's face.

"Make a sound, and I'll split your fucking head in half," Jack growled.

The kid's eyes widened, his head nodding in short, nervous bursts. "Who killed the people at the hospital?" Jack hissed.

"I… I don't… I don't know," a high-pitched voice whined.

Jack pushed the barrel tight against the part of the kid's mask that was covering his mouth. "I think you do know," Jack hissed. "I think you're trying to bullshit me. Talk to me, and you'll live. Keep up this crap, and I'll skin you alive and take my time doing it."

For emphasis, Jack removed one hand off his rifle and pulled his knife. At the sight of the blade, the guard's eyes opened even wider. "Miguel and some of the guys went to the hospital, Mister. They said they wanted the people there to join us. I don't know what happened, but the guys were joking about how they didn't put up much of a fight."

"What is Miguel after?" Jack asked.

"I don't know. He's probably told some of the other guys, but he doesn't talk to me much, Mister. I only came along because Miguel promised to feed me and there wasn't much else to do back in Midland. It's not like I am part of his inner circle."

"How many men does Miguel have?"

Evidently, Jack's prisoner was regaining his composure. He hesitated before answering, which annoyed the commander to no end. Cisco pressed the business end of his rifle to the teen's temple to loosen his tongue again. "Just a couple now," the captive continued. "Jose and two of the guys got killed in a fire today. You and the woman killed two of us over in the opening."

Jack didn't believe him. "There you go again, lying to me." The knife flashed, the point stopping just as it pierced the kid's skin right above his navel. A yelp of pain broke the silence.

"Now you listen to me, you little shit. I will gut you, right here and right now. It is the most painful way to die, the agony just enough to drive you insane without causing that puny brain of yours to overload. Stop fucking with me, or I'll shove this knife in and start twisting."

"Okay, okay! Miguel has four guys left, including me. He sent another one back to Midland to get reinforcements. He expects them to be back here in a couple of days."

Jack considered his answer, finally concluding he had heard the truth. "How long before you're relieved?"

"Dawn."

"Stand up," Jack ordered.

"Hey, wait a minute, Mister. You said you wouldn't kill me," the sentry pleaded.

"I'm not going to kill you. I'm going to enslave you. You're going to help me get some water. After we're done, I'll tie you up, and when your relief comes, you can tell them what happened."

Not having many options, the guard stood while Jack shouldered the captured rifle. It was a bolt-action deer gun, probably a 30-06.

The commander then patted the man down, finding a pouch of stale cigarette butts, a couple books of matches, and the pipe. "Aren't you a little young to be smoking?"

The kid only shrugged. "You think lung cancer is goin' to be the death of me, Mister? Really?"

Jack ignored the retort, instead confiscating a handful of rounds for the rifle and a small pocket knife, leaving the tobacco and pipe. "Let's go; walk that way," Jack commanded, gesturing with his weapon.

Staying about 10 feet behind the teenager, Jack guided his newly enlisted help to the wheelbarrow. An hour passed before all the buckets and jugs were full. "Come on; you're going to help me down the trail and through the gully. If anybody is waiting along the path, they're going to shoot you first."

Twenty minutes later they were approaching the Lanier home. Jack stopped the kid. "That's far enough. Leave the wheelbarrow behind that pile of brush."

After the youngster complied, Jack continued. "Come on; we're going back."

The repeat trip proved uneventful, the guard not interested in trying to escape. The commander decided to give him a break. "Give me your shoes."

"What?"

"Sit down and take off your shoes. I'm not going to tie you up; I'm just going to take your sneakers. I'll leave them at the end of the trail."

A minute later, Jack was stepping back along the path, a pair of smelly shoes dangling from his shoulder.

After checking on Heather, Jack unloaded the water and then thought it best to take a quick nap. Barefoot, it would take the kid a while to retrieve his shoes and then a bit longer to report into Miguel. Jack thought he had about two hours before trouble came calling. He had poked the tiger with a stick, and surely the beast would demand his revenge.

He slept, ate, checked the perimeter, and then woke Heather. She only yawned and stretched as he checked her wound. It was no worse, no better. After her next dose of meds, she sat and listened to his recounting of the night's events.

"Miguel is going to be pissed," she nodded. "You embarrassed him. He won't handle that well."

"He has come out on the short end of the stick after every encounter with me," Jack explained. "How badly does he have to be hurt before he backs off?"

Sighing, Heather's face flushed with frustration. "He was the captain of the football team, the oldest of a half-dozen children, a Marine, and always so full of himself. He doesn't give up. There's no 'quit' in him. Surely, you've encountered young men who thought they were invincible."

Indeed, Jack had dealt with his fair share of hard-charging, testosterone driven individuals. The military was full of them, both alpha males and females. "That's why I assume he'll be stopping by soon. I think we should be ready."

"What are you proposing?"

"I think he'll try and shoot up the house, or burn us out. He and his boys seem to like playing with fire. One way or the other, I think he'll be hunting scalps."

She shook her head in disagreement. "You don't know him. I don't think he'll try to hurt me."

"He already did," Jack chided, nodding toward her bandaged trunk.

"That was an accident. You saw his face. He was horrified that I'd been hit," she responded.

Standing abruptly, Jack was far from convinced. "Heather, he executed everyone at the hospital. Either he or his men have tried to kill me, three times. One of them shot at me when I went back to the pump, and then an entire patrol tried to burn me out of an office downtown. We've stolen what he considers to be his water and embarrassed one of his men. I think you're underestimating what time and the apocalypse have done to your ex."

"Maybe. Maybe not. I suppose it's possible Miguel could have changed since I went away to school. What do you think we should do? Leave? Stay here and shoot it out?"

"You can't be moved right now," Jack replied, rubbing his chin. "I'm just saying that we should both be up and ready. If my estimate of his timeline is close, he'll be here in an hour or so."

Heather didn't respond, her eyes fixated on the floor. Thinking she was merely exhausted from fighting the infection, Jack began pacing as he considered the best way to handle the imminent attack. When she spoke next, it was in a soft, distant voice. "About three weeks after the eruption, the looters began getting desperate. I couldn't fall asleep, thinking I would wake up to find one of them standing over me wielding an ax or gun. I had to fight them off…. I had to kill them. It was the hardest thing I've ever done."

More than once, Jack had wondered how she survived. Bravery was one thing, intellect under pressure another. Still, she was only one person with a substandard weapon facing overwhelming odds. Leaving the bodies in the front yard would have been a deterrent to some, but the more desperate would have not been discouraged by that sight alone. "How did you do it?" he asked.

"They were disorganized mostly. One or two at a time, desperate, hungry, crazy, not thinking clearly."

"Still," he said, shaking his head. "How did you stand watch 24 hours a day? How did you watch all sides of the house at the same time? It seems like defending this place would be very difficult for five or six people, let alone one."

His questions about the early days of her post-Yellowstone survival prompted a flood of gut-wrenching memories. She seemed reluctant to respond, almost as if she was guarding some secret. He'd sensed it from her before, writing it off to embarrassment over having to kill, or guilt assoicated with having survived. Jack had read stories of veterans who experienced bouts of depression over having been one of the few to make it back alive.

Finally, she spoke, "You are right. So, I took some steps to make security more manageable. I installed a set of mirrors, so I could watch all sides of the house at once. I would wait for any intruders to make their moves and then shoot."

"Mirrors?"

She nodded, "I removed them from abandoned cars and trucks, tore them off with a crowbar. I set them around the yard in key positions. I constructed a low-tech video surveillance system of sorts. Go look in the closet."

Frowning in puzzlement, Jack stepped to the small door and opened it. He inhaled sharply, the inside crammed full of weapons, ammo, knives, and other paraphernalia. "What the hell?"

Shrugging, Heather replied, "Yeah, I got my fair share of uninvited guests for sure. Especially at first. I think most of them still had enough functioning grey matter to realize I was eating better than they were.

Others just wanted in my pants; apparently, I am the only female left in this town. Anyway, I learned the hard way that if I only scared them off, they would eventually come back. I also discovered that if I left their weapons lying around, I was only inviting more trouble, so I started collecting whatever they left behind."

Jack counted seven long guns, five pistols, two machetes and a half-dozen fixed blade knives. It was an impressive arsenal. Given what she had indicated previously, the commander had assumed no more than three or four attempts by the black hats. As he glanced over at her, a whole new level of respect beamed in his eyes.

"You did all this with magic and mirrors?"

She laughed, "No, actually it was *lasers and mirrors*. I left my magic wand in Houston," she answered, trying to lighten the mood.

"Lasers?"

"Yes, here look at this," she replied, reaching for the nightstand drawer.

Heather removed what appeared to be an oversized ink pen. "This is a very powerful laser pointer," she explained. "You see, I worked with a bunch of nerds at NASA. There for a while, it became a competition to see who could come up with the most powerful 'lightsaber.' One of the guys was sweet on me and gave me this little beauty."

Jack still didn't get it. "You blinded the looters with a laser?"

"No, silly," she grinned. "In the kitchen, on the windowsill, you'll find an outline drawn in black marker. Turn this on, be careful not to blind yourself, and sit it precisely in that outline. Then, come back in here."

Doing as instructed, Jack switched on the laser and laid it in the outline, pointing out the window. Instantly, the living room was illuminated in a sparkling light show of twinkling green lights. Jack had never seen anything like it.

Walking up behind him, Heather pointed to the laser. "It took me all day to align the mirrors. They are set up at precise angles to reflect the laser beam all around the yard. The last mirror sends the light into that crystal hanging from the living room window, which acts as a prism. It was Mom's favorite necklace, and it has saved my life more times than I care to think about."

Jack inspected the system and began to absorb the ingenious setup. "You couldn't watch one little dot of light on the wall," Jack nodded. "So, you lit up the entire living room. That way, you would see when somebody breaks the beam. Smart. Very smart. A tripwire of light."

"If those green lights flicker, even for a second, it means somebody has crossed into the yard. I could cook, read, lie down and rest, even go to the bathroom and still be aware of what is happening outside the house. This arrangement even works during the day, but it's a little harder to see. Eventually, the mischief-makers even stopped coming when it was daylight. I guess word got around that I was a pretty good shot with Daddy's duck gun."

Chuckling, Jack stepped to the laser and switched it off. "In the Navy, we called this a force amplifier. You used technology to even the odds. I'm impressed."

"A girl's gotta do what a girl's gotta do," she grinned.

Jack was about to add more praise when Heather staggered and almost fell. Rushing to her side with a steadying hand, he said, "You need to stay off your feet while you heal, Little Miss Evil Scientist. Come on; I'll help you back to the bedroom."

"Flattery will get you nowhere, sir," she replied.

On the way, Heather continued to explain about the intricacies of her early warning device. "As long as you keep the mirrors clear of the ash, it works perfectly. We can take turns. You can sleep while I watch the light show and vice versa."

"How long do the batteries last?"

"Not that long. The laser uses a lot of power, but there are several packages of batteries in my drawer. I bought an entire cartful at Wally World the day of the eruption, and later I had to supplement my supply. Batteries were the only thing I ever looted," she disclosed, looking away from his gaze as if embarrassed by her transgression. "It's strange when you consider the way a modern-day Armageddon can affect you, isn't it? Anyway, the laser will shine for 8-10 hours, depending on the quality of the cells."

Helping her back into her bed, Jack took the chance to check her wound. Again, he found it was still the same color of irritated red around the edges, a thin layer of white puss covering much of the gash. "Well, I think the antibiotics are working. The infection seems to be in check. Another 24 hours, and those pills should turn the tide of the battle waged inside of your body. You need to rest, young lady."

"Truthfully, I haven't slept this much since the apocalypse," she sighed. "Why don't you catch some shuteye, and I'll keep watch?"

Jack was dog tired and knew major conflict was coming his way. "You don't mind?"

"No. And thank you, Commander Cisco. I'm glad I trusted you at the well."

He turned the laser back on and then checked his watch. It seemed wrong to be resting when his timeline had Miguel arriving to extract his revenge. Yet, his eyes were burning with exhaustion. He needed at least an hour of sleep and hoped his adversary had been delayed.

"Can you see it?" he called to the bedroom.

"Yes. You lay down. I'll wake you up if the beam is broken."

With his load vest and body armor still strapped to his chest, Jack flopped down on the couch. It wouldn't be as comfortable as last night's slumber, but anything would help. He would have to fight soon. He was going to need every ounce of his wits.

Chapter 36

When she noticed the laser-lights go dark, Heather startled. She waited for it to flicker, even blink back on, the signal that an intruder had entered the yard's perimeter. Instead, the beam remained off. *Damned cheap batteries,* she lamented, *I knew I shouldn't have looted them from the dollar store.* She relaxed from her high-alert status, sure the cells had died. A quick glance at her watch told her Jack had been asleep for just over two hours.

She rose quietly, his bear-like snoring a reassuring rhythm. The skirmish at the vet's office, combined with his herculean effort to retrieve the extra water had to have been exhausting. She could see it in his face. The man needed his rest.

She was weak, which made it difficult to move past him without noise, but she managed. Reaching for the laser on the windowsill, Heather froze.

There, standing in the yard where he intentionally blocked the laser's beam, stood Miguel.

She started to shout for Jack but then stopped. Her old boyfriend didn't have a weapon in his hand. He was armed with only a gloomy face and longing eyes.

He could see her through the window and mouthed the words, "I only want to talk to you. Please."

Not sure of what to do, Heather just stood there. One sound from her throat would bring Jack and that big rifle. She was sure someone would die, and there had been enough of that in Mrs. Lanier's yard.

Taking a deep breath, she nodded to the man outside and then pointed toward the back porch.

She exited the door, gently closing it behind her so as not to disturb the commander. Miguel, having his own concerns about a trap, glanced cautiously around the corner of the house. "Thank you," he said, after seeing only Heather on the stoop.

"Where is that man?" he asked, glancing at the house with suspicion.

"He's asleep," she chanced. "What do you want?"

Looking down, his response was simple. "You. I came back for you."

Not believing her ears, Heather stood with her mouth moving, trying to form words. "Miguel... that... that was so long ago. What are you talking about? This is crazy."

"I've always loved you. I never stopped, even after we broke up." Reaching for his wallet, he then produced an old photograph of Heather. "I carried this with me all through boot camp and two deployments overseas. I must have pulled it out a thousand times to look at you."

Recovering from her initial shock at his declaration, Heather's voice was gentle but firm. "I'm flattered, Miguel. Really, I am. But we wanted different futures... different lives. The canyon between us was far too wide to overcome. Breaking up was the smart thing to do."

"But I changed," he protested. "I saw a lot of the world while serving with the Marines. Through that experience, I came to understand why you didn't want to stay here in Drews. I developed a lot of respect for you during those years."

His words tugged at her heartstrings, memories of young love flooding her otherwise logical mind. There was the prom, homecoming, and those magical, star-filled nights out in the desert, talking, making out, and staring at the moon. Her life had been so much less complicated then.

They had been the most envied couple in Drews, always together, constantly having fun. Heather's friends were often jealous, Miguel's buddies always showing respect.

Miguel peered nervously toward the house. "Come with me, Heather. Just for a little while. Come with me so we can talk. I promise you'll be safe."

She stalled, on the fence, glancing back where she knew Jack was sleeping. "I don't know... so much has happened... so much water has passed under the bridge."

"Water under the bridge? Really? No, this looks more like a new man in your life, Heather. Who is he?" Miguel hissed, seeing her eyes dart back toward the man inside. "Where did he come from? What does he mean to you?"

His livid reaction forced her to take a step back, the boiling jealousy so overt and vicious. Yet, in a way, it was flattering. Part of her attraction to Miguel was his passion, his willingness to display emotion while all of the other local guys had tried to play it cool and tough. She had always known where she stood with the hot-blooded, young Latino.

"Be quiet," she snapped back. "If you wake him, somebody is going to get hurt, and there's been more than enough of that lately. He is a nice man; he has treated me like his sister." Then without knowing why, she added, "I like him."

Miguel couldn't believe his first love would choose another over him, trying desperately to rationalize her behavior. "You're alone here. You're scared most of the time. I don't blame you for letting him in your home, but now I'm back. I'm here, and I love you more than anything left in the world. Please, come with me... just for a while. I want to prove to you that I've changed."

One thing was certain in Heather's whirling mind. Miguel wasn't going to leave quietly without her. If she refused, he would raise a fuss until Jack was roused from his sleep. "No" wasn't an answer he was going to accept.

Beyond that, there was a part of her that wanted to hear what he had to say. He was the only man she'd ever felt a connection to. There had been times when she'd lay awake at night, wondering what Miguel was doing, wishing she could see his enchanting smile.

She had to go... had to hear him out. She had to know if Jack's account of the hospital assassinations and the arson at the vet's office had been accurate.

She flashed an exasperated look before responding. "You *shot* me. Remember? I can't hobble very far without my insides leaking out... thanks to you," she objected, offering one last excuse.

"You weigh nothing; I will carry you," he offered, ignoring the verbal jab and taking a step forward.

"Oh, don't be silly. I'm not a damsel to be carried off by the valiant white knight. Wait a few days until I'm feeling better, and we can visit then."

Miguel didn't want to wait, glancing around for a solution to Heather's handicap, he spied the wheelbarrow leaning against the house where Jack had left it.

Moving quickly, he rolled it next to Heather and offered, "Your chariot awaits."

It was Heather's turn to try and skirt the issue, but she couldn't come up with another excuse. Besides, Jack could wake at any second, and that would mean gunplay and probably death. Nodding, she responded, "Okay, we'll go somewhere so we can talk for a while. After I hear what you have to say, do you promise you'll bring me back here?"

"I promise," he smiled, flush with success, confident that she would never want to return to her childhood home. In a flash, he stepped close to her and scooped her off her feet. The move surprised her, a loud bark of protest coming from her throat before she could stop it. Miguel ignored the outburst, setting her gently in the wheelbarrow's bucket and then pushing it toward the street.

Heather's squeal startled Jack. He shot up in a blur, his weapon moving to his shoulder before his eyes were fully open.

For a second, he thought he might have been dreaming. Two healthy steps and he was at Heather's bedroom door, peering at her empty bed.

He turned, dashing to the kitchen, and that's when he spotted Miguel lifting and carrying her to the wheelbarrow. *What a Neanderthal!* Cisco's heart sank at the thought of Heather being in jeopardy.

The back door flew open, Jack bounding out on the porch without covering his face. The carbine came up, the optic's cross-hairs centering on the back of Miguel's head. His finger tightened on the trigger, his eyes struggling to make out the target bobbing up and down as he hauled Heather across the road.

Jack couldn't chance the shot. He might hit her. He had seen the damage his weapon could deliver, and it wasn't uncommon for the bullets to blow through a body and come out on the other side with enough energy to kill again.

With lightning quick responses, he was back inside. A mask, quick refill of his water, and a check of his weapons were all the preparations he had time for. There was no way he was going to lose Miguel's trail. He wasn't going to give the man a chance to hurt Heather... a woman he knew he respected... who was so amazingly stunning and clever. A woman who had risen out of a home barely above America's poverty line... defied the odds and completed an engineering degree... who clearly had competed professionally with many of the nation's brightest and best – after all, NASA had its pick of graduates. A woman who knew how to leverage her brainpower to secure her own safety... who apparently had defeated scalawags, rogues, and thieves singlehandedly with a duck gun, of all things. A woman to be reckoned with. It had been a long time since the commander had met such a woman. And now he was in danger of losing her, and that thought was making him see red.

"If that animal hurts her," the commander growled, jamming home the M4's magazine, his thoughts brimming with hate.

As he pulled the rifle's sling over his shoulder, Jack felt a twinge of remorse about his evolving feelings for Heather. After all, he set out on this odyssey to reunite with Mylie and his daughters. But the truth was that his wife didn't want him anymore, and he had the divorce papers to prove it. Even if Mylie had somehow beat insurmountable odds and survived the eruption, she would probably be relieved that Commander Cisco had found happiness. Heck, for all he knew, she might even have moved on *before* Yellowstone blew her top. She had felt abandoned for years, due largely to Jack's military commitment. On the other hand, the commander assured himself that he could mend his relationship with his daughters. Besides, they would like Heather, and she would adore them.

Jack was out the door a heartbeat later, moving across the yard with a simmering rage in his core. He would cut the kidnapper to pieces starting from the knees up. He had already lost one fine woman in Mylie... he wasn't prepared to lose another.

He scurried, darted, ran, and paused, moving from tree to car to building wall as he followed them. After two blocks, Miguel stopped and then let Heather stand on her own. She took two steps before stumbling in the ash. Miguel reached out to support her, and she did not resist. A minute later, she was back in the wheelbarrow again. *He's got her out in the middle of nowhere, injured and unable to maneuver without assistance,* Jack thought. *He knows she can't get away in her condition.* Cisco held his breath, his finger on the trigger, waiting for a clear shot. It never came.

As the couple in front of him finagled their way through town, Jack found there were times where he had to hang back. Wide, open spaces didn't afford any cover, and he didn't want Miguel to know he was following. The captor might kill Heather for spite, if nothing else.

By the time they reached the edge of Drews, frustration and anger were reaching a critical level, totally commandeering Cisco's brain. Twice he thought he had his man lined up, but then a last-second movement by Heather had ended the opportunity. Jack knew time was running out. If the abductor reached his lair, he would tap into reinforcements, making the rescue far more tenuous.

The commander's heart sank when Miguel turned off the two-lane highway. He was taking her to a gated community with a six-foot high stucco wall surrounding the properties inside. There was no shot, and he had no good options. Jack would have to go in and get Heather.

Cisco hung back, worried that his fury would lead him to making a strategically stupid decision. *You need to get a hold on yourself, Commander,* he chided. *You might be walking right into an ambush.* No doubt Miguel would have sentries posted around his HQ. Better to get the lay of the land and come up with a plan, especially given the size of his adversary's posse. *Surprise is your best weapon*, he mused, *it might be the difference between saving the girl and a suicide mission.*

The living room was as big as a basketball court, its embellishments gilded in gold leaf, the furniture upholstered in the most luxurious of Italian leather, the marble floors accented by Oriental rugs. A raised platform featured the kind of ornate grand piano suitable for a society gala. "This house is over 6,000 square feet of desert paradise," Miguel bragged. "It belonged to a bank president. Now, it's ours."

Heather struggled to respond, the journey having been more physically challenging than she had anticipated. She perched on an overstuffed chair, took a moment to catch her breath and replied, "Miguel, we have to talk."

"Of course," he responded, "But first, let me just give you a quick tour of our new hacienda."

"Let me catch my breath, okay?" she replied, slumping onto a chaise lounge. Miguel snapped his fingers, and one of his henchmen responded with a glass of water. Heather downed it greedily and rested for a moment in silence before complying with his request. She removed her coat and scarf. Tossing them over the chair, she breathed a sigh of exasperation, then stood and followed him.

Her exhaustion seemed to dissipate in direct proportion to the residence's opulence. She had never seen a home so lavishly furnished, and it was hard not to gawk. Soon she was strolling around the interior, pointing at this work of art or that Tiffany bauble, amazed at the extravagant decor of the manor on the other side of the tracks.

Yet, it wasn't real. She hadn't *earned* it, and neither had Miguel. She knew that to take something that she had not worked for violated everything she stood for and she said as much. "Stop, Miguel," she protested once her giddiness subsided. "I don't belong here. *Neither of us* belongs here. Don't you realize we're occupying the fruits of someone else's labor?"

"But we survived," he countered, disappointed at her reaction. "To the victor goes the spoils."

She started to protest his point, but Heather abruptly stopped. Hadn't she just made the same argument to Jack? Hadn't she just referred to the neighbor's bicycles as an example of resource reallocation? What was the difference between a garage full of bikes, a massive home, and dollar store batteries? Weren't they all living in an exaggerated "survival of the fittest" scenario? Didn't those that had toughed this thing out have an obligation to all of mankind to survive if they could... to ensure the continuation of our species whatever the cost?

Sensing her ambivalence, Miguel ordered his two men outside, hoping privacy would enable him to reach her. "We need to have a private conversation. Make sure we're not disturbed."

Heather watched the armed men leave before pivoting to face her old flame. "Oh, we need to talk all right, Miguel. How can I possibly trust you? The stories I have heard from Jack don't exactly paint you in the most favorable light. How do I know that the owners of this house died from Yellowstone's ash?" she demanded, having finally mustered the courage to ask the hard questions.

"First of all, Mr. and Mrs. Bank President are buried out in the field behind this property. I found their bones in the master bedroom where they died. They breathed the air without protection... there was blood on the sheets."

His story seemed plausible on the surface, Heather wanting to believe his words. Yet, she was still conflicted, remembering his legacy of always having to be the "big man on campus." *Of course, we have all changed since the days of chemistry, prom, and chess club,* she thought. Still, Heather recognized that she didn't survive this long after society's collapse without maintaining a cynical attitude. She decided to probe further.

"All right. Let's say that I believe you. What can you tell me about the deaths of the survivors at the hospital? Did you have anything to do with what happened to them?"

Miguel grabbed her hand and gazed at her directly in the eye as he began his narrative. "You know me, Heather. I am not an evil man. I just tried to talk to them, and they attacked us. I didn't want to hurt anybody." He paused to gauge her reaction before continuing, "But let's not talk about that. I want to focus on our future, on the life we could build together here in Drews."

"Go on," she responded, not sure whether to trust him or not, but curious about his intentions.

"While the poison in the air and water will eventually be cleansed by Mother Nature, I believe society will take hundreds of years to be reborn. There will be a vacuum of leadership, no functioning government, religion, or military organization left. No more countries, or states, or even counties."

"Let me guess. You want to take charge, to lead mankind into an era of rebirth?"

If Miguel noticed Heather's sarcasm, he didn't show it. Shaking his head, he humbly responded, "No, of course not. I'm not qualified. No one is. I merely want to live out the rest of my life in happiness. Together... with you. I want us to marry and be a part of a small, independent community we will build here in Drews. I know where there is a huge, hidden stockpile of food in Midland. With the water here at the well, we can be safe and content, surrounded by friends."

Ignoring the marriage proposal, Heather seized on the more interesting topic. "A stockpile of food? Seriously?"

"Yes, I discovered it by accident when I was out foraging. Look at me, Heather. I'm far from starving. My men are well-nourished, all of them at their pre-eruption weights. I can offer you a good life in our little village. We will start right here and spread out as our township grows."

"Why not begin with a modest subdivision? Maybe something closer to the pump? After all, it's not like we worked hard, saved for a down payment and secured a mortgage for one of these mega-mansions," she protested. "Why the need for all the extravagance?"

"Look, I am not going to deny that these are remarkable houses, but that is not the reason for my choice. This gated neighborhood will be easier to secure, and your safety is my number one priority," he responded, winking at her.

"Okay," she responded, her brain's neurons firing on overload, attempting to assimilate the data dump of information, circling back to unanswered questions. "So, what were you looking for at the hospital? Why the argument with the medical team? I know Dr. Spencer was a bit of an ass, but he was still a reasonable man."

Miguel spun away from her, his hands moving up to rub his temples. "Please, listen to me. I have a vision, Heather. What I want to create is a community that is like a Phoenix and literally rises from the ashes, right here in Drews. We can balance defense with agriculture, water resources, and everything else we need. We can lay a pipeline from the well and erect a solar pump on it when the sun becomes brighter."

"What does this have to do with the dead people at the hospital?" Heather probed, frustrated, trying to keep the conversation on point.

"That doctor came at me with an attitude – like he was some sort of God with a medical degree. When I told him I had come back for you, he became angry… told me he had already invited you to come live with his group. He hinted that I had committed crimes in order to survive, treated me as if I were some felon. I went there with the best intents of talking about what we could build together. Not only would he not hear me out, he didn't even let me in the door."

"And?"

"Well, naturally, I started getting frustrated," Miguel hesitantly admitted, staring down at his shoes to avoid eye contact, knowing that his temper had led the conversation with the doctor. "But that man disrespected me. He laughed at me, said you would never go with a loser like Miguel Campos. Instead of discussing my offer for an alliance, your doctor friend joked about me with one of his comrades… about that time when I was 10 and broke my arm and how much I blubbered while he was casting it. He was such a jerk, and then he told me I should go back where I had come from. That my 'kind' wasn't welcome in Drews anymore."

"So, you got angry and killed all those people? For disrespecting you?"

"Well," he continued, "that was not all. He boasted that they intended to partner only with people 'like them.' Successful people. Well-educated people. He bragged that they had invited only one person from the outside to join them, and that was you – to perpetuate the species."

He paused while the significance of his words sank in before continuing his story.

"I couldn't listen to that garbage, especially when it involved you. So, we began shouting at each other. One of his men shoved me, and I hit him. A shot rang out from somewhere, and soon everybody was blasting away. I swear it; I didn't go there to hurt anybody. I wanted the doctor and his people to join our community, to increase all our efforts to survive."

Heather digested his explanation, her mind moving at the speed of light. "Is that why you're after me? To help you populate some futuristic community?"

He softened, sensing her distress. "Yes. No. I mean, you're the smartest woman I know, and I still love you. You are the perfect fit. A

337

great wife, a fighter who survived, and an engineer who worked at NASA. I need you. I want you. I always have. That has never changed."

While her instincts told her she wasn't hearing the whole story, she struggled to wrap her head around everything he was spouting out. She wanted to believe his tale, that realization in itself disconcerting as she strongly suspected there was more to it. She couldn't dissect the self-important man in charge from the romantic. *He never was good at admitting his shortcomings,* she mused. He did have a point though; the idea of pooling resources certainly had merit. But could she chance her own survival on someone who could might not be able to control his emotions in a stressful situation when her tendency was to choose a course dictated by logic?

Then again, that had always been her problem with Miguel. Her mind swirling with possibilities, she started to step toward him, not sure why. Suddenly doubling over in pain, her grand gesture was aborted, her injury making itself known.

Watching her stagger and wince, Miguel moved to guide her to a nearby chair. "Your side," he said softly, slipping his shoulder under her arm to assist.

Outside, Jack was peering through the high wall of windows that formed the rear of the home. Through the commander's optic, Heather seemed to be in distress, Miguel at fault. Without the benefit of audio, Cisco could only guess at the dialogue. From what he could see, Miguel was a kidnapper and Heather the damsel in distress.

"Not on my watch!" the commander whispered under his breath. Rising on adrenaline-powered legs, Jack Cisco marched with purpose toward the house. He strode out of the desert, bold and fearless, rescue at any cost the only thought on his mind.

The first burst from his weapon tore into the nearest sentry, four rounds ripping flesh and shattering bone. The second of Miguel's guards was out of the fight a moment later.

Inside, Miguel dove for the floor, screaming for Heather to take cover. Somehow, she sensed that her person wasn't the target.

Miguel hustled to the counter and retrieved his own weapon. It was nearly a twin to Jack's carbine.

"Who *is* that son of a bitch?" he growled.

"His name is Commander Jack Cisco," Heather replied from behind the breakfast bar. "United States Navy."

"A squib? Are you kidding me? They can't fight. What is this guy's problem?"

She didn't bother answering, making the correct assumption that Miguel's question was rhetorical. Then she realized, "He probably thinks you abducted me. I didn't tell him I was leaving of my own free will. Let me talk to him. Better yet, let me leave. Otherwise, he's going to come in here after me, and somebody is going to die."

"You want *to leave* with him?" Miguel snapped, his head on a swivel, waiting for Jack to show himself.

"I want to go home and digest all you've told me. Besides, this man's my guest and a friend. There's a difference between that and wanting to leave with someone."

Miguel's eyes blazed like a man who was losing control. Shaking his head in disbelief, he countered, "I don't see any difference. I can't believe you would choose him over me!"

"I'm not choosing anyone. I'm not some desperate, frail, little thing who craves or needs a man. Let me talk to him before somebody else gets killed."

Jack's voice sounded from a different location. "Let Heather go, Miguel. Let her go, and I won't kill you."

"She doesn't want to leave with you, Squib! She came here to be with me. Get the hell out of Drews while you still can," Miguel taunted.

"Oh, yeah? You got some reinforcements to back up that big mouth of yours? Because I am telling you, you are gonna need a group rate at the local funeral parlor, bud. Let her go, or you'll be joining your friends," Jack replied, his voice now sounding like it was inside of the house.

"Jack? Jack? He didn't kidnap me. I came to talk to him of my own volition," Heather interjected.

The commander didn't believe her. "Sure ya did, Heather. And I'm Kris Kringle. Nice try, Miguel, but I didn't fall with yesterday's ash."

"No, seriously, Jack. I'm coming out. Don't shoot. We can go back to my house together. There's been enough killing," Heather pleaded.

She rose, taking a hesitant step in the direction where she'd last heard Jack's voice. "Heather, don't!" Miguel protested, reaching to grasp her arm.

The combination of the radiating pain from the gunshot wound and Miguel pulling her out of harm's way caused Heather to lose her balance. Collapsing with a yelp of pain, her head struck the granite countertop. Jack, hearing her distress, charged.

Miguel fired two shots at the blur moving at his right, both bullets punching holes in the plaster near Cisco's head. The commander snapped a return round but remained in motion, his legs pumping like pistons.

At ten feet, with a full head of steam, Jack pushed off and dove at Miguel, his body flying over an oversized sectional. He landed shoulder first into his nemesis, both men grunting from the impact as they rolled across the floor.

Miguel was on his feet first, slashing at Jack's head with a vicious thrust of his rifle butt.

Cisco ducked the blow and stepped in, his arms seizing the Marine's waist. Jack lifted, pushed, and tripped. Again, they tumbled down in a heap, both men initiating a barrage of blows, all aimed at the other's head.

The skirmish continued, a rolling ball of jabs, kicks, curses, and grunts. Jack was taller and had longer arms, allowing safer access to his target. Miguel was stronger and more compact, making him a difficult mark. Both men were focused entirely on a single goal – obliterating the other from the face of the earth.

A separation occurred, enough to allow Jack to take advantage of his reach. Three quick rabbit punches landed on his foe's face, Miguel staggering backward with each strike.

Knowing it was his best chance, Jack moved in, his killer instinct blossoming in its blind fury. Miguel was now pinned against the wall, unable to retreat any further. Cisco threw a kick, a brutal roundhouse, and two lightning fast undercuts.

Spent, Miguel couldn't resist as Jack's left forearm pinned his throat to the wall. The commander's right hand closed on the hilt of his knife.

Heather recovered just as Jack drew his steel, bloodlust burning in his eyes. "No!" she screamed as the blade cleared its sheath. "Don't!"

Despite her weakened state, Heather darted at Jack just as his arm torqued to deliver the coup de grace.

She slammed into his side as Miguel lashed out with a hard, upward thrust of his knee. The impact knocked the commander off balance, fouling Jack's aim just enough that his blade missed Miguel's throat and buried completely in the wall.

Staggering backward from the twin blows, Jack lost his grip on the knife. Hurt and bewilderment flashed on the commander's face, his mind entirely unable to process Heather's betrayal.

Miguel was down, but not out. Taking advantage of the reprise, he reached for his rifle. Jack, now staring at Heather with wide eyes, didn't notice the move.

"Stop!" she commanded. "Enough!" she barked, steadying herself between the two combatants.

"What are you doing?" Jack panted from his heaving chest as his lungs tried to catch up from both the physical and emotional turmoil.

"I was telling the truth," she responded, her voice softening. "He didn't kidnap me. I came here to talk... to get some answers from Miguel."

"You *want* to be here? Why? This man is a murderer, a power-hungry, nut job! He's tried to kill me three times!"

She shook her head, pleading, "No he's not like that. This is all a misunderstanding, and I'm trying to clear it up before more people get hurt."

Heather moved toward Jack, her tone becoming calmer still. "Come on, let's go. Let's go home until cooler heads can prevail."

Jack was willing to accept that, her pleading eyes and forced smile coaxing the rage to drain away. After he picked up his rifle, Heather wrapped her arm under his and began to turn him toward the door.

By then, Miguel's head had cleared and his voice rang out. "Heather? What are you doing? You're leaving me for him?"

Jack pivoted and found his foe now standing, back against the wall, wiping the blood from his nose. A rifle was in his hands. Heather turned to face him as well, shouting, "Stop this, Miguel. Pull your damn head out of the macho clouds and listen to me. This isn't about my picking one man over the other. You need to get that through your thick skull, right here and right now."

Her message having been delivered, she turned back to Jack just as Miguel's rifle fired.

The round struck Jack's carbine, knocking his hand from the grip when Heather screamed. Cisco's response was swift and immediate, the reaction of a man who had made the decision to kill or be killed many times before. His hand was a blur, pulling his pistol and firing.

The first .45 caliber slug slammed into Miguel's chest, the second and third destroying more bone and critical tissue. He was dead before gravity pulled his body to the floor, three streaks of crimson smearing the wall behind him.

Heather cried out, "No!" and scurried to the dead man. "No, no, no," she prayed, reaching for Miguel's face, tenderly running a finger down his cheek.

Stunned at the dizzying turn of events, Jack just stood there, none of the words forming in his throat enough. "I... I... I didn't want to...," he stammered.

Sobs racked her body as Heather kneeled next to Miguel, her tears quickly escalating to hysterics. Finally, Jack moved toward her, carefully lifting her to stand. "We should go," he whispered as gently as possible. "Let's go home."

Regaining some composure, Heather merely nodded. Jack saw it then, an emptiness behind her gaze. She was going into shock.

Heather managed less than 20 steps before she staggered. Sweeping her up in his arms, Jack began the journey back toward Mrs. Lanier's house, her head resting in silence against his shoulder.

For three days, Heather remained in bed. She ate whatever Jack brought her, hobbled to the john, and took her medication as prescribed. During that time, Jack couldn't recall her saying more than five words.

He decided to cheer her up with a bath, rising early on the fourth morning and making two trips to the well. Next, he built a roaring fire by the garage, scavenging scrap lumber from a nearby outbuilding that had collapsed during a storm.

Heating bucket after bucket, Jack filled her tub. All the while, she sat in bed and watched him, never making a sound.

The bubbles were overflowing the white porcelain clawfoot. "I drew you a bath," he beamed, stepping to her side. "I thought it might help you feel better. Your injury is healing well enough to start moving around."

She nodded, pushing back the covers and shuffling toward the bathroom. Once inside, she said a weak, "Thank you," and closed the door.

Jack stood for a moment, his heart hoping she would get back to her old self soon. Still, she'd been through a lot. He would give her time.

While she'd been bedridden, he'd done a lot of thinking. His mind was made up. He wanted to be with Heather, wanted her at his side for the rest of their lives. After she was well, he'd take her back to Carlsbad or Archie's farm. They could have a blissful life despite the post-apocalyptic setting, happy with each other and working together to rebuild what they could.

He had also determined that going slow was the best option. She had endured so much, for so long, and done so alone. This last episode with Miguel had nearly overloaded her system. He was confident the old Heather would be back soon. She was such a resilient woman.

Having used all of the water for her bath, Jack decided to refill the buckets before preparing their lunch. Pushing the wheelbarrow down the trail, he turned and glanced back toward the house. "Hope you're enjoying that soak, kiddo," he smiled.

The trip to the well was uneventful, Jack reasonably sure he and Heather were the last remaining residents in Drews. Other than the occasional drifter who might pass through town, he was confident they were now alone.

As he trekked back to the house, he noticed something new on the back porch. Stopping well short of the Lanier yard, Jack pulled the rifle from his shoulder.

Heather then appeared, stepping out the back door with her shotgun cradled in the nook of her arms.

"What's wrong?" he asked, scanning the property with suspicious eyes.

"I want you to leave," she said with a strong, cold voice. "Thank you for nursing me through this, but I'm fine now. It's time you were on your way."

Initially, he thought she was playing some kind of crummy joke, even managing a half-hearted chuckle. "Funny," he said. "You've got a better sense of humor than I imagined."

"I'm not kidding," she retorted with a deadpan face. "It's time you hit the road. You're not welcome here anymore."

With his ears suddenly burning hot, Jack took a step forward with his arms spread wide. "Why? What did I do? Why are you doing this?" he pleaded.

"I don't have to explain anything to you, Jack, and I'm not going to try. Here's your pack and gear. I filled up your water bladder and gave you some food. It's time for you to be on your way."

He couldn't believe it, absolutely shocked by her words. "But... but, Heather, I love you," he professed. "I want to spend the rest of my life with you. I can't just leave like this."

"Throughout this entire affair, neither you nor Miguel thought about me or my feelings. You were like two stud bulls fighting over the last cow. You don't love me, Jack. I'm merely the last woman left on earth."

"That's a pretty tainted point of view," he replied. "And completely off the mark. I honestly and truly care about you. I swear it, and I thought you loved me."

"Did you ask?"

"No," he responded, shaking his head. "But that's not an easy question to pose. Rejection sucks. I thought I saw love in your eyes and word and actions."

"Well, you should have done a little more research before getting your hopes up, Commander," she snapped, the exasperation clear in her tone. "Now, I'm getting cold and tired. I wish you well, Jack, but don't come back."

He started to protest, but she didn't stop to listen. Turning abruptly, she headed inside. Jack heard the door lock behind her.

He stood there for five minutes, trying to formulate a plan, trying to come up with some sort of logic or reasoning for her reaction. *What should I do now?* he asked himself. He considered storming inside, taking her into his arms and talking some sense into her. He would make her believe him. He rehearsed a long list of the reasons why he respected, admired and desired her.

It then occurred to him that it was too late; he had missed the opportunity to properly declare his love and nurture a budding relationship with this woman. Guilt and embarrassment filled his soul. Worse yet, had he been so blinded by the apocalypse that he had misread the entire situation? Was his male ego so immense that he had made faulty assumptions regarding her wants and needs? Where was it written that a woman needed a man?

He took a step toward the back door, self-doubt now overriding his desire to be with the woman inside. When he was standing beside his pack, he knew he'd arrived at a critical fork in the road.

He could either reach for his gear or the knob.

Visions of Mylie and the girls resurfaced, his mind returning to his family as the pain of Heather's rejection filled his core. "Sometimes you don't know what you've got until it's gone," he whispered.

"You've not learned a single lesson from all this," he grunted, shaking his head. "Heather probably saw the same flaws in your character as your wife. You're not doing to so well with the ladies, Commander."

Jack bent quickly and lifted his pack. After checking the straps and buckles, he then made for the garage and his bicycle.

Without a backward glance, he mounted his bike and rode away. "I wish you all the luck left in this cruel world, Heather," he whispered.

Jack turned east on Main Street, his legs pushing the cycle at an easy clip. "It's the Hill Country or bust," he sighed.

THE END

Made in the
USA
Columbia, SC